# The Pigeon Whispers

Claudia Jean Hugo

Grosvenor House
Publishing Limited

This book is published by
Grosvenor House Publishing Ltd
Link House
140 The Broadway, Tolworth, Surrey, KT6 7HT.
www.grosvenorhousepublishing.co.uk



A CIP record for this book
is available from the British Library

ISBN 978-1-80381-531-2
eBook ISBN 978-1-80381-532-9

# Dedication

To little brother and sister, beautiful nieces both, and all our pet cats and dogs, past and present.

# Acknowledgement

Sometimes you are lucky enough in life to cross paths with truly good and decent people, I was exceptionally lucky to come across two such people who nudged and cajoled this book to the finish line, I thank them both from my heart – to Ryan Zombie and Georgia Araund, the best of people.

# one

As Faye walked into a small annex to her office, she glanced at her diary to see who was her 3 o'clock - Oliver Blake. Faye remembered the phone call Oliver Blake made which was almost three weeks ago, he had sounded far too pleased with himself and had asked about the waiting room arrangements, would there be anyone else in the waiting room while he was there, would he meet anyone on the way out, apart from one person a number of years ago who consider himself famous, but who in fact Faye had never heard of, no one else had asked such questions. As it happened, Faye was able to guarantee the anonymity he wanted. In the small annex Faye opened a can of coke which she took from the fridge, drank two long gulps and not for the first time thought that two lines of coke would probably suit her better. She looked into the mirror on the wall and reapplied her neutral lipstick, it really didn't need re-applying but she wanted to look good, and so she ran a brush through her hair. Damn, she thought, I really will have to start to dye my hair. Faye had held out on what she felt was the brutal ritual of the hairdresser and the painfully long process of the hair dye, and the way hairdressers had of making you feel like a criminal because you don't have regular trims and treatments. Recently she had noticed more and more grey hairs, and as she certainly wasn't going to be one of those women who embraced their greyness, she thought she might try her hand at a home dye kit. At that point she heard a knock on the door, Oliver Blake must have arrived. Back in the main office she took an index card, attached it to a clip board and placed it together with a pen on the polished coffee table.

As she entered the waiting room, she caught the scent of something quite nice, an aftershave lotion or some man perfume, something expensive, it definitely was a pleasant change from the smell of stale cigarettes, musty clothes or BO which unfortunately for Faye was not an uncommon displeasure. Faye approved instantly, at least superficially, of this man. He stood up with outstretched hand and confidently announced that he was Oliver Blake. They shook hands and Faye introduced herself.

'Hello I'm Faye Monroe, it's very nice to meet you, please come on through.'

Faye stood back, held the waiting room door open and directed him across the small hall to the office, where she directed him to a seat on the sofa. Faye then took her seat, a very nice designer type high backed chair. Between them was a low coffee table on which there was a vase of cream roses, a long slim glass jug of water and a drinking glass, a box of tissues neatly contained in a cream ceramic tissue box holder, although thought Faye, Oliver Blake did not look like the crying type.

Oliver Blake observed his surroundings, the furniture was in good taste and while not excessively expensive it certainly wasn't cheap, the room was spacious and warm, he recognized the familiar fresh, green, spicy fragrance in the room, the scent of Diptyque 34. The walls were painted a dark blue and four large abstract paintings hung on them, the sofa he sat in was comfortable and supported his frame, he noticed a Corbusier couch against the end wall, probably the analysis couch, he would avoid that, he liked to see the eyes of those he spoke to, all in all the room met with his approval. As Faye sat down he took her in, thin but not in that awful starved way, she looked as if she was naturally thin, long titian hair, her thin frame allowed for definition of her features, high cheek bones, a full well-shaped mouth, her large eyes were the palest blue, and very alive. Her body, while thin, had good definition, smallish breasts, narrow hips, toned but not hard, she certainly was attractive, not in a bomb-shell-want-to-bonk-her-brains-out sort of way, more in a subtle way. Oliver thought she looked well bred, the kind that are brought up on pulses and lentils and tennis, the kind he would be happy to be seen with at a business dinner, he preferred a different type out of the public eye.

'I might just take a few details from you first, date of birth and so forth,' began Faye.

She has a nice voice, professional but personable thought Oliver.

'Before we do that I would like to ask you a few questions, on your website...'

No, thought Faye, that bloody website, I knew it was a bad idea. Faye had been talked into a website as the way forward and given that she needed more business after the divorce she had relented and now people had preconceived ideas about her before they ever met her.

'...you say that you have an Existential-Phenomenological approach to your work, can you explain that to me?'

Oh for crying out loud, thought Faye, I have problems understanding it myself, and now he wants me to explain it to him in a minute, I hate when they ask these stupid broad questions and then usually pretend to understand the answer I give, I really ought to tell him that I am not Wikipedia and to go Goggle it, that blasted website.

'It is quite a big area and as much as I would like to discuss philosophical ideas, I do not wish to eat into your time here,' began Faye.

'I am quite happy to use the time to understand your approach and its implications, after all if I choose to embark on therapy with you, I think it is fairly important that I understand your method, don't you agree?' Oliver asked in a very even matter of fact tone, he had no intention of letting her off that easily.

Well, thought Faye, how can I disagree with that without sounding like an inept pillock, this one is competitive, and Faye never liked the competitive ones, it just, she thought, made the whole thing miserable, may as well give him what he wants.

'Of course I agree, and I am more than happy to expand on the Existential-Phenomenology,' answered Faye. 'Existential analysis is deeply influenced by philosophical writers such as Heidegger, Sartre, Buber among others. Existential thinking in fact could be considered to be as old as the first time someone contemplated their existence, it is a form of reactionary thinking usually against pedantic and dogmatic attempts to control people. The approach is not to cure or explain, but rather to explore and describe in an attempt to understand your human condition. People are often craving answers but reject the questions. People seek certainty and security while rejecting their responsibility to seek out truths which will bring with them insecurity. The idea is to explore with an open mind the various ways in which our minds are closed. It takes courage to stand at that point of tension in our life, the tension between where we are and where we want to be, between what we are willing to do to change and what we are willing to accept for that change, what are we willing to let go of, and all the time taking account of the context of the world we inhabit and of course to accept that we are limited beings and not capable of all we might desire. It is an approach which champions individuality and freedom, freedom to be who we want to be comes at a cost, we are free to do whatever we wish but we must suffer the consequences of our free actions.'

'So we can do whatever we want once we can live with the consequences?' enquired Oliver.

'In essence yes, that is not to condone bad actions, one has to live with one's own conscience. Psychoanalysis may help reframe how you perceive your world and your actions. Since we are free it follows that we can re-choose, yet this is not without its difficulties since one's way of seeing and being in the world are inextricably linked. Change only comes when we allow ourselves to experience the existential anxiety of standing over the abyss in which self and world, past and future, change together. Exploring one's past and making connections between your actions and outcomes can help you in choosing a different future,' answered Faye.

'What kind of things from your past do you look at?' asked Oliver.

'Anything that comes up, remember while children likely have some basic level of unreflective, present-oriented consciousness, you cannot discount what was won by insight or transferred onto us as children, just because we were children does not mean that we were unaffected by our surrounding – our conditioning,' answered Faye.

'How do you discern what things are harmful and what are useful? asked Oliver.

'During the process of the analysis we might look at the analytical relationship and the transference...'

What do you mean by transference?' interrupted Oliver, although he knew full well, but he was enjoying himself watching Faye trying to impress him.

Bloody hell who cares what it is, thought Faye, but went on to explain.

'Generally speaking, transference refers to how the patient might transfer their feelings, wishes, reactions or experiences towards another person, most likely from their childhood, onto the analyst.

Yet transference is not the preserve of the therapy setting, it is in fact a universal phenomenon which might occur in any area of one's life, where the reactions to a current person echo early patterns. In existential analysis, the task is to look at the patient's interpersonal world and how it relates to their present relationships and recast it to reflect the true nature of the present without the interruption of the past.'

'How long does that take?' Oliver asked this knowing well how irritating that question must be.

Faye hated this question, people came to her after a lifetime of clutter and then expected to be fixed in three sessions. Early on in her career she had stopped giving any time frame as people immediately set that time as their ending and usually wanted to finish at that point even though they were not within an ass's roar of where they needed to be, another example of conditioning gone wrong.

'I never presume to know how long anything will take especially on only first meeting a person, it is best to allow it to run its own course,' answered Faye.

Nicely done, thought Oliver.

'Might you be able to say what slows things up in therapy, taking it as a given that the therapist is competent and not dragging it on for their own ends?' he asked.

Faye noticed that he did not have an accusatory tone when he asked this but was very matter of fact about it; nonetheless she thought there was something fishy about Oliver Blake.

'Taken as a given that the analyst is trained and competent and not money hungry,' began Faye, 'then things like the patients' resistance and defences can come into play.'

'But if you come here of your own volition,' enquired Oliver, 'how could that be resistance?'

'In psychoanalysis, resistance and defences are considered ways of being-in-the world, non-reflective strategies developed over time to deal with difficulties. As these strategies are usually developed in early childhood, they can be quite entrenched and you may be unaware of your own resistance or your defences. It is thought that defence mechanisms may have a mechanical quality to them because the person as he experiences himself is dissociated from them and suffers from them rather than being their author,' she answered.

'So what you are saying is that we are not really responsible for our actions given that our resistance and defences are not in our control?' Oliver asked this knowing well the answer he would get, he noticed she held eye contact all the time and remained very still, no fidgeting or unnecessary hand movements, he hated people who used their hands to emphasis what they were saying, it usually meant that what they had to say did not hold enough weight without the embellishment of dancing hands.

'Unlike Freudian analysts, existentialism holds the belief that human beings are free rather than determined and as such responsible for our actions. Freedom here is not a freedom out of context, as I said earlier, we are limited, but to some degree are the authors of our experience in the sense of being world-related rather than being environmentally determined beings. Analysis is about bringing the patient from the position of feeling one's experience is determined to being free,' she said while thinking that if she was so bloody free she should just tell him to cop on and get to the reason he came to see her.

'Do you consider people who come to you sick since you use the term patient?' enquired Oliver

Of course I do, screamed Faye, but only in her head.

'No, I just use that term as a matter of habit - it does not have the same meaning as in the medical setting, what would you prefer I use?' she asked, hoping to shift the direction of questioning.

'Oh it makes no difference to me as I know I am not sick, I was thinking in general as I am sure others of less certitude may find it offensive,' Oliver wanted to rattle her a bit, see how she would hold up.

It was as if Faye could feel her neurotransmitters release angry chemicals in her brain and her quickening heart rate told her adrenaline and noradrenalin were beginning to surge through her blood stream, in a millisecond she deepened her breath to counteract this effect and told herself not to react to Mr Blake. If you are so full sure you are not sick, what are you doing here and why are you trying to vex me, she thought.

'Oliver, I certainly try never to wilfully cause offence but that does not mean that people do not take offence. When it does happen, it can be very beneficial, therapeutically speaking, as it may expose a lived experience of an otherwise hidden emotion,' Faye said in her best nonchalant voice.

'Interesting,' he replied, Oliver had registered Faye's initial spark of annoyance and the ensuing regaining of control. To the untrained eye it would appear she did not anger at all, but Oliver made it a point to notice such nuances. He would have liked to have come closer to see if he could pick up the scent of her pheromones, it was a smell he enjoyed, even longed for, although he had trained himself not to long for anything, he had read that the release of these chemicals caused others to react with empathy albeit unconsciously, not Oliver, he reacted with a desire to devour. Dr Monroe could certainly take control of herself, he liked that. What's more he sensed that she prided herself on not reacting, even better, he thought.

'Is there anything in particular you would like to discuss, perhaps why you decided to come to see me?' Faye asked as she registered a very slight flare of his nostrils, like an animal picking up a scent, it gave her a slight shiver up her spine.

'My wife and I have recently separated, I must admit it was not by mutual consent, I, it now appears, mistakenly thought everything was going well but apparently, she did not and asked for a divorce after twelve years of marriage. Needless to say, it came as quite a jolt and as you can imagine I was very upset. She was adamant it was over and did not wish to seek some compromise or indeed entertain trying to work on a resolution. She moved out of our home the same day, she told me not to contact her as she needed time to clear her head and think clearly,' Oliver paused and dropped his head, he thought this would have the desired effect.

'When did this happen?' asked Faye.

'A while back, I thought I would come to terms with it all but to my own annoyance I have not,' answered Oliver.

'What do you mean when you say "to your own annoyance"? enquired Faye, somehow she was surprised by what he was saying, he did not seem the type to admit he was having trouble getting over being dumped, she thought he was coming about some obtuse existential midlife-type angst.

'As you will come to see I am not the type to dwell on things, I am very successful at what I do and tend not to cry over spilt milk, I move on, I focus on the next thing, I am in the habit of succeeding.'

'So you see your wife leaving as a failure?'

'No, I did not fail her or our marriage - she came to that decision without my input, she was the one who decided things were not as she would like.'

'Would you have been willing to change?'

'Frankly, what she wanted I could not give her, so you see it was not simply a matter of me changing, I was not the person she wanted me to be.'

What did his ex want from him, Faye wondered, probably that he wasn't such a control freak, mind you, that observation would have to wait, too much too soon is never a good idea, for lots of reasons, primarily because they never believed it and spent the rest of the time disproving you, which quite frankly was too tiresome, Faye thought. So instead of pointing out his over-controlling personality, she asked how he felt not to be the person his ex-wife wanted.

'Dr Monroe I am quite happy with the person I am, in fact it would be difficult to fault me on any level, you may think that sounds egotistical, but I am confident in my own abilities and have achieved a great deal in my life. I am not an unreasonable man, and I gave my wife a very comfortable life, she wanted for nothing and was well looked after. You see she became discontented with the very things which she previously stated gave her a great deal of contentment. She never wanted to work and was happy to be provided for, I demanded little of her, we had a fulltime housekeeper and gardener, holidays two, perhaps three times a year, with a holiday home in France. I hardly need to go on, I am sure you can conjure up a picture as to the life I am capable of providing,' Oliver delivered this in an even tone which contained none of the conceit which the words held.

Yes indeed, Faye could conjure up a picture of the life Oliver Blake could offer and the price for that life. She had often wondered what it must be like to be "taken care of" and not have to work, right now it sounded more desirable than ever, being divorced brought with it a new kind of poverty. Yes she still made money, but now all her money went to pay all the bills as there was no splitting of expenses, and these expenses did not decrease just because there was one less person, a light bulb does not care how many lives it lights up, it still wants to be paid for its trouble.

For a second, she thought he was flirting with her, it was as if he was letting her know what he could offer. God was this how desperate she was becoming, this poor man had come in devastated that his wife did a runner and in the only way he knew how, he was trying to come to terms with it. She had seen it before, now more than ever since the economic crash, all those highflyers now broke in more ways than one. When they come first, they are all about how successful they are and within no time they are a blubbering mess not able to form any connection to this new person they inhabit, this person without the wherewithal to splash two hundred grand on a car for the wife, or a bolt hole in Lake Coma. Their identities were so enmeshed in their capacity to procure that not only did they not recognize their non-omnipotent self, but they loathed this person, and this self-hate led to all sort of trouble. But Oliver Blake did not lose his money, he lost his wife, and sometimes a wife is easier than a fortune to acquire again.

After Oliver had expanded further on what a great husband he was, Faye needed to check the time, this act was always a tricky business no matter how many times you do it, she had a small digital clock on the table between herself and the patient and also her watch. Getting a glimpse of the watch was always more obvious and therefore you had to find the most opportune moment to drop your gaze to catch the small digital read-out which signalled how close you were to shutting up time. No matter how evolved the patient was, catching you looking at the time gave an unwelcomed feeling, she is no longer interested, I'm boring, I won't have enough time to say what I came to say, she's trying to get rid of me, namely rejection. And since most people came to therapy to deal with some incarnation of rejection, the end of each session was always peppered with this dance of one-upmanship. Of course everyone denied this, but then in Faye's experience most people denied most things. So as surreptitiously as possible, she noted that they only had three minutes. Faye made it a rule very early on in her career never to go over time no matter how interesting things were, then again, it was a long time since Faye was tempted to go over time.

'Oliver we are just at the time and so we will need to finish up, I would be happy to see you again if you so wish or perhaps you might like to think about it,' said Faye, not really quite sure whether she really wanted to see him again, but then again she needed all the work she could get.

Oliver was not in the habit of having others call time on him, he liked to hold that position himself, but this was only a small thing in the bigger picture. Yes he would be coming back, that was not something he needed to think about, but she need not know that.

'Yes I think I would like to return but it will depend on whether you can offer me a time which I can work with, day time will be impossible for me, I see from your website that your last appointment is eight on a Tuesday, that time would suit me,' Oliver didn't ask, he expected that time.

'Yes I work late on a Tuesday night but that eight is gone for the next few weeks,' Faye lied. The eight was not gone, but neither was the seven o' clock and she had no intention of sitting for an hour until eight, he'll take the seven, she thought.

Oliver wanted the eight o'clock slot but could not quite read whether Dr Monroe was telling the truth or just getting the upper hand about this time not being available - in fact he was rather sure she was lying, he had to decide whether or not to risk it, if he refused the seven he could end up waiting several weeks to come back and that really was not an option, taking the seven meant he ceded to her on this one. He decided to yield to her in this instance, but he certainly was not going to make a habit of this.

'Very well I will take the seven o' clock but I would hope that in a few weeks when the eight does come available you would offer it to me,' Oliver would hold her to this.

'Yes of course,' answered Faye with no intention of offering this to him unless she had someone to fill the seven o' clock session. It wasn't that she was some sort of cold-hearted cow who wouldn't put herself out for someone, but from experience, it was the ones you put yourself out for the most that abused it the most.

'So shall we say seven next Tuesday,' asked Oliver.

'Yes,' answered Faye as she handed him a sheet of paper that passed as a contract, it had the bits about confidentiality, obligation to disclose to authorities any admission or suspicion of child abuse, suicide protection, but it was the bit about the cancellation fee which people always questioned. Faye charged for a missed appointment unless she received forty-eight hours' notice. People hated this, they appeared to have no problem about her having to possibly disclose child abuse but resented having to pay for an appointment they made but did not keep. As far as Faye was concerned, it was yet another example of people not taking responsibility for themselves and acting like babies. It had happened that over the years Faye had lost patients because of this clause, but she stuck to it nonetheless, as a result she now had very few cancellations, but she also had no waiting list. There had been a time when she had a six-month waiting list, the boom had brought with it a desire for people to discuss the problems which excessive amounts of money brought. Should they buy their little darlings a new car for their sixteenth birthday, which charities are more worthy of their time and money, which was really about which charity would afford them the most publicity, should they get rid of the Polish nanny because she doesn't love the children enough and on and on.

'What way do you like to be paid,' asked Oliver.

Hard cash, Faye wanted to say, but that was too crass. She had stopped taking checks, it was no longer worth the hassle of dealing with the ones that bounced, one from a patient who had ran up a bill of twenty-two sessions, she had no intention of letting that happen again.

'Credit card or you can do a bank transfer – the fee has to be transferred prior to your appointment or you can pay as you go,' answered Faye.

'In that case, I will pay you in cash if that is acceptable?' said Oliver. It was always his intention to pay in cash as he did not want any form of payment linking him to Dr Monroe.

'That would be fine,' said Faye and it was only when she was saying goodbye and walking him to the door with her hand outstretched to shake his that she noticed he had not removed his gloves, nor did he do so before he shook her hand, which was firm but strange that he did not remove his glove. And then, for some reason Faye could not quite explain to herself, she did something she had never before done - she went into the waiting room which had a window overlooking the street, to catch a glimpse of Oliver Blake. And there he was in all his suaveness crossing the road but not before he suddenly stopped and to Faye's horror turned to look directly at her, but instead of turning away, she raised her hand, waved at him, smiling and gesturing to an oncoming traffic warden, hoping frantically that he would get what she was trying to convey and not look like the complete pillock she felt she was. He appeared to have understood as he turned and kept walking. For crying out loud, Faye thought, how could she have been so bloody stupid, she must have looked like a complete idiot, or worse still, some kind of weird psycho who likes to gawk at her patients. At that moment Faye's next patient, Mari Philips came in, Mari was great, she liked the couch which at that moment suited Faye just fine as it allowed her to close her eyes and relive the horrific scene in her head over and over again.

# two

As Oliver turned away from catching Faye staring at him, he was smirking to himself, he had lost on the time slot but most definitely he had the upper hand now. Faye had impressed him more than he had expected, under other circumstances she might be an asset to him. He had deliberately not parked on Harcourt Rd where Faye's office was, instead he had his driver Jim park around the corner on Hatch St. Jim was waiting for him and as he opened the rear door of the Bentley Continental he took out his mobile and dialled Arthur Wilson's number. When Arthur answered, Oliver simply said that it was on and hung up.

'I'm going home Jim please.' Oliver said to his driver. Home was not so far, Oliver lived on Wellington Avenue and at this time the traffic from Harcourt St to there should be fairly thin. As they drove Oliver checked his emails and made a call to his secretary Tina, there was nothing pressing which gave him time to think about Dr Faye Monroe. As Jim pulled into the drive Oliver saw that there were no other cars in the drive, except for his silver Jaguar XJ, which meant that the housekeeper and the gardener had left, which was fine as it was after five. Oliver lived, by most people's standards, in a very beautiful red brick Georgian house. He had, what the estate agent might say, sensitively restored the house leaving all the original features in this five bedroom, three storeys over a basement, four thousand square foot home. Before he got out of the car, he bid Jim a good evening and asked him to collect him at six-thirty the following morning. As Oliver climbed the six steps to the front door, he began to take his keys out when he suddenly felt concupiscent, he had not felt this way for a while, Dr Monroe had ignited his libido; Freud would have been pleased.

Like most powerful men he was driven in most areas of his life and sex was no different, he would have a woman later. He could smell that Nora had cooked, she would have left his dinner wrapped and ready to be reheated on the counter in the very expensive German-imported kitchen, which he liked because it didn't hide untidiness. Oliver liked things to be transparent and there was transparency in order.

He didn't follow the smell to the kitchen but instead went upstairs to the bedroom and began to take off his suit jacket. The bedroom was all pale greys and whites, the super-king size bed a reminder of his plans for later, but not in this bed, never in this bed. Oliver carefully hung his Brioni Vanquish II jacket on its hanger in the adjoining dressing room, followed by his trousers, his shirt went into the laundry basket for Nora to look after and when he was naked, he carefully and admiringly gazed at his refection in the long wall mirror. It would be hard not to like what he saw, he was thirty-eight with the body of a well-crafted younger man, Oliver had made it a habit to take care of himself - this was less motivated by vanity than necessity, the way Oliver saw it if he wanted to stay at the top of his game, sharp and successful, then he would have to be as body fit as he was mentally astute. The bonus of course was what was reflected back to him right now and it didn't matter a toss to him if others thought that was vanity. Irish men were ridiculously bad at taking care of themselves, thinking instead that their charm and good humour was enough to compensate for a milky-white flabby body. Not Oliver, from a very young age he knew the value of the physical and aesthetics, while admiring his reflection he reached for one of his many phones and dialled a number he knew by heart and made the arrangements to meet Silvia later on.

In the kitchen after heating up his dinner, it was shepherd's pie, he was a fan of simple good food, Oliver opened his briefcase and took out the sealed envelope which was left in the back of his car while he was in Dr Monroe's. As he ate, he took from the envelope several photos and a list outlining a day-by-day routine. Faye Monroe photographed well although in some shots she did look harried, Oliver gently traced the outline of her body with his index finger and thought if she looked harried now, wait until he had finished with her. He read through her daily activities and who she saw as he ate his dinner. She has a busy life he thought and did some interesting things, she attended two lunch-time concerts in the National Concert Hall in the last ten days, she went alone, he liked that, she also visited the National Art Museum and sat in front of the same picture for more than twenty minutes at a time, it was a newly acquired Picasso, "Woman Drinking Absinthe". Oliver was not familiar with this particular one, he would have to make a visit. She played polocrosse which he approved of, and she was part of a group called the Phenomenologists, whatever the hell that was. Probably a clique of pseudo-intellectual failures, sitting around pontificating some drivel like how they are indifferent to the fact that they are not making truckloads of money because money is dirty, and it is the experiences in life that are important. Oliver had not once come across someone who said no to money, but in his experience, it is far easier to say you are not interested in money when you don't have any.

He checked his watch, it was time to leave Faye for Silvia. He dropped his plate, knife and fork into the sink then grabbed his keys, set the alarm and shut the door behind him. He drove the Jag to within a street of Silvia's apartment, parked it and briskly walked the last of the journey, eagerly anticipating what would come next.

# three

Everything about Ina Mulhall contradicted itself, long back, short legs, short arms, long fingers, big breasts, tiny waist, small eyes, big lips, pale green eyes, light brown hair. But somehow all this combined to make her very alluring in a most unconventional way. Intellectually she was as clever as they come, sharp as a whip, a proper brain box, with such a wealth of knowledge she was like a full set of encyclopaedias. Ina could have been anything she wanted to be, but she chose the guards, no one could quite fathom why. Those close to her knew she became a guard to please her father, he was a Garda on the street all his life. One of those that valued the old school way of doing things, work your way up and all that sort of thing, he never valued Ina's huge intellect and typically she gave her life trying to please an imbecile. To be fair to the guards they quickly realised what a gem they had in Ina, and she now heads up an extremely successful forensic department in the Garda headquarters in Phoenix Park. As she waited for Faye in their usual haunt, The Copper Cow, she was reading a tome on neuropathology, she was half-way through even though she had been reading it for a few hours, and although she would never admit it to be true, her friends were all convinced that Ina had a photographic memory. It was futile playing scrabble with her as there was no word she did not know and better still none she could not spell. Just as Ina was getting into some neuropathology theory, Faye arrived.

'Hiya,' Faye said.

'Hi Faye,' answered Ina, 'what would you like, I'm having a pint?' Ina knew Faye would not have a pint she wouldn't dream of it, probably a G&T she thought.

'Gin and tonic please although I would like a nice chilled Veuve Clicquot,' said Faye.

'You could still be drinking Veuve Clicquot if you had minded your husband, it's your own fault you are reduced to gin!' Ina said in her cop-yourself-on voice. She had always liked Noel, very much indeed and thought that Faye had been mistaken in letting him go.

'God Ina don't start that again, I know you thought he was the bees' knees, but you didn't have to live with him, now shut up about him, not another word. Is Harry coming? asked Faye.

'Yeah, he's running a bit late, he said to order for him. Anything strange or startling going on?'

'I wish, but I did make a complete idiot of myself today with a patient, when he left I went to the waiting room window and looked out at him and as if he could feel me looking at him, he turned around and caught me.'

'Cringeful!'

'That's an understatement, and then I waved and pretended to be looking out for the traffic warden, who for good luck was just coming down the street'.

'What the hell were you doing looking out the window at him?'

'I don't know, it was an urge, I have never done that before, really I haven't, but there was something unnerving about him, almost intriguing, I don't know what I was expecting to see, maybe what kind of car he got into, but really I don't care about cars people drive, so I honestly don't know. He probably thinks I am some sort of weirdo.'

'Yeah, I bet he does.'

'Thank you, that helps a lot.'

'What was he like?'

'Handsome, classy, successful, clever, self-important,' answered Faye as their drinks arrived and they both clinked glasses and paused to have a drink.

'Maybe you fancied him, after all you are going through a very dry spell, and needs must,' grinned Ina.

'I'm not that desperate that I have to resort to patients and besides it's impossible. Let's change the subject, I think I might have to give up Harcourt St.' At just that moment Harry strode over to their table in that easy, playful way of his.

Harry, Ina and Faye were friends for years, they had met when they were fourteen at a swimming gala, all were useless swimmers, at least in the sense of medal potential, they called themselves "The Leftovers", but had hit it off and remained firm friends ever since.

Harry was the art director and partner in a very successful advertisement company and was great fun, if a serial womaniser; to his credit he had never hit on either Ina or Faye, not that he hadn't fantasized about it but he knew it would irrevocably change everything and he would never risk that.

'Hello you two,' beamed Harry, he was always happy it seemed. 'What have I missed?

'Faye made a fool of herself with a patient she fancies,' laughed Ina and preceded to tell Harry her version of events, with Faye occasionally throwing her eyes to heaven.

'Oh you poor thing,' sympathised Harry, 'you most feel like a right plonker.'

'Well I certainly do now, you two are no help. Harry any new conquests? smiled Faye.

'Now that you ask, there is a lovely young thing in the copy writing department.'

As Harry went on to talk about his latest infatuation, Faye was distracted by a man sitting at the bar, she was sure she had seen him before, then she remembered, it was in the museum two days ago, she had caught him looking at her for a second but quickly dismissed it, and here again now she had caught him looking at her. Faye, like most women, was used to men looking at her but she was never at ease with it, it always felt wrong to her, to be looked at. She felt that any man who did not hide the fact that they were looking at you were a little pervy and cocky. But this felt different, Faye had an intuitive sense, it was what had made her good at her job, and this felt funny to her, but she could not quite put her finger on it.

'What or who are you looking at?' asked Harry.

'No one, just a guy over there who I thought I saw before, but I realised I didn't,' said Faye, 'Let's order some food I'm starving.'

The man at the bar was aware that Faye's gaze lingered a bit too long on him and noted the flash of recognition, this was the second time and he knew he had to be careful. He prided himself on his ability to blend in and remain unnoticed, he had a lifetime of practice after all, but there was something about Faye Monroe that was different, she had a heightened sense of awareness just like him, he decided to leave.

As he was leaving, he noticed Faye walking towards the loos. When Faye was out of earshot Harry leaned in closer to Ina and said with as much shock in his delivery as he could muster.

'You'll never guess who came into the office today?'

Ina was not the guessing type.

'Just tell me Harry.'

'Daniel bloody Cohen,' Harry said, savouring each syllable as he registered the shock on Ina's face. Harry loved to shock Ina and as Ina was rather shock immune, Harry savoured this all the more.

'You're joking me, Dan Cohen, our Dan Cohen, it can't be.'

'The very one,' said Harry, 'What are we going to do about Faye.'

'What do you mean, what are we going to do, we are going to say nothing, do you hear, nothing,' answered Ina.

'Ina, we have to tell her.'

'Why?' asked Ina indignantly.

'For one he is back in Dublin at least for the next six months, his company are opening up here and want us to do the advertising campaign.'

'You told him you couldn't work for him of course.'

'No I didn't, Ina times are tough, and he is a big client, the company needs this job and quite frankly I like Dan, always have done,' said Harry.

'I don't believe you, after all that happened, after all he put Faye through, you are now going to take his money.'

'Ina it's just a job, I am not marrying the guy and besides it's not up to me to make the decision not to take him on.'

'You're a partner, you could if you wished.'

'Yes, a partner who has to consider the other partners, Ina calm down, he's in Dublin and he asked about Faye, we have to tell her, what if they bumped into each other that would be catastrophic.' reasoned Harry.

'I suppose you're right, it's just a shock, Dan Cohen, I can't believe it, yeah we have to tell her,' Ina was not a stubborn person and always relented if she could see the reason in another person's argument, it was one of her many admirable traits.

'You tell her, here she comes.'

Faye sat down just as their food arrived.

Faye I have something to tell you,' began Harry, 'Dan Cohen is in Dublin for at least the next few months and he came to the office today to talk about an advertisement campaign, we have taken him on as a client, it's too substantial a job to turn down, despite past history. He asked about you, not only that he said he would love to see you,' Harry was not one to drip feed information.

'He just told me a second ago,' added Ina.

Harry and Ina could see Faye's face pale to white and through her eyes almost see her brain processing the information and the firing of memories which they both knew could be nothing but painful.

'Really?' she whispered almost inaudibly.

Faye could feel, for the second time that day, the physiological actions of her sympathetic nervous system. It often helped Faye to focus on what was physically happening in her body, it was a coping mechanism. She thought about how the catecholamine hormones were right now causing her heart rate and breathing to increase, she could visualize the constriction in her blood vessels. She understood that an abundance of these hormones at neuroreceptor sites would trigger the classic intuitive behaviour of combat or escape. Oddly she felt like doing both, she wanted to get up and run, find Danny Cohen and kick his head in. But Faye was also practised in the ancient art of restraint, she would never allow herself such an expression of emotion, it just wasn't the way things were done, denial was the order of the day. Faye reached for her drink and slowly took a long sip, returned the glass to the table with hyper-vigilance so as not to knock over the glass or clink it against the plate, which would be a betrayal of the flux she felt inside.

'I can't believe he came to your agency, why do you think he would do that, why not use another firm, I must say I find that a bit strange,' Faye said.

'Frankly so do I,' added Ina.

'Well maybe it has something to do with my agency being the best, and I find it strange that this is your reaction,' said Harry.

'Harry, it has got nothing to do with your agency, but surely you must think it a tad strange that after all these years he walked into your office, out of nowhere, no warning, there has to something else going on,' said Faye.

'Faye's right, this is no coincidence, and let's face it he was never the spontaneous type, plus it is nearly ten years since we have seen him. What exactly did he say and how did he appear?' Ina turned to Harry practically spitting out the questions.

'He had made an appointment about two weeks ago, but I never copped the name, or gave it any notice, and when he walked in you could have knocked me over with a feather. He was very nice and acknowledged that it was strange, but that his firm had researched various agencies and that ours was selected and that he would not use us if I was uncomfortable.'

'That was big of him,' interrupted Ina, 'it wasn't your heart he broke'.

'Still, he was very upfront about the whole thing. We discussed the job and caught up a bit on the years and then he asked how you were Faye.'

'What did you say?' asked Faye.

'What do you think I told him, you were a mess and never got over him, married on the rebound, followed by a divorce, piled on ten stone and dribble when you eat!' smirked Harry.

Both Ina and Faye laughed, both knew Harry would have championed Faye to the end.

'I hate myself for asking this but what was he like, has he changed?' Faye did hate asking but then curiosity often overrode dignity.

'Faye, it's perfectly normal to ask that, you're only human remember,' reassured Ina.

'He looks good, the years have been gentle on him, athletic looking as ever, he has two children, two boys I think he said, they moved back to London three years ago,' said Harry.

'Did you tell him I was married and separated?' asked Faye.

'No, I just said you were doing great and very successful and really nothing else. Faye I wasn't going to blab to him about you, you know that,' assured Harry and then added, 'or tell him that you were going bonkers spying on patients out the window.'

'Are you going to meet him?' Ina asked, dreading the answer.

'What's the point, I have nothing to say to him, and besides if he looks that good, I might not be able to control myself,' deadpanned Faye.

'Aren't you at least a bit curious to meet him, just, well you know, to test the waters?' asked Harry.

'The waters do not need testing,' Ina glared at Harry 'and you should not be encouraging her to meet him,' turning to Faye she finished, 'don't do it to yourself, you know the effect he has on you, it will only end in misery.'

'What do you think I am going to do, see him and then jump into bed with him, please credit me with some restraint and a shred of dignity, besides he dumped me precisely because he did not want to be with me,' said Faye.

This was not exactly true and all three knew this. Faye and Dan had started dating when they were sixteen and all four pal-ed around together. They remained an item for nine years and were mad on each other; they were, by any accounts, moulded for each other. As they were getting older it was obvious that they were becoming more serious about a future together and it was at this time that unbeknownst to Faye, Dan's parents, or more accurately his mother, started to prevail on Dan. Dan was Jewish, which never mattered to anyone, in fact it was never an issue to any degree, neither he nor Faye were religious in any way, but ultimately it seemed that Dan's mother wanted him to marry a Jewish girl. It wasn't that they didn't like Faye, quite the contrary, they were very fond of her, she was a regular fixture in the Cohen household over the years, but when it came to the crunch Faye was not Jewish. Neither was it a question of Faye converting, not that she was given that option, it was a question of heritage and deeply held beliefs which ultimately were stronger than love. That last summer together Dan told Faye he was going to Israel on holidays with his parents and his sister and brother, it was their first family visit together to Israel. Faye sensed that something was a bit off with Dan when he was saying goodbye, but thought it was that he felt bad that she was not asked to go with them, she assured him she was fine with him going which she was, after all it was only two weeks. Nothing could have prepared her for what happened that summer. Dan never returned, subsequently he married an Israeli girl and remained in Israel to begin their life together.

At the time Faye felt she was dismantling, everything she had thought to be true about Dan was demolished, not a word to her, not a call, nothing. She only found out when a day after he supposedly was to be back, she had not heard from him, she called his parent's home and his sister Anna answered. Faye then had to suffer the humiliation of being told that her lover of nine years had unceremoniously dumped her in the most dramatic fashion, he was to marry a woman he had only barely met and moved half away across the world - had their relationship been that bad and she'd never realised?

Faye could not bring herself to suffer the ignominy of going to his parents for an explanation, so she really had nothing to root her disbelief in other than he was a complete fake and she a complete idiot to be taken in by his gentle nature over the years, which clearly was fraudulent. Obviously, Ina and Harry had their theories, Harry thought he was the greatest wanker who ever walked the earth, Ina thought he must have had some sort of psychotic episode which rendered him incapacitated and this would account for his completely out of character preposterous behaviour. But ultimately, he was gone, married, out of all their lives, without a word. For a long time Faye felt stunned by the absurdity of it all, she thought that there was nothing as inequitable as being cast aside without the opportunity to at least have your say. Six months later Faye received a letter from Dan, she knew it off by heart and even now could recall it word for word.

> Faye, (I can hardly use a term of affection given what I have done to you)
>
> I am so sorry, I know I am such a bastard to do to you what I did, it is no excuse to say I was pressured into it, I acted freely. There were a lot of factors at play, things I could not ignore, I had to put others needs before my own and I will regret to my death that also meant putting others ahead of you.
>
> I hope you can forgive me someday and I wish nothing but the best for you.
>
> Everything I felt for you and said to you was true and real.
>
> Full of remorse
>
> Danny

What a useless cop out of a letter.

No address or date was given, which sent a message in itself - do not contact me. With Ina and Harry, Faye analysed, dissected, poured over, theorised and ultimately destroyed the letter. Anna had as much as said that tradition dictated Dan marry a girl of Jewish faith, but even Anna didn't sound convinced herself.

Over time Faye's soreness, because she physically felt sore from the whole episode, eased and she survived it. At the root of it Faye knew that the human species are survivors and while we think we cannot live without someone, the truth is we can and do, we just live in a different way.

'I don't necessarily want to revisit the past and relive old tribulations, there is absolutely nothing to be got by that. We have both lived our lives quite well apart, it is best that we remain apart. If he asks you again about meeting me Harry, tell him I do not want to,' Faye said decisively, 'Let's not talk about it anymore it's such a stale story now.'

'Righto,' said Harry, 'let's finish up here and go dancing.'

As they were leaving Ina and Harry cautiously caught each other's eyes silently sending each other an expression of alarm.

# four

Daniel Cohen was staying in the Merrion Hotel for the time being, he could have stayed with his sister but he was wound too tight to relax there and besides Anna would only complicate things, and there was no question of him staying with his parents, things were never right between them since that trip to Israel. Meeting Harry Stuart again had completely unnerved him, not because of Harry, no Harry was very gracious given the history and did everything to put him at ease, no, the contact with Harry had made him realise the realness of his whole messy situation and also being around Harry had made him long to see Faye again.

He had not been back to Dublin in six years, the last time was for the funeral of his grandmother, it was part of the arrangement he had made with Liat's father, Uziel Nachman, stay in Israel for seven years with no trips home during this time save exceptional circumstances such as a death, work hard in the business with the view to opening an office in London, and have children. Uziel was aware he had been in a long relationship and that his marriage to Liat was not one of love but obligation, he felt that an arranged marriage such as this had as good a chance of success as a young love match and that in time Dan would grow to love Liat, and if not well, so be it. Dan was a chemist, in fact a medical chemist and hardly by chance his new father-in-law had a pharmaceutical company where finding a position for Dan would be easy. So Dan did what was expected and knuckled down to work, he was a respectful husband, the love never did come, they had two boys, Arnie and Iggy, but not a day went by when Dan didn't feel the dolour of his actions towards Faye. Almost unconsciously he could not allow himself to love Liat. Liat was brought up wealthy, accustomed to the finer things in life and had come to expect them, she was in many respects shallow and vacuous and obsessed with her appearance, and possessions. She was also brought up with the idea that her marriage would be one of her father's orchestration and so she did not object in the slightest when introduced to Dan, why would she, he was very handsome, intelligent and clearly given the arrangement, once married would be indebted to her father, which had its advantages. Dan knew that Liat had taken lovers over the years, it did not bother him, what in fact bothered him was that fact that he was not bothered. He too had had the occasional dalliance over the years but nothing of any import. Finally, three years ago, Liat's father had given the go ahead to open the London office. Dan couldn't wait to get back to Europe, he hated the middle eastern heat and despite his best efforts, and he did put in effort, he could not settle there, it was where the deal was made with Uziel and in Dan's mind would always be associated with betrayal and loss, his betrayal and loss of Faye and how he had been betrayed by his parents and ultimately realising that parental love and sacrifice was a myth, the truth lay in the primal instinct to survive, be you a parent or not.

As Dan lay on the large bed covered in luxurious linen he thought of Faye and tried to imagine how she might be ten years on. He had tried goggling her over the years but not surprisingly he found nothing other than the mention of her speaking at various events but nothing with pictures and no personal website or Facebook page, Faye had always valued privacy, so he did not expect to find anything, but looked nonetheless. The last time he tried he had discovered she had a website, with a picture, she was as beautiful as ever, even by webpage photos standards. He had such contempt for himself at how he had treated her that he dreaded meeting her but ached to see her. He had known going to Israel that there was a real possibility that he would not be coming back, but on the off chance that things would not go according to his parents' plans, he thought it best not to tell Faye anything. He knew now how utterly stupid and cowardly that was and that that which is denied always has a way of exposing itself.

What he never denied to himself was the love he had felt for Faye, he worshiped her, she was all he ever wanted, they had an ease together that didn't require questioning. Now here he was after ten years about to come back into her life, with the sole intention of getting her to love him again.

A lot depended on it.

# five

Oliver quickly checked that there was no one on the street before he took the steps up to the black door. The front door to the period house was opened, he simply pushed it in, this brought Oliver into a vestibule where there was a second locked door with an intercom to the right-hand side, Oliver pressed the intercom button and said 'Silvia' into the speaker. Almost as soon as he had said it, the door clicked open, Oliver pushed the door away from him and entered. The reception hall was elegantly decorated, it had a plush Fifth Avenue mid-century feel to it, the high-polished maple wood floor was covered with a silk rug and the piped tranquil music was like an opiate lulling you into an illusion that you were in some high-ranking diplomat's posh home and not a whorehouse. With the air of someone who had been here before, Oliver sauntered up the stairs. He turned right at the top and at the end of the hall Silvia stood smiling outside the third door on the left. All five other doors were shut, not a sound came from any room, not that that meant anything, the rooms were prodigiously sound proofed, someone could be kango hammering behind these doors, or more likely ecstatically screaming from a master and slave flogging and not a sound wave got past the high-density vulcanised rubber embedded in the walls.

'Good evening Silvia,' said Oliver as he brushed past her into the room.

'Yes, good evening,' answered Silvia in a thick Romanian accent, she had perfect English just highly accentuated. Oliver began to take off his jacket as he made his way to the bed, he noticed that she had already laid out his favourite toys, although the room was filled with all manner of intriguing objects from cages to ropes to ball and chains, blind folds, and gags, even a spanking machine. Oliver remained simple in his needs, he liked a tightly rolled newspaper, preferably The Sun, or a knotted tea towel. Silvia allowed her bath robe to slip to the floor, she was wearing cheap washed-out knickers and bra, she knew Oliver preferred them as rank as possible, she had a drawer full of worn and unwashed old underwear, these were particularly seasoned, just the thing for tonight.

As Oliver took in Silvia's beautiful body, he felt strong and in control, he was naked now and he picked up the tea towel and with powerful force hit Silvia repeatedly with it, the more she moaned and begged him to stop the more aroused he felt and the harder he struck the next time. By the time he was satiated, he was sweating and breathing heavily. After ejaculating in her face, he finished by urinating over her, he then went to the bathroom cleaned himself, got dressed and took five crisp one hundred euro notes from his wallet and put them on the bedside table. Silvia remained on the floor unmoving and silent, just as Oliver had instructed her on their first meeting, she only got up as he closed the door behind him.

As Oliver came to the bottom of the stairs there was a large well-groomed man waiting for him, with an outstretched arm he motioned to Oliver to enter into a waiting room, Oliver had been in here before, it simply meant that someone had arrived at the front door and he would have to wait until that client was out of sight, this was all part of what you paid for, discretion and anonymity.

'Apologies for the delay Sir, enjoy the rest of your evening,' said the big man as he accompanied Oliver to the front door, no foreign accent here.

Oliver was feeling very satisfied, he never questioned why he found it so pleasurable to inflict pain, there was no need to question it, he accepted it as part of him and therefore experienced no angst, people like him did not doubt themselves or question their motives, self-inquiry was for neurotic women or emasculated men. He found the popular opinion that powerful men like to be dominated amusing, powerful men were powerful simply because they dominated.

He thought about Faye, and he found himself feeling aroused again as he savoured the picture of her perdition, he would dismantle her.

# six

'You fucking ugly cow, I don't have to listen to this fucking shite, you fucking give me a good fucking report or I'll fucking rip your ugly fucking mug off,' roared Darren, spitting in Faye's face and kicking the table over before being restrained by two male orderlies. They dragged him kicking and screaming from the room out into the hall and down the corridor to the recovery room. There was something about being spat at that was worse than a belt in the jaw, it was so degrading to be on the receiving end of a lump of phlegm.

Faye worked one day a week at Mount Catherine's Hospital for the criminally insane, not that they called it that anymore, and Darren was referred for a capacity assessment to determine whether or not he was mentally fit to be tried for his crimes. It was very clear that Darren's plea of diminished capacity was a farce and Faye told him as much which led to the outburst. Early on in her career Faye was very impassioned about helping to rehabilitate those caught in the unrelenting cycle of crime and mental illness, she saw these people as victims of horrible circumstances, genetics and poor brain chemicals. Over the years that passion had waned, and it was practically extinct in her as she wiped the spit from her face.

'Are you alright?' asked Jack Donnellan, the hospital's most senior psychiatrist.

'I just saw them take a live one out of here, what happened, did you tell him his mammy never loved him, you know they don't like that,' he laughed.

If Faye's enthusiasm for the job was fading, Jack was gone into reverse, he was forty-two years working in the hospital with no notion of retiring and he was probably one of the most cynical people Faye had ever encountered and worryingly she liked him.

'No Jack, I just told him he was of sound mind,' answered Faye.

'Oh dear sweet Faye, surely you could have come up with something more inventive than that,' laughed Jack, 'come on we'll get a cup of tea.'

'Thanks, but I have to finish this report before I leave,' said Faye.

'What's the hurry, hot date now that you are a free agent,' joked Jack

'Not quite,' answered Faye, she wasn't about to tell him that she was going to meet the love of her life who unceremoniously dumped her years ago.

As Jack was turning to go Faye fought with herself over calling him back, she lost the fight.

'Jack before you go I was wondering if you wouldn't mind writing up a script for me, the usual,' she tried to sound causal but knew she sounded pathetic.

'It's been a while, I thought you got another supplier,' smiled Jack. To give Jack his due he would never judge or cast aspirations.

'You know I'd always be faithful to you Jack,' Faye answered, with a flirty gilt of her head.

'I have my pad here, I'll write it up now, is a month fine?' asked Jack.

'Plenty thanks, things are just a bit tricky at the minute, that's all,' Faye said trying to sound convincing.

'You don't have to explain,' Jack was writing the prescription out for a month's supply of Valium, as he handed it to Faye he took her hand for a second as he said, 'any time, you know that,' and turned to head out the door.

'Thanks Jack,' said Faye and she meant it.

Faye decided over the weekend it would be ridiculous not to meet Dan as she would only end up tormenting herself about him. She had arranged for Harry to give him a message saying she would be at The Ludo, a low-key place, at six o clock on Monday evening. It was now quarter to five which gave her forty-five minutes to finish the report and thirty minutes to get there. Faye was normally quite conscientious about report writing, but with her skin still crawling from the spit she had a little less rectitude than usual. Once she had signed the report she made her way down the long decrepit corridor towards the bathrooms, the building was over two hundred years old and at times what went on in there felt to Faye as antiquated as the building. Of course it was a joyless place but more than that it was as if the walls had ingurgitated the wretchedness of all those who had dwelled there at one point and now it churlishly spewed it out defiling the air and disheartening those who entered, how could people possibly mend themselves here, thought Faye.

The mirror in the bathroom was so aged it was hard to find a spot to get a clear look at yourself, which had its advantages at times. Faye put a stopper in the sink and filled it with water, which was cold and with a squirt of antibacterial soap washed her face, luckily, she had her make-up bag with her, she hardly ever brought it but she had today because of meeting Danny. Despite the pungency of the soap, she felt she could still smell the spit, yet she felt better for the wash, she quickly applied her make-up and thought she looked okay. Then she wondered how her looks had altered in ten years, that lovely youthful roundness was definitely gone, her face was now far leaner and for that probably more defined, was that good or bad she wasn't sure, probably bad but there was nothing she could do about that in the next thirty minutes. She left the hospital and walked at a brisk pace to the train, luckily one had just pulled in as she entered the station, she hopped on and took a seat opposite a woman who the years had not been kind to, her skin was ropey and puffy from too many Rothmans, she had a box in her hand, and too much booze. Faye avoided eye contact, the last thing she wanted was to give this woman an opportunity to burn her ear, she pulled out a book, opened it, dropped her head and let her mind run wild; luckily her stop was not too far otherwise she would have worked herself up into a frenzy. She wished she had time to fill the script Jack had given her, but she knew there was no chemist on the way.

As she approached the restaurant, she willed herself to turn and walk away, she knew this was a mistake, but despite all she now knew about human suffering and the pointlessness of hope she could not resist, she had learnt nothing. Our nature is to constantly recreate where we have come from and retry different versions of the same formula, each time with a vacancy of mind hoping that this time will be different. No wonder the world was in such a state, no one seemed to learn, including Faye. She went through the door of the restaurant which had an open plan set up, she scanned the tables and found him at a table close to the back wall, he too was looking expectantly towards the door and in the moment their gazes met it was as if no time had elapsed, no pain inflicted, just the two of them, no one else existed, there was no need for anyone but them. The maître d' broke the time warp with his invitation to help, help that is to seat her, not to erase the years and catapult her back to a time where the sheer cogency of love acted as a guardian against pain. She obligingly gave the tall man her coat and began to walk towards the table in a what felt like a state of suspension, what do you do in these situations, fling your arms around him and hold on to him for dear life or fling your bag at him and curse him to hell for ruining your life, but of course the civilised self takes over and you do neither. Instead, she extended her hand out in a formal gesture which she hoped conveyed a mature adult capable of a polite conversation with an ex-lover.

Harry was right, she thought, he looked good, better than good. There was a moment's silence as they both fiddled with their chairs, Dan had stood up to greet Faye, and shake her hand, he would have preferred if she had kissed him, but he thought that might be a bit much to expect and he did not dare make a move to kiss her.

'Faye thank you so much for meeting me, you look amazing, better than before, I mean not better but great, really you haven't aged a bit,' Dan was stumbling over his words and although he had rehearsed his greeting it had sounded much better in his head, hearing himself now he thought he sounded like an idiot and willed himself to shut up.

'Thank you,' answered Faye, 'I certainly feel older.'

She had recovered herself from the first sight of him after so long and now she wanted to show him she had moved on and she wanted answers.

The waiter approached their table and asked if they would like a drink. Of course they would.

'A Green Spot with one ice-cube please,' said Faye, something strong seemed a good idea.

'I'll have a Jameson and ice please,' said Dan, he was tempted to call for a double but didn't want Faye to think he was an alco, or worse still, nervous.

'It's been a long time Danny,' Faye looked straight at Dan as she spoke in an even kind tone, 'we can't sit here and pretend what happened didn't happen, the reason I came is to ask you the question that I never got the opportunity to ask you and the one that tormented me for a long time. Why, why did you do it?'

Dan had always admired the fact that Faye was forthright and didn't play the usual' try and guess what I am thinking' games, but at this precise moment he wished she wasn't so direct. He had dreaded this question and hadn't expected it quite so early in their meeting, he had hoped to endear himself a bit to her first. But he had also told himself that he would answer it as honestly as he could. The waiter returned with their drinks and he took a deep swig of the whiskey which both warmed him and settled him as it oozed its way into his bloodstream.

'Beau I..'

'Don't call me that, don't ever call me that again,' interjected Faye, with such an incredulous tone that Dan was abruptly reminded of the pain he had caused and that all informalities of their past were dead. He had called Faye, Beau, but not anymore.

'Sorry, I forgot it just slipped out.'

'Well, please don't forget again.'

'Faye I didn't go to Israel knowing that I would not come back, it all happened so quickly and then I just couldn't contact you, I wanted so much to return home to you, but I couldn't, things had gone too far and everything was arranged and backing out would have had serious consequences for everyone.'

'What happened so quickly and what would have happened if you said no?' Faye asked calmly.

'My parents had gotten into a lot of financial debt, they had invested in property, it was the boom times remember and they made loads of money and then stupidly invested the money in a high-risk investment scheme which went sour. They lost everything and still had Anna to put through university plus all the mortgage repayments. Mother has a cousin in Israel who had a very influential and rich friend who she said could help them out. He had a daughter, who was our age and wanted to get married, he wanted her to marry a European Jew, and my mother's cousin thought of me. Mother told me I would only have to meet her and go to a few parties and then I could return home, and what happened after that was completely up to me,' said Dan, it came somewhere near the truth.

Faye sat almost motionless listening and forming a picture in her head. She said nothing.

'I did not tell you because I was ashamed of my parents for asking me to do this, and I thought I would be back in two weeks and all this would be over. So I went,' again as close to the truth as he was willing to go.

Dan did not go into the details of the argument he had with his parents, he remembered the disgust he felt when they told him of their plan, he ranted and raved about the archaisms of arranged marriages, the hypocrisy of them wanting him to marry a Jew when they were practically atheists themselves, a charge they both denied, how he loved Faye and she was the only person he would ever marry. At this point he did not know about their financial mess and in the end his mother began to cry and his father pointed out how ungrateful he was, that he was causing his mother great distress in his refusal to grant her this one thing she asked. God knows it was not as if she asked for much, no she was a giver, giving to him and this family her entire life, and that if he couldn't oblige them with two measly weeks of his life, well he didn't know want kind of a son he had reared. So in the end guilt won out, guilt was as powerful a weapon used by parents among the Jews as it was among the Catholics.

'When we got there things happened so quickly. We were immediately introduced to Uziel Nachman and his daughter Liat, and I was strongly encouraged to spend all my time with Liat. I still thought I would be coming home once I had gone through the motions. There were lots of parties where Liat and I were pushed together and it soon became obvious that everyone thought of us as a couple. When I mentioned this to my parents, they just fobbed me off. Then after a week Uziel took me aside and said that he would be happy to have me as a son-in-law and that Liat was happy to accept me. I began to tell him that I could not marry Liat that I was in love with someone else, you. He indulged me while I protested but in the end, asked if I wanted to be responsible for my parents becoming destitute. This was the first I learnt about my parent's financial problems and it soon became clear what was going on. Nachman would bail my parents out in exchange for me marrying his daughter,' he didn't tell Faye that it was from Nachman that his parents had borrowed money from in the first place.

'Nachman,' he continued, 'was no fool, he could see what was happening but he was used to getting what he wanted. He painted a picture where I could have a perfectly good life married to Liat, he did not expect me to fall in love immediately, but he did expect me to respect her. I would be given a very responsible position in his pharmaceutical company and could in a short time relocate to London. This good life would mean that my parents were financially secure, and their debts taken care of and Anna would get the education she deserved. Sure I was free to return home, but this would mean that my parents would go bankrupt and there would be no money for Anna to go to the Conservatoire.'

What he didn't say was that his parents had already taken the money from Uziel Nachman and as good as guaranteed him that Dan was available for marriage. When Dan confronted his parents, they had made noises about having no choice, that they had to take the money or risk losing everything they had worked their lives for. What about his life and his future he had asked, did that not matter, he was in love with Faye and would return home to her, they had created their own problems and should fix them. This did not seem unreasonable to Dan, after all they were not living in the dark ages he could not simply be bartered as a husband. He was wrong.

That day Dan witnessed a side of his parents he wished he never had, it was not simply the coming-of-age realization that they were fallible, he had realized that a long time ago, this was different, this was a self-preservation that involved the devouring of your young. He remembered Goya's painting of *Saturn Devouring His Young* he had seen on a trip to Madrid in the Museo del Prado. Saturn, fearing being overthrown by his young, ate them at birth - at least Saturn had the good grace to ravage them as unaware babies, his parents had waited until he was in full comprehension of what they were doing to him. They told him that by refusing Liat he would be denying Anna her future, they had funded his education to a high level, given him every opportunity, equipped him with all he needed to be successful in life, Anna was just on the cusp of that, waiting to be accepted into college, she was clearly bright and a gifted pianist, it was indisputable that she would be accepted by the Conservatoire de Paris, it was just a matter of funding, huge funding.

Dan had always adored his little sister, she was more than ten years younger than him and it was true she certainly had an aptitude for music and had wanted to attend the Conservatoire ever since they had visited there on a trip to Paris when she was ten. She was dedicated beyond belief and completely enthralled to music, she existed for it. She had also immersed herself in everything French and spoke almost fluently now. In that moment he knew he would have to choose between his love for Anna and his love for Faye, and in that moment, he knew who he would choose. Faye, he knew, would recover and so would he, recovery was possible for both of them, but Anna would not recover, part of the reason he loved her so much was because of her vulnerable and ethereal nature. She did not have the necessary sagacity to withstand such a blow to her dreams, dreams which were encouraged by Dan, actively encouraged. She belonged to those in the world who needed to be shielded from the starkness of reality, perhaps it was her artistic nature where she existed on another plane to those who could not create. Her creativity took such an amount of her energy that there was none left to deal with the banality of life, she was beyond banality and to bring her into that would cause her to dismantle, not limb by limb, but thought by thought. He would not do that to Anna, he could not. And so he gave in to his parents' wish, they had dangled Anna as bait and he had taken the bait, Anna would get want she needed, but his actions would satisfy their primary motives which was to save themselves from ruin.

He marvelled at how cunning they were, what an elaborate plan they had pulled off, after all it wasn't every day that you could manage to marry off your son against his will to someone he had just met and get him to leave his country and all he knew and loved. He had never thought of his parents as monsters, they were quite ordinary really, they lived a very conservative life, his father a boring accountant, his mother a civil servant in the department of agriculture. They had had the same group of friends for years, gave and went to dinner parties a half a dozen times a year, went on a foreign holiday once a year, celebrated Christmas in the same way as all their friends, being Jewish was never an issue. People liked them, and they never flashed their money around, everything was so measured, and so too was this exchange, it was a measured exchange of their son's future so that they could keep their past. Reasoning with themselves as to their motives appeared easy as far as Dan could see and in typical Irish fashion once everything was agreed it was never mentioned again. Whether or not the absence of their only son in their lives had any meaning for them Dan never knew.

'So I did what they asked and married Liat. On every possible level I know I should have contacted you, I know what I did was cowardice. I can't even explain why I didn't, it was like I was numb, I thought by not contacting you then it wasn't happening, I could go on with the illusion that I would be going home to you soon. I suppose by contacting you it would have made it real and I did not want to hear what you would have said. I didn't want to have to confront the realness of the situation, or the realness of the hurt I was causing you.'

'I had imagined all sort of reasons why you didn't contact me, I convinced myself that you must have been brain washed or drugged in some way, that that could be the only reasonable explanation why you would cut off all contact, leave me in a state of suspension, as if we never existed. I could not contemplate any other scenario where you would deny me. But as time went by my mind became strong enough to consider the usual motive behind human behaviour, self-preservation. The boring everyday reason behind why people do what they do, self-preservation. I realised you were weak and could not take responsibility for your actions and of course by denying me a chance to seek an explanation or offer an opinion, you were able to deceive yourself into thinking what you were doing was at some level acceptable. That also put me in a position where I had no idea what was going on, racking my brains as to why you would do this, wondering what I had done that made you want to completely eradicate me from your life. I questioned everything, wondered if I had only imagined the love between us. It felt like I was going mad, I began to question my own thoughts, I doubted myself about everything. And now you are sitting in front of me confirming that what you did was to protect yourself.'

'It was as much for Anna as...' began Dan.

'Stop it, stop hiding behind your little sister, even if it was entirely for Anna, you could still have told me. Do you have any idea of how much easier that would have made things? Instead you chose to torture me.'

'I am so sorry,' Dan said this but knew how empty it must have sounded.

'Dan, I don't want your apology, not now, not ten years too late,' Faye was completely in control, she spoke with a certitude and firmness and kept her eyes on Dan all the time. She had waited a long time for this, and she wasn't going to allow him to excuse away his pathetic actions.

'I am not here for an apology, I am here to put this sorry episode of my life behind me for good, to eliminate any doubts I may have had lurking in the back of my mind, to confirm for myself that what you did was done with your full awareness and without regard for me and that it was not that I was some mad woman that you had to flee to the middle of the earth to escape.'

'It didn't feel like I was letting myself off the hook, and I certainly didn't want to escape you, I loved you, I had to deny myself you.'

'Yes, but you made that choice without me, you were not the one in the dark as to what was happening, you knew exactly what was going on, you were not an innocent in this.'

'It didn't feel like I had a choice, I felt cornered, I had to marry a woman I had only just met.'

'Quite frankly I don't buy your pretence of martyrdom, maybe you've been too long in the Middle East. Let's just say for a moment that you did marry against your will and did it in an act of self-abnegation, that in no way would have prevented you from picking up the phone or putting pen to paper and letting me know what you were doing. Jesus Dan what you did was just plain wrong and mean.'

Faye felt worn out, there was not going to be any real explanation for what had happened. Life sometimes is just wrong.

'I know, you are right, what I did was wrong. I feel so utterly inane. I feel as dry as the Judean desert that I came to hate. That desert became my nemesis, a reflection of myself, arid, fruitless and hostile, a place where nothing could flourish or thrive, a bloody wasteland. I read that throughout that desert there was a planned defence system of strongholds and secret water supplies, it was as if every time I looked at the desert it taunted me with this. I had no defence against myself, I was as dry as the desert dust, sapped of lymph.'

Dan knew how bereft of meaning his life had been but now sitting with Faye it was excruciating to think of what a life he could have had. He felt not just a stirring of what he had felt for her years before, but an avalanche of desire for her.

'That's a load of shite and sounds stupid – I don't care about the desert water supplies, speak normally will you.'

'Sorry you're right,' said Dan and realized he was laying it on too thick.

'You know, it was the things I had never questioned that troubled me the most,' said Faye.

'What do you mean?' asked Dan.

'In all our time together, I never had to question your reliability, how you would react in a crisis or how strong you were. When life does not present you with the challenges to test these things you somehow presume that you will act in a way which is commensurate with what you know. You see Dan, who I thought I knew was someone who could be relied on, someone who could not knowingly sentence someone to misery, someone, you know, brave. And you turn out to be a coward.'

Faye, more than most, was familiar with the vacillations of the human condition, she knew how impossible it was to ever really know someone, how could we possibly truly know someone else when most people had such a scant insight into themselves. Phrases like "I know I would never do such and such" drove Faye to distraction, what do we really know of our own capability until we are put in a situation which tests our own morality and held beliefs. Faye had come to accept that all humans were capable of almost anything when cornered. She knew this of Dan, but knowing and understanding are two altogether different things.

'Look,' said Faye, she was drained and wasn't sure what the point of continuing with this was.

'I am not here to reopen old wounds and I don't have the arrogant determination to pursue at all costs the truth behind your decisions. Maybe the truth is too much for us. I have experienced what I have experienced, and this is without knowing the truth, but knowing the truth will never change what I have already experienced. So what is to be done, what is to be gained here, us two rehashing our versions of reality. Let's just leave it.'

'Okay.'

Dan was not sure what she meant by leaving it, did it mean she had nothing more to say to him and therefore this was the end, they once again part, he had to stop that from happening, but he could not gauge Faye and wasn't sure what to do. He knew this could not be their final meeting.

'I would like to know how you are and what you are doing, I've often wondered about what your life was like,' Dan hoped he sounded relaxed and not nosey.

'That would take more time than we have,' smiled Faye 'Anyway, I wouldn't know where to start. Why bother with all that anyway, do you want to go dancing?'

Dan couldn't believe his ears, and he didn't' miss a beat in answering.

'Absolutely, where to?'

'There's a great dingy little place in Temple Bar, with live Jazz five nights a week, let's go.'

# seven

Martin Cleary was a bright seventeen-year-old who appeared to be a whiz on computers, it seemed he knew everything there was to know about them including how to hack into any system, but he would never hack a system because he was so paralyzed with OCD. It was all he could do to come to see Faye once a week, but he forced himself to do this, he wasn't quite sure which helped more, the CBT exercises she gave him every week or the fact that he got to sit in the same room as her for fifty minutes, he didn't care he was going to keep on coming. He was trying not to stare at her legs when she said their time was up. No! He wished his parents would spring for two sessions a week, after all they wanted him to get better; he would have to work on it.

Faye smiled at Martin as she saw him to the door, she really liked him, and was well aware that he sat ogling over her, but in that innocent teenage way, at least she hoped it was innocent. She had heard her next appointment go into the waiting room, but did not go straight into get him, she wanted a moment before she greeted Oliver Blake. She felt unsure as to whether she should bring up the embarrassing window moment or not, she decided to play it by ear. After a few minutes she went to the waiting room.

Oliver was sitting legs crossed in that very man about town sort of way, everything about him said he was fully in control. Faye wondered if he was so in control, why was he here?

'Hello Oliver, come on through,' said Faye.

Oliver rose without effort and followed Faye into the office, they took their seats, Faye crossed her legs and sat her hands in her lap. She now thought better of bringing up the window episode, she did not like the idea of explaining herself to Oliver Blake.

'You look well doctor,' said Oliver, it must be all the weekend activity he thought, he knew from Arthur that she had spent much of the weekend with Daniel Cohen. He liked to imagine what she was like in bed with men, adventurous in a conventional way, nothing too risqué for Dr Monroe.

'Thank you. How are you Oliver since we last met?' Faye said.

'I would like your opinion on why you think my wife left me without warning, when she had everything?' asked Oliver without a moment's hesitation.

'It's impossible to answer that question, for many reasons, firstly I do not know any of the circumstances of your marriage or what your relationship was like, but in my experience, it is very unlikely that someone would leave a marriage without reason.'

'What are the reasons in your experience?'

'There are a multitude, but I think it is best to perhaps focus on your relationship, why do you think she left?' Faye was not about to be finessed into saying something he could hold over her.

'That's just the thing, there was no reason. Do you believe me?'

'I believe that you feel there was no reason, but what you believe and what your wife believe may differ.'

'Is it not true to say that in therapy you only ever get one side of any story, that it is plausible that I could be making up everything I say to you, or for that matter everyone coming to see you is only giving you their version of any experience?'

'That is correct, but that does not mean that they are unable to see events from another's perspective.'

'Do you find that people are good at that, I mean really seeing things from another person's point of view?'

'In truth perhaps no, but that can become a very important part of therapy and in how we learn about ourselves, it is often through our experiences of others that we learn most about ourselves.'

'But is it not possible that someone could come here and give their version of events which may be altogether at odds with reality and then you become an unwitting accomplice and give advice based on a fabrication?

'I do not give advice, but what you are saying is possible, people very rarely give the full version of events, we tend to edit a lot of what happens in our life as a coping mechanism, but in the course of therapy there is the hope that one can eventually feel free enough to open up.'

It was Faye's experience that most people lied, lied through their teeth all the time, but you learn to factor that in, to see around the lies, just as right now she knew that Oliver was holding something back.

'I believe my wife was influenced in her decision.'

'What makes you think that?' asked Faye.

'Because I know Valeria would not have wished to leave me without being influenced, as I said she had everything and there were no signs of unhappiness, I feel she was poisoned against me.'

'Oliver sometimes it is very hard to accept the end of a relationship or marriage and we can search for all sorts of motives and reasons which may take us away from the real reason, again as a means of coping and coming to terms with a new situation. But normally there is a reason why someone wants to end a marriage. What reason did Valeria give you?'

'Her reasons were not her own, she was paraphrasing someone else, they bore no connection to our marriage.'

Oliver was watching Faye closely, but he could not detect any sense of discomfort for her, yet.

'Have you ever caused a marriage to split up because of something you said to a patient?' he asked.

'I am not in the business of splitting up marriages Oliver, but people through therapy can come to their own decision to leave a marriage,' answered Faye.

'But they come to that decision with your help, you guide them towards that decision, would that be true?' he asked.

'Therapy is a place where people arrive at their own decision, I am more of a sounding board than a guide,' answered Faye.

She could feel her annoyance rising but kept it in check, it was not unusual for spouses or partners to blame the therapist when someone becomes strong enough to confront a difficult situation in their life. A number of years back a disgruntled husband had come to her office and told her "*stay the fuck away from his wife and stop putting stupid ideas in her head*". Faye had pointed out that his wife came to her and not the other way around but did not pursue it because she feared what he might do to his wife. She never saw the woman again.

'But you might open a person's mind up to other possibilities or ideas which they did not have before coming to see you, I read on your web site that psychoeducation was an important part of therapy.'

That blasted website, thought Faye for the umpteenth time.

'Yes, it is important for all of us to have some understanding of how we approach the world and those in it, so it is possible that through therapy you come to challenge old held beliefs and form new, perhaps more constructive ideas.'

Faye wanted to say that it was by virtue of the fact that most people are stuck in old unexamined ideas that they are so miserable, mind you it didn't always follow that forming new more enlightened ideas was any guarantee of a less miserable existence.

'So someone coming to you would eventually end up thinking like you, since you would be educating them in your philosophy,' offered Oliver.

'I would not say that, everyone has their own unique view of the world, the goal of any form of education in my view is to equip the person with the tools to think for themselves and to be able to explore possibilities and see beyond the given or what is believed to be intractable.'

Faye felt Oliver was trying to set her up and then catch her out, it was a cat and mouse game and for some reason she could not extract herself, he kept drawing her in, she hated when it became competitive like this, it always made her uncomfortable and defensive. She decided to try and shift the direction this was going.

'Oliver,' she began in her best compassionate voice, 'you said you came here because you were upset about the end of your marriage...'

'I do not believe I said I was upset,' he interrupted.

'I beg your pardon, what I meant was you wanted to explore the end of the marriage.'

It was becoming clear to Faye that Oliver Blake was someone who paid attention to detail, every detail, a classic over-controller.

'Yes, and I am exploring that with you right now, after all you did say that you like your sessions to be client lead, did you not?'

'Yes of course, I am happy to discuss with you whatever you feel will help,' answered Faye.

'So to get back to how you might influence a client...' he began.

'I don't think influence is the correct term in this situation, as I said I am more of a sounding board, people are ultimately free to do whatever they wish, I cannot control what people do or how they interpret what I might say,' Faye could become as precise as Oliver Blake.

'Indeed you might say people are free but it is my belief that most people would never allow themselves the freedom afforded to them, most people conform and they conform and concede to those whom they think know better, like you for example, you are an expert in your field, so people may feel you know better than they do and consequently they act in accordance to what you might say,' Oliver could sense he was getting to Faye and he relished this.

'As I said earlier Oliver, it is not my role to tell people what to do, but to help them come to their own decisions, to examine all options and to act in accordance with their own desires,' said Faye.

'Do you believe in divorce,' asked Oliver.

Of course I bloody well believe in divorce, any normal thinking human being would believe in it, why should someone be condemned to a life of sheer agony because that was what it was, agony, to live with a person you do not want to be with, for whatever the reason, it was like death by a thousand cuts, slowly sucking the joy from the fibre of our being, turning you into a resentful hateful thing. Yes of course I believe in divorce, only narrow-minded Neanderthals didn't, because they subscribe to the best form of agony, penance. Penance for making a mistake and getting saddled with an ogre, this penance according to them was good for you, good for the soul, it made you a better person. Well Faye had never seen the living proof of this, only the broken people it created. Best not say this to Oliver.

'Why do you ask that?' she asked instead.

'Because if you believe in divorce, you are more likely to indicate to a client that it is alright to leave a marriage, as opposed to, shall we say Unity, they do not believe in divorce and so they help couples to deal with their problem and sort them out.'

'Unity is a religious organization, and so it subscribes to their religious ethos, for my part I do not allow my personal beliefs to influence how I work with people.'

'Is that possible, how can you keep them separate?'

Faye felt she could detect a slight snigger and an incredulous tone, but it was subtle.

'I can do it because I am a professional and like any professional, I am able to set aside my personal beliefs and put the client's needs first, it is never about what I want, it is about what the client wants.'

Faye could hear the sound of her own pique which only annoyed her more, she did not want to betray her feelings to this man, she felt exhausted, this was going nowhere, only round in circles.

'But for argument's sake, if there was a woman whose husband was abusing her and she was happy to stay are you saying you would not try to convince her to leave him?'

'I would try to be as supportive as possible in any decision she made. Oliver what are these questions really about?' Faye decided to deal with this head on.

'What do you mean?' Oliver looked slightly offended.

'I mean it feels to me like you are trying to catch me out in some way,' said Faye and immediately regretted it as she heard weakness in her own voice.

'I wonder why you might feel that way?' asked Oliver and Faye had the feeling that things were definitely the wrong way round.

'Oliver, you said that you believe someone convinced your wife to leave you,' Faye said.

'Yes, I do.'

'And who do you think that might be?'

'Someone like you.'

'Do you mean a therapist?' Of course you bloody well do, this is what this is all about, thought Faye.

'Yes.'

'Why do you think that?'

'I do not think it, I know it.'

'What makes you so sure?'

'She told me.'

'Do you mean your wife told you?'

'Yes, my wife told me.'

'What did she tell you?'

'She said that her therapist told her to leave me.'

'As bluntly as that, with no explanation or based on anything in particular. The reason I ask is that it would seem highly improbable that a statement like that would occur in isolation.'

'We deal with improbabilities all the time, I am sure you will agree doctor, and this was one of those times. As I have repeatedly told you she was perfectly happy, and then she went to see someone and they put idiotic ideas into her head, made her believe she was unhappy. I am sure you can be very persuasive, especially if someone is vulnerable or not as intellectually as astute as you.'

Faye did not like the way this suddenly shifted to her.

'Again, as I said earlier it is not my practice to persuade people to do things against their will or because I think it best.'

Faye thought how difficult it is to get people to change the most minuscule of bad habits, people are extremely sedimented and unwilling to change, this in Faye's opinion was because despite coming to her for help most people saw their problems only in relation to others, if others changed than everything would be fine, people were extremely reluctant to give up their old ways, so Oliver's thesis was completely flawed. In the end people did things because they wanted to, not because Faye suggested it. Of course, this truth didn't stop self-righteous plonkers from blaming Faye, in an effort to divert any responsibility from themselves, just like Oliver was doing right now.

'I do some work in the Middle East, and they have a saying there about Pigeon Whisperers, it means someone is whispering lies or ideas into someone else's ears. It seems to me therapists are like pigeon whisperers. How else can you explain a perfectly happily married woman suddenly deciding she wants to leave her husband, when the only extraneous factor was a therapist?'

'I could not begin to explain this as I do not know your wife, but there must have been an initial reason for your wife to attend therapy, she went for a reason.'

'Bloody hell he's comparing me to a pigeon whisperer, thought Faye, not really knowing what to do with it.

'It was because her mother died and she was very close to her, and she wanted to talk to someone about coming to terms with this, but it appears this was twisted and suddenly she was told she was unhappy in her marriage. Extraordinary how this shift could be made don't you think?'

'Not really, many people wait for a crisis in their life to attend therapy and then when they begin to talk many repressed or ignored issues present themselves which might well shift the focus of the therapy.'

Faye glanced at the time, great, time was up.

'We are at the time now Oliver, and need to finish up,' she said.

'I do not feel better, doctor, how do you account for that, I thought talking about these things was meant to make me feel better. Do you realise that you can make people feel worse than they did coming in here, and yet I have to pay for that privilege. It seems to me like a conspiracy.'

'I can assure you there is no conspiracy to make you feel bad, people sometimes feel bad when they reflect on their own actions or their situations,' answered Fay.

She definitely sounded patronizing but didn't care.

'So same time next week.'

'If you wish,' said Faye hoping he didn't wish, but knowing he would be here on time again next week.

'Oh, but I do wish,' said Oliver as he placed the money on Faye's desk.

As he was leaving and Faye was opening the door he turned, moved closer to her, 'If people come with one reason but the real reason is hidden, what do you think my real reason for seeing you is?' he grinned and then laughed and walked out into the hall saying 'to be continued.'

Faye knew at that moment that Oliver Blake was trouble.

# eight

Arthur Wilson was born in Rhodesia, he never adapted to its new mantle of Zimbabwe, it would always be Rhodesia to Arthur. His family left there in 1979 when he was five and came to live in Ireland, back to where his ancestors had left in 1897. His parents never got over what they had left behind in Rhodesia and lived in the constant lament of what could have been. Arthur did not subscribe to this, he believed in the here and now, very Zen he thought, and did whatever it took to ensure he had the means to live the life he wanted, not so Zen.

Arthur had done a stint in the French Foreign Legion, he achieved the rank of corporal in the Ordinary Legionnaires after fourteen months. He was not there to work up the ranks, besides all the top spots were commandeered by the French even though they only made up small minority of the Legion, no he went there to learn to endure, to be pushed to the edge, to test his limits and go beyond them, to desensitise. He had learnt by heart, as was expected, the Legionnaire's Code of Honour and he now adopted it as his only personal code, with sight alterations, as required. He worked for a few years as a mercenary, or to be more precise and politically correct, as a Private Military Consultant, in Iraq and The Congo - while the Legion gave him discipline of steel, being a PMC rewarded him with bundles of cash. He did this just long enough to accumulate a nice little cache and then packed it in, in his experience most of the mercenaries were unhinged and to trigger happy for his liking, they lacked discipline, had no Zen qualities.

Now Arthur was his own boss, had his private detective licence and was never without work. He didn't advertise like other PIs, his name circulated strictly by word of mouth, he liked to tell his clients that he took the private part of his title seriously. This, he noticed, brought peace to the client as they registered what was said and then suddenly there was nodding of heads and a visible sense of security, exactly what Arthur wished to achieve.

He had just gotten a call from Oliver Blake, he had done work for Blake for six years now, a cold, calculated shark, but he paid on time and never got emotional over anything, he had discipline. Many clients did not, they fell asunder on finding out that their wife was getting boned by their best friend even though they were giving one to her sister. Arthur often thought that the future looked bleak with all these whinging, hair-gelled wimps, ruling the world, because if you were high up in finance then you were ruling the world. It wasn't the greed that Arthur objected to, no it was the complete absence of any moral code, they were devoid of any code whatsoever, but Arthur did not judge, he carried out the orders and cashed the cheques.

Blake wanted him to shift the surveillance from Cohen to Monroe for the next few days. That was fine by Arthur, Faye Monroe was easy to survey, easy on the eye that is, in surveillance terms she was always on the move, she seems to be working out of three venues, her private practice on Harcourt St, the looney bin and she did some work for the cops in Dublin Castle. She had a busy social life, she was up and down to the stable where she kept her horse, played polocrosse, she did fencing classes occasionally, was in and out of the National Art Gallery like a yoyo and went to the lunch time concert in the National Concert Hall at least twice a week. She also met two friends regularly and now there was Cohen. Arthur knew he needed to be careful, he had caught her eye twice already now and she was no slow coach, she registered it the second time, he could not afford a third.

It was unlike him to allow this to happen once let alone twice, but he found it difficult to resist looking at her. He had never married or had a long-term girlfriend, his life was not conducive to it, he saw women from time to time, but had never succumbed to the female charm, until now he feared. He dismissed the thought completely and forced himself to be disciplined.

# nine

Ina was just finishing work, glad it was Friday and was leaving her office when her mobile rang in her pocket, it was Faye.

'How you.'

'Not good, I need to talk to you as soon as you are free.'

'What's up, is it Dan?'

'No, it's something else, where are you?'

'I'm just about to leave work.'

'Can you stay there, I could be over in a few minutes.'

'Why not meet in Figgerty's?'

'No, I hate to ask but I might need you to run a search for me.'

'What kind of search?'

'Missing person.'

'Okay come on in.'

'Thanks Ina, see you in a few minutes.'

Ina switched her computer back on and entered her password and clicked into the site for missing persons. Ina wondered what this could be about, it wasn't Faye's form to ask her to do searches or anything like that for that matter, that was why she did not hesitate to have her come in. Ina had gotten Faye some work with the guards a few years back, initially on a particular case where a psychological profile was necessary. Faye had impressed Ina's boss enough that he asked her back in on other cases and she now had a small but regular slot in the Garda teaching department. Ina knew that Faye was very grateful to her for getting the gig, she often said so, and as such she would never jeopardise either her job or Ina's by asking for favours like this.

The intercom on her desk buzzed, it was the front desk saying Faye had arrived. Ina told them to show her through. Faye arrived in looking worse for wear.

'Jesus Faye, you don't look well, what's this all about? asked Ina.

'You know that creepy client I was telling you about.'

'Faye, you have so many creepy clients,' Ina smiled.

'The one who caught me looking at him in the window.'

'Oh yeah, Mr Suave.'

'Yes him, well in his last session he was blaming his wife's therapist for her leaving him and I got the feeling he thought it was me who was the therapist. Anyway, he said something about her originally coming about her mother dying and I remembered later I had this woman who came about her dead mother but almost immediately started on about her husband, this guy sounded psycho, he controlled everything she did, she couldn't buy knickers without his permission, and that is a fact. She said that he was very wealthy, but she never saw a penny of it. He was a complete control freak about everything in the house and if things were not to his standard he would deny her food for three days, he discounted what she said and made her feel worthless, the usual abusive stuff. She came for a while and finally she decided that she had to leave him, I knew she was terrified and encouraged her to have someone with her when she told him, but he also had isolated her from her family and friends, so she really had no one.'

'How did he let her come to see you?' interrupted Ina.

'She told me that at a business dinner she had told one of the wives that she was finding it difficult to get over her mother's death, this woman told the creep that he should see to it that his wife got help with this, he never liked to be shown up, so he sanctioned it. My patient hoped telling this woman would have this effect.'

'Okay, so what happened next?'

'On that day she left my office fully intending to go through with it, I gave her my out of hours number and also a domestic abuse centre number. She had squirreled away some money, so she was alright for money. She had made an appointment for the following week. I never saw her again.'

'Did she leave him?'

'That's just it, I don't know, she never contacted me after that appointment, I did think about calling her, in fact I did twice but both times was her voice mail. And then I stopped, you know I can't keep calling someone, you never know what changes in their lives and they don't want anything more to do with me, that's their choice. And I had forgotten about her until today.'

'Do you think she was married to the creep?'

'Yes I do. Ina I am really worried and that is the only reason I am here about to give you the name of a patient.'

'Yeah I know Faye, it's fine I'm not going to blab her name around,' Ina thought all the client confidentiality stuff a tad over the top, especially when it came to court, but that was another story.

'He said his wife's name is Valeria, but my patient was Amanda Kennedy.'

'What makes you so sure they are connected?'

'I just know it, everything about him fits, what she said about him, and he is not coming to me for help I know that for certain, he is up to something, and it is not good. Can you see if anyone has reported her missing?'

'Why do you think she's missing, maybe she did leave him and moved away?'

'I think if she had she would definitely have contacted me or kept her appointment if she was able to.'

'What did you say her name was, Amanda what?'

'Kennedy.'

Ina quickly typed the name in and in seconds it came back that there was no missing person reported under that name.

'Try Amanda Blake' Faye said.

Again, no missing person under that name.

'I'll try Valeria Blake,' said Ina

'Nada' she said after a few minutes.

'I'll try other searches, like car registrations, did she have a car?'

'No, he never let her drive, but try anyway.'

Again, nothing under variations of the name.

'Did she work, belong to any clubs anything like that?' asked Ina.

'She didn't have a job, he didn't want her outside the house. She was in a tennis club, one he approved of, I think it was in Leopardstown.'

Ina's fingers were quick as lightning as she searched again. Bingo, a hit, Amanda Blake was a member of Leopardstown tennis club, membership was paid up until March the following year,

'When did you last see her? asked Ina

'It was 26th September, six weeks ago,' said Faye, she had checked Amanda Kennedy's file before coming to see Ina.

'I rang the number in her file, but the number was not in service. I had no next of kin listed and no family or friends' names. She had a brother and a sister, both of whom she had lost contact with because of her husband and both parents were now dead. Amanda came from a working-class background but had done well at school and did a diploma in business and had a good job as a private secretary in a big firm when she met her husband. He considered that he had rescued her from a life of poverty and routinely reminded her of this.'

Faye could easily visualise Oliver Blake in this role. Amanda had never called her husband by name and Faye never asked, people can be strange, but then Faye was in the business of strangeness.

'Do you know where she comes from originally?' asked Ina.

'Somewhere outside Limerick, let me think for a moment... yes Munlney, yes, I am almost sure of that.'

'Did she ever say where her brother or sister live or anything that might help to locate them?' Ina asked.

'Not really, but from what I could gather her brother was in and out of trouble, nothing too serious but enough for him to be considered undesirable by the creep, something similar with the sister, I think she had a baby when she was quite young, again undesirable for him I imagine, they may well still be living in Munlney.'

'Do you know their names?'

'No, she never gave any details like that.'

'Can you give a description, height, hair colour, that kind of thing?'

'She was very good looking, about five foot five, very slim, she was obsessed about weight, the creep would weigh her every second day to make sure she didn't gain a pound. She had long thick dark blond hair, always shiny and bouncy, you know that kind of girl-about-the-town hair.'

'Yeah I know it, go on,' moaned Ina, as she wrote down the description Faye was giving.

'She had brown eyes, clear milky-white, flawless skin, Mick Jagger lips, she had them filled. She wore a lot of makeup around her eyes, she was always very well groomed, dressed well but conservatively, Polo shirts and deck shoes, that kind of thing, she always had a string of pearls around her neck and fiddled with them a lot. She had a whopper of an engagement ring, a solitaire diamond and she had a Rolex watch. All the trappings of a wealthy life. She spoke well but when she became animated about something the Limerick accent would come through, but not often, she had herself well coached. He sent her to elocution lessons before they got married.'

'Jeepers, what a plonker.'

'Yes indeed, a prize plonker, does any of this help?' Faye asked.

'It might, there can't be that many stunners from Munlney, how long is she gone out of there?'

'She was married for twelve years and I think she was working in Dublin for a few years before, so probably around fifteen.'

'These small villages have long memories, I'll phone the local station and see if there is some auld codger still pounding the beat of the Munlney metropolis.'

Ina quickly found the phone number on-line and dialled Munlney garda station. After ten rings someone picked up, Ina thought they were probably stuffing their faces with potato wedges from the local Mace shop and only reluctantly answered the phone.

'Munlney garda station, what can I do for you?'

It was a male voice which the only image Ina could possibly associate with it was a turnip, a big narley mucky turnip. On the positive side he sounded ancient and was probably stationed in Munlney since he got out of Templemore training centre, he may even have been promoted to Sergeant, not on the merit of his outstanding police work but because the station most likely only had two garda and one had to be superior in rank to the other.

'Garda Ina Mulhall here, how's it going, I was hoping you might be able to help me with something.' Ina used her best one-of-the-lads voice, she didn't like it but experience had taught her that it can often be the quickest and most successful route to take, especially with the old timers.

'Sur we'll see what we can do, fire away.' crooned the turnip.

'I am trying to locate a female named Amanda Kennedy, she is originally from Munlney, she has a brother and sister, both parents are deceased, she's thirty-six years old and left Munlney over fifteen years ago, a very good-looking woman.'

'Where you calling from?' droned the turnip.

'Dublin,' said Ina.

This could be death as many of the culchies hated the sight of the big boys up in the big smoke.

'Right so.'

And then nothing. Ina waited, still nothing.

'Do you think you might know them, the Kennedys?' asked Ina feeling somewhat silly.

'Do you think I should know them?'

Fecking smart aleck, thought Ina, of course I don't think you should bloody well know them but there's a big possibility that you do since you most likely have been lounging like a lizard down there for the past twenty years waiting for your pension to kick in. Ina tried to keep her voice calm.

'Not at all, I was only hoping that someone down there might be able to help. Maybe someone remembers her. Her mother only died less than a year ago.'

'What was the mother's name?'

'I am afraid I don't have it,' said Ina, regretting this call.

'How about the brother or sisters?'

'Again, I don't have that information.'

For some reason the turnip was making Ina feel like a tulip.

'Not a lot to go on is there, but leave it with me and we'll see what we can do for our colleagues up in The Big Smoke, have you a number there?'

'Yes,' said Ina and she gave him her private mobile number.

'What was your name, I don't think I got it?' asked Ina.

'That's cause I didn't give it.'

Ina could hear the smirk in his voice.

'Garda Pat Ryan at your service,' he said.

'Thanks Pat, anything at all would be appreciated,' said Ina.

'No problem, Ina, I'll give you a shout if I find anything.'

'Goodbye.'

'Good luck now, take care,' Pat droned down the phone and then hung up.

'God that was like getting blood from a turnip, I wouldn't hold out much hope there, I don't expect to hear from him again. Maybe she is still living with the creep but stopped coming to you,' said Ina as she hung up.

'But that wouldn't explain him coming to me, no I do think she is gone, where is the question. The address I have for Amanda is not the same as the one he gave me, her address is Wellington Place and his is in Dalkey. I might call to Wellington Place,' Faye said.

'And what are you going to do if she answers the door, and she simply did not want any more contact with you?'

'Well at least I would know she was alive.'

'Hang on a minute, now she has gone from missing to dead,' Ina said incredulously.

'Ina, men kill their wives for lesser things than them wanting a divorce. The rejection is so incomprehensible to these men, coupled with what they see as the shear audacity of the women to want to leave them, could easy ignite enough fury to kill them. You know it happens all the time.'

'Yes, and women also kill their husbands.'

Ina believed in equal opportunity.

'Fair point, but you know as well as I do they are in the ha'penny place – men are the bigger killers. Ina you of all people know that the missing person files are full with those who are in fact killed and the killer gets away Scot free, swanning around feeling secure in the knowledge that no one will bother looking for the dead person after a while and the dead get no justice,' Faye was trying to appeal to her friend's inordinate sense of justice. 'Are you free for a little drive?'

'Faye, I think you should drop this, you have nothing to go on only a hunch.'

'Please Ina, just come with me to the house you never know what we might see, one hour is all I am asking for, come on and I will buy you dinner after.'

'I have a date as a matter of fact.'

'Really, with Bosco?' Faye said, with a broad grin.

Ina and Bosco were like the Odd Couple, he was a scatologist, they had met on a case where some guy was breaking into houses, tying women up and then forcing them to look at him as he laid out a piece of red silk which measured exactly fifty centimetres square and then defecated on the silk, he then took the four corners of the silk and tied them in a bow, lifted the silk bag of poo up and left it on the woman's stomach. He was dressed in what the women described as a baby grow, a one piece in pale blue which had buttons at the backside which allowed the material to flap down facilitating his performance. In the end it was Bosco's examination of the faeces which determined that there were traces of two antipsychotic drugs, Abilify and Zyprexa, and also a very expensive truffle oil which was found to be stocked in only two shops in Dublin, this eventually leading to the arrest of the mystery shitter. Bosco and Ina started seeing each other after this but it was virtually impossible to avoid some reference to shit when she ever mentioned him. Unfortunate really.

'Yes, with Bosco,' signed Ina

'He'll probably be shitting it if you are late, sorry, sorry I couldn't resist,' laughed Faye.

'You know that is so immature, and I am getting sick of you and Harry taking the piss.'

Ina was smiling as she said it, but she was growing very fond of the scatologist. If only he didn't examine shit for a living.

'If you come with me now, I promise never to make another smart comment about Bosco,' pleaded Faye.

'Okay, but one hour only I am meeting Bosco at nine and I have to go home to change, it's nearly six now so let's get going.'

' "Ina the Supreme" I'll give you free therapy for this,' smiled Faye as they gathered their things and headed down the back stairs to the employee car park where Ina parked her car.

'You can keep your therapy, I'll take a ticket to Baroness, they're coming to Dublin,' answered Ina.

Baroness were some heavy metal group Ina was into, Faye could never see the appeal, but Ina was a diehard metal head and had been since they were teenagers. Ina had long since given up on trying to convert her friend to this most noblest of sounds and accepted that this sublime form of music would be forever lost on her.

'I thought you said they were not playing anymore because of a car accident? asked Faye.

'It was a bus accident, but they have reformed with two new members, I'm interested to see what they will be like now,' answered Ina.

'Are there enough fans in Ireland to come here,' Faye teased.

'Never underestimate the size of the flock,' answered Ina as they popped into her car.

It was a black 1978 Austin Martin Lagonda with an orange go-faster stripe down the sides, Ina had craved this car for years and eventually bought it two years ago for a ridiculous amount of money, but for Ina it was worth every penny, she loved her Lagonda. It was everything a car should be, it had a 5.3 litre V8 engine, 3-speed automatic, telescopic shock absorbers, antiroll bar with self-levelling coil spring and shock absorber units, it was a four door, plus it was beauty personified. There was also a very limited number ever made and this for Ina was pivotal. In a world where everything was mass produced, she enjoyed having something fairly unique. Faye couldn't see the vintage beauty, she thought it just looked old fashioned.

Just as Ina drove out of the main gates of work, Arthur returned to his car. He needed to evacuate his bladder, there was a time Arthur could go for ten hours without an urge, now he had something which the doctor said was benign prostatic hyperplasia, in plain English he now needed to piss a lot. The doctor said it was probably a result of years holding off on going to the loo when he needed to, Arthur had goggled it and this wasn't true. The doc had also said he was very young for the condition and that an operation would not be wise, instead he suggested alfuzosin which was an alpha-blocker, Arthur decided against this, he didn't want his Alpha blocked thank you very much. Instead, he had started taking a plant extract, *saw palmetto*, which was recommended to him by a very nice naturopath who he did a bit of work for. Her husband was never home, she thought he might be having an affair, turns out he was, but it was with Jesus, the poor bastard was a Jesus freak and was spending vast amounts of time in churches praying - that was a first for Arthur.

As he got into his car, he noticed the back of a very nice Austin Martin driving out the avenue towards the main gates, that's the kind of car he would like to drive but in his line of business discretion took precedent over style.

He had followed the taxi Faye had taken to here and knew from background checking that it was most likely to see her friend who worked here, but they were taking their time, he hadn't gone into the building to relieve himself but found a spot behind a wall which still allowed him a view of the entrance.

It took longer than they thought to get to Wellington Road, the traffic was quite thick, Ina had gone down Haddington road, onto Pembroke road, then took Pembroke Lane until she turned onto Wellington road. It was hard not to be impressed by Wellington, a wide tree-lined road with high walls and hedges protecting the privacy of those who lived here. Not only was there ample street parking but all houses seemed to have off road parking, such was the amplitude of the front garden. Nor could you miss the plethora of luxury cars lounging along the road, Ina drove to the end of the road which brought them onto Wellington Place, which was more of these same high-end living. They found the house, the number was clear to see.

'Fancy pad,' said Ina.

'Fancy indeed,' answered Faye.

They were parked on the opposite side of the road which offered them a favourable view of the beautifully kept front gardens, hedges trimmed in that way which didn't say obsessive, even the gravel looked a cut above average gravel, and the generously proportioned steps which led to a door painted in a grey tone which said that the occupants of this house have the height of good taste.

'I want that house,' pined Faye.

'We can't just sit here hoping that the creepy guy shows up, I will go up and knock on the door,' Ina was never one to beat around the bush, besides she had a date to get to.

'What will you say if he answers?' enquired Faye.

'Oh, I'll just say I am looking for Mrs Quimpugh,' answered Ina, 'and if a housekeeper answers I'll ask for Amanda and play it by ear from there.'

'Okay I'll keep an eye out from here, if I see him coming, I'll give you a ring,' Faye was feeling quite excited by the whole thing.

Ina got out of the car and began walking across the road towards the house. Once she got to the door she gave two knocks with the lion's head door knocker, nothing so brash as a doorbell on this door she thought. Having been brought up on the other side of town, Ina had an inbred dislike for the well-heeled, she knew it was based on rudimentary conditioning and disliked it in herself, but nonetheless felt it. After less than a minute the door was opened by a pleasant looking woman in her fifties, she was wearing a black and white maid's outfit, which only strengthened Ina's dislike of anyone who would insist that the help wore a ridiculous outfit like this.

'Good evening, how may I help you?' asked the lady in black and white.

'I'm looking for Amanda, is she home?' Ina sounded relaxed and had the tone of someone who was certain in her belief that this was the right place to expect Amanda to be.

'No, I am afraid she is not at home, may I take a message?' This maid equally had the authoritative tone of a woman who saw it as her role to act as sentinel at the opulent doorway.

'To be honest,' began Ina in a more polished version of her own accent with the slight American intonation which many middle-class women had affected and one which deeply disturbed Ina, 'I am a bit concerned I haven't seen her in an age, and she hasn't been to the club in, like, forever, maybe you can tell me where I can find her?'

'I am not at liberty to say that, but should you wish, you can leave your contact details,' answered the sentinel.

'You know we girls are all a bit, like, freaked out that Mandy has been so, well, incognito, we just want to see if, like, everything is okay.'

'As I said, I can take your name and contact details.' Calm as a cucumber was the woman in black and white, Ina knew when she was being stonewalled.

'I can come round tomorrow if that was more convenient,' tried Ina.

'It is best to leave your details.'

'Is her hubby home?' Ina knew she was on shaky ground, she had to be careful not to give too much away, but she did not want to be bested by this woman.

'No, I am afraid he too is out,' she equally was not giving anything away.

'Will he be back soon?' asked Ina, hoping she would let his name slip.

'I am not aware of when he will return.'

One more go, thought Ina 'Look can you please just tell me if she is, like, alright and not ill or something awful, like, we're *sooo* like worried,' pleaded Ina.

'As I said I am not at liberty to discuss such matters, but again please feel free to leave your details.' There was no getting past this one, thought Ina.

'Okay but will you be sure to give it to her, it's like she has fallen off the face of the earth,' Ina was hoping to illicit some kind of response.

'I will write your details down.' She turned to walk away, presumably to get a pen and paper, leaving Ina on the doorstep.

'Do you mind if I use your loo, I'm simply going to explode,' Ina had already made overtures to stepping into the hall.

'Very well, but I must ask you to be quick, I have an appointment to attend.'

The maid's tone had shifted but only slightly. Ina knew she was not happy with her barging her way in, but needs must, thought Ina, who was now convinced something was amiss.

Ina took in the surroundings, scanning for a photo or a coat, anything really to tell her something about who was living here, there was nothing personal on display in the immaculately kept hall, only expensive looking furniture, and big paintings.

The maid ushered Ina to a door just to the left of the hall door, pity, thought Ina, she had hoped to get a look at the rest of the house. The door led to a loo, Ina was struck by what she considered obsessive cleanliness, everything had a sparkly effect like the ads on telly for cleaning products, the chrome sink taps looked new and the towel was perfectly creased, it must have been starched, thought Ina, to achieve that level of anal perfection, who starches towels? There were no cabinets or cupboards to inspect and nothing of a personal nature. Ina thought that if she used this toilet that it would probably smell of lavender, she didn't, she flushed it and turned on the tap to wash her hands and took great pleasure in un-creasing the towel. When she came out the impervious housekeeper was waiting, pen and paper at the ready.

'Would you like to give me your details now?' she asked with a slight emphasis on the now, one which didn't go unnoticed by Ina.

'Of course, it's Sorcha Kelly, and my number is zero eight seven eight five five five seven five four, please get her to call me tonight if possible or tomorrow at the latest, we miss her.'

'Thank you and goodbye.'

Ina was now back on the doorstep and the door was being gently but resolutely closed.

'Goodbye,' said Ina to the closing door as she turned and walked back down the steps.

Once Nora had closed the door, she raced up the stairs to the front room on the top floor to look out the window where she had a clear view of the street. She knew immediately that something was not right with this caller, and she needed more information, like the car registration. She pulled the curtains back slightly to get a look out. She watched as the woman walked towards the gate, a woman she had never seen before nor heard of. She wanted something concrete for her boss, after all she owed him a lot. When her son Joey had gotten into trouble with the guards over selling drugs at a low level and it looked as if he might go to jail, Mr Blake had intervened and now Joey was living and working in London. Mr Blake had gotten him a job, she had a lot be grateful to him for.

Ina was royally pissed off. She had wanted to whip her ID out and insist the old crow tell her where Amanda was, she also felt that this woman was on to her and had not believed a word out of her mouth. Ina did not want to look back, but she was sure she was being watched and for that reason she walked away from her car as she came out the gate, she turned left and kept walking hoping that Faye would cop what was up. As she walked, she phoned Faye and told her to stay put for a few minutes and to drive away in the opposite direction and to wait for her call. Ina kept walking down the street until she was sure she was out of sight of the house. She waited five minutes and called Faye again telling her where she was and to come collect her.

Nora could see the woman walk out and turn left, she did not get into a car but kept walking, the road had a bend a few feet down from the house and soon Nora had no sight of her. She looked along the road but saw nothing unusual, there were some cars parked but it was dark, and Nora couldn't make them out very well. She came away from the window.

Faye hated driving to begin with but even more so in Ina's contraption, it was almost impossible to turn the damn thing, probably too old for power steering. She did as Ina had instructed and pulled up awkwardly to the footpath, she thought she had put it out of gear so she could get out and let Ina in to drive, but it must have still been in gear because it gave an almighty jerk forward and then cut out.

'Jesus Faye what are you doing!' screamed Ina.

'Sorry! I thought it was out of gear, anyway I am useless at driving this car,' Faye knew better than to argue with Ina about the car.

'Okay get in. There is definitely something fishy going on, that maid or housekeeper or ninja or whatever the hell she is, is a master of nondisclosure, and I am sure she suspected me of something. She gave nothing away and never once confirmed or denied Amanda's existence.'

'Did she say anything at all?' queried Faye.

'Nope, nothing.'

'What about Oliver, did you ask about him?'

'I asked about her hubby, I didn't want to use his name in case he made it up, but nothing, I thought she might let his name slip, but she was definitely guarded.'

'Did you see anything when you went inside?'

'Nothing of value, other than a freakishly clean loo, no personal stuff and everything was in its place, fabulous furniture and paintings, but like a show house.'

'Over controller, intense need for order and cleanliness, sounds like our man. Ina he definitely did something to Amanda otherwise why was the housekeeper so tight lipped?'

'Yeah, something's not right, but remember we're still not certain this is the creep's house, we could be letting our imaginations run wild.'

'I know, what should we do now?'

'Firstly, we need to confirm that Oliver Blake lives here, that means you need to watch the house and confirm it.

'Okay do you want to stay with me?'

'No, I am already running late, why don't you call Harry, if he's not off shagging some young one, he might keep you company.'

'Good idea, I'll do that,' answered Faye, as she dialled Harry's number.

Arthur was beginning to wonder what the hell Faye was doing when he noticed a car coming from behind the building which he now presumed was the staff parking and it dawned on him that Faye and her friend could have left which meant a back exit and Faye would not have to come out the main entrance which she went in. Even still, how could he have missed them, he was here all the time and there was virtually no activity. Arthur had to concede to himself that he might have botched it. It must have been when he went to the loo, he cursed his weak prostate. He decided to call it a night, but he was not happy at all.

At about the same time, Harry noticed he had three missed calls from Faye, he would call her later, the truth was he was trying to avoid her, he felt bad about encouraging her to hook up with Dan, he of all people knew how badly affected she had been when he never came back from Israel. The percolating thoughts began to filter through and with it the guilt, he knew she never really recovered and that something had been irreparably ruptured. He couldn't quite determine the exactness of what it actually was but it had something to do with her ebullience - it was like an orange that looked so inviting but on cutting was found to be dried out. He loved Faye, she was his best friend and he knew he should have warned her off, protected her from what he knew was a strong possibility of getting hurt again by Dan. But he needed the contract Dan had promised, but that contract came with a catch which was that he would get Faye to meet with Dan. Dan had made it sound reasonable enough, he was sorry, he wanted a chance to explain, to give Faye the chance to get answers to her questions, yet Harry had an uneasy feeling, Dan was very affable but there was the implicit warning that if he did not get to meet Faye he would not get the contract. Harry reasoned with himself that Dan would eventually meet Faye if he was in Dublin even if he refused to encourage her, so why not do it, it was nothing really and get the contract?

He had gotten Ina on side regardless of her initial reaction, a reaction Harry now wished he had listened to.

The call last night had thrown him - he had thought once he hooked Dan up with Faye that that was it, but now more was expected, he wasn't sure what to do, and just at that moment Sandy or was it Sandra, sauntered into the room naked and drop-dead gorgeous and he knew exactly what he was going to do, right now at least.

# ten

Oliver had returned home the night before to find Nora waiting for him, he had told her he was going to be late and not to bother with leaving a dinner, so he knew something was amiss. He thought about what she had told him. A woman pertaining to be friends with Amanda from the tennis club had come enquiring about her, saying she missed her and was worried. Nora was shrewd enough not to disclose anything and she knew that this woman was not whom she pretended to be. Nora gave a description of the woman which was quite detailed, she liked to please, and Oliver could not fit this picture to anyone he knew. The woman had also asked about Amanda's husband but had not used a name, which most likely meant she did not know it and was fishing for a name. She had said her name was Sorcha Kelly, but again Nora did not believe this was her true name, nonetheless he would pass it onto Arthur with the phone number and have him check it out. Nora didn't get a car reg as the women left on foot.

He had thanked Nora and told her to go home. When she had left, he took his keys and went to his room where he unlocked the Louis XV Stephanoise armoire which was home to a very sophisticated surveillance system. There was a hidden camera in every room in the house and eight more divided between the front and back of the house. The monitor showed all cameras simultaneously. Oliver switched to see the front door camera only and pressed the rewind button until the time showed 6.45, Nora said she answered the door at 6.48, the monitor was clear for a few minutes until a woman walked in the gates. Oliver had never seen her before and watched the whole thing through twice, he had switched to the indoor cameras when she entered to use the toilet and he observed her nosing around the hall and her trip to the toilet was not to use it but to inspect it. He then inserted a USB stick into the port and copied what he had seen, he would pass this on to Arthur. Oliver had a slight uneasy feeling, a feeling which he did not care for. He had planned to remain in for the rest of the night but with his mood changed with this information, he decided to make a trip to see Silvia - that usually sorted any unease out.

He thought for a moment about Silvia. He didn't normally draw blood, but the last night was different, he had no desire to control his urges and his urges were strong, it would take her awhile to heal but he had compensated her well and she hadn't asked him to stop.

The knock on the door brought him back to this morning.

'Come in Arthur,' said Oliver.

'Good morning, sir,' responded Arthur as he walked into Oliver's office.

Arthur never failed to feel impressed by this office, everything about it was powerful, the huge imposing mahogany desk and high-back chair. The wood panelled walls were covered with what Arthur knew to be expensive modern art. As he walked towards the desk, Oliver motioned for him to sit down in the seat in front of the desk. Arthur pulled back the chair which even for him was heavy, Oliver did not like to make things easy for people.

'Does the name Sorcha Kelly mean anything to you?' Oliver asked.

'No, not off the top of my head but I can look into it.'

'I'd like you to take a look at this – do you recognize this woman?' Oliver had the USB stick from the night before inserted into his computer and he turned the screen so Arthur could get a good view as he pressed play.

Arthur watched as he recognized Faye's friend, he also noticed the time in the bottom right-hand corner and cursed silently to himself, he was still in the Phoenix Park waiting for Faye and this woman to come out. He had missed something and he wasn't about to tell Oliver, he needed a little time to figure out what she was up to and if Faye was also involved.

'No, but I will take a copy and get back to you on it, what was she doing?'

'She was enquiring about my wife, find out who she is and get back to me by the end of the day. Anything else to report?'

'No sir, not at this present minute.'

Oliver handed him the USB stick and turned his attention to the computer which was Arthur's cue to leave.

Arthur could tell that Oliver was miffed about something and was glad it wasn't at him, yet. He knew better than to give him half an explanation and he certainly didn't want to expose his slip up in any way, Oliver paid substantially for professionalism and results and nothing less. As Arthur left Oliver's office he passed his secretary, she had not been at her desk when he came in.

'Good morning Ms Flynn,' Arthur said, he never called her Tina, he was sure no one did, not even her mother.

'Mr Wilson,' she answered.

'Not a bad morning out there,' said Arthur.

'No, not at all,' came the answer.

'Have a good day.'

'Thank you, goodbye.'

Tina Flynn was in her early fifties with a matronly figure, her dyed brown bouffant was the height of naff perfectionism, there was never a rib of hair out of place, all cautioned to position by lavish amounts of hair lacquer, when Arthur tried to imagine what it would be like to run his fingers through it, he got a shiver down his spine. She had an arsenal full of navy-blue skirt suits and various coloured pussy-bow blouses which was her signature look, in her own way she was kind of a style icon for frosty secretaries worldwide. Tina had worked for Oliver for eighteen years, eighteen years of wholehearted devotion, Oliver was her mission in life. She surrendered herself to him like a willing victim, there was nothing she would not do for him, Arthur was sure she was in love with Oliver, the kind of cuckoo maternal love where she confuses her boss for her child for her lover, whatever it was, Arthur thought it was weird. Weird but not uncommon. She was unmarried, lived alone, no pets not even a cockatoo, had no interests outside of Oliver and she worked up to twelve hours a day, she owned her own apartment, had no mortgage or loans, she rarely used a credit card and when she did, she paid on time so as not to incur interest. She drove a white Toyota Corolla which she traded in every year for a new white Toyota Corolla. And until it was shut down a few years ago, she had two weeks holiday in the Seagaia Ocean Dome, the world's only indoor beach located in Miyazaki, Japan. The Dome featured a fake volcano, fake sand, fake fish and fauna, a steady 86 degrees Fahrenheit, and water park rides. Now she stayed at home. Arthur had done a bit of research, for his own amusement.

When Arthur returned to his car, he inserted the USB stick into his PC and began to look at the video again. Alongside the video he opened his case file and brought up the information on Ina Mulhall - she was a well-respected member of the garda force and intelligent or shrewd enough to advance through the ranks at speed, she showed exceptional intelligence in her field of forensics. She lived alone and over all abided by the laws of the land. What was she after and what did she know, Arthur wondered, it was no coincidence that Oliver had recently made contact with Faye Munroe, she must have made a connection, it was the only explanation, but what the hell was she and Mulhall up to. He decided he would go back to the hotel. Faye had spent the night there with Cohen and was most likely still there.

# eleven

As she stood in the bathroom staring into the mirror, Faye felt the familiar feeling of dread in her stomach, she felt miserable, and wished she could stop the relentless ruminating over nothing. Well, it wasn't quite nothing, she had just spent another night with Danny, and she hated herself for her own weakness, why couldn't she govern her own thoughts and have some self-restraint and dignity. She had acceded to her puerility and now whatever pleasure she got from being with Danny was tainted by the gnawing in her belly, it felt to Faye like what she thought caustic soda burning through her would feel like. And why should it feel any other way, if she was stupid enough to allow a man who dumped her brutally years before to waltz back into her life then this is want you get.

She thought about desire, the desire of pleasure as one of the fundamental motivations of all human action but for Faye this felt like a form of bondage over which she had no control. She recalled what Hume had claimed about desires and passions that they were noncognitive, purely automatic bodily responses and that reasoning in these cases is capable only of devising means to ends set by desire. But Faye knew from her own experience and that of countless others that desire breeds obsession and rancour and delivered the desiring subject more woe than pleasure.

Yet it was almost impossible to disentangle oneself from this tyranny of desire, maybe she thought, she ought to subscribe to some more enlightened philosophy which advocated the relinquishing of bodily desire as a means of freeing oneself from our more primal, base needs in an effort to be content or more evolved. Was it even possible to do this, these philosophies were based on the ancient teachings from the eastern world where they had centuries of practice of being indifferent to their desires and it seemed to be imprinted in the fabric of their being. What, she wondered, was imprinted in the fabric of her being, well it certainly was not a sense of unity with the universe or a sense of connectivity. The goals of western philosophy were predicated on individual success and lay firmly in the external world and understanding how it relates to you and therefore how you can manipulate it to best suit your own ends and not in the cultivation of the internal world as suggested in eastern thought. So basically, we are damned, constrained by the randomness of where we landed when we were thrown into the world, and from this very arbitrary act of coming into existence, our struggle begins, the struggle against our fundamental urges and desires.

Her thoughts were interrupted by the sound of room service bringing breakfast, she quickly took two Valium and washed them down with tap water and came out to find Danny eating some toast and at that very moment she had an urge to ram the toast down his throat, but she didn't, of course.

'Hey,' he said.

'I have to go, I have things to do,' said Faye.

'Oh, I thought we could do something together today.'

He could sense her distancing herself from him and he really wanted her to stay. Despite everything that had happened when he was with her, he felt the same as he had all those years before as if holding her in his arms was what he existed to do.

'I'm sorry but I have loads to catch up on.'

'Can I help with anything?'

'Thanks, but no, it's all stuff I have to do myself.'

'What about tonight, are you free?'

'I don't think so, I am meeting someone.'

'Oh, maybe tomorrow so.'

Dan was aware that he was beginning to sound pathetic, and he didn't want to scare her off, but he still wanted to meet her.

'I ate in a nice Japanese restaurant the other day and thought you might like to try it, it's on Drury St.'

'I know the one, I've eaten there loads of times, but we can go there, I'll give you a call tomorrow', Faye said as she finished getting dressed and was putting her coat on, she needed to get out of the room before she exploded. She hated that he was picking out restaurants she might like, she actually hadn't eaten in the Japanese restaurant in Drury St, but he wasn't to know that and here he was presuming that she hadn't been there, and *he* would bring her there, she didn't need him to bring her anywhere. She took her bag off the chair beside the bed and checked that her keys and phone were in it, she couldn't see her phone and was sure it had been in the bag but it wasn't there now.

'I'm sure I had my phone in my bag,' she said.

'It's on the table,' Dan said.

'That's odd, I don't know how it got out there,' she said absentmindedly and put the phone in her bag and began moving towards the door of the hotel suite.

'So you'll give me a call tomorrow,' Dan said as he got up from where he was eating his breakfast and walked over to Faye, he put both of his hands on her shoulders as he looked at her, he went to pull her into him but could feel Faye's resistance and so didn't persist. He wasn't sure what had happened, last night was great or so he had thought, but he wasn't about to force her and risk everything, he would go at her pace, it was the safest thing to do, he just hoped she wouldn't take too long. He kissed her lightly on the cheek and let go of her shoulders.

'Have a good day Faye,' he said.

'Thank you, you too,' Faye answered, and she left and closed the door gently behind her.

When she got out to the hall, she began to feel a bit better or maybe the Valium was kicking in, either way she was glad to be alone. She needed to get home. She left the hotel and hopped into a taxi just outside and gave him her address. She now lived in a rented flat in Ranelagh. She had lived in a lovely seventeen century house in Wicklow with Noel but neither could afford to buy the other out when they separated. They had bought the house before the property boom and sold it in the property slump, so they didn't make the killing most people seemed to have. She had spent so much time and care on that house and garden, she had done it without expectation of any plaudits or as a monument to taste, it was an homage to love, the love she had for Noel was coalesced into the love she had for the home they shared together, each piece of furniture, each colour selected was about their love, maybe she should have seen that as a sign that there was something amiss if in her head she had entwined her husband and her sofa into one.

They converted one of the out houses which was away from the main house into an office and Faye saw patients there. The house was everything they wanted, nestled in the middle of beautiful countryside but close enough to the city to be there in a dash, the best of both worlds everyone had said, except eventually neither world was really all that great. After they split up Faye, moved to Dublin where most of her work was but continued to travel down once a week to see her clients, she used a rented room in a monotonous office complex in the town. Over the last while she had reduced this to monthly and had hoped to stop completely but that hadn't happened yet.

The taxi pulled up in front of the house, it was divided into four flats, one in the basement the other three on each floor, she had the second floor flat. It had a large living room, a kitchen, bathroom and two bedrooms, the high ceilings gave the illusion of the rooms being larger than they actually were and it had two huge windows which allowed the living room to be flooded with light. Faye had brought some furniture with her from the house, but they sold most of it simply because neither had the room for it and it seemed pointless to put it in storage. Faye had been surprisingly dispassionate about the whole thing, once the decision had been made, she simply got on with it. She had put some effort into making the flat a place she wanted to be, but ultimately it still had the feel of a rented flat.

Just as she was walking up to the door she saw her landlady, Mrs Liggia Clayworth-Howsham, coming up from her basement flat. Mrs Clayworth-Howsham was the owner of number 64 and had lived there for thirty-six years. Her husband whom she always referred to as The Colonel, had died of old age ten years ago at ninety-three and Mrs Clayworth-Howsham prudently decided to convert the house into flats, for three reasons, as a source of income, to prevent the house falling apart and as a safeguard from isolation. Faye had taken tea, as she liked to put it, with Mrs Clayworth-Howsham on several occasions and had grown very fond of her. She was a spritely seventy-nine-year-old whose elegance was accentuated by a whippet-thin figure, she had told Faye she put her svelte figure down to the practice of eurhythmics while she was at school in England. Faye had always thought that eurhythmics was a band with the lovely Annie Lennox but discovered that it is also the harmonious body movement as a form of artistic expression, she could easily imagine

Mrs Liggia Clayworth-Howsham's body moving harmoniously across a room.

'Hello dear,' said Mrs Clayworth-Howsham.

'Hello Mrs Clayworth-Howsham,' answered Faye 'How are you?'

'Very well my dear, I am just about to go down to Blake's.' Blake's was a small family-owned betting office, Mrs Clayworth-Howsham had a penchant for the horses.

'Any good tips?'

'No, but one must amuse oneself before the dreaded OA takes a grip.' OA was old age, Mrs Clayworth-Howsham had lots of abbreviations, she also saw OA as something that started around ninety plus, not surprising given that all her family lived well into their late nineties and one aunt made it all the way to one hundred and three, not to be recommended by all accounts.

'Would you care to take tea this afternoon?'

'Unfortunately, I have something to do today and I don't expect to be back until later this evening, but thank you, but I am around tomorrow,' answered Faye.

'What about some curried eggs and a G&T tomorrow around eight?' asked Mrs Clayworth-Howsham. Mrs Clayworth-Howsham had had Faye round to supper when she first moved in and had given her curried eggs, Faye raved about them and so began the tradition of curried eggs, Faye hadn't the heart to tell her that she had gone right off them.

'Perfect, I'll look forward to it, good luck on the horses,' said Faye.

'Thank you dear, you will have the house to yourself, the men are out.' Mrs Clayworth-Howsham was as good as any security system, she watched everything like a hawk and missed nothing. The men she referred to were Pat Harvey, a fifty-eight-year-old science teacher who taught in a posh boys' school and had always lived in flats in Ranelagh since he moved to Dublin from Wexford as a young man to go to college, he never married and according to Mrs Clayworth-Howsham was most likely a virgin because he was in short supply of SA (sex appeal). He was reserved but very obliging and did a lot of maintenance work in the house which Mrs Clayworth-Howsham offered to pay him for, but he always refused saying that he enjoyed it. He had helped Faye move furniture around her flat from time to time and insisted that she leave any heavy shopping for him to bring up, he had the ground floor flat.

In the attic flat was twenty-nine-year-old Jason Tynan, a real ladies man Mrs Clayworth-Howsham had said, and she wasn't wrong. Jason, or Fabio as Faye had come to think of him as, was the polar opposite to Pat, full of confidence in his own beautifulness, superbly proportioned body and charm. He told Faye he worked in computers which was vague enough to allow you to infer whatever you liked, he could be some sort of whizz kid who came up with fantastically elaborate algorithms vital to nuclear physics or he could simply be a data entry clerk, it didn't matter, he was beautiful. And he had plenty of SA, so much so that one night not long after she had moved in, Faye, in a momentary lapse of concentration, had been seduced by his glorious perfection and slept with him.

Ina had always maintained that gorgeous men, and women for that matter, were abysmal in bed simply because they didn't have to try, Faye didn't have enough experiences of gorgeous men to verify this until Fabio. He was living proof of Ina's theory. She was mortified the next day, but she needn't have been because Fabio was completely guileless about the whole thing. Faye realized soon afterwards that for Fabio, bedding women was a routine occurrence, three, four, even five times a week. He was sweet, kind of simple-minded and Faye liked him, she liked living in this house.

Faye opened the main hall door and checked the hall table for any post, she found a few letters, all bills, and went up the stairs to her flat. After Ina had dropped her back to the flat on Tuesday, Faye had tried Harry in the hopes of cajoling him into coming on surveillance with her, but she couldn't get hold of him, which was odd as he was never without his phone. In the end she went back herself and parked a bit away from the house but where she could get a look at the driver as they turned into the driveway, luckily there was a streetlight outside the house which would help get a view in the dark. There wasn't any car in the drive when she went back there, and she had hoped she hadn't missed him while she was gone. At eleven o clock she was freezing and hungry, she hadn't thought the whole surveillance thing out very well and she didn't want to turn the car on to heat up for fear of attracting attention. At around half eleven she was feeling somewhat defeated and was contemplating calling it a night, she decided to wait until midnight and then go.

About twenty minutes later a car arrived and indicated to turn into the house, Faye could hardly contain herself and could feel the surge of excitement, or maybe it was fear, when she clearly identified the driver, there was no doubt in her mind, she was absolutely positive it was him. This confirmed to Faye that he lied about his address, and he was connected to Amanda, she decided to wait a few more minutes to see if he stayed in the house. After twenty minutes, the housekeeper came out through the gates just at the same time as a taxi pulled up, she popped in and they drove off. Faye left the car and walked towards the gate, she wasn't sure what she was looking for, but she wanted a better view. After a minute the downstairs lights went off and soon a light went on in an upstairs room, looked like he was staying in for the night. Satisfied with herself she went back to her car and drove home. She phoned Ina first thing the next morning to fill her in and they had decided that they would take a trip to Limerick on the following Saturday to see if they could locate either the brother or sister.

Faye changed out of the clothes she had on and got into a pair of jeans and a black cashmere polo neck jumper, she pulled on a pair of flat knee-high boots and her Moncler down jacket – a Christmas present from the married days. They had decided to take Faye's car as it was less conspicuous, she drove an eight-year-old Volkswagen Passat estate. Faye was to collect Ina at eleven at her house, Ina lived in Clontarf, so all going well if the traffic wasn't too bad, she would be there before eleven. Faye locked up and got into her car, luckily, she was the only person with a car in the house. Mrs Clayworth-Howsham had gotten rid of her car a few years back because The Colonel had always done most of the driving and she felt driving alone was too tiresome and neither of the men had one, Pat used the buses and Jason used taxis, this meant that Faye had use of the only off road parking spot, not only did this save money but for Faye it was the luxury of not having to look for a parking spot every time she went out or having to walk the length of the street with heavy bags in high heels.

Ina lived on Clontarf Rd in a red brick Georgian house which faced the sea, she was lucky enough to have bought her house in such a nice spot for a song, her elderly Aunt whom Ina had always been good to sold Ina the house not long before she died at a knockdown price, she did this to prevent her children getting the house and also she didn't want to leave a substantial sum of money. She had two sons and a daughter whom Ina said were vultures and were only waiting for their mother to pop her clogs to cash in on this very valuable property. When they discovered what their mother had done they were spitting fire, not only that but the will revealed that there was no money left, their mother had heavily donated to two charities, one which involved a water irrigation system in Chad and the other was to help finance small businesses in various parts of Africa - at the time of her death Ina's Aunt had helped set up a barber shop in Botswana, a video store in Nigeria, a laundry in Kenya and a pottery school in Mozambique. Ina wasn't in the slightest bit perturbed everything was legal and above board and as far as she was concerned her aunt could do what she wished with her own life and belongings. Ina was not invited to her cousin's wedding.

Faye parked outside her house and quickly ran up to the door, there was a small but very well planted front garden which Ina's Aunt had taken great care of during her life and as a tribute to her, Ina continued to care for the garden, which meant it looked well year-round. Just as Faye was about to knock on the door it opened.

'Hiya, I'm ready,' said Ina as she walked out through the door and pulled it shut behind. Ina was not a dilly dally-er.

'Okay do you want to drive?' asked Faye.

'Yeah, I'll drive,' said Ina, this suited both of them, Ina loved driving as much as Faye loathed it.

'It shouldn't take more than two and a half hours to get there if we can make it to the motorway in good time,' Ina said as she got into the driver's seat.

'Good, I hope we can find them,' said Faye, she had become increasingly convinced that something had happened to Amanda.

'Even if we don't find them, we'll probably find out something or maybe where they live.'

'Let's hope so, what if we find them and they haven't heard from her?' asked Faye.

'Let's not get ahead of ourselves, we'll see what we find today and build on that, we might even find Amanda.'

'I don't think we will but you're right, we need to wait and see what happens.'

'How did last night go with Danny?' Ina asked.

'I'm not sure, I was miserable this morning, I hate myself for being so weak and letting him back into my life, but I also want him, he's just like he used to be Ina, for moments I can almost forget what happened and it feels like we were never parted and then there are times when I look at him and feel utter revulsion both for him and myself.'

'That doesn't sound good.'

'I know it doesn't sound good Ina, I know it's completely bonkers and I know you probably think I am nutty for seeing him but it's not as easy as I thought to stay away from him.'

'I don't think you're stupid, I'm just concerned for you, he is still married you know.'

'No he's separated.'

'No he's not, I did a bit of research, and he hasn't filed for separation or divorce.'

'How do you know that?'

'It's not that hard, I have a contact in the UK who did a background search on him.'

'What, why?'

'What do you mean why, do I need to remind you of what he did and the years of ghosting you? I just think it's a bit suspicious that he has turned up after all this time and has wheedled his way back into your life, don't you think it's a bit fishy?'

'No, I don't,' Faye snapped.

'Well Faye we are going on what could be a wild goose chase because of a feeling you have about a patient, and I am going with you because I know you are not crazy, but you need to start applying some of that same reasoning to Danny.'

'What else did you find out about him?' asked Faye, she was fuming not so much at Ina but at herself for being so gullible.

'A lot of what he told you himself is true, he works for his father-in-law, has two boys and still lives in the family home.'

'Why did you have to tell me this, I would have preferred not to know.'

'No, you wouldn't, it's just hard to hear it and I don't particularly like to have to tell you, but you are my best friend and I love you and I don't want to see you getting hurt again.' Ina said this in the gentlest way, and it made Faye cry because she knew Ina was her greatest ally and would never want to hurt her.

'I know,' sobbed Faye. 'It's just so, so...' she took a tissue from her bag and blew her nose, and tried to control the tears, without success. Eventually they stopped. She felt exhausted.

'He's a liar, he told me emphatically that he was separated and that he had moved out of their home. What's he at, why after all these years would he come back and blatantly lie to me, it doesn't make sense. I mean there must be some plausible reason.'

'There's only one plausible reason for someone to lie about being married, Faye think about it, I know it's not very savoury but it's years since you've seen him, he could have had a series of affairs and you are his latest challenge.'

'That's a bit much.'

'Yeah, but plausible.'

'God do you really think that's what he is doing, I'm just another notch on his belt?'

'Well, he probably had to come to Ireland for work and saw it as an opportunity to hook back up with you but he knew he would have to convolute the lie about being separated if he was to have any chance with you, he knew that you wouldn't go near him if he was still married to her, so he told Harry he was separated to set the bait.'

'Bloody hell Ina, I was such easy prey, what's wrong with me, do you know I am considered quite good at my job, if only people knew how ridiculous I am.'

'How good you are at your job has got nothing to do with this, you are good at your job because you went to university and are clever enough to be able to adapt what you learnt to your patients, that doesn't mean nor imply that you should be able to do it for yourself. If you ask me, people in your line of work are the most unhinged of all, maybe it's the overexposure to madness,' Ina laughed.

'I know, but seriously I must have some sort of masochistic streak, maybe I like pain but can't admit it,' Faye wondered out loud. It wasn't the first time she had thought this, such were the incidents of situations where she found herself at the butt end of heartache and pain.

'You're not a masochist, you just think with your vagina and that leads you astray,' offered Ina by way of explanation.

'Ina that's disgusting. I most certainly do not think with my vagina!' Faye sounded so huffy that Ina burst out laughing. Faye followed and they laughed the way they did as children, that uncontrollable laughter, the kind of laughter which transported them away from their worries and concerns or any trouble they were going to get into, which, while it lasted, was pure and innocent, the kind of laughter that when it began to abate brought loss and regret at its end. And so they laughed and laughed until Ina said she was going to wet herself if she didn't pull the car over. As with this kind of laughter it took several attempts to stop. When they eventually did stop, they both sighed and in silence Ina started the car up again and they drove without a word for several miles. Eventually on the outskirts of Limerick, Faye spoke.

'Thank you for telling me the truth.'

'You're welcome sweetie, what are friends for only to dash your hopes and dreams,' answered Ina and they smiled at each other.

'We'll be in Munlney in a few minutes,' said Ina and they discussed their plan.

Arthur had followed the taxi Faye had taken back to her flat and didn't have long to wait before she left again this time in her car. He had been following them for over an hour now and they were on the M7, he wondered where the hell they were off to. They had just passed exit 13 for Kildare when the petrol light came on. He cursed himself for not filling up the tank, but he had not envisaged this trip down the country. He decided to stay with them for as long as possible, there was probably twenty-five to thirty miles left in the reserve, with a bit of luck they would be stopping soon. By the time they came to the toll booth at Portlaoise, Arthur knew he had to fill up or end up on the side of the road. He cursed himself for what was an amateur blunder. He was distracted lately, but he couldn't quite figure out what was the cause of this distraction, all he knew was that he better get his gear together and fast. Still cursing, he turned off onto exit 18.

Ina parked Faye's car outside Kelly's, a small grocery shop in Munlney. They both got out and walked into the shop. They had chosen this shop because it had all the appearance of being around for a millennium and probably had the same family of Kelly's running it since time immemorial. Their plan was to pose as Amanda

Kennedy's old friends who had lost touch and were trying to contact her to invite her to Ina's wedding.

When they opened the door, it brushed against the bell hanging from the ceiling and all eyes in the shop turned to look, well stare, at Ina and Faye. The shop was neither quaint nor curious, what it was was an atrocious mix of Formica, beauty board, discoloured lino and MDF everything. It had a fetid stink which reminded Faye of corned beef and damp.

'How're ye?' asked the shopkeeper, he was probably only forty but looked sixty-five, he was bald on top with longish brownish side hair, his face had what might best be described as a high colour, which was probably helped by the massive gut which jutted out from his torso like it was a whole separate entity. His shirt unfortunately couldn't quite make it all the way across the bulge, so evidence of his hirsute belly was presented to all who cared to look, and it was very difficult not to. The poor shirt which had seen better days had food stains down the front and stale sweat stains in the armpits. His bottom half mercifully wasn't visible, hidden by the Formica counter.

'Well thanks,' answered Faye, it was decided that she would do most of the talking.

'Can I get you anything?' asked the shopkeeper completely ignoring the other two customers who were there already.

'Oh, I don't want to jump the queue,' said Faye, smiling at the two women, one elderly woman, the other ancient.

'Don't worry, love, we're grand we're in no hurry,' said the older of the two.

'Thank you so much,' smiled Faye 'I'll take a packet of emeralds and two cans of coke please.'

'No bother,' said the shopkeeper and added 'ye're not from around, I know all the good-looking young ones and I haven't seen ye before.'

'You're right, actually you might be able to help us, we are trying to locate our old friend, she is from here, but we lost touch and are desperately trying to find her again, you might know her,' Faye said sounding excited in the hopes of exciting them into helping her.

'Oh, right and who might this friend ye're so *desperately* trying to find be and we'll see what we can do,' said the shop keeper, mimicking Faye when he said *desperately*.

'Her name is Amanda Kennedy, and she grew up here in Munlney but left after school about fifteen or sixteen years ago and she is gorgeous looking. She has a brother and a sister. Her mother died only a while back. Does that ring a bell?'

'Was her mother Martha Kennedy?' asked the older of the old ladies.

'I'm not sure of her name, but did she have a daughter Amanda?'

'She did and another one called Pamela, another looker and a young fella Conor, a useless yoke, nothing but trouble. All the lads were mad about Amanda, I was a few years ahead of her in school, but she was a bit different, I suppose, never went near any of us lads,' said the shopkeeper.

I'm not surprised, thought Ina.

'Have you seen her lately?' asked Faye.

'Nope, mind you she was at her mother's funeral, but that was a bit odd if you don't mind me saying.' It seemed to Faye that they had stroke gold with this shopkeeper, he was a blabbermouth.

'Really, in what way?' asked Faye, in a way which pandered to the shopkeeper's greater knowledge.

'Well, between ourselves, her mother had been sick for a while before she died, pancreatic cancer, it's one of the worst, they say you cry like a baby with the pain...' he paused for effect. Faye obliged.

'Oh god, that's awful, poor thing.'

'Yeah, and your friend, her daughter, never came near her the whole time. They say Amanda married well, someone who's loaded, well wouldn't you think with all that money that she would have helped out her poor dying mam who was riddled with cancer.'

The shopkeeper was warming to his subject becoming more energised with each utterance, he didn't require much encouragement.

'Why was that do you think?' asked Ina, they all stopped and looked at her for a moment, as she hadn't said a word, they had forgotten about her.

'Well, they say that she was ashamed of where she came from and didn't want anything to do with her family, had notions about herself you know, Munlney wasn't good enough for the likes of her. Mind you her sister Pam maintained that your man she married was a piece of work, if you know what I mean.' The shopkeeper stopped. Faye took that as her cue to flatter him to say more.

'God, I never heard that, you see we never knew the husband, what was he like?' Faye asked in a slight whisper with wide open eyes.

'Big shot, by all accounts, some say he, well I shouldn't be saying this really but ye're her friends and sure it might help that ye know, that he made his money the wrong way, if you see what I mean.'

'Oh, that's awful, what was he like at the funeral?' asked Faye.

'Well sure that's more of it, he wasn't even there. And she only barely made it in time for the burial, never came to the removal or the mass, swanned in just as she was about to be put in the ground and was gone again as quick as she came. Her own mother and all she did for her and that's the thanks she got.'

'Gosh!' said Faye for effect.

'Martha's husband, Des, was fond of the drink, he also liked the greyhound racing in Limerick, and it was common knowledge that he was heavy with his hand with all the family. Martha had a cleaning job for years in the primary school and took in ironing, she worked hard to keep food on the table for those children. A nice respectable woman who went to mass and confession and kept to herself. She had a lot to put up with, with Des and when he died, I'd say it was a relief to her, God forgive me for saying it,' the younger of the old ladies didn't pause for breath and she blessed herself before continuing on.

'He died of that disease you get in your liver from drink, what's it called again...'

'Psoriasis,' said the shopkeeper with all the authority of a consultant dermatologist and not a hepatologist, Faye didn't dare correct him.

'Yes that's it, he died of psoriasis of the liver, only himself to blame, a nasty fella really, but Martha looked after those children well.'

'Why didn't she leave him?' asked Ina in her city naiveté. The old ladies didn't reply immediately but shot Ina a look of incredulity in such perfect unison that Ina knew she had inadvertently moved into boondocks territory.

'Didn't you just hear me say that she was a respectable woman who went to mass; she wasn't some kind of hussy who just threw her husband out. Some people take the vow of matrimony very serious young lady, not like nowadays where there's no respect for the holy sacraments,' the more ancient of the two was in flying form and Faye feared that this could easily distract them from what they were here for. She knew she had to salvage it and get in before Ina got incensed and began to pontificate on spousal abuse or worse yet clergy abuse. It was clear these old girls were from a different planet to Ina.

'Is Amanda close to Pamela or Conor?' asked Faye addressing the shopkeeper, giving the old girls a chance to recover from the city heathen.

'Depends on what you mean by close, sure she never comes near the place, so I'd say she's not all that close. You couldn't blame her with Conor, he was always a pup, always in and out of trouble with the guards.'

'What kind of trouble?' asked Ina, the guard in her couldn't resist.

'Robbing and making private videos, that kind of thing, general feck acting around, but there was no real harm in him really, between ourselves I'd say he was smoking a bit of that maruanna.'

'That maruanna has them all gone mad,' said the ancient one, recovered from the assault on the holy sacraments.

'I know it's awful,' said Faye 'Do Pam and Conor live around here?'

'Pam lives in the home place and Conor comes and goes, I haven't seen him for a while, but sure he could just as easily turn up tomorrow like a bad penny, scrounging off anyone who'll put up with him.'

'Where is the home place?' asked Faye.

'Sur, it's no distance from here, just on the edge of the village, you go out of here and go to the end of the road and turn right, follow the road until you get to the crossroads, ignore it and the house is on a turn off to your right, it's a yellowish colour. Pam is usually at home she has a couple of young lads, and she doesn't work, she'll probably be at home now.' The shopkeeper seemed very sure of this.

'You've been very helpful, thank you so much, we are really hoping to locate Amanda, maybe Pam can help us,' said Faye.

'Well good luck and it's three forty-five for your coke and sweets,' said the shopkeeper. Faye paid and she and Ina turned and said goodbye to all three.

'We'll say a prayer for ye,' said the ancient one.

'We will,' added the younger one, almost like a threat.

'Wow,' said Ina just as they got outside 'what are they like, it's like a museum to everything that's bad about this county in there, gossipy, small-minded bigots, I wouldn't like to be trying to keep a secret around here.'

'I know, but look on the bright side, we know where Pamela lives now,' smiled Faye.

'No wonder Amanda got the hell out of here, I had to laugh when he said she didn't go near any of the local lads, she was smart enough to want more for herself and this is seen as being uppity,' Ina wasn't mad on country thinking.

'It can't have been any fun growing up here especially with a drunk for a father, it's so sad that she tried to do well for herself and ended up married to a man just as bad as her father. Despite all the money, her life is as miserable as her mother's.'

'People never learn,' said Ina.

'It's not that simple, Amanda did get out and clearly wanted something beyond here, but when we're not accustomed to love and care it's not always possible to recognize it and equally we get used to situations so much so that we hardly notice when we are recreating our past until it's too late. It happens all the time,' Faye felt that she could just as easily fall into this category as Amanda.

They were back in the car and following the instructions the shopkeeper gave them, it didn't take long to get to the crossroads they had been told to ignore.

'We'll go with the same line with Pamela,' said Ina.

'Okay let's hope the shopkeeper is right and that she's at home, he seemed to know a lot about her whereabouts, didn't he?'

'These guys always try to sound like they know more than they actually do, but then again somewhere like here he probably does know most of her movements.'

'Here it is, great there's a car there.'

The house was most likely built in the seventies, it looked like one of those small country council houses where the front door was at the side, with three windows in the front and a small opaque window which was the bathroom. Faye wondered did they actually think the design was good at the time, because it was horrible.

Everything about it screamed functionality, there was no concession to style; the windows were replaced at some point with white PVC, the frames were so thick they took up so much of glass space which only added to the already odd proportions. The garden was blotches of patchy grass both to the front and side of the house. There were two mountain bikes thrown on the grass along with two old tractor tyres where someone a long time ago attempted to grow some flowers, presumably, they were now full of weeds and cracking. Around the back had the same class of patchy grass and there was an old trampoline and a children's swing set that had seen better days. The net curtains on the windows were all eschew ways, everything about the house screamed hard times. Faye found it hard to associate Amanda with this house.

Ina and Faye walked to the door at the side of the house, which essentially was the front door, it too had been replaced with white PVC, one with a rose motif on the glass which was stained red and green. Ina pressed the doorbell. After a moment there was a shout from inside.

'Coming, just a minute.'

The door was opened by a smiling woman.

'How're ye,' said Pamela.

'Hello we're...' began Faye but was cut off by Pamela.

'I know your friends of Mandy, Stevie from the shop just gave me a ring and told me ye were on ye're way up.'

Better than any Twitter thought Ina.

'My name is Emma, and this is Maggie, we were hoping you might be able to help us locate Amanda, you see we lost touch and Maggie is getting married and we really wanted her to be there for old times' sake,' said Faye, as she offered her hand to Pamela, they shook hands and Ina followed Faye's lead.

'Come in, sorry about the mess I wasn't expecting anyone,' said Pamela apologetically.

'Oh, don't worry, we're sorry to burst in on you like this, we couldn't think of anything else to do,' said Faye.

'Come on into the kitchen and I'll put on the kettle.'

'Please don't go to any trouble for us,' said Ina.

'Oh, it's no trouble at all, it's nice to have a chance to talk to some adults instead of kids.'

Pamela was every bit as attractive as Amanda, thought Faye, perhaps even more so she was all the better for having no Botox or fillers. Her clothes were well worn but clean, the house was also well worn but clean. Pamela had a soft voice with a definite Limerick accent, her movements were gentle and precise just watching her put on the kettle had a grace and elegance to it. She had a sadness about her which only added to her beauty and a desire to protect her, Faye wasn't sure what she needed to be protected from, but she felt she did not want to cause this woman any pain.

Pamela took out three mugs from the press overhead the cooker and placed them on the countertop. She then took an old steel tea pot and put two heaped dessertspoons of tealeaves from a tea caddy, she made tea the old-fashioned way, and many would argue the proper way. While the tea was drawing, she put some Lincoln cream biscuits on a plate and placed them on the table where Ina and Faye were sitting.

'Do you like your tea strong or weak?' she asked.

'Weak for me please,' answered Faye.

'Strong for me please,' said Ina.

'I'll give you the first cup so,' she said looking at Faye.

Pamela placed a tea strainer over the mug and poured the tea, all three watched in a semi hypnotic state as the strainer filled with tea leaves. This little ritual was having a sedative effect on Ina and Faye, the kitchen was beginning to feel more and more like what you'd imagine a kind granny's kitchen to be. Somewhere you can collapse in a heap and have someone pour love all over you with her tea and biccies and wise words like, "don't' mind them, they don't know what they're talking about". Eventually after a sip of tea Ina spoke.

'Do you know where Amanda is?'

'Yes and no,' Pamela answered. 'The last time I saw Mandy was at our mother s funeral, she found it, well, difficult to get down to us. Don't get me wrong, it's not that she didn't want to, she did, it was, well not easy for her.'

'In what way?' asked Faye, in a voice barely more than a whisper.

'Mandy is a good person and cares for all of us but since she got married, she has had to make her life in Dublin.'

Ina could sense that Pamela was being cautious and thought she might even be a bit afraid.

'We don't know her husband, but we've heard he is bossy, and life was not easy for Amanda, is that true?' asked Ina.

'Would you believe I've only met him once, not long after they got married Mandy asked me and Paul, that's my eldest son, up to stay for a few nights while he was away. We were having such a good time we stayed a night longer and he came home before we left. He barely spoke to me, and he completely ignored Paul, it was clear he didn't want us there and that was the one and only time I met him or was in their house. Mandy felt awful about that and though she never said it I knew he told her not to invite us back, she always made excuses for him; you know, that he was very busy and under a lot of pressure with work, that sort of thing. In the early days she phoned a good bit, especially when Mam was alive but as time went on, we heard less and less from her. Mandy was very proud, and she never complained but I knew she wasn't happy. She had always wanted children even as a little girl and I think she was sad that she didn't have any herself.'

'Why was that?' asked Ina.

'She said that the time wasn't right for Oliver, but then when is the time ever right to have kids, I have three and the timing was off on each of them, but they're here now and you get on with it.' Pamela smiled as she said this but there was a resignation about it which silently said, "this is my lot now". At that moment a young boy came into the room, he was his mother's son, with all her beauty, funny how the beauty of the female can be equally beautiful in the male.

'Mam, can I play the Xbox?' he asked, taking full advantage of his mother's will being diminished in the presence of visitors.

'Okay, but only for half an hour,' Pamela said, and the boy was gone as quick as he came. 'That's Tommy my youngest.'

'How old are your boys?' asked Faye with genuine interest. People like Pamela always fascinated Faye, she would surmise about the lives they have versus the lives they could have had. Mind you, Amanda had a polar opposite life, but right now Faye would have taken Pamela's.

'Paul's fifteen, Jack's eleven and Tommy there, is seven. They're good boys really but I'm on my own so….' she just let the obvious remain unsaid.

'Mandy's Paul's godmother and she was mad about him, I had him young, and Mandy came down from Dublin every weekend to help me, that was before she got married. She was great with him and would bring lots of stuff for him. I was only seventeen, Mandy's only four years older than me but she was a natural when it came to minding Paul, she was always so calm and caring. To be honest there was loads of times when I wished she was Paul's mother, I was useless, and I couldn't wait for the weekends when Mandy would come and take over. Paul was two when she met Oliver and it didn't take long before she stopped coming every weekend and soon, she hardly came at all. I suppose I resented her for a while, but she had her own life. She missed Paul, I do know that she sent him things for a good few years and then that stopped too. I know it sounds selfish, but I really missed her, you must know you're her friends, she's the kind of person you want to be around, she's just really lovely. Once when she was down at the weekend, I was so fed up with minding Paul that I took off for the weekend with his dad, I knew I should have come back on Sunday evening so Mandy could go back to Dublin, but I didn't, I stayed away until Wednesday. When I came back Mandy was still here, she wouldn't leave Paul with Mam, so she rang in sick to work. She never said a word to me, never gave out or anything, that's the way she is. That was the last time I pulled a stunt like that I felt so bad, all she was doing for me, and I could have cost her her job.' Pamela paused for a moment before continuing on.

'Growing up she was more like a mother than Mam, poor old Mam got a raw deal when she married Des Kennedy, he was useless and eventually Mam's nerves went, she could barely string a sentence together, but she was like Mandy, really kind. I know what all the locals say about Mandy that she got too big for her boots and left us all behind but it's not like that, she was in bits when Mam died, I know she felt awful guilty that she wasn't around more, but she was afraid to go against him. When she told me she was going to leave him I was stunned but delighted for her. I thought it would mean I would see her more but that hasn't happened.'

'When did she tell you she was leaving him?' asked Faye.

'About six weeks ago. At Mam's funeral she told me she was thinking about it but made me swear not to mention it to anyone, not even Conor, Conor's our brother, then a bit later I got a call from her saying she was going through with it and asked if she could stay with me for a while. I was delighted, she could stay here forever as far as I was concerned, after all this is as much her house as mine. But she never came, she decided to leave the country instead and I got two calls from her and a card.'

'Where is she?' asked Ina, not noticing how excited she sounded.

'She asked me not to tell anyone, but to be honest I'm a bit worried, and the card she sent was a bit strange, she said she wouldn't be contacting me for a while, maybe I'm just being a bit stupid but...'

Faye could sense her trepidation, she didn't want to push her, but she didn't want her to retreat either.

'I know you're worried and maybe we can help, we're worried too we haven't seen or heard from her in ages,' Faye said.

'She's in India,' said Pamela, after only a moment's hesitation.

'India!' screeched Ina and Faye in unison.

'Yeah, I know, I thought it was mad too, she always hated going to new places, she was afraid that way, I remember when she first moved to Dublin it took all her courage. I couldn't believe it when I got a call from her saying she was in India.'

'What's she doing there?' asked Ina

'Well, I'm not sure really, it's something strange that I can't pronounce,' said Pamela

'Is it Yoga,' asked Ina.

'No,' laughed Pamela 'I can pronounce Yoga.'

'Sorry I didn't mean it that way.'

'Don't worry, no she's learning some kind of craft thing called passi something or other, wait a minute I wrote it down.' Pamela got up from the table and almost floated out of the room.

'Bloody hell, India, that's a surprise, she never said a word about India to me,' whispered Faye.

'Well India is better than dead,' said Ina.

'I know, that's if she's still in India.'

'Here it is,' Pamela said as she came back in with a piece of paper and a card in her hand. She handed the piece of paper to Faye which contained the tricky word.

'Passementerie,' read Faye aloud.

'What's that when it's at home?' said Ina.

'I haven't a clue,' said Faye, but it sounds more French than Indian.

'From what I can gather its very ornate trimmings for expensive clothes and things,' offered Pamela.

'What part of India is she in?' asked Ina.

'Somewhere in the south I think, it's on the card,' Pamela held the card in her hand up and read aloud 'Udupi.'

'Never heard of it,' said Ina.

'Me neither,' added Faye.

'So, she's doing passementerie in Udupi,' Ina said sounding baffled.

'When did you get the card from her?' asked Faye.

'About five weeks ago,' said Pamela, 'Here read it,' and she handed Faye the card.

The card had a picture of a very colourful Indian bazaar, on the bottom it read *Colours of Udupi*. Faye turned the card over and read it.

> Dear Pamela, I hope you and the boys are well, I am enjoying life here and will move to a more remote place soon so don't worry if you don't hear from me. I am fine and life is good I don't think I will ever leave here. Ireland is a life I never want to return to.
>
> Lots of love, Amanda xx

She handed the card to Ina, Ina read the card and studied it closely.

'You have been calling Amanda, Mandy is that what you always call her?' Ina asked Pamela.

'Yes, ever since we were kids, I was Pammy and she was Mandy, why do you ask?'

'She signs the card Amanda and refers to you as Pamela not Pammy, is that unusual?'

'Well, yes, it is, but I didn't pay it much heed, I just thought with all her years in Dublin she was trying to be more, I don't know, adult I suppose,' Pamela sounded a bit thrown.

'What did she call you when you spoke?'

'Pammy.'

'The card is written in print, is that her writing?'

'To be honest I don't really know, as I said we had little contact in the last ten years, I don't think I know what her writing is like, that sounds terrible not to know your sister's writing doesn't it,' Pamela now sounded sad and guilty.

'Not at all,' said Faye, 'I would be the same. You mentioned that you thought the card was strange, what was strange for you?'

'Well I know we weren't in touch much but I know she cared for me and the boys and Conor, it seemed odd that she said she will never come back here, she was never one for travelling, she liked to be at home, that's all she used to ever want, was to have her own home and family. It seems so weird that she would never want to come back. But then again, I don't really know her anymore, what I am saying is more about the Mandy I remember from growing up. We all change and maybe living with him changed her and she wants to start a new life, I can understand that. And really there is nothing for her here, what would she do here, nothing, like me. I envy her in ways, the chance to start a whole new life somewhere far from here, she's right not ever to come back, the past can bring you down. If I had the chance, I would probably do the same.' Pamela was becoming lost in her thoughts and for a moment forgot she was talking to two complete strangers.

'I'm sorry, I'm rambling off there.'

'Not at all,' said Faye.

'Do you know if Amanda has been in touch with Conor? asked Ina.

'No, well not that he has said, and he would say. He is difficult to get hold of at the best of times, if she was writing to him, it would be this address she would use, and nothing has come here for him. If she phoned him, he would have told me,' said Pamela.

'Does he live here?' asked Ina.

'On and off, Conor has some problems, things can be difficult for him,' Pamela said.

'Do you think it would be worth asking him about Amanda,' ventured Faye.

'No, he would have told me if he heard from her,' Pamela had a resolve in her voice which told Ina and Faye that Conor was off limits. Just then Tommy came back into the room.

'Mam I'm hungry.'

'Okay pet, I'll get you something to eat in a minute, go back in and I'll call you when it's ready,' answered Pamela, 'I better get their dinner on, Paul will be back any minute. I suppose this has been a waste of time for you, she'll hardly be going to your wedding,' she said to Ina.

'It beginning to look that way, it's a pity I would love to have had the chance to even ask her, do you even have a phone number?'

'No, I've no way of contacting her myself, which is kind of strange, when she was in Dublin although there wasn't much contact at least I could if I needed to, but now, well I suppose she doesn't want to be contacted.'

'Can we leave you a number just in case?' asked Faye.

'Course you can, I'll just take it down here,' Pamela reached for the piece of paper she had given Faye and got up to get a pen from the worktop, 'fire ahead.'

Faye gave Pamela her private mobile number and made a mental note to herself to change the call answering message.

'Do you mind if I take your number just on the off chance we heard anything, we can let you know,' said Faye.

'Yeah, course you can,' said Pamela and she called out her number and Faye put it into her phone.

'Thank you for your time and all your help, we really appreciate it. You know you remind me a lot of Amanda, you are very alike,' said Faye.

'Thanks, I'll take that as a compliment,' smiled Pamela.

Ina and Faye got up from the table and began to walk towards the door, just as they were at the door, Pamela spoke.

'Do you think she is alright?' It was asked in that way that you don't really want to know the answer but you can't help yourself from asking.

'I'm sure she is, it's like you said, she's starting over a new life for herself,' Faye wasn't sure if she sounded convincing to Pamela, because she didn't sound convincing to herself.

They shook hands and said goodbye. Ina and Faye walked in silence to the car and got in.

Faye spoke first.

'What do you think?'

'I think she's really sad.'

'I know, it's like she has settled for this, all hopes faded.'

'Three kids will curtail your movements. I don't know how she sticks it, I'd go barmy down here.'

'I suppose it's what she knows, you learn to live with it and tailor your dreams so as not to go completely barking mad.'

'What do you make of Amanda in India?'

'It's bizarre, and doing this passementerie thing, completely bizarre, but pretty impressive at the same time. Wouldn't it be amazing to abandon your life here and take on a whole new persona and start from scratch, but this time you are starting with awareness and deliberation, you control your starting point.'

'I don't think you can really leave your past behind.'

'I think maybe we can, after all our past is only based on our memories of it and our memories are constructed and not at all reliable, much of what we think are memories are actually fabrication, so imagine you take yourself off to a completely different environment with no contact from your past, you are less likely to stimulate your memories to begin with and secondly you can fabricate the memories you want to fit in with your new life. I think it's wonderful.'

'If it's so wonderful why do more people not do it – and what you're describing sounds delusional.'

'Maybe so but aren't we just too scared to try, staying in the same relentless grind in the hopes that things will change.'

'That's very gloomy Faye.'

'Yes, but it's the human condition to continually make the same mistakes over and over again stupidly thinking that this time it will be different.'

'God how do you give any hope to your patients?'

'Is it my job to give hope Ina or to help people see reality.'

'Yes, it is Faye, people will wither without hope – it's what keeps us going, you know that don't you?' Ina sounded worried that this fundamental truth had bypassed her friend.

'Yeah, of course I do – I'm just rambling.... Anyway, that postcard was a bit iffy.' Faye didn't think hope was all it was cracked up to be.

'Yeah, did she come across to you as someone who would want to cut all ties with her family?'

'I don't know, I think it was more that she was forced to cut ties, but it wasn't willingly, she certainly cared deeply for her family and was heartbroken when her mother died, but she was also terrified of her husband so she might want to make sure that he never finds her.'

'Everyone can be found Faye.'

'Then we can find her, it can't be that difficult to find where you can do passementerie in Udupi.'

'Faye she's no longer a missing person, we know where she is now, there's no need to do any more.'

'She hasn't been heard of in weeks.'

'Yes, but that doesn't mean anything has happened to her, people have a right to vanish without fear of their former shrink hunting them down, you have to accept that she doesn't want to be found and that you might be causing her more trouble by chasing this.'

'I know you're right but there is a part of me that still feels something happened to her.'

'Faye just let it go.'

'Okay.'

'Are you hungry, we can get something before we head back, or do you want to get back home?'

'I'm famished let's get a bite to eat, we'll still be back at a reasonable time.'

'Grand, but we'll have to go into Limerick I don't think we'll get anything here.'

As they drove into Limerick Faye couldn't quite convince herself that things were as fine as Ina maintained.

After Faye dropped Ina home, she went straight home herself. She had decided in the car that she wasn't going to leave things. After pouring herself a whiskey she waited while her computer booted up, and then she went about researching *passementerie* in Udupi. As she had thought there weren't that many hits, in fact there was only one. Apparently *passementerie* dates back to the sixteenth century with the primary role being to embellish garments, long used as evidence of wealth but the advent of the sewing machine gave it a kiss of death. To save this craft a Frenchman, Bertrand Pruneau, set up a small factory in Udupi to teach and make *passementerie*. According to his website he moved there from France twenty-six years ago and built up what seemed to be a successful business. He took on people once a year for either a six or twelve month course with the option of going on to a three-year apprenticeship. The images on his site were beautiful, there were reams of jewel-coloured tassels, braiding, and fringing, they all looked like exquisite works of art. Faye thought if this was what Amanda was doing then she would be delighted for her and a bit envious. There was a contact phone number, but it was too late in India to call now, she would call tomorrow.

Her phone beeped to say a message came in. She picked up the phone and saw that it was from Danny. She hadn't given what Ina had told her much thought, she was preoccupied with Amanda and happy to be so. Thinking about Danny lying to her was just too miserable. She read the message,

> missing you, looking forward to seeing you tomorrow, available tonight if you are free.

Ina had asked her on the way back from Limerick what she was going to do about Danny, she fobbed her off with something about definitely confronting him, but the truth was she was not really sure what she was going to do. Knowing that Danny was still married annoyed her but not enough to deaden the incogitable urge she had to be with him. But not tonight.

Arthur waited in the car outside Faye's flat, he was like an antichrist because of the petrol blunder earlier on, the only thing that was keeping him from going apoplectic was the tracking devise he had fitted to Faye's car. From this he knew that they went to Munlney outside Limerick and then into Limerick for an hour before returning to Dublin. At this moment Arthur had not a clue what they were doing there, there was nothing in Oliver Blake brief to him about Munlney, it could easily be that they were simply visiting a friend, but he would have to be sure, Blake was paying him to know not to surmise. He had planned on waiting outside Faye's for a while longer to see if she was going out again, if so he would stay on her, but once he was sure she was in for the night he would drive to Munlney and find out what today's trip was about.

# twelve

Faye was up early on Sunday morning partly because she had not slept very well but predominantly because she was anxious to make the call to India. She poured herself a strong cup of coffee from the espresso machine Harry had given her when she moved into the flat, she hoped it might go some way to easing the spitting headache she woke up with. The one whiskey which she had to help relax, had turned into four by the time she went to bed and to prevent her waking in the small hours, she took two Valium. She was paying for that now. The coffee tasted good, and she could feel her body and brain wake up. She felt like popping another few Valium but decided against it, not because she didn't want to but because she was running low and didn't want to go back so soon to Jack.

She sat at her desk and while the computer booted up, she checked her phone, Danny had called twice leaving two messages about meeting up today. Faye decided to call him later. She found the website and the contact number and dialled, there was a funny sound on the phone before it was answered, by someone speaking Hindu, Faye presumed.

Faye, speaking in very clear and slightly louder than normal - why do people do that – English, asked if Bertrand Purneau was available. The lady answered in a very clear concise upper-class British accent that he was and asked Faye to wait a moment while she got him, Faye thought she must be his wife or lover and began to imagine what she might look like, probably embellished in all manner of fine *passementerie*, her thoughts were interrupted by another clear distant voice, this time that beautiful French accent, Faye felt anything said in French sounded seductive and she always fancied herself a bit of a Francophile.

'Allo, this is Bertrand Pruneau, how can I help?'

Faye thought she would love to be helped by the beautiful Monsieur Purneau, she knew he was beautiful from his web site photo.

'Oh hello, my name is Faye Munroe, I am ringing from Ireland, I got your number from your web site, I must say your passementerie is spectacular.' Never hurts to compliment before asking for something.

'Thank you, we think so too,' answered Bertrand. Of course you do, thought Faye.

'I was hoping you might be able to help me with an important matter, you see my dear friend has gone missing and the last we heard from her was that she was going to study *passementerie* with you in Udupi, her name is Amanda Kennedy but she could be using her married name, Amanda Blake, a lady in her thirties, very beautiful.' Faye paused to allow him to answer. But he did not answer.

'I wonder can you tell me if she is studying with you?'

'Madame, I am not in the habit of becoming involved in the private lives of people.' answered Bertrand in a matter-of-fact way.

'Of course, you are not, and I apologise if it appeared that I was asking you to do so. But you see I am extremely worried about Amanda and was only hoping you could confirm if she has been there or if she is still there.' Faye did not need to fake a concerned voice because she was concerned.

'But of course, I understand your concern, but you must also understand my situation, I am not at liberty to disclose any information about my students.'

'So she is your student.'

'I did not say any such thing, I am simply stating a general fact of my policies, to say she was here or not here would be to dishonour these polices. I regret but I cannot assist you in this matter.'

'Please Monsieur Pruneau, this is very serious, and I understand and respect your position and I would not ask you if I was not desperate, no one has seen her for months, can you please just tell me has she visited there?'

'Madame I sympathise, but again regret I cannot help you, now I must go, good day.'

'One moment, can you please pass this number to her if she is there and let her decide?' Faye called out her number before she heard the click of the phone being hung up in Udupi.

Faye sat looking at the phone. She felt sure that Amanda had been there otherwise why could he not simply have said that he never heard of her, while she admired his discretion, she was cross he wouldn't just tell her yes or no, I mean really are people studying passementerie usually on the run?

Thank goodness she hadn't given in to her whiskey induced urge last night to book a flight to Udupi.

A bit dispirited from the Udupi call, she phoned Danny and they arranged to meet at his hotel at one o' clock. She had not asked him to her flat, she didn't think she would.

A minute later, there was a gentle knock on her door and she could hear the sound of footsteps walking away, it was Pat, he left the Sunday papers at her door when he had read them and he usually had them read by ten o clock, Faye opened the door and sure enough the papers were waiting all neat as a pin as if they had not been poured over in detail.

'Thanks Pat,' she shouted down the stairs.

'You're welcome,' came the response.

On her way back into the kitchen she stooped down to her CDs and chose Elgar cello concerto in E Minor, Op.85. She didn't have a big CD collection and most of it was classical or contemporary female singers.

Faye then poured another coffee, took a packet of digestive biscuits from the press, before plonking herself on the sofa with the papers. She was half-way through a story about an American evangelist who was having an affair when the phone rang. As she picked it up, she could see it was an unusual number.

'Hello,' she said.

'Hello,' came the lovely Indian-British voice Faye had heard only a half hour ago, 'This is Eesha Vattyam, you spoke with my husband Bertrand a short while ago.'

'Yes of course.'

'My husband is a very honourable man Miss Monroe and I myself am quite conflicted about speaking with you right now, but I, like you, am concerned about Amanda.'

'Bingo,' thought Faye.

'Amanda had contacted us well over a year ago about our courses and she communicated regularly with us, she expressed a very keen interest in *passementerie* and was very eager to come to us and learn the art. Subsequently she booked a course which started a year ago, and she arrived and settled in very quickly. My husband and I grew very fond of her, she was an exceedingly agreeable person and she was marvellous at *passementerie*, she had a natural talent for it. She spoke very little about her past, but you could sense something was not quite right, we of course did not pry. After about six months, one morning when we went down for breakfast, we all ate together you see, she was not there, she had left, leaving only a note saying things had changed and she was moving on. We have not seen or heard from her since.'

'But all the signs were that she was happy and enjoying her course?'

'Oh yes very much so, she often said that this was a new life for her and that she loved the *passementerie*, and you could see that she did.'

'So it would be fair to say her leaving came as a shock, and out of the blue?'

'Yes that is true, she was always so caring and polite it seemed at odds with her character that she would leave in such a way.'

'Did she take all her things with her?'

'Yes, she did not have a great deal of belongings, she arrived with one small case, but she took everything except some pieces of *passementerie* she had made, which I found quite strange as she loved those pieces, they were the first pieces she made.'

'Do you remember her saying anything which might help, anything about her past or a place she wanted to visit? asked Faye.

'No, as I said she was extremely private and we did not pry, she appeared very content with us.'

'Did you try to contact her?'

'All our communication had been by phone, and she would ring us, we did have a number for her, but it is not working now, we have tried, we have no address, we knew only that she was from Ireland.'

'Did anyone visit her while she was there?'

'Not to my knowledge, but that would not mean it didn't happen, mind you she spent almost all of her time in our centre, our house, the workshop and the student chalets are all on the same property surrounded by a high wall. Amanda rarely ventured out, she spent a vast amount of time in the workshop. She never received any letters because all letters come to the main house, and I never saw her on a phone.'

'Is there anything you can think of that might help, anything she said, anything at all?

'I am truly sorry I cannot be of more help but there is nothing I can think of that is of any significance.'

'Oh, you have been a great help, it's just sometimes we hear things, and it is only afterwards that they have any significance.'

'Yes indeed, I know what you mean, but in this case, there is nothing I can think of, she was not at all talkative.'

Faye was trying to think was there anything else which she could ask Eesha which might help.

'Did you sense she was in danger?' Faye thought she might not get the chance to ask again.

'It is difficult to say but I did feel that she was cautious for a reason, she was guarded and kept to herself, I suppose if pushed I would say she was a cautious person. I feel I have said far too much, I only wished to let you know that she was here.'

'I am very grateful that you called me, I assure you everything you have said will be held in confidence and it has been extremely helpful, please contact me at any time if you think of anything else.'

'I believe I have told you everything I can, I do so hope that Amanda is alright, I shudder to think what might have happened to her.'

'I hope she is okay too.' Faye was reluctant to let Eesha go but there was nothing else to say.

'One more thing before I go, would you like me to send you her pieces of *passementerie*, I would like someone who cares about her to have them, I have kept them safe.'

Faye was a bit taken aback, she felt a bit of a fraud posing as a friend and now she was being offered some treasured possessions, what should she do?

'Yes, please that would be very kind of you.' She had done it now, she justified it to herself by saying that they were clues to Amanda's whereabouts and that she would give them to Pamela. Faye gave Eesha her address and they bid each other goodbye.

Faye could feel a sense of foreboding build inside of her, what had started as a feeling about Amanda was now morphing into a full-scale realisation that she could actually be dead. She thought she had better ring Ina.

After two rings Ina answered.

'How are things?'

'Not good Ina, I have just gotten off the phone to Udupi - Amanda was there doing that course in *passementerie* for almost six months and then one day vanished.'

'What do you mean vanished?'

'There was a note, but it simply said she was moving on, the lady I spoke to said she was very shocked and that it was really uncharacteristic of Amanda, that while she was guarded, she was also very friendly and seemed to love it there, said it was a new beginning for her.'

'When did she leave?'

'Six months ago, same time Pamela last heard from her, Ina I have a bad feeling about this.'

'Hang on a second Faye, she left a note and she also told Pamela she wouldn't be in contact with her and not to worry.'

'I know all that, but it is still strange, why would she leave Udupi when she was happy there, maybe she's afraid and on the run?'

'Faye lots of people are on the run from their past and it is not up to you to drag her back into it.' Ina loved her friend, but she was afraid she would get herself in trouble with pursuing this.

'I am not trying to drag her back I am only trying to find out if she is alive, I think that's a bit different don't you.' Faye sounded sharper than she had intended. 'Sorry Ina I'm just concerned, I know what you mean but what if something has happened to her and she has no one to help her, it's been six months since anyone has heard from her?'

'You don't know that she could easily be in touch with people, people she knows and trusts, she could have met a man and not want to be found, especially if her husband is so controlling, you don't know what her life entails or who her friends are. Faye there are lots of explanations, just relax and let it go. You're the one who is always saying that if you tell yourself something long enough you will believe it.'

Ina was right you can be convinced of anything if you dwell on it or are told it for long enough, but Faye knew this was not the case, she knew that Amanda had no one to turn to, simply because she had told her as much in therapy, something had happened to her.

'You're right, but only up to a point. Let's just say she is really missing, what would you do?'

'The truth is that after six months it is really difficult to find someone, most missing people remain missing until such a time as they want to be found or are found accidentlly, there is rarely much police work involved. If she was using credit cards or using her passport, we might have some chance of tracing her.'

'Could you do that, check her credit cards and passport?'

'I could but without an official missing person report I have no right to go prying into people's private business.'

'That's a joke Ina, you know as well as I do that the guards are always checking into these things out of pure nosiness.'

'Yeah, I know, but I don't.'

'Ina you checked out Danny.'

'That was different, I did it for you, my friend.'

'You would be doing this for your friend, please Ina can you just check it, it would mean a lot.'

'Jesus Faye you're a pain in the arse at times, I'll check it tomorrow.' Ina knew Faye well enough that it was easier to just do this for her and hopefully it would be the end of it.

'Thank you darling, you're fabulous.'

'Yeah, yeah. Did you meet Danny last night?'

'No but I am meeting him later.'

'If you want to come over after I'll be at home,' offered Ina.

'Thanks, I'll see how I feel.'

Don't let him try to convince you he's left his wife, because he hasn't.'

'I won't Ina, thanks. If I don't talk to you later, I'll call you tomorrow, and thanks again for doing this for me.'

'You're welcome, see you later bye.'

'Bye,' and they both hung up.

Faye thought about Amanda and hoped that Ina was right and that she was shacked up somewhere with a new lover. But she couldn't quite conjure this happy image in her mind. At that moment she was having difficulty in conceptualising any happy image in her mind. She decided to run a bath and try to soak away the miserable feelings which were taking hold of her.

The bath worked no magic, other than of course she was now squeaky clean – the kind of clean that a shower can never give you.

She cringed at the thought of confronting Danny about his wife, but she thought she might as well look good doing it. She sifted through her clothes trying to decide what to wear, most of her clothes were structured in their design, clothes other women love but men just think are weird. She decided against weird and put on a very fitted black pencil skit and a cream silk blouse which flopped about nicely when a few buttons were opened, she went with a fitted cardigan rather than a blazer and finished off with some black tights and spiky heels. She looked at herself in the mirror, not quite the international woman of mystery look she was going for but not bad either. Once she had her make-up on, she put on her coat, picked her bag up from the floor and left the flat.

Arthur had been outside Faye's apartment for less than twenty minutes when she walked out to the street. Wherever she was going, she wasn't taking the car. He waited till she was about to turn the corner before he started the car, he wasn't about to follow her on foot in case she took a taxi. He followed behind her slowly and saw her answer her phone, she spoke for a few brief seconds and then returned the phone to her pocket. As she moved down towards Ranelagh's village centre she hailed a taxi, hopped in. Arthur followed them. He was not long back from Limerick and was wondering about the significance of her visit to Munlney, the GPS had registered that they stopped on the main street for fifteen minutes and then for a longer period of time in a house which he found out was belonging to a Pamela Kennedy. This name had not registered in any of his searches in this job, it might well be a friend, but they had spent such a relatively short time there that he suspected it was something else, what that was he wasn't sure, yet, but he would be. The taxi pulled up at the end of Grafton Street and Faye got out and began walking up Grafton Street, Arthur would either have to abandon his car here and risk getting clamped or go park the car because he couldn't drive up this pedestrian street, he hated pedestrian streets. He pulled into the taxi rank, got out and knocked on the window of the taxi he pulled in behind, a colossal size of a man rolled the window down, Arthur handed a fifty euro note to the huge man as he said:

'My car is behind you, I'll be back in three minutes, make sure it's not clamped and there's another fifty for you.'

'No bother,' answered the man and Arthur legged it.

Luckily it was Sunday, not many people out yet, he caught a glimpse of Faye and hurried to catch up with her, she turned and headed in the direction of The Aurelia hotel. Arthur could see her go into the hotel, he was careful not to be seen when he followed her in, she went into the main seated area and he could see Daniel Cohen waiting for her, hopefully they were going to have lunch or something which would give him time to go park the car. He waited until he saw them both pick up a menu and then he left to return to the car.

Daniel had rung Faye to ask her to meet in the Aurelia instead of his hotel, saying he was starving. He saw her coming in and was astonished to recognise the exact same feelings he had when they were kids, he felt the same surge of excitement and arousal now as he did ten years ago. He always thought Faye was beautiful, but he thought she was even more so now. He watched her walk down the steps and stop for a brief moment to search through the tables for him, when she saw him, he waved and gave her a wide smile. He thought, not for the first time, about how he had royally buggered up his life.

As she came to the table he stood up and placed his hand on the small of her back as he pulled her to him and kissed her gently on the lips. She smelt so good, he had never smelt this scent before, it was fresh and clean and woody and a complete turn on.

'You look lovely,' he said.

'Thanks, you're looking rather smart yourself.' That's the problem, thought Faye, you look so good, when she saw him across the room, he looked self-assured, like a man who knew what he was about.

'Are you hungry?'

'Yes,' said Faye, not really sure if she was or not. She did know that she felt like a drink and that in the middle of the day it was easier to order one with food.

He handed her a menu and for a moment there was silence while she looked at words in front of her. Daniel had already decided what he wanted, and Faye was doing somersaults in her head deciding whether she would confront him here or wait till later. Eventually she saw something about spinach ravioli and decided on that.

'Are you having a drink?' asked Daniel. Faye wondered if he needed one as much as she did. Not a very good sign.

'Why not, it's Sunday.'

'Yeah, I'll have a glass of red.'

'I'll have a white.'

'What did you do yesterday with Ina?'

'We went to visit someone, we're worried about a friend and were hoping this person could help.' Faye had decided not to tell Daniel about Amanda in case he thought she was demented.

'Could she?'

'Kind of, a bit I suppose. Ina told me that you have not left your wife. Is that true?'

'What, what are you talking about, what did she say?' He was flustered, he hadn't expected this.

The drinks arrived and they both paused and took a welcome gulp.

'Ina did a check on you because she thought it was fishy you simply turning up out of the blue. She checked your address and found no other address listed except your family home, and all your bills are listed to the same address.'

'What the hell ever happened to privacy, how can she do that?'

'Because she can, don't be naïve, there is no such thing as privacy anymore. Anyway, that's beside the point, did you lie to me about leaving your wife, just tell me the truth.' Faye knew immediately that he had, he looked conscience stricken, well if not conscience stricken then guilty. She felt stupid.

'Unless you give me a truthful, or at the very least a credible, explanation for lying I am leaving.'

'Don't leave Faye. I'm sorry, I did lie about moving out, but we are separated, we're not a couple and haven't been for years, it's a sham marriage, the truth is I just haven't had the courage to move out. I thought it would be easy but it's not, you must know what I mean.'

'Danny, I did get out of my marriage, and I didn't pretend to anyone I was separated when I wasn't, so no, I don't know what you mean, and not everything in life is meant to be easy.'

'I didn't mean it like that, I want to leave her, but it is complicated.'

'Jesus that is such a cliché, perhaps she doesn't understand you either.' Faye's impression of him earlier as a man of the world was vaporising.

'She actually doesn't and never has.'

'Stop Danny. I don't want to hear about your wife, and I don't give a damn if you understand each other or not, you lied to me, why are you here in Dublin spinning this story, Ina's right, it's all a bit suspect, and giving the job to Harry.'

'When the office in London had a job coming up here, I volunteered to take it, mostly I admit, in the hopes of meeting you. I had nothing to do with Harry's agency getting the job, that was a genuine coincidence, and I thought a lucky one for me. I've always wanted to tell you what really happened and yes, in truth, I hoped that one day we might get together again.' He reached out his hand to hold Faye's, but she pulled hers back. 'I hadn't planned on telling you I had separated but when Harry told me you were divorced, I saw an opportunity, I know it was wrong, but I thought if we could give us a chance then you would...'

Harry had said he didn't say anything about her being separated, thought Faye.

'I would what, ignore that you have a wife and family and slot nicely into being your mistress, it was quite handy that I was conveniently divorced, what did you think that I would be glad of anything, run back to the man who dumped me spectacularly ten years ago. My god I don't know which is worse that you thought that or that I actually did do it.' Faye took a drink hoping it would etherize the rising feeling of dread. She couldn't say what exactly she dreaded but it felt abstruse and ugly. It was also the feeling that she was going to disown herself, some part of her mind had already decided that this was not the end of seeing Danny and she dreaded that part of herself.

'Faye, seeing you again over the last few weeks has made me the happiest I've been since I left Ireland. I love you now as much as I did then, I would give anything to take back the lies and deceit, I really would, but I can't and I'm sorry for that.' Daniel believed everything he said, he only hoped that he could make Faye believe it too. He reached his hand out to take Faye's and this time she did not pull away. Daniel hoped his relief was not so evident.

The drink had not dampened Faye's dread.

Arthur had returned to his car, handed over the other fifty as promised to the big fella and driven around by Kildare Street to Stephen's Green and eventually to Clarendon Street, just behind the Aurelia. He found a parking spot easily enough and nipped in the back entrance to the hotel, it was for employees only but in Arthur's experience it was rare these days to find anyone who cared enough to check, and he was right, he sailed through as if he owned the place. He found Faye and Daniel still in the same spot, from what he could determine from their expressions all was not well in the camp. He sat down, not too close, and opened the newspaper. He checked the date on the paper, it was eleven days old, he always had a newspaper in the car, despite all the modern technology you couldn't beat the newspaper as a masterful undercover tool. And it was cheap. And reusable. He wanted to use his phone to continue his search on Pamela Kennedy, but he didn't want to risk Faye getting a look at him again.

They looked to Arthur as if they were struggling to eat the food in front of them and the conversation looked stiff. He thought that Faye looked different whenever she was with Daniel Cohen, and not in a good way. On her own, or with her friends, Arthur always thought she looked spirited and sanguine but with Cohen she seemed vague and slightly defeated. Arthur didn't like Cohen and he didn't like the effect he had on Faye. His phone beeped and he saw it was the boy.

'Yeah, I'm in the main restaurant, come in and sit opposite me.' Arthur had called Styles while he parked the car and told him to meet him in the hotel and not to come dressed like a gurrier.

Styles arrived and in fairness you would never take him for the psychopath he was. He wore what could only be described as slacks, in a dark blue and a herringbone sports jacket with a turtle-neck cream jumper - Arthur conceived that they came off someone who was misfortunate enough to have crossed paths with Styles.

'She is sitting at the fourth table on your right, long hair and she's with a dark-haired man. At her feet is a brown bag, I want you to drop it into the bag.'

'Fine.' Styles reached over and took the pen and the envelope; he slipped the envelope into the inside jacket pocket and kept the pen in his hand.

The pen concealed a powerful smart GSM microphone with a fifteen-metre radius which could be activated by simply dialling the SMS number. It also had a GPS tracker which gave a one hundred percent accurate location. Arthur had toyed with whether or not to use a bug with Faye, but the case was growing and there were too many people to keep tabs on at one time. Arthur had noticed that Faye unlike other women used the same bag all the time and it was big enough for an innocuous pen to go unnoticed amid all the other stuff that women insisted on carrying around with them. Arthur knew he could rely on Styles, he'd used him in the past without any complaints. Arthur watched as Styles passed Faye's table and saw him stumble just enough to drop the pen into her bag, it was so quick and seamless that no one would ever have noticed, he apologised and was gone in seconds. An easy earned three hundred yo-yos.

Arthur activated the device and checked to see if all was in order, he inserted an earpiece into his ear and could hear Faye's voice as clear as if she was by his side, satisfied and with Faye's voice in his head, he returned to his car confident that her whereabouts was now known to him.

# thirteen

Uziel Nachman loved his daughter but there were times when even he could not endure her need for reassurance and adoration. Liat was born beautiful and bored, neither had changed as she grew into a woman. His wealth had ensured that she didn't need to exercise her brain to succeed and between her looks and his money she could have had any man, but she chose Daniel Cohen. Uziel always suspected it was because Daniel did not want her, and that the union was forced upon him to save his family from ruin. Uziel agreed to the marriage because he valued loyalty over love, and Daniel had demonstrated this. Liat liked the fact that she had something that someone else wanted, it didn't matter that she did not know the woman Daniel loved, it only mattered that she had taken him from her, he was her possession. Daniel had worked out well over the years and had done well in the business, he had always done what he was told without question, Uziel suspected that in this case it was fear rather than loyalty, he would have preferred loyalty but it was difficult to expect loyalty from a man whose soul you owned, fear would suffice.

He had come to London at Liat's request. Now he was sitting in one of the reception rooms in her Belgravia home, the home he had bought for her when they moved from Israel. The house was expensively decorated, everything was some shade of beige or cream or white with sparkling chandeliers and shiny furniture, Uziel thought the place insipid and uninspired, one would never guess that two young boys lived here.

Liat was dressed to match the décor in cream and beige even her skin and hair was beige and cream he thought. She was fuming over Daniel's trip to Dublin and wanted to go over to make sure he was not seeing *that woman.* Of course Uziel knew about the trip, he had organized it and he knew he would be seeing the girl and there would be no question of Liat going to Dublin, her jealousy would have to contain itself on this occasion. Uziel marvelled at her capacity for jealousy, he knew she had been unfaithful on a number of occasions but he sensed that she could never accept that Daniel never fell for her charms, that he had remained immune to her. She owned him but she could not take possession of him and that tormented her and made her ever more desperate for his affection, which was in short supply.

'I want to go over Abba, what if he sees her,' she whined.

'My dear, Daniel is working on a project which is very important to me, and he went because I wished for him to go not because he chose to go, you have nothing to worry about I can assure you.'

'How can you assure me, you're not there, he could be with her right now!'

'Daniel is there with a colleague who I have instructed to keep me informed of any, shall we say extracurricular activities and so far, Daniel has spent all his time either working or sleeping.' For Uziel lies came as easily as the truth, it didn't matter to him which he told as long as it suited the circumstances.

'Really?'

'Yes really, so you have nothing to worry about. Now how about you allow your father to take you out to dinner.'

Liat beamed, got up and kissed her father on the head.

'I have just the thing to wear, I was shopping yesterday....' Her voice trailed off as she went to get ready.

Uziel found Oliver Blake name in his list of contacts on his phone and pressed call.

# fourteen

'I feel Colm is emotionally unavailable to me.'

Faye often wondered where people came up with such lines, to her they sounded like something from an American movie, but there again that did appear to be most people's frame of reference.

Ann Marie had just told Faye that she and her boyfriend Colm had bought a coffin and hauled it up two flights of stairs to their flat, once they had it installed, they each took turns at playing dead while the other had sex with the pretend dead person. Ann Marie had said she agreed to this because Colm was so insistent and she was afraid he would dump her if she refused and that she kind of enjoyed it, especially playing the dead person as it meant she didn't have to do too much.

'Well Ann Marie, it's not surprising you feel Colm is *emotionally unavailable* to you if you are playing dead with each other, dead people *are* emotionally unavailable.' Faye wanted to add Dah! but refrained. She also wanted to ask about the whole business of buying the coffin and hauling it home, but that was none of her business.

'Yeah, I suppose you're right, I'd just like him to notice me a bit more that's all.'

Poor thing, thought Faye, she hasn't a hope of getting what she wants from her wacky boyfriend, and it was probably only a matter of time before he would want to move onto the real thing, he'd asked Ann Marie to spend a few minutes in the freezer to affect a more realistic corpse.

'I understand Ann Marie, do you think you could ask him to do that?'

'No,' she was emphatic which was something.

'I understand, it's not easy is it. We are at the time now so we can talk about it further in our next session.'

'Thanks Dr Faye, do you think I'm improving?'

'Yes I do,' answered Faye, and she wanted to mean it.

Faye really liked Ann Marie, but she was a lost soul, there is only so much a person can change and for Ann Marie the change would have to be seismic and that wasn't going to happen.

As Faye opened the door for Ann Maire she knew that Oliver Blake was in the waiting room, she had heard him go in, she was more nervous than she thought she would be and tried to settle herself, she was realising how useless all the so called relaxation techniques were in practice, it's all very well and fine to pontificate about relaxing when you are already relaxed but all a bit redundant when you're scared stiff. She reasoned with herself that she had no reason to be nervy, he after all was oblivious to her suspicions, her mind was running away with itself, she would simply act normal.

No harm so, she thought, in aiding normalcy, as she popped a Valium and washed it down with a quarter can of Red Bull.

Just as she was about to go to the waiting room her phone rang, it was Ina. Faye had rung her the previous day to see if she had found out anything about Amanda, but Ina had been busy all day with drug related murder. Faye answered it.

'Hi Ina, how are you?'

'Grand thanks, listen I did a check on Amanda, and I got a hit on her passport, it shows that she did go to India but that she came back into Ireland six months ago and nothing on her has shown up since, no credit card, driving licence and her PPS number has not binged either. So it looks as if she is in Ireland but lying very low.'

'Surely if she was living here her PPS number would have to show up, even to rent a flat she would have to give her PPS number, and what is she living on, she's obviously not getting social welfare or has a job.'

'She could be using a false PPS and a lot of people rent flats below the radar and she could be working for cash, it's not that difficult to live incognito if you really want to. Listen Faye I have to run I'm late for a meeting I'll see you tonight in Finns and we can talk then.'

'Thanks Ina, see you a little after eight, bye.'

'Bye.'

Faye felt disappointed, she wasn't sure why, but she had hoped that Amanda might actually be living in some idyllic corner of India happy with her *passementerie*. But now it looked as if she was back in

Ireland but obviously hiding, probably in some rat hole afraid to register her existence. She could feel her disappointment turn to anger as she thought of the man in her waiting room, she recalled how Amanda had said that she was captivated by him when they first met, she spoke about how she felt enthralled to him. And captivated she was, just like an animal is captivated by its master, she lost her position as subject and became an object, his object, the manipulated object. She lost the ability to respond to her environment and to self-reflect, she existed as an extension of him, his needs, his desires, his wants, his urges. Amanda's nullification of herself had impressed itself deeply on Faye, rarely had she seen such a relinquishment of the self to someone else. But this was not unusual when one is oppressed. There existed from the beginning an imbalance in power which Amanda could never rebalance and this acutely affected her perceptual accuracy. She could not think for herself as she needed to be constantly vigilant so she could read her oppressor's mind lest she incur his acrimony. Of course this remains invisible to the outside world, namely because the world colludes with it through cultural conditioning, Oliver Blake is a powerful business man with a ton of money and the world admires this, he did not achieve this by not taking control, so is it not natural, even admirable, that he would bring the same control to his personal life.

Amanda had for years convinced herself that she had a lot to be grateful for, this was reinforced by those around her, how lucky she was, what a beautiful home she had, how handsome and successful her husband was, she had nothing to worry about. It was very difficult to fly in the face of this and so she pressed on. Until one day quite unceremoniously she was roused back to her senses, and she could no longer deny herself her own existence. This had happened quite unexpectedly, she had told Faye about walking in town one day when she passed a homeless man sitting outside the car park she had parked in, he was sitting on cardboard with a filthy sleeping bag and a couple of plastic bags. The man was begging and as she passed, he said, 'Any change miss an' I'll say a prayer for you.'

His words had a sense of form and force, in their function of hierarchy and in their polarities of situation. Amanda said that this encounter was a sudden bolt which brought her out of her stupor. She had explained how liberating and terrifying it felt at once, she knew in that moment that she had to get away from her husband. And for all he had done, she had no money to give the homeless man, and so she got no prayer in return.

Faye walked to the waiting room and could feel her animosity for Oliver Blake germinate inside her, she had to be careful not to allow it to become evident.

'Hello Oliver, come on through,' she said, not quite keeping the clippie tone from her voice.

'Good evening,' replied Oliver, he had not missed the tone.

Oliver was wearing what was clearly an expensive designer suit which fitted beautifully, plus he wore it with ease and dash. Faye did not like to admit it but Oliver Blake had style, a rare thing in the Irish male. He sat down and crossed his legs in that easy nonchalant way, his long lean limbs added to the elegance of movement as he sat back into the chair. Oliver Blake, thought Faye, was the kind of man who assumed control of whatever environment he was in, he had that natural authoritative air, no, she corrected herself, it was more authoritarian.

'How have you been since we last met?' asked Faye.

'Well, thank you Faye, do you mind if I call you Faye?'

'Not at all,' came Faye's curt reply.

'You seem upset, are you having a difficult day, Faye?'

Stupid of me, she thought, to give him the opportunity to have one up on me, she hated it when she became the object of attention especially by someone as calculating as Oliver Blake.

'I'm sorry if I gave you that impression but I am absolutely fine. Now tell me how you are.' Faye thought better of any further display of her displeasure and smiled openly at Oliver.

'In fact, there has been a progression since we last spoke, I received a call from my wife's sister. It was very interesting indeed.'

Faye could feel the heat rise in her body and knew she was about to start sweating, her mind began to race as all possible scenarios unfolded, the worst of which was that Pamela told him about her visit, but that was impossible, she didn't know who she really was, and Pamela had no relationship with Oliver.

'In what way did you find it interesting?' asked Faye trying to keep all traces of panic from her voice.

'Interesting insofar as she was enquiring about the whereabouts of her sister, you see she has not spoken to her in some time.' He stopped and waited.

'Is that unusual?'

'Yes, it is, she seems to believe that something might have happened to her sister, apparently two of my wife's friends visited her and led her to believe that something is amiss, that is why she contacted me to enquire about Valeria.'

Faye was definitely sweating now but kept reassuring herself that he had no idea of her involvement.

'And do you believe that something is wrong?'

'Of course not, Valeria simply did not wish to speak with her sister or these friends, whoever they are. Isn't it true that many people feel shame when they abandon their husband and marriage and find it difficult to face people because of this shame? I believe that Valeria cannot face her sister because she knows she will be told how foolish she is for walking away from a life that most would crave. Shame makes people hide, does it not?'

'In some instances, yes shame has that affect, but what makes you think Valeria feels shame, has she said this to you?'

'It's perfectly obvious to me, she was talked into doing something she really didn't want to do and now she's hiding from people, probably trying to summon up the courage to ask me to take her back.'

Faye marvelled at how he was able to say this without a hint of pomposity, did he really believe this, yes, she thought he did, a man like Oliver Blake could not comprehend that a woman whom he saw as beneath him could possibly not be eternally grateful to him and be forever beholden to him.

'Oliver that's quite a statement to make, how do you know she really didn't want to leave you or that she is now feeling ashamed, are you basing this on supposition, or has she told you this?'

'I base nothing on supposition, I am a man who deals in facts. I did not get to where I am today or achieve the things I have achieved without having an insight into human nature and human desires, or do you think Dr Monroe that that is the prerogative of your profession alone?'

So we are back to Dr Monroe, thought Faye. She was no longer worried about being found out, her fear was overtaken by indignation.

'Not at all, I think we all have the ability for insight into the human condition, but sometimes we are simply wrong, all of us, including me and those in my own profession. Sometimes we fail to see the hidden because we have become so used to taking only one perspective. Habits form and we forget that there is another way of seeing and that not all is visible unless we take up another position. Do you think that in this case you missed something of your wife's feelings, after all, it would not be unusual?' Faye could sense a slight shift in Oliver Blake, she noticed a slight tightening of his jaw, he probably noticed this himself because he quickly relaxed it.

'No, I do not, and I say that with absolute certainty. I, not too unlike yourself, like to take, shall we say, a phenomenological view of things, I go beyond what is on view or what others want me to see and I seek out the hidden, I seek out the thing people do not want me to see, because Dr Munroe as I am sure you would agree this is by far the most interesting aspect of the person, their hidden side. And everyone is hiding something, everyone. And I knew what my wife was trying to hide. She always denied her inferior origins, you see her provenance is less than favourable and while I married her knowing this, I could not produce offspring with her, this had an effect on her although she would not admit it. I know deep down she could not blame me as my reasons were valid and rested entirely on the calibre of her genes. How could she ask me to take such a risk, admittedly my own genes possibly being stronger could win out, but the risk was too high, and I will only take a carefully calculated risk. I know she left because she was ashamed that she could pollute her own child with her nidorous genes and that she denied me the chance of being a father. Such things are difficult to admit to oneself let alone talk to your sister or friends about. I think it is true to say that despite all the gains women have made they still wish to give their husband a child and feel a deep sense of failure when they cannot.'

Faye wished she was allowed to kill people. And where was he going with his *"phenomenological view"* ....

'Were you angry with her because she was not of the right pedigree to give you a child?' asked Faye.

'Ah, you misunderstand doctor, do not mistake me for the type of man who needs a child to confirm his manliness, as we can see around us any simpleton can reproduce, to me this so-called reproductive instinct is in a sense antisocial rather than social. I am not a man who gives weakly into his urges, urges need to be examined and controlled, I am not controlled by my urges, I control them. I am reminded of a line from Arthur Schopenhauer's *Sufferings of the World,*

> "If children were brought into the world by an act of pure reason alone, would the human race continue to exist? Would a man rather have so much sympathy with the coming generation, as to spare it the burden of existence? Or at any rate not take it upon himself to impose that burden upon it in cold blood."

I am not so cold-blooded or unreasonable as to have a child, no, Dr Munroe, I have no urge or desire for a child, remember all children are doomed to become adults, the majority of whom add little to the world. Valeria, I fear, fell into the category of people whose life choices are limited by social indoctrination and unexamined motives.'

Faye found herself reluctantly agreeing with Oliver Blake, she had often thought the same thing, but without the acuity to quote Schopenhauer. Still, she wasn't in the slightest bit convinced that Amanda had any major problem with not having a child, much to the disappointment of many parents, lots of people are quite content not having children and Amanda had said despite having given it some consideration, she didn't want children. Oliver Blake was spinning a story.

'You say that despite her origins you married her but knew you would not have children with her, did you tell her this when you got married or later on when she wanted to have children?'

'Are you suggesting I deceived her, not telling her I would not have a child with her until after we married?'

'No, I am just trying to establish where this guilt and shame came from, if she knew getting married then she had no expectations of having a child with you.'

'I made it very clear from the beginning that I would not require her to give me children, but as you know people think they can change you, or that you will change your mind once you are married. But I did not change my mind and I know my wife was happy with that arrangement until someone started to put ideas in her head.'

Here we go again, thought Faye.

'Perhaps you underestimate your wife, she may not have needed anyone to influence her, time alone can change even the most strongly held conventions, one could say that it is a sign of maturity to let go old ideas and embrace new ones.' In theory of course this was true but in practice, well that was an entirely different matter, but Faye wasn't about to say this to Oliver Blake.

'I don't make a habit of underestimating people. But I do take on board what you are saying, but it is also true that changes in perspectives most often are arrived at through dialogue with others, listening to others' opinions and taking on their ideas, surely you cannot deny that. And while my wife had some laudable qualities, I could not attribute her with the mental acumen to arrive at her decision alone.'

Smug moron, thought Faye.

'Well Oliver, we don't need to have mental acumen to know when something is wrong, we call this instinct.' Faye knew she was sounding a bit snippy, but she didn't care, 'maybe your wife simply just felt things were wrong for her and wanted to leave you, this isn't quantum physics, people know when things don't feel right without ever having to speak with someone else. In fact, they normally only speak to others as a means of confirming for themselves what they already know to be true. I think you are reading too much into how your wife arrived at the decision as a way of avoiding the actual decision itself. It seems very clear that you find it inconceivable that anyone would leave you, this might suggest an egocentric perspective which...'

Faye was cut off by Oliver Blake and at that very instant, even before he spoke, she felt a rivet of fear which told her she had gone too far, his immaculate composed veneer shattered for a second and she saw in his eyes a malevolence which convinced her that he was capable of anything. She was afraid, afraid for herself alone with this man.

'Just a moment, are you saying that I am an egomaniac?' He heard the malice in his own voice and saw the fear in her eyes, calm down, this is not the time, bide your time he told himself, fix this. In an instant he regained his poise. And then with a light-hearted tone accompanied by his well-practiced grin which said *"I'm only joking but I nearly had you"* he went on to say, 'Well of course you are not, you're only doing your job trying to help me to come to terms with my wife leaving me, I know I might sound a bit imperious, sometimes I forget that not everyone is adversarial. I apologise if I came across rude, I didn't mean to. I really am upset about Valeria, and I find it difficult to accept, as you said, that she left me.' As he said this, he looked down to his hands which lay one on top of the other on his lap, he admired his manicured nails as he gently ran his left thumb over the crest on the signet ring he wore on the little finger of his right hand. He looked at the lion and the coat of arms, the motto of the Blake family was *Ensuivant la Verite*, By Following the Truth, this motto was originally a war cry and Oliver still liked to think of it as that. He felt he had hit the right cord when he looked up at Faye and saw that there was no longer fear in her eyes, he saw only compassion and for the briefest of moments he felt aroused, he allowed himself a moment to visualise the compassionate Dr Monroe prostrated naked with opened legs across his bed, her mouth prised open and filled with a rubber ball, her body flailing against the plastic ties which are holding her in such a spectacular position, her eyes this time filled with fear as he approaches her with his simple but most favourite toy, a screw driver.

'I understand, it is difficult to understand why people do what they do, but if you can, it is best to focus on your life now rather than fighting against what is done.' Faye was certain this show of emotion was all a pretence but what was real was that momentary flash of contempt and she knew better than to fuel it. He was obviously trying to hide it with this inane rejected husband act, and he was hiding it for a reason. There was something about the way he dropped his head which felt to Faye like a rehearsed movement acted out to elicit a desired effect, and when he lifted his head again, he was lost in thought for a moment and whatever he was thinking about, Faye felt it wasn't good.

As much as she wanted him out of her office, he was a link to Amanda, she didn't want to alienate him, best to placate him.

'Have you spoken to your wife about how you feel, she may not realise that the break-up is affecting you as badly as it is?' she continued.

'I think she knows I am upset, some things are obvious, have you ever had someone leave you Faye?'

Faye was slightly taken aback by the question, not that people never asked her personal questions, they did, but he may as well have said: *you know what it's like to be dumped.*

'I think it's hard to get through life without experiencing some form of rejection. Oliver it might be beneficial to think about speaking with your wife to help you move on, if you find that difficult you might wish to ask her to come here with you.' Faye never did this as a practice, but she wanted to see how he would react.

'Yes, I suppose you are right, most people experience rejection, you seem to have dealt with it well or maybe it was long enough ago to have gotten over it but then again it can take you by surprise when you least expect it.' He smiled at Faye before glancing at his Breitling watch which always kept perfect time and now it was time to go.

'I see our time is up doctor, shall we say the same time next week?'

So he wants to ignore my question, thought Faye and although she knew it was maybe best to let it lie, she didn't.

'You haven't answered my question,' she said.

'Yes well, I don't think even you would be able for that.' And with that he stood up and walked to the desk as he carefully removed folded banknotes from the inside suit pocket, placed it on the desk and turned to move towards the door. Faye followed him and made sure she got to the door first so she could open it, and just as she was opening it she said, 'If you change your mind, I might surprise you in what I am able for.'

'I'm sure you might Dr Munroe, I'm sure you might, good night.' Oliver looked directly at Faye as he spoke before turning and sauntering off leaving Faye feeling like she had just propositioned him.

She shuddered. How, she asked herself, had that happened. Bloody hell.

As she turned and walked towards her desk, she saw the money he had left there and went to pick it up, the notes were crisp and looked new or else he ironed them, which she thought quite possible.

As she got ready to leave, she had a feeling of fear and to her own disgust a slight sense of pleasure, she needed her head examined, she thought.

As Oliver walked to his car, he wondered what Faye actually knew, Arthur had told him of her visit to Pamela, he had to admit that this surprised him, he hadn't expected this but was a little impressed. She had made a connection, he wondered what it was, what had he said that triggered the connection, he had been careful but obviously not careful enough and again today he allowed himself to react. Ultimately, he was satisfied that she knew nothing.

# fifteen

Faye was already at a table when Ina arrived, she had ordered a bottle of wine and began pouring into one of the two empty glasses as Ina approached.

'You look a bit rattled,' said Ina as she sat down in the chair opposite Faye and reached for the glass of wine.

'I just had the creep, Ina he definitely did something to his wife and I think he knows I know something, he said he got a call from Pamela asking about Amanda after she had a visit from two friends, and for a briefest moment in the session he became enraged, but caught himself, but from the look in his eyes I have no doubt he's a psychopath and then at ...'

'Slow down Faye, one thing at a time,' Ina had her Garda voice on as if she was dealing with a delirious person who had just witnessed a series of unlikely events and needed reining in. Faye hated it when she used that voice on her.

'Ina, I am not a wacky witness, you just need to keep up with ...'

'I didn't say you were wacky but now that you say it you do sound a ...'

'Oh feck off,' laughed Faye.

'Okay what exactly did he say about Pamela?'

'Just as I said, that she called him asking about Amanda after a visit from two friends.'

'Did he call Pamela by name?'

'No, he just said his wife's sister, it's kind of strange that Pamela called him especially after what she said about him.'

'Maybe we made her worry about Amanda, but that doesn't mean he knows it was you or me, I mean it's normal he would mention it because it's out of the blue for him too, but I think you're being a bit paranoid about him knowing it was you, there's no way he could know, remember Pamela hasn't a clue who we are.'

'I know but there was something about the way he said it that I got the feeling he knew ...'

'But how would he know?'

'He's a very resourceful man Ina.'

'Now you're running away with yourself, that would mean that he has you under surveillance which in all honesty is a bit of a stretch.'

'Yeah, but what if he had, it's easy enough nowadays, a GPS thing attached to my car would tell him we were there. Can I bring my car in to have your lads have a look at it?'

'Faye I don't think ...'

'Please Ina it would be done in a minute.'

'It actually takes more than a minute, but I'll have a look at it myself first, okay.'

'Thanks Ina.'

'What's keeping his lordship, I want to order, I'm starved.'

'You know Harry, he'll be here any minute.'

'What's the story with Danny, did you ask him about his wife?'

'Yes I did, and he admitted that he hadn't moved out but that the marriage was over.'

'A likely story.'

'I know and I'm not sure I believe him but I want to, I know I'm a joke, I can hardly bear myself.'

'Hello sweet things.' Neither Faye nor Ina had noticed that Harry had arrived, he sat in the chair between them, picked up the last empty glass and made a motion to Faye to fill him up, which she did.

'What are you two so engrossed in?' he asked in a conspiratorial tone as he took a sip of wine and nodded in appreciation of the good choice.

'I'm just telling Ina what a complete twit I am, Danny hasn't left his wife.'

'Jesus when did he tell you?'

'He didn't, Ina found out.'

'How?' asked Harry as he turned towards Ina with an accusatory tone.

'How do you think,' answered Ina sounding annoyed.

'Well then why did you do it, why not let her have a little fling in peace?'

'Because Harry there is no such thing as a peaceful fling, much wants more.'

'So,' said Harry turning to Faye looking at her very sympathetically 'now that Sherlock here has ruined it for you, what are you going to do?'

'That's where my deranged self comes into play, I choose to believe him when he told me that although he hasn't actually physically left her that the marriage is over.'

'Oh, I see, a case of wilful blindness.'

'Yes.'

'Well,' said Harry cheerfully 'I'm all for wilful blindness, and I personally have no ideological problem with a little dalliance with a married woman, I say go for it Faye.'

'Can we order some food?' grumbled Ina.

'Yes madam we can.' Harry said sounding very pleased with himself.

'Harry you are so full of shit.' Ina dropped her gaze from Harry to the menu.

'Now more importantly how is it, I mean after all these years was it a bit weird?' asked Harry.

'That's part of the problem, it's so bloody good and that's all I'm going to say, now let's order.'

'How good?' enquired Harry with a smirk.

'Harry, will you stop encouraging her, this will end badly, and we all know that no matter what these kind of men say they never, or very rarely, leave their wife and that's because they don't need to, they have their bread buttered on both sides, the best of both worlds. Faye, you have no idea what's really going on with him and his wife, she could be a saint for all we know ...'

'Well, she's definitely not that I can tell you ...' Harry stopped abruptly when he realised his own stupidity and saw Ina and Faye turn to look at him with their mouths open. Blast it. These two don't miss a beat.

'What the hell does that mean, what do you know about his wife?' Ina was practically spitting.

'Nothing, I'm just saying that she probably isn't s saint, from what Dan has said to...'

'No Harry that's not what it sounded like, Jesus have you met her?' blurted Ina.

'No! of course not,' Harry was aware that he was sounding defensive and guilty, he had to fix this.

'Harry, please is there something you haven't told us?' Faye sounded wounded and Harry's heart sank, he hated lying to them. Maybe he should just tell them. After all he hadn't done anything really wrong, just a couple of things that were not quite right. No, some things were best left unsaid.

'The only thing I didn't tell you was that Dan spoke to me a bit about his wife and that she sounds like a battle axe and I didn't think you'd want to hear about it Faye so I said nothing, that's it.' Harry felt confident that he sounded believable.

'When have you ever not told us that kind of stuff, you're always gagging at the bit to tell us any smidgen of dirt on anyone' Ina was not convinced Harry was telling the truth.

'I know but this was different, I thought it would be hurtful for you Faye if I told you.' Harry turned to Faye sounding as concerned as he actually felt, but his concern was more for himself than for Faye at that moment.

'Okay it's fine Harry, you're probably right, I don't really want to know anything about her, it just makes it all a bit too real,' said Faye.

'Anything else you're not telling us?' asked Ina rather crossly.

'No, no there isn't,' answered Harry.

'I mean I've no problem with anyone having an affair, god they're crucial really, but I suppose I never saw myself as the other woman.' Faye said absentmindedly and the other two forgot what they had been saying as they turned to Faye.

'You don't have to be, you know, just stop seeing him, it's not rocket science, you're not attached to him in any way, it's your choice.' Ina could never understand why women got themselves into these types of situations.

'You're right Ina I could just walk away but it's not as easy as you make it sound. I don't know if it's unfinished business and a desire to understand what happened years ago or if I really just want to be with him,' said Faye.

'Which does it feel more like?' asked Harry.

'Probably unfinished business, after all I've been getting on with my life perfectly well without him it's not as if I was wilting away pining for him or felt I could never love anyone else – I think who we love is accidental, often just down to circumstances and timing. Maybe I want him to want me and see what he left behind and regret it, you know like I'm the eighth wonder of the world and he suddenly realises what a complete and utter idiot he was in leaving me.'

'That's not good for you Faye,' said Ina.

'Well of course it's not, revenge is never good for you, but it is sweet,' said Harry.

'You're right Ina, it's not as if I really want to be this kind of pathetic women, but there you are, I am,' said Faye.

'You don't have to be,' persisted Ina.

'God, will you give it a rest, Faye you're doing nothing wrong, sleeping with an old boyfriend is not a crime...,' said Harry.

'A married ex', interrupted Ina.

'...we want what we can't have that's what keeps us eager, it keeps the oomph in things ...'

At that moment the waiter arrived and asked if they were ready to order or if they needed more time.

They were ready to order.

Arthur had been listening to Faye and her friends' conversation with interest. He himself had no ethical issue with sleeping with a married woman, mind you he also knew that he would never ask a married woman to leave her husband for him because if she did the dirt on her husband, it only set a precedent and she could quite possibly do the same to him. He had once been quite taken with a six-foot red-haired woman from Sligo called Roseanne, she had the most tremendous natural breasts he had ever come across, and he had come across quite a few sets, she was married to a sheep farmer and had hired him to try to locate her mother. Roseanne was one of those misfortunates who was born to an unmarried woman in sixties Ireland when it was less of a crime to kill someone than it was to do what came naturally between a man and a woman, to have sex, unmarried sex that is, and even when you were married you were bound by the *Casti Connubii* from Rome which meant that sex was purely for procreation and otherwise sinful, unless of course you were an ordained member of the catholic church and then you could shag away - man, woman, child or beast.

Arthur often wondered about big families of twelve or thirteen, whether the parents were such staunch Catholics that they saw it as their duty to produce more fodder for god's army or did they simply enjoy a shag and hadn't a clue how to prevent an unwanted sprog, given that contraception was illegal until 1980. Unless of course you were part of the educated who knew how to navigate the loophole in obtaining contraception, condoms could not be offered for sale, but a buyer could be *invited to treat* to buy it or if you donated to family planning associations you could be given contraception as a *gift*.

But the reality on the ground was that it was unavailable to the majority of randy Irish men and women. Roseanne was one of the multitudes of unwanted Irish babies, but she was lucky enough to be adopted by an English couple who had retired to Ireland and were longing for a baby. Back then obtaining a baby for adoption was not the complicated affair it is today, being a catholic and a *donation* smoothed the way. Roseanne was a happy child, and her adopted parents thought it best not to tell her she was not biologically theirs, after all it didn't matter, they reasoned, because they loved her as much as if they had made her. But Roseanne began to wonder if all was not as it seemed when at the age of seventeen in biology class they were learning about inherited physical characteristics and one girl shouted across the class that Roseanne must be adopted as she was the complete opposite to her parents in appearance. That night Roseanne noticed for the first time that she was indeed different, she was six foot tall and had been since aged fifteen, had the previously mentioned big bosom, blue eyes and mad red hair. Her parents, as she knew them to be, were both small, her mother five foot one and her father five foot five, both were dark-haired, and both had brown eyes and neither ever burnt in the sun unlike Roseanne who turned the deepest shade of pink and then blistered. She wondered how she could have been so unobservant and eventually put it down to being too happy; she resolved there and then never to be so happy again, and she wasn't. Arthur had found her mother through death records which seem fitting as it allowed Roseanne to maintain her mantel of misery. He had an affair with her and for some unfathomable reason had fallen for her, he often suspected it was because she demanded absolutely nothing of him, no pressure to see her or to love her, she was completely unambiguous in that respect, if he ever wanted to settle with someone, she was the type, even if a bit melancholy.

But now he had to get over to Faye's and remove the tracker from her car, thankfully he had put the bug in her bag. It was getting dark now, so he decided to go there and do it before she came home. As he drove there, he allowed himself to reminisce on Roseanne.

# sixteen

Faye sat at the table she had bought from a friend who specialised in lovely mid-century furniture, she brought it with her after the divorce even though it was a bit big for her kitchen, but she couldn't bear to part with it, she felt she had parted with enough. She was drinking a strong coffee and eating toast smeared with butter and pink grapefruit marmalade, fine cut, she hated big chunks of peel on her bread, this marmalade was like eating caviar for breakfast. They hadn't stayed out late last night as they all had work today but had still managed to drink too much. She was just dismissing a thought she was having about doing a detox when there was a knock on her door. She answered the door to find her landlady.

'Good morning Mrs Clayworth-Howsham, come in,' said Faye as she opened the door back and ushered Mrs Clayworth-Howsham into the flat.

'Oh thank you my dear, I have told you, you really ought to call me Liggia.'

'Yes, yes I will,' said Faye and she hadn't a notion of it, the idea of calling Mrs Clayworth-Howsham Liggia was absurd.

'I do hope I am not interrupting you, I can come back if you are in a rush, but I have noticed you leave a little later on Wednesdays.'

Of course you have, thought Faye.

'Yes I'm in the hospital on Wednesdays, late start, late finish.'

'You are such a good girl curing all those people.'

Faye had long since stopped trying to convince Mrs Clayworth-Howsham that whatever she did it certainly wasn't to cure people.

'May I sit down, my legs are not nearly as resolute as they once were?' asked Mrs Clayworth-Howsham.

'Of course, here, please sit down,' said Faye as she directed her through to the kitchen and pulled the chair out for Mrs Clayworth-Howsham. 'Would you like a coffee there's some in the pot?'

'Oh, that would be lovely my dear.'

Faye poured the coffee into a china cup with saucer, such were the things Mrs Clayworth-Howsham was accustomed to.

'You know I don't like to pry into your life, or the boys' lives, but I do like to keep an eye on things, as you know it comes from my years with The Colonel, he was big fan of covert operations.'

Mrs Clayworth-Howsham's husband Edward had been in the Wavy Navy, the volunteer reserve force of the Royal Navy in the UK, she had told Faye that they gotten the name because the strips on their uniform were wavy as opposed to straight for the regulars. The Colonel apparently always lamented the loss of this distinctive insignia in 1951 when regulars and the reserves merged. When they came to Ireland the colonel sold Pommery champagne, Faye had expressed surprise that they had managed to make a living on selling champagne in Ireland thirty years ago. Mrs Clayworth-Howsham had assured her that they had managed very well indeed, more people than you might have expected were slugging down flutes of bubbly. Once The Colonel retired from this he took it upon himself to become the chief duck feeder in St Stephen's Green Park, he would collect leftover bread from three different bakeries in the city late each evening, pack two old post bags he had managed to get hold of and head off to the park everyday ostensibly to feed the ducks, but Mrs Clayworth-Howsham said that he was keeping a great many things under surveillance and this had taught her the importance of keeping one's eyes open. And so she had kept her eyes open the previous night.

'I was sitting in the drawing room last evening when I heard a peculiar sound, like steel against concrete. I had a discreet peep out the window and to my horror there was a well-built man fumbling around the underneath side of your car. He appeared to be trying to locate something and eventually he did, put whatever it was in his pocket and took off without by or leave.'

She was sounding quite indignant and well she may as he was on her property, uninvited.

Faye was riveted, yes she had said to Ina about her car being bugged but on some level, she didn't believe it, but now this was confirmation of her fanciful ideas, as Ina was inclined to call them.

'Did you manage to get a look at him, what was he like, you said he was well-built ...'

'No need to fret my dear,' said Mrs Clayworth-Howsham as she reached into her bag and removed a digital camera. 'I have captured him on camera, The Colonel was quite a fan of these tiny digital things,' she said as she astutely clicked and pressed until she had the picture on the screen. Faye looked at it and immediately felt the pit of her stomach churn, she had seen this man before, he was in the restaurant a couple of weeks ago looking at her, who the hell is he, she wondered.

'Do you know this intruder?'

'No I do not, can I borrow this so I can print it out?'

'No need I have printed a copy already,' and Mrs Clayworth-Howsham again went to her bag and removed an envelope with very high-quality photographs of the intruder at work on the car and also a good front shot of him as he got up to go. Faye marvelled at her landlady and hoped she would be as resourceful when she was her age.

'Mrs Clayworth-Howsham you are a gem, thank you so much, I'll show these to Ina and see what she comes up with.'

'Should I be concerned for you my dear, you're not in any kind of trouble?' Mrs Clayworth-Howsham sounded very genuinely concerned, she always felt Faye was a bit, shall we say, vagarious, after all she did sleep with Jason. Mrs Clayworth-Howsham never mentioned this to Faye, she wouldn't dream of it, and as fond as she was of Jason, really Faye ought to know better.

'Oh god no it's nothing like that!' Faye heard the shrill in her own voice and started to wonder if she actually was in trouble.

'You can always talk to me, if you need anything,' said Mrs Clayworth-Howsham now fully convinced that Faye was indeed in trouble.

'I know, thank you, but really there's nothing to tell, this must be some sort of mistake,' said Faye feeling very close to her landlady at that moment, as well as to tears.

'I know you are busy, I'll leave now, I will keep an eye out for any unusual activity,' she got up from the chair and made towards the door. 'Thank you for the coffee, be careful my dear.'

'I will and thank you again.' Faye opened the door for her landlady and watched as she went down the stairs; she looked as though she was gliding.

Bloody hell she thought as she phoned Ina, I am being bugged, how bizarre, it has to be creepo Oliver Blake.

'What's up?' Ina said answering the phone.

'What's up is that I am being bugged, I was right, there was a bug in my car, Mrs C took a photo of a man removing something from...'

'Shut up Faye and hang up and don't speak to anyone until I get there,' and she hung up.

Faye was left a bit shunned and then thought what Ina had thought, where there's one bug there could be two.

It took Ina fifteen minutes to get to Faye's and when she did arrive, she had Malcolm McCarthy with her. He was a fairly nondescript looking man in his late twenties, pale skinned with gelled dark brown hair, he wore a cheap dark navy suit which hung limply from his almost skeleton frame. Malcolm was Ina's trainee, he thought Ina was a demigod and would do literally anything for her, Faye and Harry were always wishing they had a Malcolm. Ina knocked lightly on the door and when Faye opened it she motioned to her not to speak in that universal index finger to the mouth signal. She then caught hold of Faye's arm and motioned her out of the room and down the stairs leaving Malcolm in the flat. When they got to the bottom of the stairs Ina turned in the direction of the back door and headed for the back garden, once they were outside, they went to the bottom of the garden where there was a table and seats. Faye often came out here for a sneaky cigarette and also because Mrs Clayworth-Howsham was a superb gardener and had done a lovely job of the back.

Faye didn't dare utter a word until, at last, Ina spoke.

'Tell me what Mrs C saw.'

'She saw a man take something from the bottom of my car and then bugger off. She got a photo of him too.'

'Really, she's quite the sleuth your Mrs C.'

'I know she's marvellous, here take a look.' Faye hand Ina the photos.

'When did you print these?'

'I didn't Mrs C did.'

'Impressive. He certainly looks like he's up to something.'

'Ina, I've seen him before, he was at the Copper Cow a few weeks ago, the reason I remarked on him was because I had noticed him looking at me in the museum a week before and he was definitely looking at me in the Copper Cow.'

'I think it's a bit strange that a couple of hours after you asked me to look at your car for a bug, Dinjo here is removing what is quite probably a tracking device, that's why Malcolm is looking to see if there are other bugs in your flat.'

'Yes, but we were in the Copper Cow last night when I said it.'

'There might be something in your clothes or bag. We'll go up now and look at your clothes and bag, don't speak while you're in there okay.'

'Yeah of course, Ina do you believe me now that this is to do with Amanda?'

'When I was looking into Daniel I did a quick search on Oliver Blake, nothing in particular showed up, but he has been involved with some companies that have been investigated by RAW, that's India's external intelligence agency - they obtain and analyse information about foreign governments, corporations, and persons in order to advise Indian foreign policymakers. I wasn't able to get much information, but it had something to do with illegal chemicals.' Ina didn't tell her friend that she also found a link between Oliver Blake and Daniel's father-in-law. These guys were serious contenders, not to be trifled with. It was because of this that Ina came over without question.

'God, maybe he's some sort of international chemicals dealer.'

'Settle down Faye, let's not get ahead of ourselves, come on upstairs.'

When they went back into the flat Malcolm was busy picking things up, checking them and leaving them down again in exactly the same spot, when he saw Ina, he simply shook his head, Faye presumed nothing had been found. Ina and Faye went into her bedroom as agreed, the door was closed as it was bit of a mess, Ina checked the clothes Faye had been wearing the previous night and found nothing, she then took Faye's bag and emptied the contents onto the bed, full of the usual rubbish, Ina's faced pleaded with Faye to see if there was anything among the contents which did not belong there. Faye shifted through the stuff and could account for almost all of it, there were two pens which was not unusual in itself but she remembered looking for a pen when she was in the hospital and had none, one of the secretaries gave her one, she picked that pen out easily as it had a drugs company logo on it, the other pen could be hers but it was the only thing she wasn't certain about. She pointed it out to Ina. Ina picked it up and twisted it apart, raising her eyebrows she nodded to Faye, she had found something, she took it out to the dining room table and beckoned Malcolm over, together they examined the tiny device and Malcolm wrote some things down. Then they put it back together, Ina placed the pen on the table and directed both Faye and Malcolm to follow her out and down the stairs back into the garden.

'What do you think Malcolm?' asked Ina.

'It's a GSM smart bug with a tracker,' Malcolm was confident about his bugs.

'I thought so,' said Ina, apparently Ina was bug confident too.

'What can it do?' asked Faye

'It's a bug that allows your conversations to be heard and also it has a GPS built in so your location can be determined. Malcolm, I imagine it has up to fifteen-metre radius, what do you think?'

'Exactly that boss,' nodded Malcolm, as always impressed by his boss.

'Faye where were you this morning when you were talking to Mrs C?'

'In the kitchen.'

'Good and was your bedroom door closed at that time.' Ina had taken on her police voice.

'Yes, yes it was I remember because it's a mess and I can't bear to be looking at it ...'

'I don't think it would have picked up your conversation, what do you think Malcolm?' Ina asked as she turned to Malcolm.

'No. I estimate the distance to be twenty-five to thirty meters max and with the door closed it would not pick up the conversation.' He said this in a precise and matter-of-fact manner which left no room for doubt, Faye found him strangely reassuring.

'Good, Malcolm you go back up and continue the search, I'll be up in a few minutes.'

'Yes boss.' Malcolm quietly left.

'Now we have to decide what to do with it, we could use it to draw this guy out or we could just get rid of it,' said Ina.

'What do you suggest?'

'We have a conversation which sounds cryptic enough for him to follow you somewhere fairly secluded so I can get a look at his car reg and run a check on it, see if we can find out who we are dealing with, maybe even put a tracker on his car,' said Ina sounding slightly more excited than she meant to.

'That sounds like a good idea, where would we go?'

'Let me think about it, I have to get back to the office, I shouldn't be here I'm supposed to be getting ready for a meeting in forty minutes. Leave the bag at home and give me a call later and we'll decide what to do.'

'Fine, I'm working late tonight, how about we meet in the Copper Cow at half eight?'

'Perfect, oh yeah, better let Malcolm have a look at your phone before we go.'

'God, do you think it's bugged too?'

'Who knows, up to an hour ago I thought it ludicrous that *you* could be bugged at all.'

'I know!' said Faye as both she and Ina got up and went back up to the flat.

Malcolm had not found anything else and gave the all-clear on Faye's phone then leaving the bag with the bug behind, all three left the flat and went downstairs in silence. Once down Malcolm continued in silence to the car while Ina remained behind for a moment.

'Are you meeting Daniel today?'

'We have no plans, he did say he would call, why do you ask?'

'Better not to speak to him until we find out a bit more.'

'You don't think he's involved do you?'

'I'm just saying to be careful, we don't know what's going on and all this started with his return on the scene.'

'Bloody Bolsheviks Ina I don't think Danny would want to bug me, that's a bit of a stretch even for me.' Even as Faye was saying this she was beginning to wonder if he was in fact involved somehow, Ina was right, it did all start when he came back. No, she thought, it's just a coincidence, but she couldn't quite shake off the doubt that had seeded itself.

'I hope you're right but for the moment let's not take any chances, I have to go, I'll see you later.'

Ina walked towards the car wondering what the hell was going on, who was bugging Faye and why, she was convinced Daniel Cohen was involved but like Faye had no idea how. And Harry, she felt sure, knew something but wasn't talking. He was easy to sort out, she thought.

Faye watched Ina leave and for a moment felt completely alone, she quickly shrugged the feeling off and hoped she'd get a taxi quickly as she was running late for work.

Daniel had just gotten off the phone from a call from his father-in-law, he hated the man and even more so since he had discovered what he was involved in. When Daniel had discovered that Uziel's company was selling chemicals which potentially could be used in illegal chemical weapons he hesitantly approached his father-in-law about his concerns and was swiftly made aware that any investigation into the company would implicate Daniel, after all Uziel reminded him he was a ten percent shareholder and on the board. About five years earlier, Uziel had told Daniel that he wanted him to have more of a stake in the company, implying that one day the company would be Liat's and so made him a shareholder, as for being on the board he was never asked to attend a meeting. It had meant very little to Daniel and his normal pedantic existence was not interrupted. He came to realise that Uziel's uncharacteristic show of largesse towards him was about Uziel looking after Uziel. And now once again Daniel doing Uziel's bidding.

The only saving grace this time was that he was home in Dublin and seeing Faye. Every feeling he ever had for her was still there and ten years had only made her ten years better, she was different, but she was also the same. He ached to see her. She had always been so easy to be in love with, demanding of nothing, she never went out of her way to disagree with you and never cared if you forgot or remembered her birthday, either way she was sanguine and because of this he had never forgotten an occasion. She was the perfect lover, Daniel thought about how she completely surrendered to the act and allowed her body to respond without any interruptions from her head which made her body acquiescent and responsive, yielding and alive, lovemaking with Faye required nothing more than a reciprocal surrender and for him this was his bliss, his ecstasy. And she didn't speak, Liat could never resist giving him instructions, she was the same inside the bedroom as out, always issuing orders 'don't put it there put it here, it's too hot, it's too cold, faster, slower' and he as usual could never get it right, either inside or outside the bedroom. Since being with Faye again the thought of ever sleeping with Liat again made him shudder.

Daniel knew Faye was not feeling the same way about him, she was not going to trust him so easily, but time was running out, he hadn't wanted to involve his sister but she was home at the moment and somehow, he supposed, not unlike a puppy, Annie had always managed to have a transformative effect on Daniel making him look better than he actual was, something about their interaction always endeared people to Daniel in a way that never replicated itself without Annie's ministration. Unfortunately, this also meant he would probably have to see his parents, he had been hoping to avoid them. He felt an overwhelming feeling of self-pity as he wondered how things had come to this. But then of course he knew exactly how and why.

# seventeen

An old psychiatrist long since dead used to say to Faye that while there was no verifiable proof and that it was best not to say it too many, the full moon caused more erratic behaviour in patients. Faye had noticed when she looked at her dairy the symbol of the full moon on today's date, she hoped she had her quota of crazy for today given the bizarre events of her morning and that her friend's prediction would not realise. Although she knew the futility of hope, she still hoped for a relatively normal day. By the end of the day, she reminded herself again of the pointlessness of hope, it was a stinker of a day.

She had just come from seeing Andrew, a thirty-year-old farmer's son. Andrew suffered from Erotomania, a condition which was also known, quite nicely Faye thought, as *love obsessed*. The problem was that the object of Andrew's love was not impressed and because Andrew had broken a barring order on several occasions plus plagued this woman with love letters, flowers and eventually abducted her believing that she really wanted to go with him but was too shy to admit it - he was serving year two of a five years' sentence.

Faye didn't like to resort to the classic idea that lack of maternal love was the root of all evil – but in this case, it certainly seemed plausible that this lack drove Andrew in his misguided pursuit of love. What made matters worse was that the object of his affections was Sarah Rafferty, a popular talk show host on a local radio channel, a channel which was constantly being played in the hospital because it gave hourly updates on the deaths, something most of the patients were eager to hear. Andrew was particularly upset today because Sarah told her listeners that she would be away for the following two weeks as she was getting married. Andrew was initially inconsolable which Faye took to be a good sign, a sign that he might be coming to accept that Sarah was gone, an overture towards acceptance but this was short lived and Andrew became so spellbound with the notion that Sarah was sending him a message, the message of course being that she really wanted to marry him, that Faye had to call for help when she refused his request to give him a lift into town. Love, thought Faye, was a complicated thing.

As Andrew was screaming to be let out, Jack popped his head into Faye's room.

'Love hurts, ay Faye?'

'Yes, it certainly does, poor old Andrew, if only he could love someone who would love him back, he would be fine.'

'Ah my dear Faye, his kind of love never works like that, he will only love those who are beyond his reach, and thus recreate forever more the unreturned love he had for his mama.'

'The Irish mammy has a lot to answer for.'

'Yes, and I thank her for she has kept me in work for years and so she will you, don't be so quick to knock her,' Jack laughed and added 'How's your own mama, the lovely Mrs Monroe?'

Jack had briefly met Faye's mother a few years back when she uncharacteristically called to see Faye at the hospital, she had, regrettably Faye thought, somehow managed to make a good impression on Jack and he occasionally asked after her.

'Oh, she's fine,' Faye lied.

'She's a very attractive woman and charming as a silver-washed Fritillary butterfly,' Jack had a wistful tone to his voice and he spoke as though there was no one else present, mind you this was not uncommon for him and Faye thought her mother was anything but as charming as a butterfly, more dolly bird than butterfly.

'Jack, do you have the file I asked you about?' best to bring him back to reality and away from Mrs Monroe.

'Oh yes, yes indeed I do, here it is,' and he handed Faye one of the files from a bundle he was carrying under his arm.

'Are you okay for everything else?' Jack gave Faye a wink as he asked this.

Faye was relieved and thankful he asked as she did not want to ask him so soon to write another script, but this was manna.

'Actually, I am a bit low,' began Faye.

'Say no more my dear,' and with that Jack took his prescription pad out and scribbled the crucial scribbles.

'Thank you, Jack,'.

'Mon plaisir cherie, your poison is just a tad more difficult to get hold of than mine,' Jack liked single malt whiskey.

'Give Mrs Monroe my best,' and with that he was gone.

Faye looked at the script and silently vowed she would stop – but not just now.

It was just gone half seven, she still had her notes to write up which would take more than an hour, she decided to leave them, she would do them later tonight. If she left now she would get to a late opening chemist before meeting Ina. With that she put on her coat and bent down for her bag, only to remember that she didn't have it with her.

As she was leaving, she thought about Andrew and the horror of always loving those who will never love you back, she knew a little about what that felt like.

Arthur watched as Faye walked through the hospital gates, quickly running his eyes up and down, no sign of her bag. He was relieved to see she didn't have it, he was afraid she might have found the pen, but he now thought she had just left her bag at home. While he had managed to get the tracker from the car, removing the pen from her bag would be a bit trickier but he would have to get it back now that she was getting suspicious. He hadn't told Oliver Blake and hoped he could avoid that. He followed a reasonable distance behind and watched as she went into a chemist, she was out again in less than three minutes. He followed her as she continued walking in the direction of town. After about half an hour she went into the Copper Cow, Arthur parked and waited.

Ina was waiting for Faye in the Copper Cow.

'How'ya,' she said as she spotted Faye.

'Hi Ina, are you here long?'

'No just got here before you, I'm starved though, I hardly had time to eat all day. Are you hungry?'

'Yeah, I'm going to have the burger and chips, I need some comfort food.'

Ina couldn't see any stray waiter around and so she went to the bar to put in their order - she was going to have the burger and chips as well along with two cokes. They both thought that they were better off staying as clear-headed as possible.

'So, I've been thinking,' said Ina as she returned from the bar with their drinks, 'when we finish, you go back to your flat and make sure you're in range of the pen, I'll phone you and you say you will meet me at eleven o' clock tonight. Then we both drive to Island Point separately, I'll stay back, and you just sit in the car, and we wait to see if someone shows up. If they do, I'll get the reg plates.'

'How long will we wait?'

'If someone is following you, we'll know soon enough, I'll text you when I have the car reg and then you drive home.'

'Won't it look a bit odd if he does show up that the person I am there to meet doesn't?'

'No, bring your bag and I will phone you and all you say is "OK we'll met another time", our man will hear this and we're fine.'

'Alright, do you want to do it tonight?'

'Yeah, the sooner the better...'

Faye's phone rang and she made a face as if she was eating a lime.

'It's Bunty,' she said to Ina in a voice as if she had swallowed the lime. 'I'll just let her leave a message.'

'Have you seen her lately?' asked Ina.

'Not for a month or so, I must be due an interrogation, I wish she had abandoned me as a child.'

'I thought she had.'

'Yeah, but now that she hasn't got Greg, I've become her quarry.'

'I thought you always were.'

'Yeah, but now, I get her undiluted attention. I don't know why she keeps up the charade, it's farcical and she's become more of a caricature of herself the older she's getting, and she's years away from dying.'

They both laughed, it was the only thing to do where Faye's mother was concerned.

'No sign of Greg inviting her out for a long holiday?' asked Ina.

'That self-absorbed, pompous, megalomaniac hasn't even phoned her, Dad told me on the q.t the last time I was over. Nothing's changed, he was always the same but now that he has such a big knob job in NASA, he has forgotten us little people. Don't get me wrong, I'm delighted I don't have to suffer him anymore. Of course mother is making all manner of excuses for him, she could never allow herself to admit what a selfish git he is, but there again she has only herself to blame, she created the monster with all that messianic adoration, no child could turn out right after all that weird love.'

'Mind you, I think Greg was born a dickhead, he was never short of highfalutin notions about himself.'

'I know, his capacity to love himself is impressive,' laughed Faye.

'Being such a boy genius gave him some case for selflove I suppose.'

'He isn't a bloody genius, just very, very good at exams - I don't think he ever had an original thought, just very good at regurgitating other people's ideas.'

Faye had a sore spot when it came to her brother, all her life she had to hear what a genius he was, how clever he was, how gifted he was, how bloody marvellous he was, and so on. Do parents ever stop to think how this sort of nonsense affects the non-genius' of the family. And Greg of course was like a peacock among crows, preening and extolling in his own greatness which made it very easy not to like him, not that he cared, he was so uppity that he hardly registered Faye's existence, let alone cared what she thought about him. He now worked in the US for NASA as a nuclear physicist, Faye always thought it sounded far more impressive than it really was, probably a lot of egos banging on about atoms, neutrons and protons.

'How's he getting on in America?'

'Bunty says that he is already singling himself out as a cut above the rest, but I doubt that, there is far more competition there to be the best, who knows it might have a humbling effect on him,' Faye threw her eyes to heaven.

'Yeah right, humble and Greg do not bed fellows make.'

'Of course mother is making all sorts of excuses for why he is not calling or hasn't been home to visit for nearly two years, always defending the worm.'

'I kind of feel sorry for her, it must be hard for her.'

'Ina don't feel sorry for her, she's taken it out on Mary and me.'

'How's Mary, I haven't seen her for a while?'

'Neither have I, we must organise a night with her.'

Mary was Faye's older sister, Mary was not her given name she had been christened Marilyn, yes that made her Marilyn Monroe, after their mother's favourite actress, all three were called after

Bunty's favourite Hollywood stars. Greg after Gregory Peck, Bunty always gave him the full complement of his name and that was why Faye always called him Greg, she was called after Faye Dunaway, it could have been worse Faye often thought, she could have been the first born. Bunty had grand hopes for Marilyn, in her mad head she assumed by giving her child her idol's name that she would miraculously morph into *the* Marilyn Monroe. The reality was altogether a different matter, at eighteen Marilyn changed her name by deed poll to Mary, to the delight of Faye, no name could be so utterly mundane and abhorrent to their mother. Mary could not have resembled *the* Marilyn Monroe less, in fact she was the very antithesis of *the* Marilyn Monroe, again to Faye's delight. Mary was gay and had once described herself to Faye as a chapstick lesbian which was to say she was a bit of a tomboy, she'd rather wear chapstick than lipstick. She wore her hair in a short pixie style, dyed jet black and apart from her school uniform, Faye could never remember seeing Mary in a skirt, let alone a billowing white number - she had a wardrobe of skinny jeans, white shirts and converse sneakers. Mary lived in Cork which meant Faye did not see her as often as she would like, Faye adored Mary and still had a childlike admiration for her and how rebellious she was, and no matter how disenchanted Bunty was by Faye, her profound sense of being betrayed by Mary was monumental. Faye had once suggested to Mary that she should go to therapy to deal with their mothers active dislike of her, Mary, probably quite rightly declined, saying that no amount of therapy would make their mother less ridiculous and anyway their mothers lack of love had not stopped her from doing what she wanted in her life nor had it stopped her from loving others or being loved, really she conclude their mother was simply a silly woman and there was no talking ones way out of that. Proof, Mary said, that we are our own people despite our parents and that we can decide who we want to be ourselves. And if ever there was proof of a well-adjusted normal lovely human being, Faye thought, you couldn't find a better example than Mary.

'Has she told Bunty that she's getting married?' asked Ina.

Mary had been going out with Denise Long for fifteen years and if Mary could be described as a chapstick lesbian then Denise was without doubt a lipstick lesbian, she was of the drop-dead gorgeous species. Ina and Faye had often said that they could easily go gay for the delectable Denise.

'No, she's going to wait till the last possible moment to save herself the grief which will undoubtedly be immense. Dad knows and agrees that it was best to wait to tell Bunty.'

'Will she go to the wedding?'

'Wild horses wouldn't keep her away, she'll be torn between playing the role of the long-suffering mother and out doing Denise in the beauty stakes, oh god yes she'll definitely be there.'

'What about Greg, is he coming home for it?' asked Ina with a mouth full of burger.

'Mary asked him but in his usual self-important way he told her that he was working on something, and I quote *"very critical to the future of mankind"* so he may not be able to tear himself away for something as frivolous as his sister's wedding. Plonker. Mary said he's probably working on some kind of toilet paper that doesn't float in space,' Faye laughed as she finished off her chips.

'But it's quite close, isn't it?'

'Yeah, two weeks' time.'

'Are you bringing a date?' Ina asked with some trepidation, hoping that she wouldn't say Danny.

'I've asked Harry to be my date, Mary really wants you and him there, you are coming aren't you, you got your invite, didn't you?'

'Yeah, I'm definitely coming, a Monroe wedding, that would be unmissable,' exclaimed Ina.

'That's what I'm afraid of.'

'Look on the bright side, you are not a silly bridesmaid.'

'There is that and it will be visually lovely, apart from the delectable Denise herself, her taste is flawless, which drives mother cracked. We'll just have to make the best of it for Mary.'

'Don't worry it will be great,' offered Ina knowing full well that it was going to be hell.

'We better get the skids under us if we are to do this tonight,' said Faye.

'OK let's go.'

Both women got to their feet and put on their coats.

'Have you told Mary about Dan?' Ina knew that Mary would not take that news well.

'No, there's nothing really to tell and she has enough on her plate at the moment. I'll get this,' said Faye wanting to get away from these questions and she went to the bar to pay the bill.

'Thanks,' said Ina as Faye returned and they walked towards the door, she got the message and changed the conversation. 'So you know what to do when you get back and any communication with me, do it by text. Okay?'

'Yes, everything is fine,' answered Faye as she glanced around the room, she had the feeling that she was being watched but there was no sign of the man in the pictures.

'Do you want a lift home?' Ina asked.

'No thanks, I'll get a taxi.' Ina lived on the other side of town, and it would be a horrible inconvenience to have to drop Faye off, but Ina always offered.

Faye flagged an oncoming taxi which pulled into the footpath.

'I'll talk to you later,' and she waved goodbye to Ina.

'How'ya luv, where to this evening?' asked the driver.

Faye gave him the address and started to listen to the long message her mother left. She was incensed, Greg had called to make arrangements for his visit home, he was coming to the wedding. She wanted to know if Faye knew about this abomination of a wedding and if she did how could she have kept it from her own mother, she didn't expect anything else from Marilyn and of course it took Gregory, the only one who considered her feelings, to tell her. And then she got cut off.

Bloody hell thought Faye now it's really going to be hell, poor Mary, she better ring her to give her the heads up.

Mary's phone rang three times and then she picked up.

'Hello little sister, how are you?'

'Grand, have you heard from Bunty?'

'No, why?'

'She knows, the prince told her and he's coming home for it. She rang earlier and left a long ranting message, you can only imagine.'

'Unfortunately, I can. Not to worry, I was going to tell her on Friday anyway, you know, give her some time to get some Botox and whatever other poison she uses to feed her Peter Pan complex.'

'Do you want me to ring her before you call her, not that I think I can do any good, but it might soften her up a bit?'

'I suppose it can't hurt, I really don't care how keyed up she is, but for Denise's sake, I don't want Bunty to be on high doh on the day. Denise comes from such a normal family, she doesn't really get our malfunctional lot.'

'Probably just as well that she doesn't.'

'True, okay give her a buzz and work your charm on her.'

'Bunty is impervious to my charm, but I'll do my best.'

'Thanks sweetie. Give me a call when mission impossible is completed,' they both laughed as they hung up.

'Here we are luv, that'll be a fiver.' Faye hardly noticed that she was home, she paid the man and got out.

She had the feeling again that she was being watched and looked around before she put her key in the door, she saw nothing curious.

Faye was no sooner in the door when she heard Mrs Clayworth-Howsham.

'Good evening dear, I thought I ought to check to see how you are given the morning's events.'

'I am very well Mrs C thanks for asking, Ina is helping to get to the bottom of things, and she is very thorough. I expect it all to be resolved very soon. I will be going out later on so don't be alarmed.'

'Oh my dear I would never keep tabs on you, you must come and go as you please.' Mrs Clayworth-Howsham sounded wounded and hoped she hadn't over-stepped the mark with Faye, she certainly didn't want her to feel she had to report her comings and goings, after all she already tracked her movements, more by accident than intent of course.

'I know, it's just on this occasion I wanted you to be aware I was going out again, as you say given the goings on, of course I know you're not keeping tabs on me.' Faye reassured Mrs Clayworth-Howsham while smiling to herself thinking about how she could be a most reliable witness to all the residents' comings and goings.

'Why thank you my dear, now I shan't keep you any longer, I am sure you had a long day curing all those poor creatures in the asylum.'

No point saying anything, thought Faye.

'Goodnight Mrs Clayworth-Howsham.'

'Goodnight, dear.'

Mrs Clayworth-Howsham went down, and Faye went up.

As she opened the door to her flat Faye felt exhausted not only at the prospect of going out again or having to placate her mother but at the thought of Amanda, she was certain that all this was connected in some way to her, she hoped that tonight would shed some light on how.

She texted Ina to say she was home and as she waited for her call back took a coke from the fridge and opened a packet of chocolate ring biscuits, it never mattered how much she ate, Faye always needed chocolate after a meal, or for that matter before a meal.

Her phone rang, it was Ina, and before she answered she went into her bedroom where the pen was and then answered saying hello.

'OK you're in range just answer simply yes or no,' said Ina.

'Yes'

'Now just say you'll meet me there at 11.30, repeat the location and then hang up.'

Faye did as she was told. She looked at the alarm clock, it was 10.30, she estimated that it would take less than thirty minutes to drive to Island Point at this time of night which gave her a half hour to kill. No point starting my notes she thought and to get it over with she decided to return her mother's call, she closed her bedroom door plus the living room door and made the call from the kitchen out of the bug's range, no point giving the eavesdropper an insight into her warped family life.

Bunty answered after about ten rings, Faye immediately knew she was fuming and torn between answering and wanting to punish Faye by not. Faye also knew she would eventually answer, her desire to rant would eclipse her taciturnity.

'So, you finally deigned to return my call, I don't know what I did to deserve that kind of treatment.'

And so it begins, thought Faye, Bunty mostly affected a faux posh accent which she had perfected or murdered, whichever way you want to look at it, but when she was raving it took on a whole new level of affectation, Faye found it mortifying.

'Mother, you must be so excited that Greg is coming home,' said Faye, in an attempt to appease.

'Well of course I am and why wouldn't I be, Gregory is the only one who has any consideration for my sensitive disposition and what with him being so incredibly busy, he still found time in his hectic schedule to think of his beloved mother, if only his sisters were a fraction as considerate as he is it would make my life all the more bearable. But oh no! So thoughtless not even to tell your own mother that her daughter is to get married, however horrific the circumstances, but I will put my own feelings aside and do as I always do, make sacrifices for my children despite their ungrateful nature, I cannot begin to impress on you the extent of my discommode...'

Faye wanted to correct her use of discommode but thought better of it.

'... I spoke with your Aunt Shirley and my heaven she could not believe it, her very words were, "Bunty darling, after all you have done for those children", of course she doesn't include Gregory in that, as you know your aunt dotes on Gregory and why wouldn't she. No, no there is no point trying to right a wrong now, your conduct says it all...'

Faye had made no attempt to say anything, but Bunty wouldn't let a little thing like reality interfere with her notions.

'...however bad you are on this occasion your sister is opprobrious, I shudder to think how this will affect my constitution long term...'

Faye was now convinced that Bunty was reading this from a script she had prepared earlier, it wasn't that she was not capable of ranting for an age without taking a breath, it was her use of the word *opprobrious* which gave her away. Bunty was not capable of coming up with a word like that offhandedly and she was very fond of her thesaurus, a Christmas present four years ago from Aunt Shirley, who was herself a carbon copy of Bunty. Shirley claimed that her own thesaurus, the Oxford edition of course, had changed her life, she and Bunty advocated lifelong education of the variety which made you appear intelligent when you might not actually be. Faye hoped she was coming to the end of it.

'...and where is this abomination taking place?'

Finally, thought Faye.

'Actually, in one of your favourite hotels, The Embassy, Mary thought it would be nice for you,' lied Faye, in fact Denise who is an interior designer had done some work for the hotel and they gave her a great deal.

'She needn't do me any favours, and quite frankly I am surprised a hotel of that calibre would have such a wedding, now your sister has ruined that hotel for me forever, she has no consideration.'

'It's a good excuse to go shopping and buy something lovely,' said Faye hoping to get her into her favourite domain - herself.

'Oh, I don't think I could possibly buy something new, it wouldn't seem proper, I'll just wear some old thing from the back of the wardrobe.'

'I'm sure Denise's mother will be going all out, it's going to be a very glamorous wedding.'

'Oh indeed, and I am sure she has had plenty of notice and time to search for the perfect outfit unlike me, only told in the eleventh' hour, you wouldn't understand given your own disinterest in your appearance. You simply cannot throw an outfit together, colour coordination, fabrics, jewellery, my goodness the hat, no, regrettably, I was not given ample time to do an outfit justice, Shirley said as much.'

How am I related to her, thought Faye.

'Mother I'm sure with Aunt Shirley's help you can muster something, after all you have set a very high standard, people will have certain expectations of you.' Faye felt like chewing her own thumbs off.

'I hardly need your aunt's help, more likely the other way around, but yes, you are correct I have garnered a reputation as someone who takes care of themselves. We will have to see, I may be able to find the time, after all someone in this family has to put a good face on this fiasco. I shudder to think what your sister will appear in. And you, are you going on a diet?'

Bunty never missed an opportunity to comment on Faye's weight despite the fact that Faye was a perfectly normal size, Bunty always veered towards the anorexic herself and wished the same for her daughters, although she fed Greg like there was a famine coming.

Ignoring her, Faye made a loud knock on the table feigning the arrival of a visitor, Faye couldn't ignore the irony of this act since it was from Bunty that she learnt it, but it was a testimony to Bunty's "lifelong education" that she fell for it every time.

'You have someone at the door, it's rude to keep them waiting. I will speak to you tomorrow,' Bunty said, the last bit by way of a treat.

Faye looked at her phone for a moment thinking how demented her mother was before she took her coat from the back of chair in the living room. As she put the coat on, she thought that she hadn't asked Ina whether or not she should bring her bag with the bug, she quickly texted her to ask and in seconds got a "yes" reply. It was time to go.

She reversed out of the driveway onto a very quiet street, there were a few cars parked, she hoped that whoever was bugging her would be following now, but no cars appeared to follow her. As she pulled off her street the traffic began to thicken, and it was more difficult to detect if she was being followed.

It was ten to eleven, Faye was on time, she was soon on Clontarf Road and took the left turn for Island View. Ina was right to pick this place, thought Faye, there was only one way in, so you were sure to spot anyone who drove in. The View had for years been a great spot for kids to hang out and smoke and drink and get a kiss, but today very few kids went there probably because now they were allowed to drink and kiss at home. Island View was built in the sixties as a warehousing depot, but it never took off and even in the boom was not redeveloped, Faye remembered reading that there were problems with the deeds and so it remained the same, a dingy hangout with some of the old containers turned into heroin houses. It was completely dark, the city council had long since stopped any funding for lighting up what they called a carbuncle on an otherwise beautiful inlet, understandable unless you lived in one of the containers. She parked almost in the centre, the lights from the car lit up the bleakness, Faye pressed the button for central locking. There were about six other cars parked, all looked empty, after about two minutes Faye saw a car drive in, turn to the left and park. Faye waited.

After thirteen minutes Ina rang.

'Hi, now just say "what happened" said Ina, Faye obliged.

'Now just say okay and hang up then drive home but wait a few minutes to go, I'll contact you in a bit,' Ina hung up.

Ina had arrived earlier and left her car on the street and walked into The View, she had memories of this place as a trainee guard on street duty, the call outs which usually meant some poor devil had overdosed, there was never any real trouble here, the druggies just came here to flake out and plug into oblivion. Ina thought these druggies were the closest thing to zombies she would ever see, they were like the living dead, it was pointless bringing them down to the station, they could hardly string two words together and that was when they were sober, everything about them slowed to a horrible kelpie-like stated, it took an age for their brain cells to connect to make a sentence. Ina recalled one drug addict telling her that every waking moment was hell because all you ever thought about was your next fix and it didn't matter what you had to do to get it, getting it was the mission.

She had said that the fix was no longer pleasurable, in fact it quickly stopped being pleasurable and became about relief, a short abeyance from the unbearable yearning.

And here she was again. She had found a spot to hide behind one of the trailers, apart from a few clapped-out cars and the trailers there was nothing else and all was quiet tonight, they were either in the trailers or out on the mission. She had brought a pro DSLR camera from work, technically she should not be using this camera, there again, technically, she shouldn't be doing this either. The camera was everything you wanted for these kind of situations when your subject may not stand still and smile for you, it was fast and managed to take good shots of even the most erratically moving subject. Ina had taken a camera course through work and now considered herself quite a nifty photographer.

She had hunkered herself down and positioned the camera to be able to take a clear shot of anyone entering The View. Not long after Faye had arrived, another car pulled in and turned to the left which gave Ina a clear shot of him as the driver's side was facing her. Ina could tell immediately that it was the same man from the photos Mrs C had taken, who the hell was he, she thought. She took a few more shots of the car and the number plate, the camera's internal flash was able to take the number with crystal clarity. He didn't wait long to leave once Faye had gone. Ina waited a few minutes before she too left and made her way back to her car and drove home. Ina didn't waste any time in uploading the pictures. She logged into CAP, their police software programme, Ina had high clearance and had access to all search programmes. She entered the car registration and waited a moment while it sheared through data to offer up a name, Arthur Wilson. Ina opened up another search page in CAP and typed in Arthur Wilson in the search bar and waited while all notions of privacy were dissolved by the grinding of bites and whatever the hell else computers did to gain access to all areas of someone's life. Ina had no qualms about this.

She rang Faye once she had read through the information CAP dutifully provided. Faye answered after one ring, she was eager.

'What did you see?' asked Faye.

'You safe to talk?'

'Yeah, I'm outside.'

'Are you smoking?' asked Ina as indignant as you like, knowing there was only one reason Faye would be outside at this time of night.

'Just one, I think given the circumstances it's warranted, don't you?'

'No I don't and it's never just one with you, you know that.'

'Ina what did you find out?' Faye knew she was right, she was an all or nothing smoker and had successfully packed them in after years of a twenty-a-day delicious habit.

'It's all very weird, the guy is an ex-French Legionnaire, born in Zimbabwe, did a stint as a mercenary in Iraq and the Congo and is now a private detective. Clean as a cucumber as far as convictions go, not even a parking ticket, he has a handgun licence, not your average Joe.'

'What's his name?'

'Arthur Wilson, ring any bells?'

'None, so the likelihood is that he is working for someone, must be Oliver Blake.'

'Maybe, and I imagine a guy like this would not come cheap, he doesn't advertise which means he gets his work the old-fashioned way, which means he is probably good.'

'Bloody hell, what can we do about him?'

'Nothing, he's not doing anything illegal.

'We need to find out for sure if it is Blake he is working for, I'm going to have to follow him.'

'Hang on a second, you need to think this through, we need a plan. We don't know who we are dealing with.'

Faye liked that Ina was using *we,* but she was determined to press ahead with this until she found Amanda.

'Okay any suggestions.'

'I have an address for him, I might be able to put Malcolm on him for a little while, it's better that you or I don't try to tail him in case he sees us. I suspect Arthur Wilson is no slow coach, better to put Malcolm on the job and see what he comes up with.'

'Great, Ina thanks. What about the bug, will I take it with me to work tomorrow?'

'Yeah do, the less reason we give him to be suspicious the better and we can use it to our advantage, just remember to be careful when it's in earshot.'

'Will do.'

'Okay we'll talk tomorrow, go to bed and stop smoking!'

'I will,' laughed Faye, 'Bye.'

'Bye'

Faye decided to have one more cigarette before going to bed.

# eighteen

A week had passed before Ina could spare Malcolm, or more precisely sneak him off to follow Arthur Wilson, she had to be careful, she didn't want to get Malcolm in trouble and so had decided not to tell him anything other than to give him the instruction to follow Wilson and document his movements. She checked each day and on Thursday evening got confirmation that he had visited the office of one Oliver Blake, she sent Malcolm back to official work on Friday.

Ina phoned Faye early Friday morning to tell her.

'Hi Ina, how're you?' asked Faye

'Grand, listen Malcolm made the connection, Wilson went to Oliver Blake office yesterday evening and stayed for less than an hour and left. I think it's fair to assume now that Blake has hired Arthur Wilson to follow you.'

'Okay, I suppose I knew it but now that it's confirmed it makes it so real, what the hell does he want from me, he obviously blames me for Amanda leaving him, but what does he plan on doing to me, chop me up into little bits.'

'Don't joke about it Faye, this guy is no fool, he's seriously wealthy and that kind of money doesn't come without influence,' cautioned Ina.

'You're right I know, but still, he's hardly going to kill me, is he?' Faye wasn't sure and hoped Ina might reassure her a bit.

'Who knows what he is thinking but it's best to be vigilant, listen I have to go I'm at work and the boss is on his way in, see you later, bye.' She hadn't time to wait for a reply.

Ina was never very good at being reassuring.

Faye was a bit lost in thought when her phone rang, she answered it without looking at the number assuming it was Ina again.

'Good morning,' said Danny.

'Good morning.' Faye had not seen him since the previous weekend and she had avoided his calls during the week, she was terrified she was going to blurt out an invitation to Mary's wedding, which would be disastrous, Bunty would be transfixed and make a show of everyone, it wasn't that she was ever concerned about Faye's heartbreak, no, she was incensed because she took it as a personal insult that a daughter of hers was not good enough for one of the Cohens. Bunty also felt that the Cohens thought themselves a cut above the rest, and while in reality they probably were, the real source of Bunty's irk was her envy, she wanted the Cohens life.

'I've missed you, can't wait to see you tonight, what time are you finished work, we could go to that French movie in the IFI and then for sushi, what do you think?'

How normal this sounds, thought Faye, making plans for the weekend with your lover, only for the fact that he is married and probably not going to be around for very long more. She was feeling bad about having to lie to him and also because a movie and sushi was far more enticing than going to her parent's house. Bunty had insisted that as the parents of the bride, for despite Denise also being a bride, she considered herself the official mother of the bride, it was the proper thing to do to have Denise's parents for a pre-wedding dinner, as directed by Emily Post in her definitive guide to Wedding Etiquette. Mary had asked Faye to come, and she couldn't refuse, bringing Danny would certainly spice things up, but things were probably going to be spicy enough without an uppity Cohen.

'I would love to, but I can't, in fact I'm flat out all this weekend and really won't be able to see you till next week,' Faye didn't need to fake her feelings, she genuinely was disappointed.

'No way, what are you doing that you can't spare a few hours to meet up?'

For no apparent reason Faye suddenly felt really cross, perhaps it was the slight indignant tone she picked up in Danny, who the hell does he think he is, coming back here after all these years and expecting her to drop her life and attend to him, she doesn't have to answer to him, let him scurry off back to his wife.

'Danny, my life didn't come to a standstill just because you came back, I have things on and I certainly don't have to account for my actions to you, I'll give you a call next week, now I have to go I'm late for work,' Faye couldn't keep the peeved tone out of her voice, but then she hadn't tried.

'Faye, I didn't mean...'began Danny.

'I really do have to go, I'll talk to you next week,' and with that Faye hung up.

Faye's head was pounding. She went to her bag and took out the Valium and swallowed two down without water. She was running late, she quickly went into the bathroom and slapped on some make-up. She had original planned on going to her parents straight from work, but she hadn't the time now to organise clothes to bring with her. She would just nip back after work and change.

Just as she was locking her door, her phone signalled a message, she took it out and saw it was from Danny, it read *sorry I didn't mean to upset you xxx D*. This only made her crosser still.

As she was leaving the front door, she had a quick look at the hall table where Mrs C, or whoever found the post, put all the letters. She hadn't looked last night and along with a telephone bill was a failure to deliver docket from a courier company called The Pigeon Carriers, according to this docket there was a parcel for Faye. Mrs C must have been out when the delivery man came, otherwise she would have signed for it, one of the perks of having the landlady in situ.

Faye couldn't think of who would be sending her a parcel, and had never heard of The Pigeon Carriers, but she knew she wouldn't get to it today and that would mean it would be Monday, maybe, she thought, Mrs C might be in and sign for it. She darted across the hall and knocked on Mrs C's door, she waited a moment before she heard the sound of footsteps. Mrs Clayworth-Howsham opened the door and even early in the morning she looked elegant and serene, Faye silently vowed to work on her serenity.

'Good morning my dear,' said Mrs Clayworth-Howsham in her lovely melodise way.

'Good morning, Mrs C I hate to bother you but by any chance are you going to be in today, it's just that there's a parcel for me and I won't be able to get it until Monday.'

'Good grief my dear it would be no trouble at all, I am going down the high street and would be delighted to sign for your parcel when I get back.'

'Oh, you're such a darling, take a taxi on me as a thank you,' Faye took out her purse and began to take twenty euros out.'

'Goodness gracious me please put your money away, I will be taking a taxi at any rate. Now give me the notification slip and you get yourself off to work, I can see you are pressed for time.' Mrs Clayworth-Howsham put out her skeleton hand which was covered in translucent skin, skin which had not a sign of a liver spot. Faye handed her the slip and noticed her own hands which were a bit dry, she silently vowed to work on her dry hands.

'Thank you so much, I will phone them now, what time will I say you will be here from?

'I except to be back in by eleven o clock so any time from then would suffice.'

'Thank you so much, that's great,' said Faye as she entered the number from the docket into her phone.

'Have a good day my dear' said Mrs Clayworth-Howsham, she thought Faye looked a bit worn out and sad, such a lovely girl if only she could meet a nice young man, now that would make all the difference, just as meeting The Colonel had for her. Mrs Clayworth-Howsham returned to her flat thinking fond thoughts of her beloved husband.

By the time Faye arrived at work her head was splitting, she longed to take another two Valium but resisted knowing that she would probably need them more over the weekend. She popped open a can of Red Bull and took a few gulps, she didn't like it in the slightest, but it had the desired effect of filling her bloodstream with caffeine. She was still a bit unnerved by this morning's news as she looked at her diary, she had a new patient first thing and after that her day was full of anxiety ridden souls, it seemed to Faye that the world was turning into one mass of hysteria. She listened to her answering machine and took down the numbers of those enquiring about an appointment. There was a message from Oliver Blake, he had called at eight this morning asking for Faye to call him. What the hell does he want, thought Faye, the last two sessions had been agony, a cat and mouse charade, she wanted rid of him but knew she couldn't and somehow, she felt Oliver Blake knew this too.

Faye heard her first patient go into the waiting room, taking another few swigs of Red Bull, she checked his name again and put some water and glasses on the table before going out to get him.

Eugene Klein was sitting rather geekily on the sofa, looking the very opposite of relaxed, not quite out on the edge but almost, his hands were clasped tightly together, and his back was as stiff as a poker. Faye was used to this kind of posture, not many people relished coming to see her, she was probably only a little further up from the dentist in terms of people-you-most-dislike-going-to-see. Eugene Klein dwelled in the average department, no Vogue material here, average height, average looks, average dress, the kind of person who would get away with a crime because of his averageness, he would simply not be noticed.

'Good morning Eugene, I'm Faye Monroe, it's nice to meet you,' said Faye in a voice which portrayed authority and kindness.

'Yeah hello,' said Eugene sounding a bit raw, as if he had a rough night, his voice didn't quite fit with his external appearance.

'Come on through and take a seat,' Faye motioned him to the seat opposite her and as she sat down, she took out her writing pad and wrote Eugene's name down.

'I'm just going to take your details firstly if that's alright.'

'Yeah sure.'

Faye quickly went through the usual questions and then looked up from the writing pad to ask how she could help him, but before she had a chance he asked, 'Is that all the details?'

'Yes.'

'D'you not need a next of kin?'

'No, not really, why do you ask?'

'Well, I read like, online, that it's one of the questions you people ask.'

'Do you want to give one?'

'Well, I thought like, I was supposed to.'

'Not if you don't wish to, but if there is a reason then by all means you certainly can.'

'What about...well...like you know...if someone...was like, you know suicidal...'

'If you wish to give a name in case of this please do.'

'Well...wouldn't you need to have someone, like to contact if I was, you know, suicidal?'

Faye thought he really wanted to give her a name, perhaps he was hoping she might contact someone for him.

'Is there someone you would wish to know if you were suicidal?'

'Like I suppose so...if I gave a name...what would have to happen for you to, you know, contact them?'

'The only reason I would contact your next of kin is in the event that you were actively suicidal, and I felt you were a high risk, I am obliged by law to seek help for you.'

'Would you tell me if you were going to make that call?'

'Yes, I would make every attempt to let you know.'

'What does that mean like "every attempt"?'

'If you were to tell me you were going to kill yourself and left without giving me a chance to seek help for you then I would be left with no choice but to make the call without informing you, but I am informing you now, so in effect you would know.'

'So, it would only be if I was going to kill myself that you would make the call.'

'Yes.'

'So can I not, you know, talk about how I like feel because you will make a call.'

'Of course, you can talk about suicidal thoughts and urges and perhaps you might be able to get some help from that, but you shouldn't feel afraid of speaking openly about your feelings.'

'Hey, I didn't like say I was suicidal, but I should like be allowed to kill myself if I want to, shouldn't I?'

'Eugene, I have to follow the law of the land and that requires me to intervene to help keep you safe if necessary.'

'How often do you like make the call?'

'Very rarely in fact.'

'So, you would tell me before you called?'

'As I said I would make every attempt to. So do you wish to give me a name and number, if you prefer you don't have to.'

'OK I'll give you the name of my next of kin, it's Amanda Blake.'

'Amanda Blake' repeated Faye, saying this name made her mouth go dry.

'What is your relationship to this person?' asked Faye.

'She's like my next of kin.'

'Is she related?' pressed Faye.

'Does it matter, she's my next of kin full stop.' He said this in a matter-of-fact sort of way which was also charged with the message not to ask again.

'No, do you have a number?' asked Faye.

Eugene gave a number without hesitation; it was a number he knew by heart, a number he was used to dialling thought Faye, but then his age group never dialled, everything is saved in contacts, but he knew it, possibly for emergencies. Faye didn't recognize the number, but then she wouldn't. Her head was going nineteen to the dozen. Was this *her* Amanda Blake?

'Eugene how might I help you?' she asked calmly.

'I dunno.'

Nothing.

'Well why did you decide to come to see me?'

'I dunno.'

Nothing.

'Well, you appear concerned about suicide, have you been having any suicidal thoughts?'

'Dunno.'

Nothing.

'How have you been feeling lately?'

'Dunno.'

And so it went. Eugene Klein had done all the talking he had come to do and now he was punching in the time.

The minutes passed like excruciatingly slow torture, all the while Faye's mind was frantically trying to make connections between this Eugene Klein and Amanda, she had never mentioned him to her, she was sure of this because Amanda had mentioned so few people in her life.

Time continued to tick by with nothing more than a "Dunno" from Eugene Klein, at last the fifty minutes was up. There was no way Faye was going to suggest another appointment.

Eugene dug into the pocket of his jeans and produced two crumpled fifty-euro notes and gently placed them on the table before surprising Faye by asking her for an appointment for the following week. She gave him a time, thinking that next week she would put him on the couch, at least she wouldn't have to keep her eyes open between the "Dunno's".

The moment he left Faye was tempted to dial the number he had given her and would have done had she had the time, but the day went without an opportunity to do so. By the time she had finished at half five she just had enough time to get home, change and get over to her parents. Before she left, she wrote the number Eugene Klein had given her into her diary and switched off the lights and heat, she normally gave the office a quick clean on Friday evening, not that it ever got very dirty but she had missed that last couple of Friday cleanings and she noticed that the floor was getting a bit grubby and a bit of dusting wouldn't have gone astray. She decided to ignore it.

# nineteen

It was twenty past eight when the taxi Faye had taken pulled up outside her parent's home, she was twenty minutes late, she sat for a moment after forking out twenty-four euro for yet another taxi and thought about staying in the car and getting him to drive off but the image of Mary spurred her out of the taxi. As the car pulled off, she stood for a moment in the freezing cold before going in through the gates, the place looked like something out of a home insurance ad, everything preened and prettified and soulless. She didn't have a key, Bunty didn't believe in giving her children a key to her house, so she rang the bell. As she waited, the contents of the parcel Mrs C had kindly collected for her started to meddle with her mind, if she was to survive the night, she would have to block them out. As the door opened Bunty appeared in all her finery, lots of gold and diamonds, her hair was done to perfection, that is to say not a strand of hair was unescorted, her hair moved in unison like Mao's Red Army. Faye thought that her mother probably had looked well half an hour before she finished getting ready, all she piled on after that time was just over the top.

'I asked you to be on time, it's the least you could have done, it's not like I ask a lot of you, but I suppose something more important came up for you, come in and take your coat off quickly, I see you brought nothing, not that I expected anything but I hope I had taught you better manners than to come to someone's house with your hands hanging. Your hair looks a bit lank, really Faye why do you insist on vexing me, you know this is an important and difficult night for me, I'm making a very big effort given the circumstances.' Bunty didn't pause for air, she had the lungs of a Himalayan Sherpa.

Faye took off her coat and waited for some comment about her dress, she thought she looked perfectly fine, she was wearing a lovely soft grey cashmere dress to the knee, it was understated but with an edge, at least that was what the sales assistant had told Faye when she was buying it. Around her neck she had an Alexander McQueen printed silk chiffon scarf tied in a knot at the side and a pair of patent knee high boots. She wore no jewellery, she had an aversion to it, probably from years of exposure to her mother's jewellery overkill. Bunty had a belief in the power of gold and diamond jewellery that was unrivalled, there was virtually no problem in Bunty's life that couldn't be resolved by a piece of jewellery. Bunty had made her husband aware of this very early on in their marriage, which probably accounted for her not inconsequential collection, her problem was always which pieces to show off and so more often than not she tried to wear them all at once.

'Is that a new dress?' Bunty asked as she looked Faye up and down.

'No.'

'I didn't think so, it looks a bit tired.'

Cow, thought Faye.

'Let's go in,' said Faye.

Bunty hadn't quite finished her rant but Faye wasn't going to give her the chance to and so she walked ahead of her mother into the sitting room, although Bunty called it the drawing room.

The room was warm and decorated in the style of Louis XVI, with a lot of fluted columns, carved friezes, oak and laurel leaf, wreaths, and other various neoclassical attempts to imitate Versailles, not surprisingly Bunty loved Marie Antoinette.

Mary was sitting on the not very comfortable gold and dark red three-seater lounge, Faye caught her eye immediately and her pretend smile told Faye that things were not good. Best get a drink thought Faye.

'Hello everyone,' said Faye as she quickly scanned the room. Denise was looking sensational on one of the matching chairs to the lounge, she managed to make the room look good. Faye's father was sitting beside Mary looking achingly uneasy but attempting joviality, which for a sombre man was always a mistake.

Opposite on another Louis XVI style lounge sat Denise's parents, the very antithesis of Faye's parents, all elegance and ease. The introductions were made, and dinner was served.

By the time Faye was phoning for another taxi she wanted to chew her own eyelids off, the evening had been excruciating. Bunty was in rare form and with a few too many brandies she was unbearable in her attempts to impress John and Cynthia. Faye spent the entire evening cringing, Denise's parents were gracious throughout, but you could tell they were probably thinking what kind of family was their daughter marrying in to.

Mary came to the door with Faye when the taxi arrived.

'Thanks for coming sweetie,' said Mary, as she kissed Faye goodnight.

'That was the worst I've seen her for a long time,' said Faye.

'I know, I told Denise to warn John and Cynthia, they're really nice and won't be the slightest bit put off by Bunty, they probably find her a bit of a novelty really.'

'She's that alright,' laughed Faye, 'I thought I was going to choke when she came out with "Isn't it great that every religion has the feast of Christmas".'

'I know, that was priceless.'

'What is she going to be like tomorrow. Are you all set, do you need me to do anything, I feel a bit useless really, I haven't done a thing for you.'

'Don't worry, there's nothing to do Denise has everything sorted, it's what she does, I haven't done much myself as it happens.'

'Good, now I don't feel so bad, are you nervous?'

'Not in the slightest and I've decided not to think about Bunty, let her do her thing.'

The taxi blew the horn.

'I better go, see you tomorrow, sleep well.'

'Bye Faye.'

As she got into the taxi Faye quickly forgot the evening events and began to think again of the contents of the parcel. The night was bitterly cold, even more so than normal for November and there was a fog down through the city, normally Faye enjoyed the eeriness which this created but tonight it made her feel slightly unnerved. As soon as she arrived back at her flat she lit the gas heater, the flat was freezing, in her rush to get out earlier on she had forgotten to set the heating - as lovely as the flat was it was bitterly cold at this time of year, really it was cold year-round, just worse in the winter. Mrs C had put in wood burning stoves in the open fireplaces and when Faye had the time to light them and remembered to buy fuel, they did heat the flat wonderfully, but that was a rare event and so she relied on the smelly gas heater. After she pulled the heater closer to her seat, she opened the low Mastercraft black and gold sideboard and took out a classical collection CD and popped it on.

When Faye had arrived home from work earlier that evening, she had found the parcel outside her door, it had Indian stamps on it, the moment she saw it she remembered that Eesha Vattyam had said she would send her Amanda's belongings. Faye thought for a moment that she shouldn't open the parcel that it really should go to her sister Pamela, but she reasoned with herself that at this point it was essential that she open it and so without delay she took a scissors to the packaging tape and opened the box. The parcel was bigger than she had expected, on top was a small envelope which had, in beautiful handwriting, Faye's name. Faye opened the envelope, it was luxurious to the touch, and carefully removed a card which had a butterfly motif engraved in gold with a gold boarder edge, in the same lovely handwriting was written.

Dear Ms Monroe,

Enclosed you will find Amanda's belongings which she left behind; it is my wish that you return these to her. Should you see her please convey my best wishes.

Regards

Eesha

Eesha had clearly taken great care in wrapping the contents, each individual item was wrapped separately in a heavy quality cream tissue paper. The first item Faye unwrapped was what she presumed to be a piece of passementerie, Faye thought it was truly lovely, it was like a braid in green, gold and red silk. Faye imagined that this was possibly a practice piece as it was only about ten centimetres long. The next piece was a more elaborate woven piece with what looked like strands of silk chenille, silk and silver wire wrapped cords meandering back and forth through the silk weft which formed an interlocking pattern.

In all there were twelve of these beautiful pieces all different designs and colours. Faye unwrapped a larger heavier piece next which was different, it was an embroidered piece, gold on black velvet. Amanda was very accomplished at this Faye thought, but it was the images which were compelling. The first piece looked like a fifteenth century painting, it depicted a man eating his own arm, the next two pieces were also embroidered, and they both looked like a Dali painting and another, which again looked like a fifteenth century painting had a heap of bodies on what looked like a raft. The last piece was a portrait of a woman in fifteenth century dress, Faye had thought it looked like Elizabeth Báthory but wasn't sure. There was also a book of French poetry, in French, another two books on passementerie, also in French, and a small book on Greek Mythology, and that was it.

Faye had placed the contents on the dining table and left them while she went to the party and now she sat in front of them she picked up each piece of passementerie and turned them over in her hands, feeling the texture and marvelling at the intricacy and craftsmanship of the work. She could almost feel the work and love that went into making these objects. Out of nowhere she felt a sudden pang of sadness and the prickling of tears in her eyes, but she forced herself not to cry. She put the passementerie aside and began to look at the embroidered pieces, she started with the image of the woman and entered Elizabeth Báthory into Google and clicked on images. There was no doubting it, the image was of Elizabeth Báthory, the most infamous female serial killer of all time. Faye read about how she was accused of torturing and killing hundreds of girls between 1585 and 1610. The highest number of victims cited during Báthory's trial was 650. Stories alluded to her vampire-like tendencies, most famously the tale that she bathed in the blood of virgins to retain her youth. According to all testimonies at her trial, Báthory's initial victims were the adolescent daughters of local peasants, many of whom were lured by offers of well-paid work as maidservants in the castle. Later, she is said to have killed daughters of the lesser gentry, abductions were also reported. The atrocities described most consistently included severe beatings, burning or mutilation of hands, biting the flesh off the faces, arms and other body parts, freezing or starving to death. The use of needles was also mentioned by the collaborators in court. She was quite something, thought Faye. But why did Amanda spend what must have been days, if not weeks, working on embroidering this woman, Faye hadn't the faintest idea.

Next, she took out the embroidered image of the man eating his own arms and Googled "painting of man eating his own arm". While the computer did its thing, she went to the kitchen and opened the fridge, she looked inside but there was no wine or beer so she took out a small can of tonic water. From the press over the sink, she took down a bottle of Bombay gin and poured a generous measure into a glass, cut a slice of lemon and took the ice tray from the freezer section of the fridge - the ice was rock hard, she had to pound it a few times on the counter top to get the cubes to pop out, every time she did this she swore she would buy a new, better ice tray which wasn't so bloody resistant. With the ice in the glass, she popped open the can of tonic water and poured it over the gin, lemon and ice, gave it a bit of a stir by swishing it around in the glass. As she went back to the table she took a sip, it tasted good.

On the screen were lots of results but it didn't take long to find the image she was looking for, it was a painting by a fourteenth century Italian painter, Bartolomeo Passarotti, called *Magiatore De Braccio*. She looked at other images of his work and they were all a bit strange with a freakish tone to them. Faye liked them because they depicted the hedonistic side of human beings. Amanda had done an excellent job with the image, it was near perfect in its replication, the man, who looked like a peasant wearing a red hat was holding up his right arm with his left arm and was eating a chunk of flesh he had taken from his right arm. Again, Faye hadn't the foggiest idea why Amanda chose this image.

The pieces which Faye thought definitely looked like Dali turned out to be so, after scrolling through images she found the two she was looking for, one was called *Autumnal Cannibalism* and the second was called *Soft Construction with Boiled Beans*, only Dali could call a painting that thought Faye.

Faye had to read what they were about because she couldn't quite make out what was going on, they were typically Dali, all fantasy and surrealism.

*Autumnal Cannibalism* depicts two interconnected figures within a scenic landscape, delicately devouring one another with disconcerting civility. The setting for the scene is the plain of Empordà, the region of Catalonia where the artist was born. Although the characters lack any distinguishable facial features, they are nonetheless sexualised, the male, who can be made out is on the right, dips his spoon into his partner's right breast, while the woman, on the left, gracefully reaches around her companion to cut the flesh that is actually her own elongated left breast thrown over the male's shoulder. *Soft Construction with Boiled Beans*, an allegorical response to the Spanish Civil War of 1936-1939, is a garish and gruesome depiction of a body destroying itself. In this painting Dali predicts the violence, anxiety, and doom many Spaniards felt during Franco's later rule. As Faye studied both paintings closer, she could begin to see what was going on more clearly, she thought them provocative and seductive, especially *Autumnal Cannibalism*.

Faye thought about these two entwined figures, he delicately eating his lover and she gracefully eating herself, there was something exquisite in this act, it belied what was actually happening and instead gave a sense of refinement. Faye felt captivated by the painting and thinking about its actuality, she felt the allure of it, she wasn't sure why and that unsteadied her a bit.

Dali, she thought, must have had a fascinating view of the world, she didn't know a lot about him except that he was called after his dead brother who had died nine months prior to Dali's birth. When he was five, Dalí was taken to his brother's grave and told by his parents that he was his brother's reincarnation, a concept which he came to believe. That would have had to have an interesting effect on your development.

The last tapestry was more difficult to find, it pictured a pile of naked and semi naked people on a raft which appears to have been just washed ashore. The bodies were lying on top of one another, and some appeared to be dead. Faye trawled through a ton of images and put many different combinations in the search bar, eventually she found it. Once again, Amanda had done a stellar job, the painting was called *The Raft of the Medusa* 1818–1819 by the French Romantic painter Théodore Géricault whose work has become an icon of French Romanticism. It depicts a moment from the aftermath of the wreck of the French naval frigate *Méduse*, which ran aground off the coast of todays Mauritania. At least 147 people were set adrift on a hurriedly constructed raft, all but 15 died in the 13 days before their rescue, and those who survived endured starvation and dehydration and practised cannibalism. Although the *Méduse* was carrying 400 people, including 160 crew, there was space for only about 250 in the boat. The remainder of the ship's complement—at least 147 men and one woman—were piled onto a hastily-built raft that partially submerged once it was loaded. Seventeen crew members opted to stay aboard the grounded *Méduse*. The captain and crew aboard the other boats intended to tow the raft, but after only a few miles the raft was turned loose. For sustenance, the crew of the raft had only a bag of ship's biscuits (consumed on the first day), two casks of water (lost overboard during fighting) and a few cases of wine. According to one critic, the raft carried the survivors "to the frontiers of human experience. Crazed, parched and starved, they slaughtered mutineers, ate their dead companions and killed the weakest." After 13 days, on 17$^{th}$ July 1816, the raft was rescued by the *Argus* by chance—no particular search effort was made by the French for the raft. By this time only 15 men were still alive; the others had been killed or thrown overboard by their comrades, died of starvation, or thrown themselves into the sea in despair. The incident became a huge public embarrassment for the French monarchy, and an international scandal, but it fascinated the young artist, and before he began work on the final painting, he undertook extensive research and produced many preparatory sketches. He interviewed two of the survivors and constructed a detailed scale model of the raft. His efforts took him to morgues and hospitals where he could view, first-hand, the colour and texture of the flesh of the dying and dead. As the artist had anticipated, the painting proved highly controversial. At its first appearance in the 1819 Paris Salon it attracted passionate praise and condemnation in equal measure. Unlike the Dalí, this painting depicted horror and suffering in a more straightforward way, there was nothing obscure about this painting, it clearly portrayed pain, terror and revulsion.

Faye placed all four of the tapestries out on the table and gazed over them, all illustrated some variation of eating human flesh, either one's own or another's. What did it mean, wondered Faye, she was unsure what Amanda's fascination with this subject was, she certainly had given no indication of any interest in this when she came to see her. What if she was trying to deliver a message, at that moment Faye felt nauseous, the rousing music of Carmina Burana's *O Fortona Fortune Plango Vultera* filled the room, contributing to Faye's feelings of perturbation, her mind jumping to all sorts of conjectures, none of which were good. She picked up the books and flicked through the passementerie ones, nothing of any significance. The book of poetry had a bookmark on a poem by Xavier Fornenet called *Un Pauvre Houteux*, the last lines were underlined with a blue pen and hand-written in English was "*when you are hungry eat your own hand*". Faye found a translation of the poem on-line, it was about poverty and the shame of poverty and in the end, he eats his own hand, she couldn't find any interpretation of the poem, but it seems the bit Amanda was interested in was eating your own hand. There was nothing else marked in the book and no other poem had been underlined or notated. The book on Greek myths had a similar bookmark which opened on the myth of Erysichthon. He once ordered all trees in the sacred grove of the goddess Demeter to be cut down. One huge oak was covered with votive wreaths, a symbol of every prayer Demeter had granted, and so men refused to cut it down. Erysichthon grabbed an axe and cut it down himself, killing a dryad nymph in the process, prompting the other nymphs to demand that Demeter punish Erysichton. Demter responded and punished Erysichthon by entreating Limos, the spirit of unrelenting and insatiable hunger, to place herself in his stomach. Food acted like fuel on a fire; the more he ate, the hungrier he got. Erysichthon sold all his possessions to buy food, but was still hungry. At last, he sold his own daughter Mestra into slavery. Mestra was freed from slavery by her former lover Poseidon, who gave her the gift of shapeshifting into any creature at will to escape her bonds. Erysichthon used her shape-shifting ability to sell her numerous times to make money to feed himself, but no amount of food was enough. Eventually, Erysichthon ate himself in hunger.

Bloody hell, Faye thought, this was all very bizarre and now, with the sound of Edvard Greg's *Peer Gynt Opus 46* building to a massive crescendo, she could feel her heart pounding in her chest, she felt like she was going to explode, she was suddenly roasting and caught for breath, she couldn't stop her mind from racing and jumping to all sort of scenarios, she knew she would have to force herself to settle or anxiety would grip her with its vice-like claws. She walked to the large window and opened the sash window to allow some cool air on her face, it was bracing but had the desired effect, she could feel herself calm. Leaving the window slightly open, she got her bag from the table and took out a packet of Marlboro Lights and a lighter, breaking her own rule she lit one up inside and went back to the window, inhaled deeply and blew the smoke out the window. She felt better, the band of tightness across her chest had eased, her thoughts had slowed, and she was able to think clearly again. Either Amanda had a fascination with autosarcophagy, which was weird in itself, or her intricate needle work had another purpose, perhaps to communicate something or to deal with something, but what? For the first time, Faye began to question if she really knew Amanda at all, maybe she did have another side which she kept hidden, maybe Oliver Blake was not the weirdo she thought he was, what if she had it the wrong way round. She felt exhausted and cursed aloud when she saw the time, it was ten to three and she had to get up early for Mary's wedding. Faye decided not to bother with ablutions and went straight to bed, she was going to look dire in the morning, she thought.

At the same time Daniel thought that the hotel room had lost all its shine and original appeal, its soullessness ridiculed him as he lay awake in bed unable to sleep despite the time, the vacuous room had become a constant reminder of his own feelings of emptiness and loneliness. Only when Faye was here with him did the room come alive but as soon as she left it began to mock him again, Faye was never going to stay here, she had her own home, a home she had not invited him to. He had hoped that she would have asked him to Mary's wedding, it would have helped to consolidate his position. He knew from Harry about the wedding but not only had Faye not invited him, she hadn't even told him about it. This only added to his fear that she was still very wary of him, not that he could really blame her, but he hoped nonetheless that she might be coming round. He had gotten another call from Uziel today and as usual he was not happy with Daniel, he wanted all aspects of the job in Dublin wrapped up quicker than he originally agreed. Daniel had no doubt that this was down to Liat, she without doubt was getting on to Uziel about him being in

Dublin. But Uziel was caught, he had to allow Daniel to remain until the job was done and he had every intention of staying the duration. The thought of ever having to leave Faye again was heart breaking for him, he could feel the pressure of tears behind his eyes knowing the inevitability of his return to London. He let the tears flow.

# twenty

The wolf whistle was long and drawn out.

Dressed for the wedding in a J Mendel's deep claret chiffon gown which was exquisitely draped and gathered with a thigh-high split and strappy sandals, Faye was coming down the stairs from her flat when she was met with the notes of Jason's primitive approval.

'Looking sharp, where you off to?' Jason comments, no matter how innocent sounding, always seemed to be laced with roguishness.

'My sister's wedding,' answered Faye, it was impossible not to be charmed by him and she couldn't help but be pleased by his approval.

'I have a tux and could be ready in a jiffy,' he said playfully.

'Thanks, but I have a date.'

'Lucky bugger, give me a call later if you need help getting out of that dress, it looks complicated,' he managed to sound genuinely concerned.

Faye laughed.

'Thanks Jason, I'll keep that in mind, see you later.'

'Enjoy,' and with that he was out the door.

Faye knocked on Mrs C's door, she had told Faye she could borrow one of her fur coats for the wedding. After a moment, the door opened.

'Oh, my goodness dear you look wonderful, what a splendid dress and the colour is simply divine on you.'

'Thank you.'

'Now let me get you that coat, you decided on the beaver, didn't you?'

'Yes, I think so, the brown one that looks almost stripped.'

'Yes, that is the beaver, here it is my dear,' said Mrs Clayworth-Howsham as she returned with a large fur coat and handed it to Faye.

Faye slipped into the coat and despite the initial chill of the silk lining against her skin she could feel the warmth of the coat, she ran her hands over the fur and hugged herself relishing the sheer sumptuousness.

'It feels so lovely, I promise to take great care of it,' she said.

'I'm sure you will, The Colonel bought me that coat for our twentieth wedding anniversary, I wore it to all the operas and to the Berlin Philharmonic on a visit there one Christmas, now when was that again....' Mrs Clayworth-Howsham thought for a moment and then said '...doesn't matter I am getting a bit forgetful, I once was able to recall all important dates but now.... ah never mind, I am delaying you with my ramblings.' Mrs Clayworth-Howsham had told Faye this story when she was picking out the coat, but she couldn't remind her of that, it would only make Mrs C feel bad.

'Not at all, I love to hear about all you got up to with The Colonel, but I do have to run, Harry is outside, thank you for the coat, it's so kind of you.'

'Not at all, now enjoy yourself.'

'I will, thank you.'

Faye was glad of the fur when she opened the front door, it was bitterly cold. As she took the steps down, she could feel the cold coming up through the light sole of her sandals, as beautiful and expensive as they were, they were no defence against this damp. Harry had texted her to say he was outside, she was glad to be able to jump straight into the taxi.

'Howya, nice fur,' said Harry as Faye got in.

'Yes, it's Mrs C's, a present from The Colonel, how come I never got presents like this from husbands or lovers?' asked Faye.

'Mrs C obviously has that rare and elusive quality which enchants men and makes them bend to her every whim,' answered Harry.

'I know, some women just have it, I wish I did, life might be a bit easier.'

'Oh, I think you have it in spades, but you don't know how to use it.' Despite their years of friendship Harry had always found Faye immensely attractive and he was never happier than on these occasions playing the role of her escort to fancy occasions where she didn't want to bring a stranger.

'What does that mean, I "don't know how to use it"?' asked Faye indignantly.

'I suppose you were never much of a flirter, were you?'

'I suppose not, I think I ought to start cultivating the art and go after a well-heeled man, this love business isn't all it's cracked up to be.'

'Oh, don't give up on love just yet, you never know what's in store for you, maybe even today?' Harry knew she was alluding to Dan, but he didn't really want to talk about him, so he deliberately steered the conversation. He had recently been talking to Dan and had quite innocently told him about today and the wedding, it was clear Faye had not told him and now Harry didn't want to have to tell Faye about his big mouth.

'Yeah, you never know, mind you, what do you think are the chances of either of us meeting someone at this wedding?'

'We always have each other,' and Harry meant this sincerely.

'Oh, here we are, Harry this is going to be an ordeal...'

'I know - I can't wait, I'm really looking forward to having a nice chat with Greg and the Yankee girlfriend...'

'God I'd forgotten about him, he is going to be unbearable.'

Harry paid for the taxi, and they got out at the front entrance, because of the cold there was no one hanging about, not even the diehard smokers. Harry held onto Faye as they went into the foyer and just as they began to see the wedding party, Faye turned to Harry and looked straight into his eyes.

'Promise me you won't desert me for some young one.' Harry felt a tug in the base of his stomach, there were times when Faye appeared so vulnerable that his heart would crack and right now was one of those times. He wanted to wrap her up and whisk her off somewhere else, but he wasn't the whisking off type, and she wasn't the type to be whisked off.

'I promise,' he answered just as a gorgeous young waitress came over to take their coats, her legs went on forever and he almost forgot his promise.

'May I take your coats?' she asked in an Eastern European accent.

Harry was one of those who was thrilled with the influx during the boom of the thousands of migrant workers from Eastern Europe because it meant really beautiful women now walked among the humble Irish male, who it has to be said are not the most pulchritudinous of the species.

'Yes please Sophie,' answered Harry as he removed his coat and handed it to Sophie, it said it on her name badge, he then turned to

Faye who was smiling at him in a way that said, "give it a rest". He smiled back at her as he helped her off with her coat.

'Thanks Harry, oh there's Ina.'

Harry instantly forgot about Sophie when he watched Faye walk towards Ina, she looked amazing, he thought.

'Hi Faye, you look gorgeous, that dress is lovely on you,' said Ina.

'Thanks Ina, you're looking great yourself,' said Faye as she turned towards Bosco and gave him a kiss on the cheek.

'Ina, you should doll yourself up more often it really suits you, she looks great doesn't she Bosco?' said Harry.

'Yes, she looks great,' said Bosco slightly uncomfortable, he was not the outwardly demonstrative type.

'Hi Har, looking sharp in the tux,' said Ina to Harry.

'I try,' answered Harry puffing out his chest. 'Howya Bosco?' he put out his hand and the two men shook hands.

'Now let's form a plan, you're not to bugger off and leave me with my family, once the formalities are over, we'll all sit together, no wandering off and not coming back okay,' said Faye.

'Faye relax, we're not going to leave you, you know that, anyway I didn't get all dressed up to go home, we're here for the night.' Ina knew Faye was always a bit wobbly at family dos, she hated them and with good reason, Bunty usually ended up humiliating her in some shape or form.

'Yes sweetie, we're not going to miss any of this, now let's get some drinks, I saw a lovely lady swanning around with a tray of bubbly a minute ago,' said Harry as he scanned the now growing crowd for the lovely lady with drinks.

'Have you your speech done?' asked Ina.

Mary had asked Faye to say a few words, there was only going to be Faye and Denise's sister speaking as Mary could not bear to think about what her father might say and so they decided to keep it to two. Denise's father was a bit put out but took it with good grace.

'Yes, I think it's actually quite nice really, short and sweet, you won't have to suffer me for long,' answered Faye.

'Good,' said Harry 'There's nothing as bad as long boring wedding speeches.'

Just then there was the ringing of a bell which signalled it was time to take your seats. It was going to be a Humanistic ceremony and the main function room was done to perfection. The chairs were arranged in a large semicircle garlanded with ivy and white roses, as were the tables, the centre pieces very spectacular, tall vases of white peonies with ivy draping down and scented candles everywhere. At the top of the room in the opening of the circle was a small platform and eight chairs, two for the brides, four for the parents (a concession to Bunty) and two for the (kind of) bridesmaids. No one had seen the brides yet, they had decided to spend the morning together in their room, each one helping the other prepare for matrimony. Just as they began to take their seats Faye spotted her brother with her parents and another woman whom Faye presumed to be Greg's girlfriend. Wanting to avoid them for as long as possible Faye doubled back out of the room making for the loos.

'Where are you going?' asked Harry.

'Avoiding the loonies, see you after the ceremony,' answered Faye as she darted off.

She ducked into the loos and looked in the mirror, not too bad, better than she hoped for the night before, she had decided not to say anything to Ina about Amanda's parcel until after the wedding, but she couldn't keep it from her mind. After a few minutes she left the bathrooms and, on her way, back to the function room was completely taken aback when she caught sight of Oliver Blake, he had not seen her and she was intent on keeping it that way, the last thing she wanted was to bump into him, she ducked back into the loos again. Her heart was pounding, what were the chances of him being here today, she wondered, but this was definitely a place he would frequent. He was probably here for some business meeting, she was beginning to fret, if she stayed here much longer she would miss Mary and Denise coming in, she had to chance going out again. Slowly she opened the door and took a quick look out, the coast was clear, keeping her eyes straight ahead in the direction of the function room she walked quickly and got to the room without event. When she went in it was full and everyone was in their seat, Bunty caught her eye and gave her a disapproving look which said get into your seat fast, Faye chose to ignore her gaze.

She was only just in her seat when the string quartet started to play Pachelbel's Canon in D Major to herald the arrival of the brides. Mary and Denise entered the room holding each other's hands and looking exultant, both were wearing long white dresses, each one the perfect choice. Faye looked at Mary and was filled with love and admiration for her, she could feel tears welling up in her eyes, they looked so happy and at ease with each other. Faye could not remember feeling that way on her own wedding day. They came to the centre of the platform, and both read pieces they had written in honour of the other, it was all so beautiful and poignant. Then the civil celebrant, a large busted, heavily tattooed woman with cropped blue hair who looked like she was some sort of shaman, began to read from a large red covered book of love poems and sonnets. Her voice boomed across the room commanding to be heard, she managed to make each love poem sound as if it was written especially for Mary and Denise, everyone was transfixed. Denise's sister Pauline spoke next, the shaman was a hard act to follow, but she did well.

As she was finishing speaking Oliver Blake slinked into the back of the room and stood waiting to catch Faye's eye, he didn't have to wait long she looked straight at him, and he delighted in the jolt his presence clearly gave her. That was all he wanted to do, he smiled at her and quietly left.

Faye was reeling from the sight, what was he playing at, this was no coincidence she felt sure of that, she was completely absorbed in thought when she suddenly felt Mary gently nudge her arm.

'It's time for your bit sweetie,' she whispered to Faye.

Faye stood up and for a moment was a bit disorientated, she looked out at the crowd and instantly and completely lost her nerve, she couldn't think of a thing to say and even if she could her mouth felt like sandpaper, no sound would come, she had her speech written out in her bag but she hadn't the wherewithal at that moment to retrieve the sheet of paper. Paralyzed and feeling all eyes on her, pleading with her to get it together and say something, but she couldn't oblige. She knew what she must look like and knew the embarrassment everyone was feeling on her behalf, it seemed like an eternity and in mortification terms it was.

Mary was asking her quietly if she was alright, but Faye couldn't answer, couldn't speak and couldn't flee, if only she could faint it would be a welcome escape but the amount of adrenaline shooting through her could awaken the dead, there was no chance of fainting. Then she heard it.

'Tell that silly girl to sit down, she can't do anything right.' Bunty was whispering out loud, audible to the entire room.

'It's okay Faye, come sit down,' Mary's voice was so sympathetic Faye thought she might burst into tears, slowly she felt herself bend her knees enough to land on the chair.

The shaman came to the rescue, she hopped to her feet and bellowed to the entire room...

'And now to the exchange of the vows, we ask Mary and Denise to stand and share with us the vows they have written for this most special of occasions.'

As Mary stood, she slipped her hand out of Faye's and Faye suddenly came back to life, she looked out to the crowd and found Harry and Ina's eyes, they clearly said "Oh Fuck!". She had never had a problem with speaking in front of people, she forced herself to smile and squeeze back the tears which were about to leak out, she wasn't sure which was worse, the sight of Oliver Blake or her mother's caustic tongue. Oliver Blake's presence had flummoxed her, he was playing with her, but how did he get that moment so right, how could he have possibly known that she was speaking at that moment, she racked her brain to remember if she had mentioned it in earshot of the bug, she may have, but she wasn't sure. What a mess she thought, and Bunty could curl up and die for all she cared about her at that moment.

'.... I promise to love you till my last breath leaves my body,' Denise was gazing into Mary's eyes as she finished her vows.

'You may kiss the brides!!', whooped the shaman.

Everyone shot to their feet and clapped the happy couple, Faye stood and was glad of the movement, she had completely missed the vows.

The crowd was on the move now, kissing and congratulating the brides.

'What happened to you up there, you looked like you saw a ghost,' Ina was beside Faye whispering urgently to her.

'Worse than a ghost, Oliver Blake waltzed in cool as you like to the back of the room grinning up at me like a crackpot.'

'Oliver Blake, what the hell is he doing here?'

'Messing with my head that's what. I saw him earlier out in the lobby on my way back from the loo and just thought he was here for some meeting or something, but then in he comes, that's no bloody coincidence, is it?'

'No not really....'

'Faye, you poor darling what happened, I wanted to go up and save you but that might have made things worse. I bet you wanted the ground to open up and swallow you.' Harry had arrived to do the autopsy on the catastrophic episode.

'Yeah, Harry I did,' answered Faye.

'What happened?' asked Harry.

'A patient came into the back of the room...'

'Remember the one who caught her looking out the window at him,' added Ina.

'Oh yeah, him, does he have the hots for you or something?' asked Harry.

'No....'

'Great speech Fade, one for the annuals.' Gregory had made his way over to Faye to gloat.

'Thanks Grosser, nice to know I can always count on you for support.' Faye had always hated being called Fade by Gregory it was the short version of *Fade Away Faye*, and it felt stupid calling him Grosser at this hour of her life but there was something about being around him that always brought out the sullen teenager in her.

'Marilyn should have asked me to speak, at least I would have managed to say something...'

'Hi Greg, nice to see you again,' interjected Harry with his hand outstretched to Gregory.

'It's Gregory. You still in the same job Stuart? And not waiting for an answer he continued…

'As you probably know I'm with NASA now, can't really discuss the nature of my work, Homeland Security etc, keeping the world safe for all of you. Of course, I've been approached by Harvard to take up a position there, but I'm not quite ready to leave the rough and tumble, high octane life for academia just yet. Hate to say it but Ireland is parochial and a dead-end career wise, not enough brain power, small population excreta, no need to tell you what you already know,' droned Gregory.

Such a dick head thought everyone except Greg.

'He is so sought after,' came a high pitch, highly intonated voice from behind Greg.

'Oh let me do the introductions, this is Camilla Ponsonby-Smythe III, Camilla went to Harvard and is currently the CEO of Ponsonby-Smyth Incorporated, she comes from one of the oldest families in New England, her mother does the most extraordinary charitable works, hosts one of the most popular and sought after New Year's Eve Charitable Balls in the entire country, her father is Hank Ponsonby-Smyth IV, you most probably have heard of him, an outstanding industrialist, employs over four thousand people. Camilla, this is my sister Faye, may I apologise on her behalf for making such a spectacle of herself during the speeches, luckily, I had forewarned Camilla of your peculiar manner, Fade, but nonetheless, shame on you.' Like his mother Gregory never stopped for a breath during his soliloquies.

'Oh Gregory, don't be so hard on your sister, these things can happen to some people, it is not to be ridiculed but sympathised with,' said Camilla Ponsonby-Smythe III as she put her hand out to Faye with the most saccharine of smiles. She had a fish handshake, Faye wanted to wipe her hand on her dress but restrained.

Camilla Ponsonby-Smythe III had WASP written all over her, she was a woman used to the very best of things in life, while her looks were average, she made the very best of them, her hair was sleek and black and looked as if she had just had it done, it was that big American hair, all shiny and bouncy. She was coat rail thin, probably only had solid food at the weekends and kale juice the rest of the time, her make-up was perfect, and she had clear blue eyes which when she smiled did not light up. She had met Greg at a friend's party and surprised herself by liking him, he was, despite his provenance, her match. He was ambitious, had a superior sense of himself which many people are too weak to admit to, intelligent, ruthless and good looking to boot. It didn't matter that he was not from money, he was from another country so no one of consequence would know, he hardly required any grooming for her life, he had already done such a good job himself and importantly, she would always have the upper hand, because life had taught her that those with the money always do.

Ignoring everyone else Camilla turned to Gregory.

'We really ought to circulate.' And she began to move away.

'Yes dear,' answered Gregory and before pushing off said to Faye, 'At least one of us in this family will make a good marriage, Camilla and I will marry next year, in New York of course, but don't feel you have to come, you'd be out of your depth anyway, it would be a very civilized affair, with a church of course, not like this shambolic state of affairs. Of course my parents will not come because of my mother's fear of flying and Marilyn will be no doubt too busy, but no matter. I will be marrying into one of the most powerful families in America, of course it was always my destiny to triumph, looks like I got the quota of good sense for the entire family.' And with those words he turned and pranced after his future wife.

'It's hard to know what to say really,' said Ina.

'I know, it's worse he's getting,' said Harry.

'I never met anyone like them before,' added Bosco sheepishly, not wanting to insult Faye.

'Aren't you lucky Bosco, imagine having the misfortune to have him as your brother, sanctimonious turnip.'

'Mind you he's always good for a laugh and if ever there was a perfect match it's those two, she's a tight faced pull through for a rifle, and oh so very pleased with herself,' said Harry taking off her accent.

They all laughed.

'I can't believe he brought her with him to the wedding,' said Ina.

'Oh, I'm sure it was to vet us, a little reconnaissance to see if anyone of us you be fit to attend their wedding,' answered Faye

'Clearly none of you measured up,' laughed Harry.

'It's going to be a long day,' said Faye.

'There's only one answer,' said Ina, 'Drink'.

'Good plan, let's get started, now where is that lovely young thing...' said Harry as he wandered off into the crowd for the leggy waitress.

Faye had almost forgotten about the earlier embarrassment, the embarrassment of having Greg as a brother fairly well trumped all other embarrassments, until she saw Bunty making a bee line for her, she grabbed Ina's arm and said, 'Don't go anywhere Bunty's on the war path, may as well get it over and done with.'

'Okay so,' answered Ina.

'Hello Mrs Munroe, I must say you are looking particularly well, you've lost a load of weight and that colour does wonders for you, doesn't it Bosco?' Ina turned to poor Bosco and saw the colour drain from his face.

'Ah, eem, yeah, really suits you, ah yeah, lovely,' and that was all he could manage.

Bunty lapped up the compliments, before moving in for the kill.

'You made a show of us up there today, bad enough that your sister broke with proper protocol and had *you* instead of your father to speak, and look where that got her, Gregory agrees completely, if Marilyn really wanted to be different why not choose Gregory, he would have been the perfect choice, can't you do anything right...'

'Ah now that's a bit rough Mrs Monroe, I mean poor auld Faye didn't want that to happen to her, sure you didn't Faye?' Faye and Ina were staring at Bosco in awe, it was completely out of character for him to contradict anyone, yet alone the formidable Bunty Monroe.

'No Bosco you're right, of course I didn't want that to happen,' Faye smiled at Bosco, which probably emboldened him because he went on to say ...

'Now I think that should be the end of it and we all should enjoy the day instead of upsetting people.'

'Well, I was only pointing out that public speaking is not one of her strong points and she is best to avoid it,' said Bunty indignantly to Bosco and making sure she had the last word followed this with...

'Now I must find Gregory and his wonderful Camilla, at least they know the proper decorum for a wedding.' And with that she about turned and hightailed off in search of her super-son.

'Thank you, Bosco, that was so sweet of you. I feel like a damsel rescued from distress,' smiled Faye.

'My hero,' said Ina as she reached up to kiss him on the cheek.

Wherever the earlier valour had come from it had now vanished and his cheeks turned bright red, but the smile revealed his pleasure in this rare form of attention.

Harry arrived back.

'Look what I managed to get my hands on!' he beamed holding up two bottles of Moêt.

'Well done, Har, now let's find somewhere to sit, these shoes are killing me,' said Ina.

Faye decided Oliver Blake could wait until tomorrow.

# twenty-one

When Oliver Blake left the hotel, he was sure that he had rattled Faye enough for the moment, while he enjoyed his meetings with her, more so than he had anticipated – he found her very interesting, there was no doubting her intelligence, she was clearly very clever and he suspected if one could be moved by such things, that she was a good shrink. She had surprised him a few times with her very sharp and accurate assessments, not that he would ever concede this to her, but time was running out, he couldn't indulge himself for much longer, things had to move on.

Arthur had told him about the wedding and had managed, in his own way, to find out the schedule of the day so Oliver was able to choose the most opportune moment to ambush her; it couldn't have worked out better he thought, nothing like a bit of public humiliation to balance things out.

From the hotel, he drove to his office and once he was seated behind his desk took out the file with the photocopies of the monthly bank transfers Arthur had given him not long after he hired him for this job. He then added the new photocopy Arthur secured for him, it had the exact same dates as the other two and only confirmed what he already knew, that Faye Munroe, Daniel Cohen and Harry Stuart were each paying €200 per month into the account for nearly eighteen years. The insignificance of the amount only made Oliver marvel more at the sheer stupidity of people and what they were willing to do unquestioningly, leaving themselves exposed to... well, to people like him. He cared little for what the Americans might call collateral damage, he would use whomever he needed to, to get to Faye Monroe and whose lives were destroyed or effected was of no consequence to him.

He carefully returned the file to its place and locked the drawer, as he always did. As he was leaving, he took a moment to stop at

Tina's desk and opened up her computer, typed in the password and did an internet history check, nothing out of place, he had once found that she booked a personal flight while at work, he disapproved of this and told her as much. He hadn't found any further indiscretions.

His phone buzzed, he took it out and saw from the screen that it was Uziel Nachman, what did he want now, he thought.

'Uziel, how are you?' Oliver asked the question in a way that left Uziel in no doubt that anything other than being fine would not be entertained.

'Well thank you Oliver, and you, I trust you are well.'

'Yes, very well indeed, now how can I help you?'

'I am sorry to bother you, but I was wondering when you might be finished with Cohen, not that I want him back, but you see... it's my daughter...well she is getting...shall we say, a little anxious and has mooted something about going over there. Of course I told her there was no need, but you know how headstrong women can sometimes get.' Uziel tried to lighten the tone by laughing at his own comment, it was met with stony silence.

Uziel feared few men, but Oliver Blake was one he did. But he was caught, he was beholden to him because Blake had gotten him out of a sticky situation with Her Majesty's Customs and Excise two years ago and now he had to pay his debt, he had no intention of reneging, but Liat was becoming very persistent, he thought if he had a time frame for Daniel's return, it would be easier to contain her. He already regretted his call.

'As agreed, he will be finished when I no longer require him. I would be very displeased should your daughter arrive in Dublin Uziel.'

'Yes of course Oliver, I can assure you she will not. And keep Daniel as long as you need. I know you are busy, so I won't hold you any longer.'

'Good to hear from you Uziel, now take care.'

Uziel wasn't sure whether Oliver meant the "take care" as a threat but it was best to assume it was.

'You too Oliver, goodbye.'

'Goodbye,' as Oliver hung up, he felt a surge of anger at the old man, could he not keep his daughter under control, Uziel had shown his weakness in making this call, he would need to get a reminder of his obligations, Oliver made a mental note to have Arthur make a call to Uziel.

His present anger combined with seeing Faye in distress had left him feeling very concupiscent, he hadn't planned or booked a visit to Silvia tonight, but his carnal desire was strong. He decided he would treat himself to a street girl, he liked these because they were so vulnerable, once you had them in the car there was virtually nothing you could not do to them and getting them in the car was never a problem.

He called Jim.

'Yes boss,' said Jim as he answered on the first ring.

'Can you bring round the BMW, I'm in the office, I'll meet you outside Dwyer's,' said Oliver.

'Right away boss,' and Jim hung up.

Oliver was a cautious man and kept a five-year-old BMW 3 Series, the kind of car jumped-up, gel-haired, cheap-suited wannabes drive, which was perfect for soliciting a street whore. It was not registered in his name, and he only ever used it on these kinds of occasions. He got into his Bentley and drove the short drive to Dwyer's, he spotted Jim immediately, Oliver pulled up beside him and hopped out at the same time as Jim did.

'Meet me outside Tara street station at 10pm,' said Oliver.

'Yes boss,' answered Jim and got into the Bentley.

Try as he may, Oliver had not succeeded in getting Jim to refer to him as Sir and not boss, but in this case, he did not labour it as Jim was too valuable to get upset about these things, Oliver prided himself on knowing what he should let go of and when not to.

The inside of the Beemer was as he had directed Jim to keep it, it had empty cans of Monster and discarded red top newspapers, crisp bags and other miscellaneous things such as a basketball, an empty CD case of *Top Ten Tips On Closing The Deal*, an old jumper. The car was a mess so the orange rope on the floor in the back did not look out of place, nor did the clothes hanger.

Taking out one of his phones, he made a call that lasted less than thirty seconds. After a quick stop he drove to the north of the city to a place he knew well, to a place many men knew well, a place once known as Monto, a place when in its heyday was reputed to have had the highest number of prostitutes in Europe - this was made all the more possible by the high number of British barracks in the city at that time, young men away from home had needs which called to be met. Today it still was home to the kind of street prostitutes which Oliver was fond of. He allowed himself the time to drive around by Abbey Street, Tabolt Street and Amiens Street to survey what was on offer. He noticed how young some of the girls were, too young for him, he didn't like immature bodies, he liked women fully developed, preferably with flesh on their bones, not too much but they had to have a softness around their bones, no sharp edges.

As he drove down Tabolt Street he saw her, yes, she would do very nicely, he thought, most likely in her early thirties, well built, almost athletic but not quite. Her hair was long and dark, but it was her breasts which caught his eye, they were pushed high up probably with the aid of some kind of bra, but they had a milky texture to them which excited him. He slowed down completely and let the window down, she was on the driver's side so he didn't have to lean over the passenger's seat, he would never do this, always turning the car in the right direction if needs be. He caught her attention, and she sauntered over in those slut shoes, Oliver always thought they were a ridiculous choice of foot attire for this most precarious of professions as there was no way that a whore could ever run away from a punter in them. He liked the way she moved. She leaned in the window.

'What would you like luv?' although the "luv" was clearly Dublin her accent was Russian, good thought Oliver.

'Some fun.'

'What kind of fun?'

'The fun kind.'

'And what is that luv?'

'Get in and find out.'

She hesitated for a split second and then got in.

'Mind if we take a short drive, somewhere more discreet?'

'Not too far, I am on the clock you know.'

Oliver handed her three fifty-euro bills, you could get a blow job for thirty and full sex for eighty, so this was more than enough to keep her sweet, for now.

'That should cover it,' said Oliver.

'Oh sure,' and she quickly folded the money and slipped it into her shoe.

It didn't take Oliver long to get to where he wanted to go, Fir Tree Park, a park which had swings and see-saws but not a place you would bring your children, but a park, nonetheless. It had other uses and tonight Oliver would use the cover of the Fir Trees to have his kind of fun.

He found a quiet spot and pulled the car in under a tree, there was still some light, just enough.

'Take off your bottom clothes only,' he told her.

It didn't take long as she only had a skimpy skirt and knickers. She left the shoes on.

'And the shoes,' he said.

'I like them on,' she ventured.

'I want them off.'

She did as she was told. He reached over her and pulled a handle which allowed the back of the passenger's seat to collapse completely back, he had the seat customised to this spec; it meant that the back of the chair slipped neatly into place with the back seat which created a relatively flat bed.

'I want you to lie on your belly and with your arms above your head.'

'You like it doggie style, okay.'

'And no more speaking.' Oliver then reached back to get the orange rope from the back, it was approximately an inch thick, and he had already tied four knots in it. From the driver's side door, he took out two plastic cable ties, with the girl lying flat he pulled up a steel ring about the size of a teacup saucer from the back seat and with very quick movements he tied her wrists together with one cable tie and slipped the other around the ring and then around the first cable tie, he pulled them tight, too tight.

'Hey that hurts!' cried the girl.

'I told you not to speak,' and he prized open her mouth and stuffed a dirty rag from the seat into her mouth. She began to wriggle and twist, Oliver gently took her head and turned it towards him and whispered, 'You will only make it worse for yourself if you resist, the best thing for you is to relax and let me get to work and it will be over far quicker, but remember either way I will have my money's worth, so be clever and stop moving.' He could see the fear registering in her eyes and feel her relax under his touch, wise girl. Her fear was arousing, and his anticipation was growing. He gazed for a moment at her bare bottom and relished the smooth white plumpness, he did not have much room in the car to swing so he would have to keep the rope short, no matter, it would have the desired effect. He raised his arm and with a quick swift movement slapped her bottom with the rope making sure one of the knots made contact, the girl's screams were muffled, and he repeated this a number of times until he drew blood, then he stopped. Very gently, he ran his hand across the damaged tissue and could feel the heat of the stinging flesh, he brought his hand to his mouth and licked the blood from his palm, savouring the metallic taste. Slowly, he lowered his mouth to her and ran his tongue across a trickle of blood which was running down towards her thigh, he opened his mouth wide and bit hard into her buttocks. He wanted to bite harder, but he restrained himself, instead he bit into two other spots, he could hear the girl's whimpering, ignoring her, he bit into her three more times, the last bite drew flesh. He was finished. He took out a Stanley knife from the glove compartment and cut the cable ties. Before he removed the rag from her mouth, he spoke to her.

'I am going to take this out now, I know you are an intelligent woman and will not utter a sound, am I right?'

Terrified, she nodded, she thought she heard a sound from behind the back seat but wasn't sure, she wasn't going to take any chances.

'Good.'

He removed the rag and she gingerly got to her knees.

'It's better if you get out of the car here otherwise you are going to have to sit down and that might not be advisable just yet. Do you wish to get out here?'

'Yeah,' she whispered.

With her back to the front window-screen she managed to open the door and get out of the car, Oliver had picked up her skirt, knickers and shoes, making sure the money was still in the shoe and handed them to her, like a gentleman.

'Goodnight,' he said and reached over to close the door and drove away. Had he bothered to look in the rear-view mirror, he would have witnessed the woeful sight of the woman in tears struggling to get her clothes on while wincing in pain. Oliver Blake never looked back.

# twenty-two

I need my head examined thought Faye as she woke on Sunday morning, she cringed as she recalled the night before, she had bumped into Jason in the early hours on the stairs, he was coming home from a night on the town and between one thing and another, he was now beside her in her bed. She nudged his shoulder to wake him up, he slowly opened his eyes and with the innocence of a mind free from angst, immediately grinned.

'Ready for round four?' he said.

'No, ready for you to go, you need to get up now Jason,' said Faye.

'What, no breakfast and good morning kiss,' Jason laughed, but was now up and on his way to getting dressed.

Good thought Faye at least he got a hint, but she needn't have worried, Jason was only ever interested in night-time activities, the daylight was for other things, and they did not include Faye.

Faye was in the kitchen dressed in an oversized biscuit-coloured jumper which almost met her knees, her hair was down and tossed and the remnants of make-up from the day before gave her a risqué look. When Jason came to the door he smiled appreciatively.

'Looking good Faye, thanks for last night - ten out of ten, as usual. I'm off now, see you.' He blew her a kiss before turning and leaving.

'Bye Jason'.

The coffee was ready, and she poured herself a cup. She groaned out loud as she recalled the day before and the spectacle she had made of herself at the speeches. Together, with Harry, Ina, and Bosco Faye had spent the evening drinking until they were all completely potted. It was like a dream to her now, but she had a flash of Harry trying to kiss her, surely not, she thought.

She walked with her cup in her bare feet to the living room and sat on the couch, as she sipped piping hot coffee, her eyes came to rest on the box sent from India. She took out the tapestries again, Ina was coming over later to have a look, Faye had only told her that the package arrived and had discussed it no further.

At four that afternoon Ina arrived.

'You look worse for wear,' she said as she greeted Faye at the door.

'I know, how are you?' asked Faye.

'As you can imagine, my head would be pounding it I hadn't swallowed four Panadol, what time did we finish up?'

'It was about half four,' Faye decided not to tell her about Jason, she had her quota of humiliation for now.

'It was great in the end, wasn't it?'

'It was actually.'

'And what the hell was up with Harry trying to kiss you!'

'Oh God! I thought that was a dream,' they both laughed, 'I think he must have mistaken me for one of the girls he was eyeing up all night.'

'Maybe, but it didn't look like that...'

'Stop it, don't say another word, it's too weird, like your brother kissing you.'

'You mean like Greg...'

'Oh well not quite as completely and utterly repulsive as that... what an awful image, thanks Ina...' Faye scrunched up her eyes and shook her head, as if to rid herself of the image.

Ina roared laughing.

'Let's forget about that shall we. Do you want anything, coffee or something?'

'Do you have a coke?'

'Yep, they're in the fridge, help yourself.'

While Ina went to the kitchen, Faye turned the music down and hit the repeat button, she was listening to the sad tones of Mariza, the Portuguese Fado singer.

Ina returned to the living room drinking a can of coke.

'So, let's have a look at the stuff you got in the package.'

'I've laid it all out on the table, come here, just look at them for a moment.'

Faye stood back as Ina took a pair of rubber gloves from her pockets and slipped them on with the ease that comes with any habit,

Ina then set about examining Amanda's belongings. Faye had laid them all out on the table, so each item was visible. Faye watched Ina as she examined, scrutinized and absorbed the details of the embroidered pieces. She read the pieces from the books which were opened and flicked through the books on passementerie, she held the same pieces of passementerie in her hands with a reverence which Faye appreciated. After almost fifteen minutes she spoke in almost a whisper.

'Whatever this is, it's not good, what do you know about these images?'

Faye told Ina about researching the images, she offered no opinion just the facts, wanting Ina to make her own inferences.

'What do you think?' asked Ina.

'Well, there is certainly a theme here, a flesh-eating theme, either eating oneself or others, self-cannibalism or autosarcophagy and cannibalism.'

'I never heard of self-cannibalism,' said Ina.

'Well, in fact we're all kind of involved in auto-cannibalism, eating your nails, people pick at their scabs and eat them, even licking ourselves means we are eating our own skin, biting our lips or sucking the blood on a finger if we get a pin prick, all that kind of thing.'

'That's very off putting to think of it like that.'

'Yeah, but autosarcophagy as a practice is very rare and has been documented only a few number of times in psychological and psychiatric literature. Cannibalism is far more common. Most acts of cannibalism are, to a degree, motivated by a desire to express power or control over the victim. Cannibalism is the ultimate expression of dominance over another person. Aggressive cannibalism includes acts of cannibalism that are motivated by feelings of hostility or fear, creating an overriding need to exert power, revenge or control over the victim by consuming him or her.'

'That's quite an act of revenge. Do you remember the case of the German woman, Anna Zimmerman, in a fit of rage and the desire for revenge, she killed her boyfriend and cut up his body and froze him in bits. Then over time, she would defrost a bit of him, cook him and him to her two children.'

'Tasty. Aggressive cannibalism is probably the most common form of cannibalism and often overlaps with other types, especially spiritual, ritualistic and sexual cannibalism,' said Faye.

'What do you think is going on here?'

'I don't really know, spiritual and ritualistic cannibalism is usually associated with tribal power, it was used in an effort to scare off possible invading enemies and to get rid of captured enemies of war and slaves, that kind of thing. Apparently, a lot of cannibalistic tribes believed that eating your enemy meant you also consumed the spirit and skills of your victim.'

'Nice,' said Ina.

'I know'.

'What about sexual cannibalism?'

'It is considered to be a psychosexual disorder, usually involving a person sexualising the consumption of another person's flesh. A form of sexual sadism really and can be associated with necrophilia.'

'That's so freaky, what is so wrong with good plain sex?'

'It's not everyone's cup of tea, there's no accounting for what some people get their kicks from. There was a study done in America where they surveyed several groups of people, they were asked questions about cannibalism and sexual interests. The results found that people were more likely to eat someone that they were sexually attracted to than not, which suggests that there might be a significant sexual component to cannibalism.'

'"Your honour I only ate her because I loved her",' laughed Ina. 'What's the thinking behind why people do it?'

'The jury's out on that, theories range from the over nurturing of a child during the first few months of their life to sudden stress, but there's scant evidence to support most theories. One expert believes that a child, following weaning from the breast, experiences separation anxiety and fantasises about devouring their mother.'

'I know lots of people who would like to devour their mother,' deadpanned Ina.

'That's true,' laughed Faye, 'anyway the theory goes that a person who has experienced this separation may regress back to this stage in adulthood, possible due to a traumatic experience and this in turn leads that person to seek out the fulfilment they were denied by indulging in cannibalism.'

'That's a bit extreme wouldn't you say, just because your mother took the boob away.'

'Ina, never underestimate the ingenuity of the human mind to deal with intolerable situations, people go to extremes to make the intolerable tolerable.'

'More like deranged maniacs.'

'One man's derangement is another man's ingenuity. Maybe I'm completely wrong about all this, it could be that this is all symbolic and not meant to be taken literally, which probably makes more sense when you think about it, what are the chances we are dealing with cannibalism?'

'Yeah, you're probably right, so what does all this symbolise?'

'In myths and legends, it is most often attributed to evil characters or as extreme retribution for some wrong. Maybe Amanda feels wronged or feels she is being devoured or eaten alive by someone, or that her life is not what she would like it to be, and it is eating her alive... who knows, it could be anything, but what exactly, I do not know.'

'Well, it has to mean something because no one would go to this much trouble or time doing this unless it has some meaning,' offered Ina.

'I agree. Ina, a young man came to see me the other day and gave his next of kin as Amanda Blake and gave a phone number.'

'She's not the only Amanda Blake in the country.'

'I know, call me paranoid but he was a bit insistent on giving a next of kin name which is highly unusual.'

'Did you call the number?'

'No, I nearly did but didn't have time and since then I have been a bit iffy about it'.

'Do you have the number?'

'Yeah, it's in my diary,' Faye went to her bedroom to get her bag and pulled out the diary and found the number as she walked back to Ina. 'Here it is, will I write it down for you?'

'Yes, I will run it through the system.'

Faye wrote the number on a small ring binder notepad that lay on the table, tore the page out and handed it to Ina.

'Thanks Ina, you know the more I think about Oliver Blake having me followed the madder I get, the bloody cheek of him, I know you said he could be dangerous, but I can't simply let him do what he likes.'

'These kinds of men generally do whatever they like and remember he doesn't know that you know what he's up to.'

'That's true.'

'What are you going to do with all this?' asked Ina as she pointed to the table.

'I better hold on to it for a while, I can't really give it to Pamela, anyway Arthur Wilson would be on to me, he probably knows we visited her already.'

'You might be right, better keep her out of it for now. Anyway, they're not exactly the kind of thing you would like on general display.'

'I don't know, I think they're really lovely,' said Faye as she looked at Amanda's hand work.

'Yeah, you would.'

'Ina, I didn't use gloves when I handled them and I have given them quite a mauling, I never thought to put on gloves,' said Faye.

'I don't think it matters, just use gloves putting them away and it's better not to do too much handling of them.'

'You got an address for the private detective, didn't you?'

'Yeah and going by the swish area and size of the house he is on very good money, he lives in Bridemoor in a very nice, detached house, nothing too flash but a solid house, lives alone.'

'He's the key.'

'What do you mean?'

'Just think about, he's the one snooping and gathering the information for Blake, so it's reasonable to assume he has some idea of what's going on...'

'Maybe, maybe not, information can be useless unless you know how to use it, he might know nothing.

'Unlikely though.'

'Maybe, but that's beside the point, it's not as if you can waltz up to him and ask him what he's up to.'

'Two can play at his game, he's following me and eavesdropping on me when I've done nothing wrong, why should he be allowed to do that?' Faye could feel herself becoming angry.

'Faye, the rights and wrongs of things have got nothing to do with anything, you better than most know that nothing works that way, it's what you can get away with and the richer you are the more you get away with. I know you're miffed with all this but being right holds no sway, so don't be stupid.'

'I wasn't planning on being stupid.'

'Well, what were you planning?'

'Nothing really,' Faye lied 'but I can't just sit back and allow them to meddle in my life and what about Amanda, she's still missing ...'

'I know but remember she has not been officially reported missing, all I am saying is that we don't want to get all gung-ho, we have to think it through.'

'And meanwhile Amanda could be in mortal danger...'

'Relax, there's also the possibility that she's fine and just left her sleazy husband...'

Faye raised her eyebrows and gave Ina an incredulous look.

'Okay maybe she's not fine. But our hands are tied, we have no real evidence of any wrongdoing, so we have to be careful.'

'This is how people get away with murder.'

'Who are you telling, I have to deal with this kind of thing every day. If it's any consolation, people do make mistakes and that's how we catch them.'

'But it's usually after the fact, after they have killed someone or after they have committed a crime, I don't want to wait for that. If I don't act, I could be allowing something awful to be happening right now.'

'What do you propose doing, remember this isn't some movie where things just conveniently fall into place, this is real life?' Ina made no attempt to disguise her agitation.

'I know that,' said Faye calmly, there was no point getting annoyed with Ina she was only trying to help, 'we can still use the bug to our advantage, I just can't think of anything right now, which is bloody frustrating and probably not helped by the fact that we're tired and hungover. Why don't we sleep on it, something might pop onto our heads.'

'Yeah, you're right, where's the bug anyway?'

'In my car,' Faye had left it in the car the day before and was not planning on retrieving it just yet.

'Good, listen I better be going. Bosco is still at my place we're going to watch a film and get a takeaway later, you're welcome to join us if you like.'

'Thanks Ina, but I think I'll give it a miss tonight, I'm wacked and I've work tomorrow. I'm so glad Mary and Denise didn't have a two-day thing. Greg is such a plonker and his fiancée is not much better.'

'They're such twats, are they staying long?'

'God no! I'd say they can't wait to leave; Bunty is having a *special* dinner for them tonight, you can only imagine what that will be like.'

'And you weren't invited!'

'No, in fact she made it quite clear that she didn't want me barging in on their *special* time together, she said she can see me any day of the week but that she only rarely gets to see her beloved son and that she wanted to savour each moment of her time with him and basically didn't want me distracting from that.'

'You must be gutted,' laughed Ina.

'Devastated. Anyway, thanks for coming over, I better let you get back to the lovely Bosco, you two seem to be getting serious, are you?'

'I suppose, he's easy to be with and he understands the job so there's no sulking when I have to cancel or something like that.' Ina wasn't sentimental but she did like Bosco more than she cared to admit, even to herself.

'Well for what's it worth, I really like him.'

'Thanks, so do I.'

'Oh, Ina methinks you are falling in love,' teased Faye.

'Enough of this, I'm off.' Ina got up and put her coat on and started to move to the door.

'I'll walk you down,' said Faye.

'No need, stay where you are, I'll talk to you tomorrow, bye.'

'Bye Ina.'

Faye felt a pang of sadness as she watched the door close and her dearest friend leave on her way to a man who clearly adored her, there was jealousy there as well, jealous of the ordinariness of it and also the loveliness of it. Here she was with a family that didn't want her, nor she them, a man who said he loved her but is married to another woman, a patient who was having her followed and a penchant for Valium, she thought it was best not to contemplate on this too much. She needed to do something, anything to make her feel that she was alive and purposeful, she picked up the address of the detective Arthur Wilson and decided to take a trip. Why should she be the only one being followed?

It didn't take long to organise herself, leaving the door to her flat open she ran downstairs to the car and took the bug out of the glove compartment, the car was like an ice box, so she decided to turn it on to heat up. She ran back up to her flat, placed the bug on the table and put five CDs in her player and set them to play in rotation. There was easily six hours of playing time, she didn't think she would be that long but to be on the safe side she hit the replay button. It was so cold outside she waited a few minutes longer while the car warmed up and decided to make a pot of coffee to bring with her in a flask, she also popped a packet of custard cream biscuits into her bag and her camera for good measure. She was careful when leaving to close the door really quietly, she could hear the music outside the door. She hoped Arthur Wilson didn't like classical music.

It took her a good forty-five minutes to find the house, Ina had been right it was a very nice house in a very smart area, there was a car parked in the drive, she recognized it from the night in Island Point, so Mr Wilson was at home. Faye thought about going up and knocking on the door and inviting herself into his life as he had come into hers uninvited, but now was not the time. There were lights on in two of the downstairs windows and none on upstairs, as far as she could make out. Faye was parked on the opposite side of the road to his entrance but because the walls were low she got a good view into the front, it was not a big front but it was well kept, a neatly trimmed lawn, even for winter, with a five foot Portuguese laurel hedge on either side dividing the neighbours from him, the hedge on the road side was about three foot high and a well raked pebbled driveway.

Faye poured herself a cup of coffee from the flask and had a few biscuits, she was getting cold but didn't want to turn on the car, it would look strange. She was nicely sandwiched in between two other cars, the street was full of parked cars, so she didn't stick out. She waited. She wasn't entirely sure what she was waiting for, but anything was preferable to the torment of sitting alone in her flat. Danny had called three times, but she had not answered any of the calls, she knew he would want to meet tonight and while she wanted to see him, she had decided that she was too readily available to him and he was taking it for granted, which she supposed was only normal but nonetheless it was no harm to make herself scarce. She only hoped that she would maintain her resolve.

After about an hour and with her feet gone numb, Arthur Wilson appeared at the door, it was quarter past seven and dark, but Faye could see him clearly because he must have a sensor light, as the moment he stepped out into the porch the light came on. Faye got a good look at him, he was a big man probably six two, he looked fit, not all bulked up, but definitely toned, short dark hair, rugged features, his clothes fitted well, probably a left-over army habit, he had a bag with him, it looked like a computer case. He got into his car and reversed out on to the road, he went in the same direction Faye was pointed and she instantly decided to follow him. She stayed back, following the wisdom garnered from the great and the good of Hollywood films. She reminded herself that he was the professional at this and that he knew her car, her advantage, she told herself, was that he would not be expecting her to be following him.

He drove down to the East Well, along Alward Road over to Fairtown and into Donworth, it was easy enough to stay back with a car between them because it was Sunday, and the traffic was not too heavy. He slowed down on a street that had a few dingy looking shops, he came to a stop which slightly threw Faye, but luckily, she was able to stop and pull in where she was, it all looked innocent enough. Faye took out her camera and had a look through the long lens to see things a bit better. After a moment Arthur stepped out of his car with the ease of a fit person, a man who didn't have to make any concessions to an ache or a pain, he stood by his car, erect and at the ready, he didn't look like he would ever slouch, thought Faye. After less than a minute, a scrawny young man approached Arthur Wilson, Faye started to click on the camera, they spoke briefly before Arthur handed him what looked to be an envelope. The young man shoved it quickly into the pocket of his tatty tracksuit bottoms and then scuttled off. Arthur got back into his car and Faye could see him taking his phone out and making a call. She was reeling a bit from the surprise of recognising the young man, it was Eugene Klein, the silent patient who gave Amanda Blake as his next of kin. No wonder, thought Faye, he was so eager to give a name and number he was obviously paid to do just that by Oliver Blake, but for what purpose, he obviously wanted her to call the number. As she was running various scenarios in her head, she nearly missed that Arthur had started his car and was pulling out. She quickly put the camera down, turned the ignition and waited to pull out but Arthur did a u-turn, it was going to be hard to do the same immediately, so she waited until he was up the road a bit and turned, after a minute or two she could see him again. It looked as if he was going back the same way he came and sure enough he was returning home, when they arrived, he pulled into his driveway and Faye passed on, she thought about parking and waiting but it was now half past eight and she was exhausted, so she continued driving.

Danny had tried calling again, when she was almost in town she slowed down and pulled into the side path and called him back.

'Faye,' he answered after the first ring in an excited tone 'I was beginning to give up on you calling me back.'

He sounded so genuinely relieved that she called, Faye felt bad for ignoring his calls.

'I was busy, I told you that,' she said softly.

'I know it's just that I miss you, do you want to come over tonight?' he asked tentatively.

'I'm actually in town and I haven't eaten, have you?'

'No, do you want to get something now?'

'Yeah, do you fancy Japanese?'

'Perfect, how about Rocu, how far away are you?'

'I'm in my car so I have to find parking...'

'Why not come to the hotel and use the hotel car park, I have a space I don't use, and we can walk to the restaurant.'

'Okay, I should be there in less than ten minutes, I'll meet you in the lobby.'

'Great, see you in a bit.'

Faye thought how nice it was to drive in the city on a Sunday, getting to the hotel and parking was effortless. As she entered the lobby from the car park, she quickly caught sight of Danny, he had a face that held your gaze, it gave little and everything away at once, depending on what you wanted to see. When he registered her presence she could tell, not with her mind but from a felt sense, almost at a primordial level, the depth of his feelings for her, at least in the moment. He cupped her face with his hands and lifted her face up slightly before kissing her on the lips. Faye loved when he did this, at that moment she wanted to dissolve into him, to be consumed by him, like the confluence of two streams, she wanted to be him.

'God it's so good to see you, I've missed you,' said Danny.

'I've missed you too,' and she didn't just mean the past few days 'Let's just get room service.'

'That's fine by me.'

# twenty-three

It was Tuesday evening and Oliver Blake was due any minute for his session with Faye, she tried not to rehearse what she would say to him, she wanted to play it cool and let him lead, if he didn't bring up the wedding then she was not going to either.

The outer door opened and closed, he had arrived on time, to the minute.

Faye wished she had a secretary who would just usher him in, instead she had to go out and get him.

Try as she may, she could not quite manage a cheery voice, she was aware that her greeting sounded forced and sour.

'Is everything okay Dr Monroe, you sound a bit off?' Oliver knew he was in command and relished Faye's discomfort.

Here we go again thought Faye, she didn't feel like playing his game but then what alternative did she have?

'I am perfectly fine, but thank you for asking,' Faye thought she sounded a bit more cordial, but only a bit. She ushered him into the room and thought how well-groomed he always looked, always self-contained, she could do with a dose of his unflappableness.

'I've had an interesting week,' he said as soon as he sat down.

I bet you have, thought Faye.

'Really?' she said.

'Yes, I think my wife might want a reconciliation,' he thrilled at the shift in her demeanour, he had snared her, now he would wait.

Faye had not expected this, and all thoughts of the wedding evaporated, the possibility that Amanda was alive and well buoyed her, but she was also aware that it could just as easily be one of Oliver prevarications. She took a moment before replying.

'How do you feel about that?' resorting to what must be the most worn-out phrase in therapy.

'Honestly, I am not altogether surprised, it was only a matter of time really before she would come begging for forgiveness, the whole singleton life wasn't all it was cracked up to be I suspect. Now she wants to come home, she misses me and realises that she made a terrible mistake.'

'She said this?'

'You sound doubtful, do you not believe me?'

'No not at all but sometimes we interpret things the way we would like them to be, it's a natural bias.'

'Bias or not she wants me to take her back.'

'What are your thoughts on that?'

'I haven't decided yet, I wanted to discuss it with you first, see what you thought?'

Faye didn't believe this for a second, he was being derisive.

'Oliver, it has nothing to do with what I think, it's entirely your decision and you are clearly very able to make that decision for yourself.'

'I know that, but do you think it would be healthy for me, she did leave me, even though it was not entirely her decision.'

He never missed a chance to get that particular jab in.

'It's important to take into account that your wife decided to leave you for her own particular reasons and those reasons may still be present in your relationship were you to get back together, I think it would be important to explore these in any discussion on a reconciliation.'

Oliver's eyes never left Faye, gauging her every gesture and expression, he hoped that his intense gaze would fluster her.

'How do you suggest we do that?'

Faye felt goaded, as usual he was after something. She decided to change direction.

'Do you want to get back with you wife?'

'Perhaps.'

'Well perhaps you should decide that first.'

'That's why I'm here.'

'Have you met with her?'

'No, she phoned me.'

'Why not arrange to meet her, talk things out and see how you feel after that.'

'It's not easy to come back from the hurt. Forgiveness is not easy, and truth be told I don't put much stock in forgiveness, I see it as a way of letting people off and people don't learn from being let off - they learn from pain and suffering. I'm not sure I want to forgive her for leaving, I would like to make her pay for what she has done, revenge is a whole lot more appealing to me than forgiveness.'

Faye knew that what he said was what most people thought but haven't the gumption to admit it, people are always feigning forgiveness and covertly extracting their revenge, and this was nowhere truer than with a reconciling couple.

You can never underestimate the urge for revenge. Faye didn't doubt for a moment that Oliver Blake inclinations towards revenge would be impressive.

'When you say, "make her pay" what do you mean by that?' Faye's mind conjured up all sorts of things he might do and quite a few involved eating human flesh, she felt a bit fidgety but resisted the urge to shift in her chair.

'Believe me I can think of lots of things, I am limited only by my imagination,' Oliver smiled and raised his eyebrows, teasing her.

'It's one thing to imagine doing something, it's quite a big leap to actually doing it, we can't be put on trial for our thoughts, but we can for our actions.'

'Don't worry, I don't plan on doing anything illegal, but then revenge is rarely illegal, society allows us lots of scope for acceptable cruelty, all walks of life are full of it from the moment we are born - the too busy parents withholding their love or attention from their child, the teacher's public humiliation of a pupil in class, the power hungry school principal asserting their authority over children, the washed-up college lecturer envying the bright, fresh young students making him so bitter that he won't give praise or encouragement where it is due but instead ridicules and makes cutting hurtful jabs which cut to the core of the student. And on to the workplace and relationships and so on and on it goes... people are always acting out vengeful thoughts with the sole purpose of making another person's life miserable, all the while justifying their actions to themselves and others.'

He had a point, thought Faye.

'People waste such a lot of time convincing themselves that they were morally justified in their actions... why is it so difficult for people just to accept that they are not as pure as they like to think and that they get pleasure from hurting others. It's a fallacy and one I don't resort to in my life, I know I do things which are inimical to others, but I can handle that. I don't try to pretend I am something I'm not. That is why I can say to you that I want revenge for the hurt my wife caused me – it's a way of balancing the books if you like.'

Oliver's almost lackadaisical delivery gave nothing away, Faye wondered if he was in fact a psychopath, while he wasn't far off the mark in what he said, it was the way he said it - cold-bloodedly. The thought came to her that this man could easily slit her throat open, wipe the blade clean and saunter casually to his car never to give her a second thought. For the first time she thought she should leave Amanda to her own devices. Oliver Blake was a dangerous man. So far, apart from being followed, she was safe, best not to push her luck. And yet there was a part of her that couldn't let it go, she wasn't arrogant enough to call that part moral obligation or duty, she wasn't sure what it was, maybe it was old fashioned curiosity or stupidity, whatever it was it was tugging at her to keep going. It was a fault she knew - sometimes she just couldn't let go.

'Oliver, if you are so comfortable with being vengeful, I'm not entirely sure why you are here. You are correct in that many people have vengeful thoughts and some act on them, but a lot of people struggle with them, and I suppose they seek help in understanding and dealing with that part of themselves, but if you are happy with it there is no angst, no motivation for change.'

'Surely you realise Dr Monroe that the motivation for change is seldom from within but imposed by others on us, in every situation be it work, home, a social group you belong to, wherever people converge, someone will always elect themselves as the adjudicator of how others should behave, the rights and wrongs according to their, let's face it, usually limited experience, and others subjugate to this false dictator. They fear being pushed outside the pack which only emboldens the dictator even more, compounding his or her position as arbiter supreme. So while I may be comfortable with who I am, others may not be and sometimes that requires my attention.'

What the hell does that mean exactly, wondered Faye, probably knee capping someone who dared challenge the inimitable Oliver Blake to change, well probably not kneecapping, he was a bit too finessed for that, more likely to be some form of weird humiliation or bankrupting them...he was definitely capable of that. He was looking far too pleased with himself, she thought.

'Oliver, I know you have made it clear what you think of forgiveness, but while you might not forgive her, have you thought of not taking revenge?'

Faye didn't think that Oliver would be a big fan of that, few enough were, but she thought it might be worth enquiring.

He looked at her as if he was reading her thoughts and smiled at her as if to say, "you poor thing you haven't a clue".

'No.'

She waited. Nothing.

'Okay, do you want to think about it now?'

'No.'

'Do you plan on reconciling with you wife?'

'I am not sure if reconcile is the correct term to use, but yes I most likely will take her back.'

'And after that, what happens?'

'What happens is that she will have learnt her lesson and conduct herself as my wife ought to. No doubt you don't agree, you perhaps think we might benefit from...what do you call it...couples therapy.' He said this as if the very words caused an offensive taste in his mouth.

'No, I don't think that,' said Faye, as much as she would like to see if Amanda really was alright, she knew that Oliver Blake was not a man to concede or compromise, his self-interest made the needs or wishes of others redundant, he was intransigent.

Oliver had to admit to himself that he was surprised by her answer.

'Why is that?' he asked.

'Why do you think?' answered Faye.

'I have no idea,' he lied.

'It's just what I think, but you don't have to put any weight on it. We are nearly at the time, so we need to finish up. Now that your wife is back in your life, do you wish to continue seeing me?' Faye asked this to try to gauge his motives, she wanted him out of her life, but she didn't want to be clueless as to what was going on.

Oliver was not ready to give Faye up just yet...no he would continue to come, for now.

'I think it beneficial to return – I like to see things to fruition.'

'Okay, same time next week so?'

'Yes.'

He stood up with consummate ease and walked to the desk where he put the money. As he turned towards the door he paused and turned to Faye.

'I thought you looked very nice on Saturday, I hope I didn't put you off by appearing at the door, I saw you in the lobby and I'm afraid my curiosity got the better of me and I couldn't resist taking a peek.'

Faye was taken aback by the gentle way he said it, she almost believed him.

'Oh, it's no problem, it's a small town, hard to avoid occasionally bumping into a client.'

'I suppose you get to know so much about your clients and they get to know nothing about you, it's hard to resist a little inquisitiveness.'

Except in your case where you have taken your inquisitiveness to a freakishly invasive level, thought Faye.

'Yes indeed,' said Faye as she opened the door, she was anxious to end this chit chat it was creepily uncomfortable.

'I can see I upset you, you think it was wrong of me to intrude on you last Saturday'.

He sounded sincere.

'Not at all, it's fine really, don't give it another thought,' lied Faye.

'Okay, but I meant what I said, you did look very well,' he gave her a gamely smile.

Bloody hell this is so friggin' weird, thought Faye, he's acting like a completely different person, almost school boyish, and to her own annoyance, she was a bit chuffed by the compliment.

'Thank you,' she answered sounding slightly flustered, she couldn't look at him, so she turned towards the door which only contributed to the awkwardness of the situation. At last, he motioned towards leaving, but just before he left, he turned back to face Faye.

'You really ought to wear that colour more,' he grinned and walked away.

Faye's head was reeling. She was completely capsized by him.

She closed the door and sat down at her desk, she suddenly and without warning wanted to cry. Everything seemed chaotic, it felt as if she had control of nothing, it was suffocating, she overcame the desire to cry and instructed herself to pull herself together, this made her smile, the phrase was at once absurd and yet so apt.

She took her phone out and checked the messages, Harry had tried twice to contact her. Harry would be a good tonic. She rang him back.

'Hello sweetie,' said Harry.

'Hi Har, I missed your calls, I was working,'

'No bother, are you finished, do you want to get a bite to eat?'

'I'd love to, where do you want to go?'

'There's a new Mexican opened near work, how about that?'

'Perfect, I have a few work calls to make which won't take long, I could be there in forty minutes.'

'Grand, I'll meet you outside my office, it's only a minute from there.'

'Okay bye.'

Forty minutes later Harry was on the footpath outside his building having a cigarette while he waited for Faye. He had just taken his first drag when he saw Faye coming down the street. She looked lovely, so unaware of herself, he had always found her lovely ever since they were youngsters hanging out together, but she was with Danny, so he kept his feelings to himself, and when Danny left, she was still his for years and by that time he valued his friendship with her over any romantic dalliances.

'Are you back on them full time?' asked Faye as she nodded to the cigarettes.

'Not really... I don't know maybe,' he laughed.

'I'll join you and we can both be not-really-smoking together.'

Harry took the pack of cigarettes out of his smart jacket pocket and with the dexterity of a seasoned smoker had the cigarette out and lit in Faye's mouth in seconds.

Faye took a long deep drag on the cigarette with her eyes almost closed and slowly exhaled the smoke.

'I think I'll always be not-really-smoking,' she smiled up at Harry.

'Yeah, me too, come on,' he put his arm around her and pulled her into him and they began to walk towards the restaurant, it was dry but bitterly cold so standing around for any length of time was miserable.

'What are the reports on this place?'

'Well, the food is supposed to be really good, but the decor is a bit iffy.'

'I'm famished, it will have to be awful for me not to eat it.'

Harry had been right, it was literally only a minute from his office, they took a moment outside the door to finish off their cigarettes before going in.

They were hit by a welcome blast of heat and the food smelt really good. A very hip looking man came over and asked if it was to eat in or take away, once he established it was to eat in, he took Harry and Faye to a small table at the rear of the room. It wasn't a very big place, but they had certainly optimised on tables they were crammed in. It was about three quarters full, which one might suppose was not bad for a cold Tuesday night.

Between the Mexican music, the sizzle from the hot skillets arriving at tables and the cackle of people chattering it was noisy but in a good fun sort of way.

'God you wouldn't want to be too heavy coming in here,' said Harry as he squeezed himself in between the chair and table.

'I know it's a bit squishy, but it smells really good,' Faye was already looking at the menu.

'Will we have a margarita?' asked Harry.

'I don't see why not, might as well get into the spirit of it.'

'Now where is that hipster waiter?' said Harry as he looked around the room.

When Harry looked back at Faye she was crying.

'God what's wrong Faye?' asked Harry.

'Damn,' said Faye as she rubbed the tears away, 'I'm mortified, this is ridiculous.'

'It's not ridiculous, but what's going on, this is so unlike you.'

The hipster waiter had come to the table but seeing Faye crying he did an about turn and left.

'Call him back, let's order those margaritas,' her voice was shaky as she tried to sound light-hearted.

Harry did as he was asked, and they both ordered their food as well as the margaritas.

'So what's up?'

'Harry, I feel like a fecking idiot, blubbering like this in public, I'm just a bit...I don't know a bit all over the shop...'

'Is it your hormones maybe?' ventured Harry.

'No, it's not my hormones, why do men always think it's hormones. It's lots of things, the wedding, my awful mother, that creepy patient and... I suppose Danny. I know you like him, but Ina thinks I'm mad seeing him again and truth be told she's right, I am mad...but it's so difficult for me to stay away from him.' It felt good to talk to Harry so Faye continued. 'Two nights ago, he said he wanted to get a divorce and marry me and move back here. Harry, I think I'm falling in love with him again and want to believe him and forget the past, but I know I should be cautious, take Ina's advice and stop seeing him. What's wrong with me Harry?'

Harry's heart sank as he heard the pain in Faye's voice. He wanted to make things right for her, but he also knew that in an indirect way he was responsible for her pain. Perhaps he should tell her, he thought he knew the risk he was taking by telling her, but he couldn't stand by any longer and leave her vulnerable to what he felt certain would happen.

'Faye sweetie, there's something I have to tell you,' began Harry.

Fifteen minutes later Harry followed Faye out of the Mexican restaurant, none the wiser on what the food was like, their order remained untouched, as did the Margaritas.

It was freezing outside, but Faye took no notice as she hurried to try to get a taxi.

'Faye I am so sorry, please don't...'

'Harry go home, don't follow me,' Faye didn't turn around as she spoke.

'I'll call you later,' Harry wasn't sure she heard, he was speaking to her back.

Moments later he saw her get into a taxi. She didn't look out at him as the car drove past him.

He had never felt so utterly miserable, he should never have opened his big mouth.

# twenty-four

Daniel looked at the caller id on his phone, he was sitting on an armchair in his hotel room with a glass of whiskey in his hand and the Financial Times on his lap, he never quite knew why he read this paper, he was bored stiff by most of what was in it, but in the same way that fear was behind most of his actions, he was afraid not to read it. He thought about not answering his father-in-law but then thought better of it.

'Hello Uziel.'

'Good evening Daniel, I really don't like to have to be calling you on this matter, but you left me with no choice since you have not kept me abreast of matters, as we had agreed. Where do things stand, is she snared?' asked Uziel

Daniel thought what a horrible word *snared* was and hated Uziel even more for using it. But he also knew that Uziel chose all his words with care and in that word lay the unsaid. Daniel had toyed with lying to Uziel but thought better of it.

'Yes, I think she is,' answered Daniel.

'Good, we can call this to a close soon, you are needed back here. Is that clear?'

'Yes,' said Daniel.

'Oh, and Daniel, call your wife,' and with that Uziel hung up.

For a moment Daniel stared at the phone and then flung his glass with the remains of the whiskey across the room, it made a satisfying crashing sound as it hit the wall.

'Damn him!' he shouted to no one but himself.

His mind went to the weekend he had just spent with Faye and the giddy idea that this could go on forever. He marvelled at his own stupidity and his chimerical ideas.

Just then his phone rang. It was Faye. Daniel was thrilled, but only for a second, until he thought about what he had to do.

'This is a nice surprise,' he said as he answered the call.

'Are you in your hotel?' asked Faye.

'Yes, do...'

'Can I come over?' asked Faye.

'Of course, will I...'

'Fine I'll be there in a few minutes, I'll come up,' Faye hung up.

Daniel thought she sounded a bit off but maybe she was just anxious to see him, which delighted him.

When Faye got into the taxi after leaving Harry, her head was addled. She had given the driver her home address, but on the way changed her mind and called Danny, she couldn't imagine getting a wink of sleep until she saw him, and she certainly wasn't going to have this conversation on the phone.

And now as the taxi pulled up outside the hotel, she was frazzled with rage. She paid the driver and leapt out of the car. She was oblivious to everyone as she made her way across the lobby to the lifts. She pressed the button and in that redundant way pressed it again, and again, finally her frustration got the better of her and she took the stairs. By the time she reached the third floor she was winded but didn't notice. Her knock on Danny's door was sharp and loud. He opened it and greeted her with a broad grin.

Faye pushed past him into the room she now knew well, but wished she had never set foot in.

'Harry told me why you came back,' she was still a bit breathless from the stairs.

'What do you mean...I came back for work...' began Danny.

'Stop Danny', said Faye as she put up her hand. 'Stop taking me for some kind of idiot. Is this your way of getting your kicks, did you think you might not have done a good enough job the first-time round of humiliating me. Why all the lies about marriage and moving back here when you never had any intention of it...'

'They weren't lies...' began Danny.

'Yes, they were. Don't stand here and tell me you weren't lying. What's wrong with you, why would you do this?' Faye could feel tears smarting behind her eyes, but she was determined not to cry.

'Faye, please believe me, everything I said to you was true...'

'No, it wasn't, you have no intention of getting a divorce or moving back here, have you?' asked Faye.

'Believe me I want to, there's nothing I want more, but... I....well... I can't,' said Danny.

'Then what is all this about, I just don't understand why you came back here, and the way you did it – why did you have to involve Harry, did you want to poison our friendship, and then to bring up Belfast, that's the worst part. We all agreed that that would remain in the past forever...'

'I know... I just got...desperate...I was afraid that if Harry didn't encourage you to see me you never would have...'

'Fine but why did you want to meet up again when you clearly are married and have every intention of staying so?'

'I wanted to try to make up for the past and...'

'By coming back into my life only to dump me again...'

'No, no I never wanted that, never, I know it looks awful but...'

'No Danny, it doesn't look awful, it is awful – you know there must be something wrong with you to do this, when were you planning on leaving anyway? You know what, I don't really care, it doesn't matter because this is the last time I ever want to see you.'

'Please Faye don't say that I never intended to hurt you, I would never do that.'

'But that's exactly what you did, but I don't understand why, why after all these years did you decide you wanted to see me, it doesn't make sense.'

'I know and I can't really explain it, I really wanted to see you, I've always wanted to see you Faye and try to make up for the past, I realise this is not the right way, but I didn't know any other way.'

'That's just rubbish, if you wanted to make up for the past you could have just met me to talk, but it's clear your intention from the start was to get me to sleep with you. How's that making up for the past?' Faye was exhausted and could feel herself wane under the sheer wretchedness of it all.

'Look Daniel I'm going to leave, and I never want to see you again,' she sounded matter of fact, there was nothing left to say.

'Please don't go like this, wait let's just take a moment...'

'No amount of talking will change anything, it's pointless to keep talking, we've said what has to be said and any more talk is only going to be the same thing again. I'm tired I want to go home.' Faye started to walk towards the door and Daniel stepped haplessly out of her way.

Daniel stood staring at the closed door, and he felt completely defeated and if he was honest, a complete shit. He knew what he had done was woeful, but he really had no choice – he was protecting Faye, or so he told himself. He looked around the room and thought that he would be leaving sooner than he thought, he dropped his head and roared silently into his hands.

Faye left the hotel lobby in a bit of a daze, not taking the slightest notice of the man she knew was Arthur Wilson, sitting facing the door reading a book on cooking for one. Arthur could see her through the window as she waited for a taxi, she looked bothered, he thought, something about her made him feel sad for her. He did his job and what was asked of him but that didn't mean he agreed with what he did, and Faye Monroe was a case in point, she was a sitting duck in Oliver Blake's game. He got up and put his book under his arm and made for his car. He could see Faye get into a taxi, luckily, he was faced in the right direction to follow. Looks like she's going home, he thought.

As Faye got out of the taxi Arthur could see, even from a distance, that she was crying. He turned off the car.

The door had double locks on when Faye went to open it, it was later than she thought, just as well, the chances of running into anyone was slim at this time. Sure enough when she got in all was quiet in the hall, it was as cold inside as outside, these old houses were impossible to heat, at least on Mrs C's budget. When Faye entered her flat, she could feel the warmer air against her skin, she had put the heating on a timer that morning thinking she would be home long ago, but it was nice that the flat was warm, not that it actually made her feel any less miserable, but at least it didn't add to her misery.

She went to the kitchen and mixed herself a gin and tonic and took a bag of crisps from the press, more for comfort than hunger. Back in the living room she collapsed down onto the sofa and thought about the last couple of hours. Well, she thought, she definitely knew where she stood now with regards to Danny, tonight really put pay to her silly pipe dreams of them together happy ever after. She felt such an idiot even thinking about it now. As she slouched back into the sofa her eyes came to rest on the package from India and was hit with the thought that Danny was connected in some way to Oliver Blake. She couldn't quite fathom out in what way, but then it was too much of a coincidence that he came back just as Oliver Blake started seeing her, she wouldn't put it past him. And Harry, could he be connected, surely not, but then she hadn't expected his bombshell from earlier. She got up and went to her bag to get her phone. She called Harry.

'Faye, I'm so glad you....' said Harry immediately.

'Harry if I ask you a question will you answer me honestly?' asked Faye.

'Of course!' said Harry.

'Do you know a man called Oliver Blake?'

'No, no I don't,' said Harry.

'Are you sure?'

'Yes Faye, I don't know him, really I don't, why do you...'

'Okay bye,' said Faye and hung up.

She thought for a moment and rang Danny.

'Faye, I'm so...'

'Danny, I think you owe me an honest answer to a question, will you do that much?' asked Faye.

'Yes,' said Danny, any hopes of her reconsidering vanished when he heard the determined note in her voice.

'Do you know a man called Oliver Blake?'

'No, I don't think so.'

'Are you sure?'

'Yeah, I don't know anyone of that name personally,' he answered honestly.

'But you might know him through work is that what you are saying?'

'No not really, I am fairly good on names, even ones I meet through work.'

'Okay, what about a man called Arthur Wilson?'

'No, again the same thing, why do you ask, who are they?' Danny asked.

'It doesn't matter, bye.' Faye hung up.

She looked at the package again and this time thought she was just jumping to conclusions, it was a bit farfetched. The G&T was helping to take the edge off, she thought I'll just have another one and then go to bed. In the kitchen she noticed the bag of crisps on the table she had forgotten them and now decided against them – she really had no appetite. Back in the living room she put on Michael Ortega, his piano music was suitably depressing. Round and round went the same thoughts in her head, each new one just another version of the last one, why had she allowed herself to fall for him again after all she had told herself over the past ten years, ten years of toughing up down the swanny, she could hardly bear her own gullibility. In the end she couldn't put up with herself anymore and went to bed.

Arthur only waited for a few minutes after he saw Faye's light go out. He could hear soft sobs from the bug, and while he still felt sad for her, he was reeling from the phone call to Daniel Cohen, she had asked him if he knew him. How the hell did she find out about him and how much did she know. Being in the dark was not a position he savoured. He certainly wasn't going to tell Oliver Blake about this. He drove home in botheration.

# twenty-five

Faye woke the next morning feeling dreadful, sleep hadn't helped, it rarely helped with reality.

She lifted herself up in the bed, she longed to stay in bed and sleep for the next ten years, but she had the hospital today – the curse of the self-employed – there's no ringing in sick. Her body felt cumbrous as she flung her legs onto the floor, it was stone cold against the soles of her feet, normally this would prompt a quick retraction and search for socks but today she couldn't care less. The tiled bathroom floor was even colder - as Faye sat on the loo she could see her refection in the mirror in front of her, not the most flattering position for a mirror but it was there when she first arrived and was the only full-length mirror in the flat, so it remained there. Somehow the loo looked drab and hostile, it was normally a cheerful room but not today. Her reflection looked broken and jaded. Maybe a coffee will help, she thought.

The kitchen was just as dull as the loo, probably as much to do with the dull skies as her mood. She took the moka coffee pot, well technically espresso maker, and unscrewed the top, she hadn't cleaned it out from yesterday morning, once she had emptied the old coffee granules out and refilled it with water and coffee, she turned on the cooker. Leaning against the sink as she waited, she was trying to make a decision as to whether to have toast or not, it seemed like a monumental task, in the end she decided to have some.

There was some brown bread in the bread bin, but it was a bit old and had a bit of mould on it, Faye hadn't done a grocery shop for a while. She cut off the bit with the mould and put it in the toaster, her ex-husband would have had a conniption with her doing this, he was convinced she was going to die from eating out of date food – but she hadn't died yet, people were far too fussy about these things.

While the toast and coffee were doing their thing, Faye went to the bedroom to get her bag hoping she might have a Valium left, knowing she almost certainly hadn't didn't stop her looking, there must be something comforting in the looking, those brief moments of hope which made fools of people. Before she even picked up her bag, she was hit by what she had done – the bug was on the table she had forgotten all about it the night before when she made the calls to Harry and Danny and mentioned Arthur Wilson and Oliver. How had things come to this, I can't even talk in my own flat, she thought and decided she had better call Ina.

After a quick shower she dressed and went back to the kitchen, the toast was burnt, the toaster was dodgy, no matter what setting you turned it to, unless you stood over it, the bread burnt. With a knife she scraped off the burnt surfaces and buttered it, the coffee helped disguise the charred taste, a bit.

With her hair still wet from the shower she pulled it back into a rough bun at the back of her head, put on her coat and scarf and left, leaving behind her bag with the bug in it. At the bottom of the stairs Pat was fumbling to carry two awkward looking bags, whatever was in them looked lumpy and sharp.

'Good morning, Pat, you seem overloaded there, can you manage - do you need a hand?' asked Faye hoping that he didn't, she really hadn't time to help him.

'Oh, hiya Faye, yeah no I'm grand, just some stuff for an experiment with the lads today, looks worse than it is, they're actually light enough, but thanks anyway. I've a taxi waiting outside – can I drop you off on the way, it's freezing brass monkeys out there?' asked Pat.

'No thanks, oh well actually yeah that would be great, I'm in the hospital so I can continue on from your school, it's on the way.'

'Grand, come on so.'

They walked out together to the street where the taxi waited, noticing the cumbersome bags, the driver popped open the boot and Pat dumped the bags in.

'Thanks friend,' said Pat to the driver.

'How's school Pat?' asked Faye when they were in the car.

'Oh grand, good yeah,' answered Pat, 'we have a few bright sparks up for the Young Scientist Competition, they look good too.'

Faye knew that Pat's students always entered the Young Scientist Competition and always did very well, he had a lot of winners nationally and a few that went on to do really well internationally. In another life, if Pat had more confidence in himself, Faye felt sure he would have invented something marvellous or found the cure for something – but there again we all might do better, had we another life.

'That's great Pat, I'm sure you are a very inspiring teacher and a great help, those boys are lucky to have such good teacher.'

'Ah now, they do most of it themselves – they're good lads.'

Pat hated flattery, it made him deeply uncomfortable, and he was glad when the school gates came into view, and he could escape it.

'Ah well here we are, good to see you Faye, good luck now.' And with that he was out of the car, removed the bags from the boot and shoved a tenner in the window to the driver and was gone before he could get his change.

Poor Pat, thought Faye, and then thought better of it as she looked in the school grounds. The perfectly manicured lawns with an avenue of mature lime trees leading to a beautiful eighteen century building, it was so welcoming looking, Pat could while away his days flapping around Bunsen burners and examining fruit flies under a microscope and he was right, the boys here were for the most part motivated to succeed, just like generations before them, Pat was probably on the pig's back, living a charmed life with no one stalking or eavesdropping on him. Faye's pity turned to envy.

By the time they arrived at the hospital Faye was positively depressed. The hospital grounds were the complete antithesis of Pat's school, unwelcoming, unkempt and those inside had the opposite of motivation towards success. Walking to her office, well the room she used when she was here, Faye could hear the string of profanities she had come accustomed to from the far end of the hall – someone else was not having a good day.

In the office, which it has to be said was fairly depressing, the paint was peeling from damp and the furniture was horrible stuff from the seventies, such a pity they hadn't hung onto the old nineteen century furniture, but some kind of Formica awakening took place in the seventies, and everything was replaced with it. Faye thought it had to be the most lifeless material ever manufactured.

As she sat down, she took her phone out to call Ina. She had switched it off the night before and now she saw that Harry had rung umpteen times between last night and this morning. Danny hadn't called – not surprisingly, he was such a defeatist.

She pressed Ina's number and let it ring, it was answered just before the answering machine came on.

'Ina it's me I need...'

'Sorry Faye, it's not Ina it's me Bosco, I just answered it because she couldn't get to it.'

'Oh fine, Bosco, how are you?'

'Never better thanks and yourself?'

'Good thanks, sorry Bosco I'm actually at work I was hoping for a quick word with Ina before I get started.'

'Oh yeah sure, hang on a sec and I'll get her,' after a moment Ina came on the phone.

'Sorry Ina you're obviously at home...'

'It's fine I've taken today off, we're going to a family thing at Bosco's, was it important?'

'No, no it's nothing I was just ringing for a chat, I'll talk to you tomorrow or Friday, have a nice time.'

'Yeah thanks, see you.'

'Bye Ina.'

Faye was not only feeling envious of Pat but now she was thinking about what a nice life Ina had with Bosco - Ina had told her before that his family were lovely and she didn't want to mess up her day with offloading on her.

Somehow, she had to get to the bottom of this whole business, she was tired and fed up with being afraid. As she thought about it, she decided what she was going to do. But for the moment she had a day's work in front of her.

At least the screaming had stopped, for the time being.

At the end of the day Faye went straight home, picking up two trays of sushi on the way. By the time she had eaten it was half eight. She needed to get going before it got too late. Quickly changing into jeans and a warm jumper, she pulled on her coat and took with her the bag and the bug. The car keys were on the table, picking them up she went down and got into the car. She knew where she was going this time, so it didn't take long to get to Arthur Wilson's house. His car was in the drive.

Faye found a parking spot a bit down from his house and before she could change her mind she got out and marched right up to his door and pressed the bell. She heard footsteps, there was still time to run, but somehow, she stood still.

There was a moment's quiet, Faye had spotted the peep hole and so stood out of its view, she knew he was looking through it, better to give him a bit of a surprise she thought.

Arthur opened the door.

'Hello. Arthur Wilson, I believe you know who I am,' said Faye.

Arthur had to admit he was surprised, he hadn't expected this, she had gumption, he'd give her that.

Faye held out her hand to show him the bug.

'You planted this in my bag and have been listening in on my life without permission, I don't think the Gardai are going to like that.'

'I don't know what you are talking about, this is madness,' bluffed Arthur.

'No this is not madness, madness is you thinking you can get away with this - I know you are working for Oliver Blake, I think it's in your best interest to talk to me, as you know, my friend is a policewoman, better me than her. You've managed to keep a low profile all these years, do you really want to jeopardise all that, or have Oliver Blake find out, I just want a few answers,' Faye sounded remarkably in control - even to herself.

Arthur gave a quick look over Faye's shoulder.

'Don't worry I am here alone, but my friend knows I am here,' she sounded believable.

'Come in,' said Arthur as he stood back and opened the door to allow Faye in.

The hall was like something out of an interior design magazine, clearly there was money in snooping.

Arthur ushered her into a room to the left of the front door, again it was classical stylish, under other circumstances Faye would have liked to discuss the decor but not tonight. It smelt good too.

'Can I offer you something, a drink, I was just about to mix one for myself before you called.'

Sounds like a good idea, thought Faye but she declined.

Arthur walked to a very snazzy drinks trolley, there were lots of bottles of spirits, cut crystal glasses of various sizes, an ice bucket and cocktail shaker, just like something in an old Hollywood movie. Arthur poured himself a brandy. Faye didn't recognise the label.

They both sat down opposite each other. There was a moment's silence, now that Faye was in, she was thrown off a bit.

Arthur looked at Faye, not for the first time, but this was the first time he openly took her in – he thought how entirely different it is to look at someone when they are looking at you as opposed to when they are unaware of your gaze. She held his eye, and this made him see her in a different way. This was not good for his job. Better not to see the person. Arthur needed to think of her as his paycheck – but he couldn't look away – there was something otherworldly and hermetic about her, like she had seen too much or felt too much, Arthur had seen this before in men he had met in Iraq, they sealed themselves off, couldn't take anymore. She looked a bit at sea, the bravado she had at the door was gone. He had to admit he was intrigued as to how she found him. His intrigue was soon assuaged.

Faye took three photos from her bag and placed them under his nose. One was the photo Mrs C had taken, the second was of him in his car in Island Point and the last one was him handing the envelope to Eugene Klein.

'You take a good photo, Miss Monroe, but I am not sure why you are showing these to me, it looks a bit like you're the one doing the following.'

'Believe me Mr Wilson, I was oblivious to your existence until I discovered that you were following and bugging me, which is illegal, as I am sure as a registered private investigator you know. I have no problem going to the guards with this – you could get five years in jail you know.'

Arthur simply smiled.

'I want to know why Oliver Blake hired you to follow me?'

'I don't know what you are talking about.'

'Look we can go around in circles all night, I know it was Blake, I have proof, I am willing to ignore your part if you tell me what you know about his wife.'

'Look Miss Monroe, you are out of your depth here and if you don't mind me saying a bit, I don't know, erratic. These pictures prove nothing, and you will have trouble getting any guard to take you seriously. Let me give you a bit of advice, go home, forget all this, maybe get some help with...you know...these strange ideas, you have let your imagination get the better of you.'

'Oh, for crying out loud don't' try and fob me off as some nutter - how do you explain the photos?'

'I don't have to explain my movements to you and that's all you have here, last time I checked it wasn't against the law to meet someone for a chat or to park my car in a public place, as for this one,' he pointed to Mrs C's photo, 'it's what you can't see that's important, I was walking with my young nephew and the ball he was kicking along went under that car, all I was doing was getting it back, nothing more, no big conspiracy against you. Are you sure you're okay, you know, you're not on any medication or anything like that – I could call someone for you.'

Faye looked at him and wanted to scream at him, tell him she was the sanest person she knew, that she was cursed with sanity and awareness and that she knew what he was trying to do, that Freud had a name for it. But she decided against it, because she also realised that it was so easy for him to wriggle out of this, what she had was flimsy and she couldn't prove he planted the bug – it was a game of one-up-man-ship, and he had the upper hand.

'Arthur, I know you bugged me, and I know you work for Oliver Blake, now why not rethink and take a moment and just tell me what you know because if you don't this will not end well for you.' She sounded almost menacing. Almost.

'Faye, now that we are on first name terms, I can't help you and I want to as you seem so...for the want of a better word – desperate. But I don't have a clue what's going on for you.'

'Okay,' she said as she stood up, 'I'll go now,' she walked towards the door.

Arthur stood as well, he didn't want her to go, but knew it was best to let her. He followed her to the door, out into the hall where he passed her in order to open the door. As she left, she turned and looked at him.

'You haven't heard the last of this.' Now she sounded like a prissy teacher who was sore because a student got the better of her. She regretted saying it.

'Good night, Faye.' Faye detected a trace of pity or was it sadness.

'Fuck, fuck, fuck, fuck, fuck,' Faye was sitting in her car, she wanted to bang her head on the steering wheel, but it wasn't in her to be so dramatic, she was always able to control any urge like that – in fact it was never an urge, more a desire to be free enough to let rip. She started the car and headed home. That had gone spectacularly arse ways. Ina was going to blow a gasket.

# twenty-six

It was Monday evening by the time Faye got to talk with Ina, Bosco was steadily becoming more of a permanent fixture in her life which was great, but it meant Ina was not nearly as available as she used to be. They met at a pub near Ina's which meant Faye had to either drive and not drink or drink and get a taxi, she decided she needed a drink. Faye was waiting in a quiet corner of the pub when Ina came in, she was radiant, thought Faye, love suited her.

'Hiya, what are you having?' asked Ina.

'Am, ah, a G&T please or no, maybe I'll have a whiskey, ah no go ahead with the G&T, it's so bloody cold, actually I'll have the whiskey, a Green Spot please.'

'Are you sure now?'

'Yeah, yeah.'

Ina went to get the drinks and returned with two bags of crisps and two bags of salted peanuts.

'How did the family thing go with Bosco?' asked Faye.

'It was grand, they're that rare thing – normal, very easy going and relaxed, I really enjoyed it.'

'Sounds serious.'

'Well, we have talked about him moving in with me.'

'Wow Ina, that is serious, for you I mean, you've never lived with a man before, I'm delighted for you. Bosco is lovely.' Faye genuinely felt so happy for her friend, it wasn't that Ina had been unlucky in love, more that the right man had never come along. She had never been heartbroken or distraught from a bad relationship, nor had she ever pined after the great love, but now it seems her love had come.

'Thanks, I think he's lovely too.' And that was about as close as Ina ever got to a proclamation of love.

'What's up with you, you don't look great, if you don't mind me saying.'

'I know. I think I might have done something stupid.'

'Go on.'

'Well, it's finished with Danny, and I had a fight with Harry, and I was so fed up with everything and being followed and all that stuff, I went to Arthur Wilson's house to confront him...'

'Hang on a second you went to his house, please tell me you didn't actually talk to him.' Ina was getting excited and not in a good way.

'Well yeah, I did go in and talk to him, I thought I could get him to tell me why he was following me.'

'And how did that work out for you.'

'Not well, he tried to insinuate that I was bonkers.'

'Maybe he wasn't far off the mark. I mean really Faye what were you thinking and why didn't you call me first.'

'I tried to, but you were with Bosco, and I didn't want to be bothering you. Ina, I had to do something I was sick of being in the dark.'

'Are you any the wiser now?'

'No actually, but it does mean he can't follow me anymore and anyway he knew I knew about him because I mentioned his name on the phone to Danny, so it really made no odds.'

'Why did you tell Danny about him?'

Faye went on to tell Ina about what Harry had told her, leaving out the bit she didn't need to know, and about confronting Danny.

'I don't get why Harry just didn't tell you Dan approached him, it's not really a big deal. I knew he was hiding something, and you thought it was a bit of a coincidence that Dan ended up using his company – Faye I think there's more to it than that, why after all these years come back and get Harry to convince you, how did he even know Harry and you were still friends?'

'Harry said that he was desperate for the job because things have not been going well at work, he felt like he was using me to get an influx of cash into the company and that's why he said nothing – because he was ashamed.'

'And so he bloody well should be! Do you think Dan knew that Harry's company was strapped, he must have, otherwise he wouldn't have felt so cock sure of himself coming to Har, which means he had access to privy information.'

'I did wonder if it was all related to Oliver Blake, I asked both Harry and Danny if they knew him – both said they didn't.'

'Well, we can't believe either of them for now. We need to talk to Harry and get out of him exactly what happened. I'm going to call him right now and get him over here.'

'No Ina I don't want to talk to...'

'Faye, it's Harry, whatever he did was probably harmless enough, but he thinks it's a bigger thing than it really is – you know what he's like.' She took out her mobile and called Harry, he answered after two rings.

'Harry I'm with Faye in the pub down from my place, Ryan's, she told me what happened, will you come over so we can sort it out.' Ina knew Harry would only be gagging to get things sorted.

'Yeah, I'll come immediately, see you in about fifteen minutes.'

'Grand, see ye.'

Ina hung up and put her phone back in her pocket. She turned her full attention to Faye.

'Now tell me exactly what happened with Arthur Wilson.'

Faye did as asked, leaving nothing out.

'The thing is Faye, he's right in what he said, he hasn't broken any law that we can prove, we know it's a cock and bull story about walking with his nephew and yeah it all adds up from our end, but we have no proof of any of it. Now he knows we are on to him so he will be ultra-careful. I think it's fair to say we've lost him.'

'I'm sorry Ina I thought he might... I don't know, buckle under the pressure from my, you know, super advanced interrogating skills... he definitely is working for Oliver Blake. He was very composed, but he kind of missed a beat every time I mentioned Blake.'

'He's probably worried about how Blake would react if he finds out you found the bug, shabby work on Wilson's part.'

Just then Harry arrived, he was standing at the table before Ina and Faye realised he was in the pub.

'Hi Harry,' said Ina.

'Hiya Ina,' and turning to Faye, 'Hi Faye, how're you? He was cautious in the same way kids are cautious the first time they venture to speak to their parents after getting a telling off over something.

While Faye was really angry with Harry for what he did, she didn't have the heart to stay cross with him, there was enough other stuff to be upset about and besides he looked so miserable it seemed unnecessarily cruel to prolong his suffering, plus she just didn't want to be fighting with Harry. So she smiled at him.

'Hi Harry, it's your round.'

Grown men have a peculiar tendency to act like boys when things unexpectedly go their way – Harry became giddy.

'Yeah, no problem, what are you having, have anything you want, really...' his voice slightly boy soprano.

'Calm down buckaroo, we're both having a Green Spot,' said practical Ina.

'Grand, I'll get them,' said Harry and he turned to go to the bar, but not before beaming over at Faye.

'God you've made his day, he's practically floating to the bar,' said Ina.

'Do you think he's broke or that the company are going down the tubes?'

'No idea, but lots are, we'll just ask him.'

The pub was beginning to fill up, a lot of young couples, probably in for a few quiet drinks before heading into a week of racing and tail chasing. Faye thought they all looked a bit jaded; it just happens – life not living up to expectations.

Harry came back with the drinks, three whiskeys. He sat down and they clinked their glasses, it was an automatic reaction, they always did it, no salutation, just clink, clink.

Ina got straight to it.

'Harry, tell me when and how Dan initially made contact with you and what he said.'

'I know I should have told you but...'

'Harry, just tell us the details.' Ina interrupted any display of repentance, time enough for that later, or better again just forget it as far as Ina was concerned.

'Okay, he phoned me in the office about a month before I told you about him, he spoke only about business and said he was going to be in Dublin the following week and that he wanted to meet to discuss a project they wanted advertising for. I said it was a bit weird after all these years and that it felt, you know, wrong, me doing business with him after what had happened. He was saying the same thing and that it wasn't him who decided on the agency, it was his boss and when he was researching it, he discovered I was a partner. He acknowledged that it must be uncomfortable but that he had to do as directed by his boss and thought it was better to deal with me.'

'Did he ask about Faye?'

'No, at that time he said he wanted to keep it professional, he actually said it might be better not to say anything to you Faye. He never asked anything about her at all. So, we made an arrangement to meet when he was over, which was only a few days later as it turned out. I got the call on the Friday, and he was over on the Monday. At first, he just spoke about this project, looking back it was all a bit vague, anyway he soon brought you up Faye and he started asking about you, general things like work, marriage, where you were living now that kind of thing, then he said he wanted to meet you. I said I didn't want to get involved but that I thought you would not want to meet him. I thought you wouldn't, was I right Faye?' He looked to Faye, but it was Ina who answered.

'Of course you were right she didn't want to meet him, anyway, go on.'

'Then it all got a bit strange, he said he wanted me to help him get Faye to meet him, I said I wouldn't do that, that it was underhanded, then he said he would expose me to my partners at work if I didn't help him'

'Expose you for what?' asked Faye.

'About a year ago I borrowed some money from the business without telling the partners, it was when I was selling my old flat and buying my new place, I was a bit short of money at the time. I have since paid it all back and no one is any the wiser – somehow Dan knew about it, how I don't know when the other partners didn't even know.'

'That means he, or someone he knows, has access to your agencies' accounts and your personal accounts, that is how they would have made the link,' said Ina.

'How?' asked Harry a bit of the boy soprano back in his voice.

'Easy enough these days, to any good hacker it would be a piece of cake.'

'But surely the banks have secure systems?'

'If you use online banking, it's your system that is accessed not the banks,' deadpanned Ina.

'God that's a bloody nightmare...' began Harry.

'Go on with the story Harry,' said Ina.

'Oh yeah, well basically he threatened to dob me in it if I didn't get Faye to meet him and to talk him up a bit, he said all I had to do was encourage you,' he said looking at Faye, 'to meet him and if I did that, I was safe. I know I'm such a shit for doing it, but I was bricking it, if the partners found out it would be hell.'

'He threatened you, doesn't sound like Dan, but then people change, what was he like when he was making this threat?' asked Ina.

'Well, he seemed a bit out of his depth to be honest, you could tell he was not very comfortable doing it – at the time I put it down to a kind of desperate act. He went on about his unhappy marriage and the pressure from his father-in-law, who apparently is his boss. He said he didn't want to do this, but that he would have to follow through if I didn't help him.'

'Why not contact Faye directly?'

'I asked him that and he said that he was afraid she wouldn't meet him and that his chances were much higher this way.'

'And how has he been since, when you are working on the advertising job?' asked Ina.

'That's the other thing, there was no job, that was all a ploy. I haven't seen him since, but he did tell me to keep the pretence up about the job. He phoned twice and I did tell him about Mary's wedding but nothing else.'

'Harry why the hell did you not tell us that!' Ina demanded.

'I told you why, I know I shouldn't have, but I don't know, I just didn't think it was a big deal.'

'Of course it was a big deal, mucking around with people's lives is a big deal,' said Ina.

'I know, I know Ina you're right, and I am sorry.'

'Bit late for sorry,' said Ina.

Harry looked at Faye, there was no doubt he was sorry, he was also afraid that he had gone too far and that Faye would never trust him again – she didn't look angry or disappointed, it was worse than that, it was a look of resignation which made him feel outside the pack, outside their pack – not a place he wanted to be. He should have just told them from the beginning, and he thought if he wasn't so bloody vain about his work and lifestyle, he probably would have, but pride got in the way.

'Harry is there anything else you haven't told us?' asked Ina.

'No absolutely nothing, I promise you Ina and don't look at me like that!'

'Like what, I'm not looking at you any sort of way, this is my normal look.'

'Yeah, your normal look when you don't believe someone.'

'You've given us reason not to believe you.'

'I know but I'm telling you the truth now,' Harry's was beginning to sound a bit desperate.

'Okay, okay I believe you,' said Ina.

'So do I,' said Faye.

'Thanks,' said Harry, relieved.

'Now don't sulk,' said Ina.

'I'm not sulking,' said Harry indignantly.

There was a moment of silence. Then they laughed. After all what were the choices, they could to and fro about the rights and wrongs of it, but really none of them wanted to do that. They were friends and wanted to stay friends and to do that, things had to be allowed to slip quietly away. Of course everything left a bit of a stain.

'Harry, who is Danny's father-in-law?' asked Faye.

'His name is, I'm not sure of how to pronounce it, Uziel Nachman, I googled him, he has a big pharmaceutical company in Israel with offices in London and I think in India. Sounds like Dan is completely under his thumb.'

Ina took out a pen and a small black note pad, like the ones you see detectives use in movies, obviously they also use them in real life.

'If Dan was a bit out of his depth, as you say, when he was threatening you, it might mean that he was being forced to do it by someone else, and he's not the type to hack computers is he?' asked Ina.

'No, but then his father-in-law getting him to hook up with an ex-girlfriend, that doesn't make sense either,' said Faye.

'We're missing something, some connection. Dan comes over here, gets you back and then what – as you said Faye, he clearly hadn't a notion of leaving his wife – so what did he want, what was all the threatening Harry about?'

'This is all personal stuff; I mean Danny had no interest in Harry's firm and I'm a nobody when it comes to anything really. But I don't think Danny did this of his own volition, I'm not sticking up for him but it's just not him,' said Faye.

'But who then?' asked Harry.

Ina and Faye looked at each other both thinking but neither saying the name Oliver Blake. Harry noticed the exchange and wasn't content to be out of the telepathic loop.

'Who are you two thinking of?' he asked.

'No one you would know and it's a bit convoluted,' said Ina.

'And you think I'm too thick to keep up, anyway I know who it is, it's that man you asked if I knew the other night isn't it Faye, Oliver something or other. Who is he? said Harry.

'I don't really know who he is to be honest, but if he is connected then this is getting more and more bizarre and a bit scary,' said Faye.

As she thought of Danny and the whole palaver he went on with, the more she thought Oliver Blake was connected – what the connection was she wasn't sure, but she felt it might be something to do with Danny's father-in-law. The bigger picture was lost to her, but as she, in the grand scheme of things, was a nobody then this had to be personal. This meant that Oliver Blake had gone to great lengths to – Faye wasn't sure what his motive was and could only come back to her original idea – to punish her because his wife came to see her and then gave him the heave ho, he blamed her.

'What do you mean scary, are you in danger Faye?' Harry sounded alarmed.

'To be honest I'm not sure,' she answered.

'What the hell's going on,' demanded Harry.

'Look calm down Harry, Faye's fine. Now we have to think this through, right now no one knows we have made any connections, assuming there are any. Arthur Wilson only knows that you're on to Blake not Dan so we could use this,' said Ina.

'Who is Arthur Wilson?' asked Harry as he flopped back into the chair and threw open his arms.

'A private investigator who's been following me and bugging me,' said Faye in that way you get when the idea of something so off the wall becomes familiar.

'What the hell! a PI following and bugging you, this is mad, what have you done?' asked Harry.

'Nothing, well nothing that I am aware of at any rate. I found the bug and got photos of him, well Mrs C got the first photos and then we set him up and got more photos and then I went to his house but that didn't go so well...' Faye was belting it out.

'Hang on a second, you set this guy up and went to see him and old Mrs C was taking photos, Christ almighty start from the beginning,' and as an afterthought, 'Why didn't you tell me about all this,' he sounded a bit put out.

'I have an idea,' said Ina ignoring Harry.

'If Harry rings Dan and tells him you are really upset Faye and that he's worried and that he should meet you to sort things out. Then Faye you get some answers. What we really want to know is who put him up to this and why.'

'Are you alright with that Faye?' asked Harry

'Yeah, Ina's right, he knows something and let's face it, he used me to some end, and I want to know why,' said Faye.

Faye didn't relish meeting Danny again, especially now knowing that he had set her up from the start and that nothing he said was remotely true. She didn't like to think about what a fool she felt for believing him, but she wasn't going to think about that now.

'Harry, you ring him and make a big deal about how upset she is and all that and tell him she wants to meet to discuss it,' said Ina.

'When and where?' asked Harry.

'What do you think Faye, might be best at his hotel, it's better than somewhere public and I don't think it's a good idea to have him over to yours,' said Ina.

'Yeah, the hotel is probably the best option. Why not make it for tomorrow evening, I'm finished work around five so say seven,' said Faye.

'Right so, ring him Harry,' ordered Ina.

'Now this minute!' said Harry, taken a bit of guard.

'Yeah now, do you have his number?' asked Ina.

'Yeah, it's in my phone, so I just say that she came over and that she's a mess and I think he needs to sort it – is that the gist of it?' asked Harry.

'Yeah, be very concerned, don't let him wriggle out of meeting her,' said Ina.

'Alright,' Harry took his phone out of the inside breast pocket of his jacket and scrolled down through the numbers until he found Dan's. He pressed the dial button. Dan answered after two rings. After less than a minute Harry had made the arrangements for the following evening.

'He didn't need much persuading, he jumped at the chance of meeting you Faye,' said Harry.

'I bet he did. Harry, can you meet Faye and go with her to the hotel and wait for her and then I'll meet you both back at yours Faye, how is that?' said Ina.

'No problem, I'll collect you at your flat and come with you to the hotel,' said Harry.

'There's no need to come to the flat beforehand, I can meet you at the hotel,' said Faye.

'It's no bother,' said Harry.

'Let him,' said Ina 'It's the least he could do,' and she smirked at him.

'Right, one for the road,' said Harry and got up to go to the bar.

# twenty-seven

Ina spent the best part of Monday morning methodically working through screen after screen of information. She was working on the premise that there was a connection between Oliver Blake, Uziel Nachman and Dan. Ina had also asked Harry and Faye for access to their bank and email accounts to see if there were any red flags. She had Malcolm working on it too, he was looking at both Nachman and William's companies and who they did business with, who they banked with, who their investors and board members were, where they went on holidays, where they stayed when in London, anything which might connect them. Ina often marvelled at the amount of information available to Joe Bloggs once they knew how to look for it and since the attacks on the Twin Towers, law enforcers worldwide were given incredible access to information. Ina had mixed feelings about this. Today she was all for it.

She didn't ask Malcolm to look at Harry or Faye's stuff, she kept that to herself. She assured them that she would only look at anything she felt was necessary, although neither had asked for this assurance.

Both Nachman and Blake were incredibly wealthy men and with that wealth comes a lot of clout – and from what Ina could gather neither of these two men were prone to acts of philanthropy. While Nachman was in pharmaceutical manufacture, Blake was what Ina supposed you might call a venture capitalist, but he played with the big fish. He was not offering funds to small start-ups, from what Ina could gather he went into established industries and bankrolled them for certain types of expansions, investments or takeovers which might be difficult to get past shareholders. A lot the investments appeared to take place in the Middle and Far East. After some cross-checking Malcolm found a link, Blake had put up finance for Nachman, not for his main company, but what appeared to be a new subsidiary company. There was no record of the actual amount of money but going by other amounts that Blake put up, it was well into the millions. The first date Malcolm could find was eight years ago and Blake seemed to be involved with Nachman ever since, it looked as if Nachman was starting a new business every couple of years. Malcolm was able to assess the companies Blake invested in through VCAI, an organization which represented venture capitalists in India, he found that Blake also had offices in Berlin and New Delhi, it was more difficult to access information from these offices, at least officially. Malcolm told Ina he could "get in a back door" if she wished, she did, if he was very careful. Malcolm bent down to grab his rucksack and took out a computer, Ina noticed that he had another one left in the bag and thought for a moment of the other life of Malcolm.

While Malcolm set about getting in the back door, Ina began running Faye and Harry through the system, this, as expected, yielded nothing. Ina brought up their bank account details and began checking them - it didn't take long before she spotted that they both had a monthly standing order of €200 going to the same account. When she checked further, she discovered that the standing order was years old, going back over ten years. There was no name on the receiver's account, but the bank was in Belfast, after a bit of probing she found the name Martin Stockdale. Ina had never heard this name and wondered what his connection to Harry and Faye was, she printed off his address. Ina was lost in thought when Malcolm interrupted her to tell her that there was money coming in from Nachman's company in India to both Blake's Berlin and New Delhi offices, so it appeared money went out to Nachman from the Dublin office and back into the Berlin and New Delhi offices. There was more money coming back to Blake than going out to Nachman. Malcolm felt that it could be money laundering or else loans at very high interest rates to Nachman, either way they were linked together, and Blake was at the helm.

Ina asked Malcolm if he had looked at Daniel's bank accounts, he hadn't, but said he would do it now, it wouldn't take long.

While he was doing that Ina started searching for anything on Martin Stockdale. Turns out Martin was a small-time crook – lots of driving offences, parking tickets, reneging on child support payments to two separate mothers, shop lifting, car robbery, impersonating a priest and trespassing. He hadn't spent any time in jail, having come up with court fines on all occasions. He had several different jobs over the years from caretaker in a block of flats, odd jobs in supermarkets and a job in a tyre repair place but for the most part he was signing on the dole. Ina brought up a photo of him, his image certainly did not match the impression she had made of him from her reading. He looked younger than his forty-five years and had the look of a shy post office clerk who won't dream of removing a pencil from work let alone robbing a car. What was his connection to Faye and Harry? It was more than mildly disturbing, while they were all friends Ina had always thought that she and Faye were closer and that if there was anything worrying either of them it would be to each other they would go to first. When Danny left, Ina was sure Faye spoke to her more than Harry about how distraught she was, not that Faye was given to outbursts of emotion, but if it was going to be in front of anyone Ina was sure it would be her. Ina, like Faye, was not overly demonstrative with her feelings but it was only Faye she ever spoke to about her father, never Harry or Danny. Ina felt hurt, she was on the outside of this and wondered what else she was on the outside of. She was about to feel worse.

Malcolm had printed off Daniel's bank statements as Ina had asked. He had three accounts, a work one, and two personal ones, one of which was a joint account with his wife. It was from his personal account that Ina saw the same amount going to Martin Stockdale. So, the three of them were paying €200 a month to this man for years. Ina gave Malcolm Stockdale's bank account number and asked him to check it and any other accounts he might have. Ina racked her brain to come up with a connection, it had to be something that happened ten or more years ago, she couldn't think of anything they didn't do all together.

Ina had never felt so let down in her life, these were her best friends, and the three others were part of something she was clearly not part of.

Malcolm had found Stockdale's account and there was no record of any other activity except three monthly standing orders for €200 each, the money was always withdrawn as soon as it was lodged. He had another account which he used for everything else, mostly social welfare lodgements and on rare occasions, wage payments.

Ina thought it could be only one thing, blackmail of some sort, why else would the three be paying this low life thousands over the past ten years, but for what? It was the only thing that she could think of that Faye and Harry would keep from her, what had they done, what had Stockdale on them, she had absolutely no clue. She hated not knowing.

Her phone rang, it was her boss looking for her, she was late for a meeting.

Before shutting down her computer, she printed off what she had found on Stockdale and shoved it into her bag and stomped out.

Faye had woken that morning feeling rotten and for reasons that were now beyond her, she went for a run. It had been freezing out, there was frost on the car windows, and it glistened on the tree. It took her ages to warm up probably because she was not quite running, more of a shuffle really, she was only five minutes out when she was passed by a group of bouncy women in their twenties, all in lycra gear showing off their well-toned bodies with bouncy hair to match. It was the kind of hair that no matter what way you moved your head it came back to a perfect style, someone told her it was professionally blow-dried hair that behaved so well. But who on earth could have their hair blow-dried at this hour of the day? In the end she packed it in and went home before she had gotten to the park where she was going to have a real run. She mainly gave up because she caught an unexpected glimpse of herself in a shop window and she looked demented. She hadn't realised she was quite so unfit but marvelled at her own surprise since she did absolutely nothing to keep fit.

Later that morning at work, she was listening to a story she had heard umpteen times before from the same person. People, she reasoned, needed to hear their story over and over to help make sense of it, on the other hand, it could be argued that repeating the same story which inevitably was about suffering only kept you reliving old pain, such is the human condition. It was sad to listen to this woman who was in her mid-fifties, caught in the same reel of existence which had not changed since her childhood, repeating her life over and over just in a different set of circumstances. She knew she was unhappy but could not see that she was the common denominator in her story. Faye thought this woman would have to tell these stories for a long time to come.

The day dragged. But when it was time to leave, she was queasy at the thoughts of meeting Danny.

When she got home, Harry was already waiting for her. Mrs C had let him in and was chatting to him in her front room, Mrs C loved Harry, she found him *so charming.* They heard Faye come in the front door and called out to her.

'We're in here dear,' said Mrs C.

'Hello Mrs C how are you, hi Harry, I wasn't expecting you so early.'

'I know, I finished work early and rather than go home I came straight here, and your lovely landlady has been very gracious and regaling me with stories of her flamboyant life,' Harry was smiling at both women.

'Oh Harry, it is always a pleasure to chat with you,' said Mrs C, half flirting, Faye thought.

They chatted for a few more minutes and then Faye said that they were going out and she needed to get ready. Harry and Faye said goodbye to Mrs C and went up to the flat. It was cold and felt more so coming from Mrs C's warm and cosy room. Faye lit the gas fire and turned it to high. She wished Harry had not come so early, she would have liked a half hour or so to herself. Harry, she guessed, was trying his best to make it up to her. She told Harry to help himself to whatever was there while she went to her bedroom. She was half tempted to doll herself up, but she really didn't have the enthusiasm for it. Harry was muttering something she couldn't quite make out; she was having second thoughts about meeting Danny. No matter how much she tried to tell herself that he didn't matter to her, she couldn't quite believe it, the truth was he had succeeded in making her just as miserable as he had done ten years ago. After staring into the wardrobe for a few minutes, she finally took out a red pants suit and got dressed.

'Wow! That will show him what he missed,' said Harry approvingly as Faye came into the sitting room.

Faye felt like bawling but of course didn't.

'Sorry Faye I didn't mean ...'

'It's alright Harry, it's just this whole thing is kind of surreal and weird, I mean what are the chances of Danny coming to you for work at the same time all this other stuff is going on with private detectives and being followed. He set me up, for whatever reason, I'm not entirely sure why. Why did Danny mention Belfast to you, do you think there is some connection, I was thinking we should tell Ina, see what she thinks?'

'I think he only said it to scare me, which it did, but it can't have anything to do with him coming back here, as for telling Ina, she'll go ballistic'.

'You're probably right but I still think Ina should have all the facts.'

'Faye, we gave her our bank details she will have seen the monthly payments,' Harry had just thought that Ina was surely going to see the direct debts and most definitely get suspicious.

'Oh god yeah, that completely slipped my mind, is this our past coming back to seek retribution, I don't believe in all that but there is something off about all this'.

'I have just blocked Belfast out, but maybe you are right we should tell Ina, we should have told her at the time.'

'This is insane, Ina is not going to be happy about it, maybe we will say nothing, after all we don't want to put her in a compromising position, it's not fair to her'.

'I know, maybe say nothing and see if she brings anything up about the payments.'

'And if she does, are we going to tell her the truth?'

'We could tell her it is compromising information and see if she wants to know.'

'How the hell did things come to this. Anyway, we better get going.'

'Faye, you don't have to meet Danny, I don't give a rat's arse if he tells the partners about the money, I could go in and rough him up a bit.'

'Harry that's hilarious, you going to rough him up a bit is kind of hard to imagine, you are too, I don't know, posh or urbane or something, to get rough, but thanks for the offer,' Faye was laughing.

'You shouldn't doubt my prowess, there's an animal inside me. But really, maybe you should leave it, he's no good and it will only upset you more.'

'At this stage I don't think that's possible and besides, if he knows something I want to see can I get it out of him. I'll be fine, come on let's go.'

They both put on their coats and headed out. They took a taxi.

'How are you going to play it when you get there?' asked Harry.

'The best way is probably to pretend I want to get back with him and come on all miserable, can't live without him and if we are going to make it work, we need to trust each other and see if I can get anything out of him.'

'I'm so sorry you have to do that,' Harry didn't like the idea of Faye having to put herself through this and smooch up to this creep.

'Have you any better ideas, because I don't.'

'Not really but it's just that I hate thinking of you having to be near him,' he reached over and took Faye's hand and squeezed it gently in silence.

When they had arrived at the hotel, Harry wanted to go upstairs and wait outside the door, but Faye insisted he stay in the lobby.

'Be careful with your heart,' said Harry and kissed Faye on her forehead.

As Faye stood outside Danny's hotel room door, she felt how shabby the whole thing was, she knocked gently hoping he was gone. Her luck was out, he answered.

'Come in please,' said Danny as he moved aside to allow Faye to come in. As Faye walked into the room, she was struck by how unremarkable she now found the room. It was a fairly swish hotel and when she came here first, she had liked the contemporary décor, now it just looked soulless, a place of no consequence, no personal meaning, nothing to reflect the occupants, the room was indifferent to the occupants and would remain indifferent to all its future occupants. Faye wished she could be equally as indifferent to Danny as the room was, but that was not the case.

'Faye I am so glad you're here, I wanted to explain things to you, it was never my intention to hurt you...' Danny was speaking but Faye was not listening to his excuses, she had had enough of him, he looked pitiable and weak.

'Oh my god would you just shut up, I can't bear to hear another word out of your lying mouth, I'm going, this is ridiculous. I'm ridiculous for coming here, I need my head examined!'

Faye turned and walked towards the door, what in reality was only a few feet felt like a long mile, with each step she was becoming more breathless, it felt like Danny was sucking the life out of her, draining her of the person she had grown used to being, she didn't feel herself with him, he made her someone she despised. She wasn't going to go back to that. She vaguely heard him mumbling something as she walked down the corridor past the lift, she took the stairs to pump some oxygen into her lungs, to breathe herself back.

By the time she got to the lobby she was giddy.

Harry stood up as she came towards him.

'That was quick. Faye, you look at bit funny...'

'Let's go,' Faye didn't wait for an answer and quickly walked outside where she continued to walk faster and faster.

'Slow down Faye, what's wrong, what happened, where are you heading?'

'Anywhere,' Faye sounded strange to herself, like she was in charge of herself again, like she knew what she was about, but she didn't.

As she walked, she thought about what had just happened, it was never easy to understand one's behaviour with full clarity, driven as we are by impulses, urges and feelings which are never easily explained or understood but something had propelled her out of that room. She knew going in what the goal was and while she didn't necessarily like it, she had gone of her own volition, no one coerced her. What she did know was that had she stayed there and gone through with the charade of getting back with him, she would be somehow lost, it was a feeling of course, but a feeling that spread through her like an electric shock. She had in fact wanted to stay more than anything else, wanted to be with Danny to recreate what they had all those years ago, to forget all that had gone in between, marriages, children, pain, obliterate it all and just be the two of them. Ridiculous. Ridiculous that she would still want this, ridiculous that she would even think this. So her only choice was to get out, she couldn't trust herself around him. Pathetic, she thought.

'Faye are you okay?' asked Harry.

'Do you want to go clubbing?' Faye asked after a few minutes.

Not quite what Harry had expected.

'Why not,' said Harry, thinking that dancing was infinitely better than talking about it.

Later in the early hours of the following day as she quietly crept in, Faye found an envelope with her name on it on the hall floor. It was a short and sobering note.

> It was my father-in-law, Uziel Nachman, who told me to come here and to look you up and rekindle things – he never told me why. He is a dangerous man.
>
> I am truly sorry.
>
> Danny

A bit later that same morning, Oliver was reading the update from Arthur Wilson. Oliver was ready to wind things up, it hadn't quite gone to plan, Nachman's son-in-law was pathetic and clearly wasn't up to much. According to Arthur, Faye was unravelling, drinking a lot and acting irrationally – well at least that was something. Anyway, he was losing interest in her.

# twenty-eight

Faye answered on the first ring from Ina.

'I think we need to meet. I'm free this morning, are you?' Ina asked.

'I could do nine, would that suit?'

'Yes, that's fine, where's the easiest to meet?'

'Can you come into town?'

'Yeah, what about Nash's?'

'Perfect, I'll see you at nine'

'Okay bye.'

Faye knew Ina was mad about something, at this point it could be any number of things.

It was nearly eight o clock, Faye decided to walk, it would be quicker at this time with all the school runs.

When she got to Nash's, Ina was already there with Harry.

'Good morning, I didn't expect you Har,' Faye said.

'I asked him to come so I could talk to the two of you,' replied Ina.

The waiter arrived with three coffees and croissants.

'I won't beat around the bush,' began Ina, 'but when I was looking into this whole thing for you Faye, I came across something strange. You two and Dan have been paying two hundred quid a month to some low life up the North, for years, now maybe it's none of my business, but you asked me to help, and this is curious so I'm asking you, what's it for?'

Both Faye and Harry remained silent. Both playing out scenarios of telling the truth or not, not daring to look at each other.

'You're both unusually quiet, if you're not going to tell me that's fine, I may as well go,' said Ina.

Finally, Harry spoke 'It's not that we don't want to tell you but I'm not sure you really want to know.'

'What's that supposed to mean, I can only imagine that it's some kind of extortion?'

Faye looked at Harry 'I want to tell her.'

'Yeah, me too.'

Between them, Harry and Faye told Ina the reason for the monthly payment.

Years earlier when they were all about twenty, they had been members of a voluntary organisation which often took young volunteers on trips to far-flung corners of the world in exchange for a few hours' work every day. They had joined in the hopes of getting to go on one of these trips. Eventually they were chosen for a trip, but it was to Belfast, not quite what they had hoped for, they didn't even get to fly. Nonetheless they decided to go – it was a week away from home, only Ina couldn't go because she was in training while the others were on long summer holidays from college.

The work entailed cleaning old tools which were going to be sent to Africa – supposedly to rescue the continent from poverty. It was all a bit of fun until the last night when a local volunteer Johnny, asked Harry, Faye and Danny if they wanted to go to a party at his friend's house. They went and that's when things went terribly wrong. There were only three others, two men and a woman, at the party and before long the two men started to fight, beating each other until one was out cold on the flat of his back. They couldn't wake him, there was a lot of shouting and bawling, eventually the girl said the guy was dead, she couldn't hear him breathing or get a pulse.

Harry, Ina and Danny were terrified and insisted on calling the police. That's when Johnny turned on them, took out a Stanley knife and told them that it was manslaughter and that they would all be considered guilty. When Harry and Danny tried to stand up to him saying they had nothing to hide as they had done nothing wrong, Johnny said he would tell the police it was them who beat up the guy and killed him, the girl chimed in to say she would say the same. After a lot of arguing, Johnny offered them a way out, he would look after the body, and they could buy his silence with monthly payments. At this point Harry, Faye and Danny were terrified and agreed, details were exchanged, and more threats made by Johnny should they think of reneging.

The three left the next day and swore never to talk about it to each other or tell anyone.

'Oh my god, you eejits,' said Ina, 'Sounds like you were royally set up, how were you sure that the guy was dead and not just playing dead?'

'I have thought about that over the years and the possibility that we were tricked, but he looked dead at the time,' said Faye.

'This guy "Johnny" who you keep in the lap of luxury is a low-life crook and this is exactly the kind of stunt he would pull. There is no way that guy was dead, he was in on it with the girl,' said Ina.

'Ina, you're probably right but we were kids at the time and frightened out of our minds and just wanted to get the hell out of there. It was hell coming up with that money back then, but fear is a powerful motivator and then over the years, I just didn't want to think about it, and really forgot about it,' said Harry.

'You just can't go on paying this scumbag, you have to confront him. Any private detective could have found what I found, we have to assume Arthur Wilson made this connection and probably got Dan to tell all.' Now that Ina had heard the story, she was no longer upset. She was now incensed that someone had made fools out of her friends for years.

'Ina, how can you be so sure the guy wasn't dead?' asked Faye, this had tormented her for years, but she never dared mention it to anyone and, like Harry, had buried it deep so she didn't have to think about it. The idea that it was all a hoax was beyond palliative; she also felt the sting of her own misguidedness.

'Sweetie, trust me, I am sure.'

'When Dan came to me in the beginning and wanted me to set him up with Faye, he brought up Belfast, as a kind of threat,' Harry told Ina.

'And I got this note from Danny this morning,' Faye took out the note, put it on the table for the other two to read.

'Oliver and Nachman knew each other and Nachman is in a lot of debt to Oliver, this is how Dan is involved,' said Ina.

'What does it mean?' asked Harry.

'I'm not really sure, but it looks like Blake has some sort of personal vendetta against you Faye,' said Ina as she looked at Faye.

'He said his wife is back on the scene – but I'm not convinced – where has she been hiding, could she really be dead, I have to get into his house,' said Faye.

'Hold your horses Miss Marple, that is not going to happen,' Ina was firm. 'We need to think this through Faye, one thing at a time. I suggest we start with our Belfast friend and sort that out because Blake might want to use it against you. This guy withdraws the money the day after it goes in from the same cash machine around the same time every month – we need to be there and catch him – we can contact the PSNI...'

'Hang on a minute, are you talking about involving the guards, we could get into a shit load of trouble Ina,' said Harry nervously.

'No, you won't, you've done nothing wrong except being gullible twats,' Ina tried not to think about the fact that they actually thought someone had died and did nothing.

'Thanks Ina,' said Harry.

'Ina, don't you think we should leave the guards out of it for now just in case...'

'Faye, I guarantee you there's nothing to worry about, no one died.'

It was such a relief to hear that, but Faye still couldn't help worrying after all the years of practice.

'Leave it with me for a few days and I will suss it out below the radar, okay?' Ina was sensing their fear.

'I feel like a right plonker now, paying out all that money to that piece of shit for nothing,' Harry's fear had morphed into indignation.

'You should have told me about this when it happened,' said Ina softly.

'I wish we had,' replied Faye and reached over to hold Ina's hand, 'I really wish we had, I am so sorry.'

'Me too,' said Harry.

'What's done is done,' said Ina, ever the pragmatist. 'How did last night go with Dan?'

'I couldn't do it in the end, when I went up to his room, I felt sick,' said Faye.

'I understand,' said Ina.

'He's a bollocks,' said Harry sagely.

'I better go, I have work,' said Faye.

‘Okay but promise me you won’t do anything or contact anyone until we talk again, I can come over this evening, we’ll have more time to figure this out,’ said Ina.

‘I promise,’ said Faye as she kissed Ina on the cheek.

They all stood up to go and walked out arranging to meet again that evening at Faye’s flat.

Faye’s phone rang, it was her mother, she couldn’t deal with her now and rejected the call. She was looking forward to work, it would be a relief to listen to other people’s problems and get a break from her own.

Ina went to her office after leaving her friends, feeling better now that she knew what the money was about, but also wondering at her friends’ complete and utter stupidity – she couldn’t fathom how they had fallen for the hoax so easily and worse still, to have continued to pay out for years. But she also felt fiercely protective of them and was determined to get the scumbag.

Once back in the office she phoned an old college friend who had married a girl from the North, he moved there and was working for the PSNI. She found his number easily enough and called him.

‘Derek, it’s Ina Mulhall’.

‘Ina! Long time no hear, how are things down your way.’

‘Good and you, are you keeping out of trouble?’

‘You know me, good as gold. What can I do for you Ina?’

Ina always liked that about Derek, he got to the point fast.

Ina filled him in on Martin Stockdale, leaving out that it was her friends who were hoodwinked by him. She asked if he would back her up in confronting Stockdale, she would be out of her jurisdiction and was not after an arrest but to put the frighteners on him, let him know we are on to him, threaten to charge him for fraud by false representation, exhortation, you know the form. Derek seemed amused by the whole thing and was happy to help Ina, he said he would do it for her to save her a trip. Ina thanked him and gave him the date and time he usually withdrew the money, which happened to be in a few days. Ina chatted with Derek for a bit longer and he said he would be in touch to let her know how it went.

Ina got up from her desk to go get a coffee and went by Malcolm’s desk to see if he wanted a cuppa.

Malcolm had photos laid out on his desk which caught Ina's attention.

'What are these?' she asked as she picked one up.

'They came in from Vice yesterday, they wanted us to take a look and to check if there was anything similar on the system.'

The pictures were all similar, naked women with bites on the buttocks, thighs and belly.

'Who, what, are these pictures of?' asked Ina.

'Well, they're all girls on the game who got bitten by their punter– apparently one woman went to A&E last week, bleeding pretty badly after someone bit her. The doc on duty called the guards and when they questioned her, she reluctantly said it was some john who picked her up, tied her, beat her and bit a chunk out of her.'

'Before or after sex?'

'Weird thing, no sex involved, also she thought there might have been two of them in the car but couldn't be sure, she thought she heard a sound in the back.'

'These bites look really deep.'

'They are, he took a bite of the flesh'

'Who are the other three?'

'Same story with them - punter picks them up, ties and gags them and then yum, yum, they had to go to A&E for stitches too'

'When did this start?'

'Well, the first one is from nearly two years ago,' he said as he pointed to one of the photos on his desk, 'and the last one was a week ago – course there's probably a lot more – most girls on the job won't go to the hospital unless they're in dire straits.'

'Yeah, that's true. Have you found anything else?'

'Not a lot. I've read the interviews and they all are similar – the guy pulls up alongside the girls and asks them to get into the car and then drives to a quiet park. He drops back the front seat – sounds like a custom job as they said it goes completely flat – then flips them over and ties their wrists to some sort of ring one woman said, and then beats them with a knotted rope – again one of the women saw it – when he finishes the beating, he bites a chunk out of them. Always pays them and then kicks them out and drives away.'

'Charming.' Ina thought of the tapestries in Faye's flat. She rang Faye, it went to her voice mail, she was probably with patients thought Ina. She left a message asking Faye to phone her as soon as possible.

Ina asked Malcolm for the name and contact details of the girl who got bitten a week ago, grabbed her stuff and headed out to find her.

# twenty-nine

Oliver was sitting in his study at home, he was not happy. Things had not followed his plan. Faye had left a message cancelling their appointment that evening, offering the same time next week, no excuse given, who does she think she is cancelling him, and she hadn't phoned the "next of kin" number. What was she up to? He wasn't going to wait a week.

Arthur was starting to irk him and Nachman would have to make things right, the ante had just gone up, Oliver was no longer feeling charitable. He could feel the ebullience of rage ferment in his gut, he had learnt to control this, now was not the time to slip up. Yet the heat of the rage needed to be heeded, why should he ignore it, why shouldn't he take what he wanted, no one stands in my way, he thought. He wanted to crush Faye Monroe, smash her obtuse head in with his bare hands, wreck her face, he wanted to feel her skull smatter in his hands.

He rang Silvia, her answering machine said she was away for a month. He forced himself not to smash his phone against the wall. Calm down, you have the power, you are invincible, no one gets to dump you. Oliver calmed as he decided to get a street girl. Again, he looked at his phone and rang Jim to arrange to meet him at six thirty with the BMW, made a second call, it was feeding time.

Ina arrived at Faye's at half eight and tried to piece together what they knew; she told Faye about the women who were bitten and about her friend in Belfast. All they really had was a lot of tenuous connections but no proof of anything and a growing sense of fear, things were unravelling and could go sideways very easily. At around 9pm, Malcom rang Ina to say that he was on his way back from the A&E, another woman was admitted at nineteen forty-five that evening in a bad state – she had been bitten. Five very substantial chunks with visible teeth marks, her thighs, stomach and buttocks. Sounded like that same MO, seat dropped back, tied hands, beaten with a rope, bitten and then pushed out. The girl is not talking, she looks terrified, I think he might have threatened her. He told Ina that she needed over 100 stitches. Ina thanked Malcolm for the call and hung up.

'I think we can rule Blake out for the women in the park, another woman was brought in this evening at seven forty-five, didn't you have him at seven?' asked Ina.

'No, not this evening. I cancelled him, I wanted to talk with you first. Ina, do you think I should report Amanda missing?'

'No, that would be career suicide for you, let's just hold on a minute. I'll talk to the girl who came in tonight, see if I can get any kind of a description and we don't want to do anything until Derek gives us the all clear, luckily the payment would normally go out tomorrow, so we'll know the day after. You stopped that payment, didn't you?' asked Ina

'Yes, and so did Harry, but I suppose Danny is still paying.'

'Who cares about him, let him pay.'

'Fair enough. So, we do nothing. What about that number for Amanda, the next-of-kin number, did you get anything on it?'

'No, not really, the number is a pay as you go, not registered to anyone. I didn't call and I don't think we should at the minute, god only knows who will answer, better to know who you are calling before making the call.'

'Yeah, I suppose – so we do nothing?'

'For now, we have no choice Faye. Are you okay on your own tonight, I can stay?'

'Jeepers no. I'm fine, you go home and thanks for all your help, and for the whole Belfast thing, I wanted to apologize about that...'

Ina cut in. 'No need, water under the bridge, no point in dwelling on these things. Okay, so I'll head off now, I have an early start tomorrow.'

Faye walked Ina down to the front door, they hugged each other tightly and said good night.

The next few days went by in a bit of a blur for Faye, she went to work and home and nothing much aside from that. Ina had spoken to the poor girl who had been bitten, the girl was a bit dazed, and afraid to talk, but said the car was an old BMW and very dirty inside, that the man was definitely well off and smelled of expensive cologne. She wasn't able, or more likely was afraid, to give any description and said she wouldn't be able to recognize him again and besides she didn't want to press any charges.

Derek contacted Ina and told her that Martin Stockdale had confidently sauntered up to insert his bank card into the machine, as usual. Derek had wasted no time in letting him know the score, telling him that he had gotten a tip off that Stockdale was involved with a murder case he was looking into, that this person could no longer suffer the guilt, nor could they afford to keep paying him. Derek told Ina that he could almost see the cogs of Stockdale's brain trying to work out his options, in the end he chose the wise decision and told Derek the truth, that he had set up the Taigs from down South, that it was only a prank but they were stupid enough to fall for it and kept sending the money. How could he refuse that kind of free money, he asked Derek in all earnestness. Derek told him that he had committed a serious crime that would carry a hefty jail sentence. Stockdale cleverly said he had very worthwhile information on crimes going on in the city and struck a bargain with Derek. Derek thanked Ina; he now had a valuable snitch.

Ina met Harry and Faye at the weekend for a drink and told them about Stockdale, both were a bit dazed by the banality of this encounter, how simple it all sounded, why had they not done this themselves, secrets and guilt are compelling paralysers.

Faye felt, after all that had happened, she still was none the wiser as to what had happened to Amanda or if she was safe. Oliver had rung back after she cancelled his appointment looking for something sooner than the following Tuesday. She told him she hadn't anything else and he reluctantly agreed to the Tuesday. Faye resolved that this would be her last appointment with him.

# thirty

Endings in therapy, as well as life, can be tricky but this was going to be trickier than most. Oliver was in the waiting room, five to seven, punctual as always.

Faye went into the waiting room, and immediately knew something was amiss, the animus was palpable.

Oliver did not speak until he was seated, without crossing his legs, which was unusual.

'I didn't appreciate you cancelling my appointment last week, do you think I have nothing better to do with my time, when I make an arrangement, I expect it to be honoured. You owe me an explanation. What do you have to say for yourself?' Both his tone and manner were rancorous.

Something snapped in Faye, maybe it was years of enduring this kind of condescension from her mother, the last weeks of being on the edge all the time or she simply had enough, as they say.

'Don't speak to me like that, I'm not one of your minions, I don't owe you anything. No wonder your wife left you if you spoke to her like that,' it was out before she knew what she had said.

'How fucking dare you! Wives leave their husbands because of the likes of you, you fill their head with poison, not giving a damn about the other side of the story, how the fuck do you live with yourself!' he was practically hissing the words out.

'Women come to you, who the fuck knows why, for help I suppose and want do you do? Well, you are the pigeon whispering lies and rubbish into their ears, convincing them that they are better off single. They can't survive without their husbands, but you convinced them they can, you know nothing about them except what they choose to tell you. Are you happy with yourself, this is what you do, destroy people's lives! You listen to one side of a story and presume it to be true and tell people to leave their husbands, do you get off on that? I bet you do because you have never managed to maintain a relationship, you want to sabotage everyone else's chance of happiness. Your marriage ended because you refuse to tailor yourself to accommodate anyone needs except your own, you drove Daniel Cohen to the other side of the world to marry a stranger to get away from you and you sleep around like a common whore – and you think you can advise others on relationships, you're a fraud and a prick tease, looking out the window at me, I see how you look at me.'

Faye could feel rage and humiliation curdle in her belly and the horror of stinging tears behind her eyes– was he right about her?

'You talk about honesty, and you left a man dead and covered it up, how honest is that Dr Monroe?'

'He wasn't dead, it was a set up,' Faye could hear the contrition in her voice.

Ah, so she knows, thought Oliver.

'But you didn't know that until recently, what kind of person leaves a man dead. Tut tut doc.'

Oliver laughed because he could feel Faye's ache, yes this was satisfying, he would like to taste the ache.

'You know Cohen came to Dublin because I demanded it, no, he wasn't here out of love for you, he didn't even want to come. But how quickly your smugness and conceit had you believing he never got over you, that he came back because he realise what he missed, yes that was the story he was told to tell.'

Faye's head was reeling, without fear of consequences she shouted at Oliver.

'You freak! I know what you are. You think you're powerful and in control but you're pathetic. You're perverse, you get your kicks from eating the flesh of women, poor defenceless prostitutes, such a big man, is that why Amanda left you, she couldn't take your depravity anymore, couldn't bear to be with you, couldn't stand the sight of you, you killed her didn't you, didn't you?' she shouted.

Oliver was out of his chair and in seconds had Faye pinned to the wall with his hand to her throat.

'You little cunt, I could gut you here right now,' his face was pressed up against Faye's, his glee had twisted back to rage, how did she know about the whores. He needed to be careful, but he didn't want to quell his fervour.

Faye could feel Oliver's breath against her face, she was terrified, she had gone too far. She felt limp in contrast to the immense energy and strength she could feel from him. Years earlier she had taken a self-defence course, when you are this close to your assaulter, they told the women to knee the man in the balls. There was no way in hell she could do that now, too overcome with fear, fight and flight were not an option, all she could do was freeze. Another example of the incongruity of the classroom and reality.

Oliver came closer to Faye and licked her cheek slowly, growled and bared his teeth, opening his mouth in a motion to bite.

Faye braced herself for what she knew was coming, she tried to turn away from his snarl but couldn't, his grip was too tight, too tight for her to scream or make an utterance. Why hadn't she kept her mouth shut, she thought of all the times she had told women to speak up for themselves, he was right she did destroy lives.

She could feel his teeth against her cheek, the wetness of his spit and then the pressure of the bite, her stomach turned, and she could feel bile surge to her throat. And then nothing. He pulled back.

Oliver yearned to bite her and rip the flesh from her face. But there was too much to lose, restraint, he thought.

'I am giving you a gift here, I could take from you what I want, but I will leave you your face. You take wives from their husbands and now I have what I came for from you, my '*jouissance*' to coin your Lacan. I've taken my bliss, your marrow, my bliss is that you will be left stained forever by me, fallow and broken. I've played you and so did Amanda.'

He released her and let her buckle and fold. He walked to the table, took out his wallet and left the fee on the table. As he was about to leave, he turned and said,

'Best session ever doc,' grinned playfully and left.

# thirty-one

It was five months since "that day" as Faye had come to know it. Life had become reduced, constrained, pathologised, the ordinariness of taking a breath became overwhelming in its significance. Not that she was suicidal exactly, but should death swing by, she most likely would open the door.

Faye continued to work because she had no other means, but in a real sense she wondered how it was she had emerged from "that day". She had brief moments when her focus allowed her to forget, but aside from these moments, she chastised herself relentlessly, despite a respectable Valium habit.

Faye was on her way to meet Ina and Harry, she had told them only that she had stopped seeing Oliver Blake and that he admitted that he blamed her for his wife leaving him and wanted revenge, but that this was the end of it, quits. Nothing further to be done. Faye didn't tell them about what he had done or said, she felt a deep sense of disquiet within her and was jittery about everything. Life was shit, but she kept this to herself.

Faye was spending too much time thinking about Oliver Blake's revenge and thought of what Francis Bacon said, *"A man that studieth revenge, keeps his own wounds green, which otherwise would heal, and do well."* She didn't want revenge, or maybe she did, but she thought Oliver Blake's capacity for revenge was at an impressive level, did she really deserve this mauling? She knew enough about revenge not to discount how beguiling it can be, even though revenge was rarely sweet except when the revenger delivers their message to the offender, only then in their eyes are the scales of justice balanced again. She had received Oliver Blake's message loud and clear and could only hope he felt vindicated.

Ina had phoned Faye earlier in the day to tell her she had news and was asking Harry to join them. Faye arrived at the Copper Cow at six, Harry and Ina were already seated in their *usual spot*, both had drinks and Faye noticed that they had ordered for her too, a whiskey.

'Hiya Faye, got you a whiskey, hope that's alright,' said Harry.

'Of course, Harry, thanks. How are you two?' asked Faye as she sat in beside Ina.

'Not a bother,' answered Harry.

'Fine, I have some horrible news Faye,' said Ina.

Faye's heart sank. 'What news?'

'You know we're still investigating the women who were bitten, trying to tie it to Blake, but since the last case five months ago there haven't been any, probably because you put the frighteners on him...'

Not bloody likely, thought Faye.

'...well, we have our system flagged to spot any case where bites on the body show up and yesterday, we got a hit. A young prostitute was admitted to St Ambroise's A&E with severe bites, like whole chunks were taken. I went to talk to her, and well, she was in a bad way, she could hardly talk, but her description matches the others. But she said when she got into the car, it was only the two of them and after he parked up and started biting her, a woman came out from behind the back seat and joined in with him, biting her too. Remember another one of the girls had thought they heard someone in the back? Unfortunately, she died this morning, by the time she was admitted to St Ambroise's she had lost too much blood and the doctor said she would have needed a lot of skin grafting.'

Faye was listening, hearing, but not believing even though she knew it was true, if she didn't believe, would that make it not true?

'Ina that's murder, he has killed a woman. Can you arrest him or bring him in for questioning?' pleaded Harry.

'No, not really. Unless someone reports that stuff as done to them against their will it can be seen as consensual, and none of the women would press charges, including this poor woman who died. She didn't want to report it, told me it was a hazard of the job. Also, there's no way of linking it directly to Blake, even if he was questioned, he could plausibly deny it, say he knew nothing of it, have us for harassing him without probable cause that sort of thing. No, unfortunately we have nothing solid to run with... no DNA because they washed where they bite with bleach. Same as all the stuff with you Faye, it's all circumstantial,' Ina sounded deflated herself, working these kinds of crimes was disheartening at best.

'All we can hope for is that he will eventually make a mistake,' Ina said it but didn't hold much hope.

'Do you think it's my fault, that I caused this in some way, I fed into this in some way....?'

'No Faye! And stop that nutty thinking, you did your best for her, he's a psycho who abuses women left, right and centre and maybe you helped his wife build up the courage to leave. This girl's death is nothing to do with you, you were not part of her life, remember that. Don't let him into your head, you've been weird ever since that day you stopped seeing him. I don't know what he said to you, but you have to get it together,' Harry never sounded so convinced of what he was saying.

He was deeply worried about Faye, more and more all the time and he had spoken to Ina about her, both felt she was on the edge, and now this, he couldn't let her slip over. He wouldn't let her slip. Then something in Faye snapped and over her whiskey she began to cry. It was the first time she had cried since that day.

Harry and Ina both stayed with Faye in her flat that night and in the morning, they agreed to go to the funeral of this girl whom none of them had known, but they wanted to pay their respects to her and acknowledge her ending. Faye asked Harry to return Amanda's belongings which were boxed in the living room to her sister, she wanted to move on. She felt a deep sadness, but it was real and easier to bear than the dread. She felt hopeful.

Things were slowly getting better for Faye, she consumed herself with her work, she was determined to redress any, perceived or real, harm she might have caused. She took on more work with the Garda and was accepted to do a research study in Psychological Autopsy, better to work with the dead she thought. She did not allow herself to think about Dan and did not allow herself to forget Amanda or the girls who were hurt.

It was Friday evening, and she was meeting Harry to discuss Ina's hen party, well not really a hen, it was only going to be the three of them, but they wanted it to be very special. Faye felt good as she locked up her office, so lost in thoughts of her lovely Ina getting married that she did not see the Bentley parked outside her building, but there was no mistaking the voice she heard calling her name. Her heart quickened.

She turned in the direction of the voice and saw Amanda in the back of the Bentley, the window rolled all the way down. Faye moved closer to the car.

'Hello Faye, you don't look so well, can I get you some help?' she asked in a breezy way, and she stepped out of the car. Both women were about the same height, but Faye felt as if Amanda was towering over her, lording over her.

Faye never heard her speak like this, full of sneery confidence. She looked different too, not the broken-down woman who came to her with stories of her fear, this Amanda was polished, sleek and shiny and more than slightly fearsome.

'Hello Amanda,' what should I say, thought Faye, that you've been on my mind every day, that I've been searching for you, thinking you were dead, worried stupid about you. That your husband nearly destroyed me too, just like he did you. But none of that seemed right to say. Something was seriously off.

'Faye, I wanted you to know that I'm fine and I don't want you to take this personally, but we just picked your name randomly out of some kind of psychotherapy directory, we wanted to prove how easy it is to lie to a shrink and well,' she paused, 'fuck with you,' another pause, 'for our own amusement.' It all started when Oliver's brother, who by the way he is very fond of, told us his wife was leaving him after going to see someone like your good self and we saw how it was destroying him. Naughty, naughty Faye destroying people's lives. And that's when we hatched our game, and what an elaborate game it became.'

Faye's head was addled, she heard what Amanda was saying but couldn't bring herself to believe it. She started to feel sweaty all over, she could feel her heart pelting through her chest, she was trying to breathe but couldn't. She should walk away but couldn't, she was stumped, both from stupefaction and curiosity. Had she just said she was playing with her.

'I have to say Faye, you were a superb contestant, we never expected to have so much fun, you were such a good sport, a worthy foe,' Amanda threw her head back laughing as if they were sharing some great joke.

'We had to call in a lot of favours, from India to Israel to Limerick, to make it work and let's be honest, make a few threats too, oh but my goodness it was all worth it,' she winked at Faye, like a couple of pals colluding with each other.

'Faye, may I give you a little advice?' Amanda said this at the same time as she reached across and gently moved a stray hair from Faye's face.

Dumbfounded, Faye stood still and allowed her to adjust her hair, while all the events of the past months were on rewind in her head and this time with Amanda's voiceover saying "oh yes that was part of our game, oh yes that too..."

Amanda didn't wait for Faye to answer her.

'You underestimate women, you presumed I was weak and docile, if only you knew how little sway my darling Oliver has over me. I take what I want, as do most women, if we are truthful. Never belittle women Faye, you took the lazy option, confirmation bias, I believe you people call it,' her tone began to take on a minacious edge, Faye heard it and wanted to scream.

In an elegant turn Amanda was back in the car.

'But the game is over now, and I warn you not to stay playing, or I will have my pound of flesh.'

And with that the window went up and the car drove slowly off, leaving Faye on the side of the street.

# About the Author

Claudia Jean Hugo lives in the outlying fields of Norway, because this is where sheep share the same roaming rights as people. She lives with an exceptionally well behaved Bassett Hound and a cat with diabetes mellitus.

Married and divorced three times she now revels in her own company.

Claudia Jean trained as a sheep shearer and wool handler and, before travel was taboo, spent four months' of the year sheep shearing in New Zealand, now she writes instead of working.

She is a keen marbles player and once was the Reine Marbles Champion. She nibbles on kippers and caviar and dreams in Italian.

She admits to a mortal dread of turtles, she doesn't know why, and probably should go to therapy for it, but has an equal mortal dread of therapy.

# About the Author

www.ingramcontent.com/pod-product-compliance
Lightning Source LLC
Chambersburg PA
CBHW030552310726
48979CB00011B/2127/J
*9781803815312*